Famous ADOPTED People

a novel

alice stephens

un

The Unnamed Press
Los Angeles, CA

AN UNNAMED PRESS BOOK

Copyright © 2018 Alice Stephens

www.unnamedpress.com

Unnamed Press, and the colophon, are registered trademarks of Unnamed Media LLC.

Library of Congress Cataloging-in-Publication Data
Stephens, Alice, 1967- author.
Famous adopted people : a novel / by Alice Stephens.
Los Angeles : Unnamed Press, 2018.
LCCN 2018033188 | ISBN 9781944700744 (pbk.)
LCC PS3619.T476675 F36 2018 | DDC 813/.6--dc23
LC record available at https://lccn.loc.gov/2018033188

Designed & typeset by Jaya Nicely

This book is a work of fiction. Names, characters, places and incidents are wholly fictional or are used fictitiously. Any resemblance to actual events or persons, living or dead, is entirely coincidental.

Distributed by Publishers Group West
Manufactured in the United States of America
First Edition

For my mom and dad, Betsy and Ralph Stephens

Famous
ADOPTED
People

Chapter 1

"And when she could hide him no longer she took for him a basket made of bulrushes, and daubed it with bitumen and pitch; and she put the child in it and placed it among the reeds at the river's brink... And the child grew, and she brought him to Pharaoh's daughter, and he became her son..."

–Exodus 2:3, 10

If it wasn't for Mindy, I might have been dead a long time ago, and now here she was in the Dunkin' Donuts in downtown Seoul, chewing on the lip of her Styrofoam cup of coffee, telling me to go home. Booze-bloated brain sloshing in sickening waves inside the hard hollow of my skull, stomach a sulfuric cauldron bubbling with acid and bile, I was just trying to keep myself from barfing all over the sesame tofu ring that I had ordered as a joke.

"Mindy, I'm sorry," I said between clenched teeth, the smell of her coffee digging sharply into my nostrils. "I know it's an important day for you—"

"Uh-uh," she cut me off. I knew she was nervous because the dimple underneath her right eye was winking at me, a facial tic that came on only when she was stressed. Best friends since we were eight years old, I knew everything about her, just as she knew everything about me. Which is why I couldn't believe what she said next. "You have never cared about anyone but yourself. How many years I wasted defending you to my mother, to Trip, to the whole fucking world."

"C'mon, Min Hee," I wheedled, "I was just having some fun."

"That's all you ever have," she hissed at me, heart-shaped mouth broken into two as she bared her teeth in disgust. "It's all you care about. You can't even stay sober for a few days! You can't say no, even when saying yes puts you and me into danger. We're not in America, Li-li. We're in Asia. Drug laws are no joke."

"It was just a line of something," I defended myself, pushing the vile tofu doughnut away.

"What if you'd been arrested? You know what today means to me. What if we had to run around trying to get you out of jail today? Today of all days?"

"Well, I wasn't arrested," I retorted, wiping away white parentheses of gummy spit from the corners of my mouth with a crumpled napkin. "I'm a little hungover, yeah, but I'm ready to go! I won't throw up all over the *hyeon gwan*."

"You're not coming with us, Lisa." Her voice trembled, and a clumsy, sideways glance confirmed that she was crying. "This is the most important day of my life, and I won't let you ruin it."

The seriousness of the situation seeped through the sickening headache that fogged my brain. I clutched at her arm, sloshing her coffee. "I want to be here for you. I am here for you."

"It's too late," she sniffed, dabbing at the coffee that had soaked into the sleeve of her cream angora sweater, probably leaving a permanent stain. "My parents are so pissed off at you, I doubt they'll speak to you again."

"C'mon, Mindy, I've been practicing my Korean. *Mannaseo bangapsuemnida.*" I bowed so low that I banged my head on the table.

"You don't get it, Lisa, do you? You did not give one goddamn thought to me last night. First you beg me to go out with you, when you knew I just wanted to chill out in the room, watch some stupid hotel cable and get an early night's sleep. Then you insist on hanging out with some shady-looking *jopok*-type guy who you'd apparently already arranged to meet at the bar, asking to stay for one more drink and then one more, and next thing I know, you're doing shots of Johnnie Walker and snorting lines! Even when I walked out on you, you didn't follow! So then I'm worried about you, tossing and turning in bed until you finally get back to the room, and then you snored so loudly I couldn't fall asleep! I'm a wreck today!" She took a deep breath, and spread her hands—obstetrician hands now that pulled babies out of their mothers' bodies—on her thighs, the gumball-sized yellow diamond of her engagement ring winking luridly. "Go back to Japan, Lisa. My dad says he'll pay the penalty on your ticket. You're not serious about finding your birth mother, and you're obviously not interested in helping me. You've wasted your life away, every opportunity that has ever been given to you. Your parents gave you such a precious gift, and you just threw it in their faces."

Not even Mindy's mother, Margaret, would have ever put it that way. "Are you fucking serious, Mindy? I can't believe those words just came out of your mouth."

She stared up at the fluorescent lights striping the ceiling, the whites of her eyes shining like pearls. "What have you ever done to make your parents proud, Lisa? You say you want to be a writer, you talk about it all the time, but you have fuck all to show for it."

Her words were hot little needles, pricking deep into my heart. The geometric angles of the hard plastic seats and tables began to melt and spread into formless blobs of beige and orange. I hated to have anyone see they could make me cry, even Mindy, so I pretended to be very interested in flicking the sesame seeds off my untouched pastry. "I know you think that I've just been partying in Japan, but I've not. I'm writing. A lot. I've filled up at least half a dozen notebooks since I started living in Fukuoka."

Mindy snorted incredulously. "Filled them up with what?"

"With observations. Scenes, sketches, thoughts," I responded tentatively.

"That's all?" she sneered. She had never been so cruel, so belittling, so mean. She had always been the sunshine yang to my dark and troubled yin, but now her light had been eclipsed by dark malice and she was all furious foe. "I thought you were working on a novel."

"The journals are the seeds of the novel, like the preliminary sketches that an artist does before a painting, or the storyboards a director makes for a movie."

She took a big, deliberative bite of her jelly doughnut, a dark clot of filling squelching out the other end, and goaded me: "So basically all the time you told me you were working on a novel, you've been lying." She wiped the white powder from her lips, but not the contemptuous frown. "Stop always hiding in the shadows, Lisa. If you don't have what it takes to be a writer, then quit pretending you're going to be a writer. You're old enough to know that just saying something doesn't make it so, and quite frankly your big talk about writing the Great Adoption Novel is getting a little embarrassing at this point."

"What the fuck?" Anger welled up, more overpowering even than the nausea of my hangover. "Fine, Mindy, you know what? Fuck you!" I leapt from my seat with an alacrity that sent black stars swimming away from the center of my vision. "I don't know what you're looking for, what kind of happiness you think you are going to get from meeting the woman who gave you up. She gave you up, Mindy!"

Mindy flinched away from me, probably because what I was saying was so hurtful, so uncalled for, so out of character after almost twenty years of unconditional love, but maybe also because of my vomity breath.

"She sent you across the Pacific Ocean to a foreign country to ensure that you'd never come around again, but you're too dumb to take the hint. You know, there are real disasters in the world, like that tsunami and nuclear meltdown in Fukushima that happened a few weeks ago—quite near me, Mindy!—and has killed thousands and may kill thousands more, without you having to go out there and make your own. But I guess deep down you're still a little drama queen who hasn't had enough heartbreak in your life, so you have to manufacture it yourself." Her eyes louvered shut, slivered lids dropped to shield her from the ugly reality of me. "Tell your father I don't need his charity, I can damn well get home on my own. Tell your mother she can unclench her rectal muscles now, 'cause I'm outta here. Have a nice life, cunt!"

Whirling away from her, I almost knocked the blue contacts out of a woman's surgically restructured eyes when I thumped into her, chest to chest. Without stopping, I rushed out the doors as Mindy began to abjectly apologize to the woman in Korean.

Back in the hotel room, I curved over the toilet for a quick puke, my yin-yang pendant, a gift to me from Mindy, dinging at the undercarriage of my jaw. After rinsing out my mouth, I scrabbled at the clasp, but I hadn't taken the necklace off in more than ten years, and it seemed as if the silver was rusted shut. *A perfect metaphor for our relationship, corroded and useless,* I thought in disgust as I gathered up whatever clothes of mine I could find scattered around the floor, my suitcase already semi-packed, since I had never unpacked it. Cramming hotel toiletries into a side pocket, I listened, half in dread and half in hope, for Mindy's key rattling in the door, her familiar call of "Li-li," the only pet name I had in the world, but it didn't come. Marching through the lobby, wheeled suitcase bumping at my heels, I expected Howard or Margaret Stamwell to be lurking behind the stately celadon floor vases, or hiding behind an unfurled copy of the *Korea Herald*, confirming with their own eyes that I was leaving their lives, finally, after almost two decades of a friendship that they had never liked. But they were nowhere in sight, and I rolled my suitcase out the heavy, brass-trimmed glass doors, held open by a man in a heavy, brass-trimmed uniform that emphasized he was just an extension of the door, and stood lost and foolish at the corner of the busy avenue, with nowhere left to go.

Dragging my wobbly suitcase through the tide of black-suited salarymen and secretaries in sensible heels, I plodded down the long blocks of tidy, well-swept sidewalks assiduously attended to by face-masked workers in neon uniforms, past the sleek, cosmopolitan, any-where-in-the-world facades of skyscrapers and luxury shops, before slipping through a crevice into a warren of back alleys that stank of garlic and piss, the chipped and uneven paving scattered with ciga-rette butts, loogies, and convenience-store wrappers. Somehow my feet knew where to go, even when my mind didn't. The first time I blundered into Spaghetti Kyu Bok's, it had been complete serendip-ity. When Mindy and I searched for it the next day, we passed the same jade jewelry shop four times and I was just about to admit defeat when we stumbled upon it. Today, I discovered that if I just didn't think about it, I could find my way there.

But when I staggered up to the door, the windows were dark and the neon sign of the bowl with three squiggles rising from the rim was turned off. It was that sign that just two days ago had drawn me out of the cheek-chapping early-spring wind and through the steam-be-dewed glass door. Seoul had changed a lot even in the seven years since I'd last visited, seeming shinier, taller, more prosperous. Still, cracking the slick surface of steel-and-glass buildings were tiny fis-sures, like the one the wind chased me down, where a whole other layer of city existed: the noisy, dirty, crowded, stinky, dilapidated fun-dament that festered beneath the brand-new glitz. Pinched, mazelike lanes were lined with crumbling, squat concrete buildings narrowly sliced into cramped stores crammed with sun-faded plastic sandals, knockoff Nike socks, sour-smelling cages bursting with cockatoos and budgies, weird bamboo implements, dented aluminum cooking ware, and cheap pleather goods. The bright blare of the neon bowl among the drab and faded storefronts irresistibly drew me toward it, promising a hot meal for my empty belly and shelter from the wind that blew from the frozen tundra of the Siberian steppes, through the stinging sands of the Gobi Desert, over the snow-packed reaches of China, and right down the neck of my useless down sweater, which had seemed so warm and cozy in Fukuoka. A grizzled man with a cheerful smile half occluded by the silken wisps of a Confucian beard ushered me with a bow to the counter. It was late morning, and the little shop was empty but for a gray-haired woman wearing a pink apron emblazoned with a teddy bear hugging a kitten, slumped in a chair in front of a big-screen TV, peeling lumpy bulbs of garlic. Shaking my head at the Korean menu the man gallantly presented me, I asked in English, "What's good to eat here?"

Smiling widely to reveal a rickety line of teeth scrimshawed with rot, he announced, "Spaghetti."

"Spaghetti! Why not? When in Rome," I said, laughing and shimmying onto a stool.

He said something to the woman. She sighed heavily and put her chin in her hand, staring hard at the TV. It was a moment of high drama: a beautiful young girl was sobbing painfully, while a rugged, much older man with an oily Ronald Reagan pompadour sneered at her in the background.

I pointed to the glass-fronted fridge stacked with beer bottles and carefully pronounced, "*Maekju juseyo.*" That much Korean I knew. It was early to be drinking, but I was nervous about my meeting with Miss Cho of MotherFinders, who knew I was coming to Korea with Mindy and had emailed me to ask that I meet her that afternoon, before Mindy and her parents arrived from the States. I didn't tell Mindy about Miss Cho's request because she had enough on her mind as it was; besides, I was pretty sure the agency hadn't found my mother, or else I would have received a glossy packet detailing the wide array of expensive services MotherFinders offered for facilitating reunions.

He spoke again to the woman, this time barking a command. She put her hands on her knees with slow deliberation and heaved herself off the chair with a low grunt. As she ducked beneath the counter, he turned again to me with an apologetic grin. Reaching up to a shelf, he brandished a brown bottle with a gold label. He smiled encouragingly, asking if I wanted it instead of beer. Once again, I wondered, "Why not?" and waved my hand to indicate that he should bring it down. He filled a ceramic flask and brought it to me on a tray with a shallow ceramic cup, which he poured full. I raised the cup to him, pronouncing my favorite Korean phrase, *"Geonbae."*

Disappearing into a cloud of steam, he and the woman stepped around each other in the small wedge of a kitchen. There was a soft, soothing burbling of boiling water, and I wished I could mute the dramatic sobs and emotion-cracked hysteria of the TV. Just as I poured myself a third thimble of the rice liquor, the man placed a vast bowl of noodle soup in front of me. "Spaghetti," he said, and nodded proudly.

"Oh, yeah!" I chuckled to myself, clapping my hands in a bow over the bowl before spooling the noodles into my pursed lips with steel chopsticks. "Delicious!" I assured the man, who hovered like a misty moon behind the heat threading up from the soup.

"Guksu," he said, nodding his silvery head toward the bowl. *"Guksu."*

"Guksu," I obediently repeated, giving him a thumbs-up. *"Oishii!"*

Immediately, the bobbing moon froze like a reflection in a still lake. *"Nihonjin?"*

"Huh? Oh, no, no." I shivered my head in denial, squinting earnestly at the man. "Not Japanese. American."

He guffawed approvingly into the baby-fine fringe of hair that hung from his chin. "America, America."

I brought Mindy to the restaurant the next day, while Margaret and Howard were sleeping off their jet lag. Proficient in Korean, Mindy learned that his name was Kyu Bok, that the dour woman in the cutesy apron was his wife, and that they had four children: one a successful factory manager who had bought this noodle shop for his parents, another a no-good party boy who drove a taxi, and two married daughters. Before coming to Seoul, Kyu Bok and his wife had been farmers down south. He was glad to leave that life, he said, holding out hands that were scarred and crooked, a ring finger abruptly ending at the second knuckle, but he missed his home village. A bullet of a woman with a kinked helmet of badly permed hair, his wife watched us with arms crossed tightly over her teddy-bear-aproned chest, face blank and hard as steel; even Mindy could not breach her fortress of hostility.

Crumpling down on top of my suitcase, I tucked my body under the narrow ceramic ledge that served as the awning over the restaurant, trying to keep out of the way of the scooters, motorcycles, and occasional car that nosed down the sidewalk-less alley. Arms trussing my legs close against my stomach, I rested my forehead on my knees, trying to will myself to sleep, until the gentle strains of "Sakura" intruded upon the anxiety-ridden narrative of my chaotic thoughts. Finally, Mindy was calling to apologize. Fumbling open my phone, I croaked, "Hello," the hollow echo of my own voice bouncing back from the satellite slowly orbiting miles above in the void of outer space.

"Miss Lisa?" His voice was small, strained, as if he were crouching in a cupboard, whispering.

"Oh, Kenji." I squeezed my eyes shut. My back was killing me and my thighs were numb. "How are you?"

"Bad," he said. Silence.

"Why? What's happened?" I asked.

His voice came back. "Kocho-sensei talked... What?"

The shitty reception had us talking over each other. "No, nothing," I said, just as he began again, "Kocho-sensei talked with..."

"Go ahead, Kenji," I said impatiently.

"Kocho-sensei talked with my mother and father. The police will come tomorrow."

"The what? The police?!" I gasped just as Kyu Bok arrived, his wife trailing after him. Surprised to see me there, he grappled with his ring of keys, his wife plopping down plastic bags heavy with vegetables with a fretful sigh. "What for?"

"To ask about the sex."

"Shit! You told them...?" My heart, weak and fluttery from the rivers of alcohol that had been pumping through it, flopped with the feebleness of a guppy that had jumped out of its fishbowl.

"Some things," he said glumly. "I am sorry, Miss Lisa, but I said something to Mori-sensei. I cannot tell too much lie to him. He is my—"

"What'd you say?" I cut him off viciously. I knew what Mori-sensei was to him. His baseball coach: priest, father figure, and teacher rolled into one irresistible force.

"I say—I said the night a person saw me go to your apartment was only the one time."

"You told him we had sex that night?"

"Yes. Tomorrow I must tell the police."

I didn't know about the age of consent in Japan (why hadn't I found out?), but I had heard of foreign teachers being arrested and deported for engaging in sexual relations with their students. I knew I couldn't go back. "Look, Kenji, you have to do something for me."

"Do something...?" he echoed, an echo to my echo.

"Yes. You have to go to my apartment and get my stuff together and mail it to me."

"What? I do not understand."

"My stuff, in my apartment!" I raised my voice, as if it were just a matter of his hearing clearly. "You must send it to me. Through the mail. Not all of it, of course, just... just..." Just what? My mind raced. Three years of books culled from Kinokuniyas around Japan. The blue-and-white bathrobe nicked from an *onsen* in Futsukaichi. The sandalwood bowls from Thailand, lacquer water puppet from Vietnam, hand-tailored batik dress from Malaysia. The dog-eared copy of *A Confederacy of Dunces*. The Hello Kitty bathroom slippers. The Imari ware sake flask and cups. The *purikura* albums. I squeezed my eyes shut against the thump of my own heart, the clamor of my chaotic mind. There was, after all, only one thing that was crucial. "My journals, Kenji, it's very important that you send them to me. There's a whole pile of pink Campus notebooks, three years' worth of them." I was babbling. "You'll find them in a stack in the futon closet. Send them all."

Kyu Bok's wife corralled a cloud of dust out the door with a bamboo-twig broom, deliberately sweeping it my way.

"Miss Lisa, you will not come back to here?" Did he sound relieved or disappointed? I squeezed the phone against my throbbing ear as a moped sputtered by.

"Kenji, I... I would love to return, but don't you see? It's no use. It's just easier if I don't go back. There is nothing important for me in Fukuoka anymore, except for you and my journals, I mean my notebooks." No use confusing him. "I'd just rather not go through the Japanese justice system." I sighed, sludgy blood squelching through my temples. "Surely you can understand that?"

He couldn't, because he probably couldn't even understand what I was saying. And he was only seventeen years old and had likely never been in trouble once in his whole life, except for not studying hard enough or for showing insufficient spirit as a member of the baseball team.

"But, Miss Lisa, I want you to come back."

"It'll be OK for you, Kenji. You did nothing wrong. It was all my fault. Just tell the police that I made you do it. Tell them I threatened your grade or something like that. Please understand, though, I just can't go back. Do you understand?"

"*Do you understand?*" mocked the satellite backwash of my voice.

Silence. A passing granny tapped me disapprovingly with the rubber tip of a slender bamboo cane.

"Kenji?"

"OK, Miss Lisa," he finally said.

"Please don't forget about the notebooks, Kenji. You can take anything of mine you want from the apartment. All my books, my CDs. But not the CD player, that's the school's. As soon as I hang up, I'm going to text you my address in America. Let me know when you have mailed the notebooks. Thank you, Kenji. I'll wait for you in America. When you graduate university, you can come and we can live together." Why was I saying that? I was such a coward. Why couldn't I just say a proper good-bye?

"Miss Lisa." His voice suddenly came through loud and clear. "I love you."

"Oh, Kenji," I half sobbed, feeling like a lower life-form than the cockroach that had just trundled out of a drainpipe near my feet. "I miss you terribly too. We'll find a way. I promise. *Kyousukete.*"

"Bye, Miss Lisa. I lo—"

I quickly hung up. This was all Mindy's fault. If she hadn't made me come to Seoul, Kenji and I would have stuck with our plan to sneak off to Nagasaki together for a few nights, and he wouldn't have been seen by some unknown informant coming out of my apartment.

As I unkinked my numb limbs, Kyu Bok's wife again came to the door to empty a bucket of dirty water. The water splashed against the pavement, spattering my legs, gurgling with a sickly burp down the drainpipe from which the cockroach had come. She blocked my way as I tried to hobble into the restaurant, first pointing to the wet floor and then at the sign on the door that listed the restaurant's hours, the ink faded into inscrutable hieroglyphics. Hoping to gain Kyu Bok's attention, I pleaded loudly with her. "Please let me in. *Juseyo!*"

Her face tightened into a walnut of wrinkles as she scowled contemptuously, firmly sliding the door shut in my face. Customer service, I noticed, was not a major concern to the small-business owner in Korea. Or at least not for this customer. My junior year of college, I had studied in China, where everyone was eager to accept me as their own, just at face value. They insisted that I was an overseas Chinese, and even when I told them I was born in Korea, they still treated me like a returning hero. But here, in the country of my birth, all I got were closed hearts, unwelcoming grunts, and slammed doors.

To kill time, I wandered toward the main street, where I could buy a beverage with which to wash down some Advil. As I was scanning the shelves of weird soft drinks for something that would actually taste like a soft drink should and not like old toenails or the burned bottom of a coffeepot, I realized that it was about now that Mindy was meeting her birth mother.

It was for this meeting that I had come to Korea. Just a few weeks ago, she had called me in a state of euphoria. I too was in a more banal state of euphoria, wailing away at karaoke long after my bedtime on a school night. "They've found her, Lisa," she quavered.

"Found who?" I asked, drunkenly pulling on the door of the karaoke box rather than pushing it, as Aussie Tim belted out "Like a Virgin" in my ear.

"*Her*. My mother."

Out in the hallway, I pretended to be confused even though I knew exactly what she was talking about. "Margaret was missing?"

"Come on, Lisa, I'm not joking!"

"They found your old lady, huh? That's great! I'm so happy for you!" I lied.

"I know, I can hardly believe it," she said in a rush, her astonishment, and maybe the stretch of planet that curved between us, making her take what I said at face value. "I keep pinching myself to make sure I'm not dreaming. When is the school year over for you?"

"For me? Why?"

"I want you to come to Seoul. MotherFinders is setting up a meeting with her. I want you to be there too."

"What do Margaret and Howard think about my being there?" I realized I hadn't brought my beer out into the hallway with me and opened the door to the karaoke box, Samantha shrieking, "And now, the end is near..." I frantically pointed at my glass to indicate that someone should pass it to me. Beer slopped onto my shirt as I cradled the glass in the crook of an arm while closing the door again. "What? Sorry, I didn't hear you."

"Mom agreed that it would be nice if you were there too. She and Dad completely get that you're the only person in the world who understands what I'm going through. They even want to pay for your plane ticket."

Yeah, right. I could just see them *begging* Mindy to buy me a plane ticket to Seoul. "What about Trip?"

"What about Trip?" she asked defensively.

"Will he go as well?"

"No. He can't. His law firm won't give him the vacation time."

That sounded suspicious to me, since his daddy owned the firm. "Really?"

"He needs to save up vacation for our honeymoon. But he's totally on board with this. Much more than you are."

"Which is why maybe he should go..." The school year would be over in three weeks, with a short break before the start of the new school year, during which time Kenji and I had planned an excursion to Nagasaki. It was to be the first time we spent the night together. He'd already told his parents an elaborate lie about a graduation trip with classmates.

"Look, Lisa, if you don't want to be there for me..."

"I had plans to do some traveling, Mindy," I whined. "With a guy." Of course, I hadn't told anyone, not even Mindy—*especially* not Mindy—about Kenji.

"Lisa Sarah Pearl, I am begging you. I don't think I can do this without you. Please, please, please, if you never do anything else for me in my life, do this."

"What about all the wedding crap? Don't you need to be there?" Mindy and Trip were getting married in June.

Her laugh was wild, the cackle of a woman on the edge. "Everything has been arranged for months now! Besides, his mother will be able to take care of last-minute details. She's practically running the show anyway."

A girl staggered out of one of the rooms, her hand held up to her mouth. It'd be a miracle if she made it to the bathroom in time.

"What's she like? Your mother?"

"MotherFinders didn't send much information. Her name is Paik Su Bin, and she lives in Suwon, a suburb of Seoul. That's all I know so far—that's all I know about her." Her voice cracked, broke up, came back together again.

"Min Hee, are you crying?"

"Yes, I'm fucking crying!" she gasped. "I'm freaking out here. I'm going to meet my mother!"

The door to the karaoke box slammed open. "Yo, Lisa! Is 'Oops!... I Did It Again' yours? It's on!"

"All right, Mindy, of course I'll be there. School ends in three weeks. Have your dad send me the ticket. There are direct flights from Fukuoka."

We are a peculiar tribe, adoptees, with something that rankles at the very core of our beings, a little burr buried somewhere deep in the tender seat of our souls. For some, it is only a pinprick; for others, it is a raw outrage that can never be soothed. But for all of us, deep down we know the truth, that we are an abomination of nature, for what could be more unnatural, more against the laws of nature, than the adopted child? Human identity is forged upon genetic history, and from the very first we find our place in society through family, the one true thing in an ever-shifting world; nations may come and go, leaders fall and rise, but family is forever. Adoption challenges those fundamental notions of belonging, subverting the sacred primacy of the bloodline, testing the boundaries of love, probing the depths of the very definition of what it means to be a mother, a father, and a child. The adopted child is a lie, her family a fiction. She learns this early, from the rude inquiries of other people, the loose talk of "real" mothers and fathers, the misty-eyed sentimentality of well-meaning strangers rhapsodizing about rescue and second chances. While her parents tell her adoption is an act of love, the world tells her something else. You know that moment in every sitcom when one of the characters is told that he is adopted? The goggled eyes, the *boinggg* of the sound track, the mirthful guffaws from the audience as the unthinkable horror of the accusation sinks in. It's all a ploy, of course. The character is never adopted—the writers would never be so cruel. Every adopted person sits through that scene with a smile frozen on her face, mind suspended until that painful and tired old gag passes and she can once again be one with the audience, chuckling at the foibles of their beloved and deeply flawed favorite characters. The pervasiveness of that tired old joke in sitcoms, comics, and other popular entertainment reveals the profound anxiety with which the general public views adoption. Many adopted children can pass by blending in with their families, but the transracial adoptee is immediately identifiable by a different skin tone, eye shape, texture of hair, as if branded with an *A* for *Adopted*, there for all to see. It is, sometimes, all they see.

I don't recall the exact moment when, as eight-year-olds at Korean Kamp, Mindy and I met, but I do remember feeling really lucky that this porcelain-skinned princess with swept-back Cindy Crawford hair and brightly hued Benetton outfits had chosen me out of all the other girls in the cabin as her most favored friend, saving a place for me next to her during every mealtime, picking me as her partner for paired activities, inviting me to sit on her bunk bed, where we giggled and whispered until the counselors told us it was time to go to sleep.

When my mom and Mindy's parents came to fetch us on the last day of camp, it turned out they recognized each other from adoptee orientations, and that not only had Mindy and I come through the same adoption agency, but we had also arrived in America on the same plane. As further evidence that she and I were destined to be best friends, we lived just a short Metrobus ride down Wisconsin Avenue from each other, the Stamwells in Georgetown and my mom and me in Bethesda.

Mindy couldn't have come at a better time for me, because the night before I met her, while tucking me into bed under a limp, coffee-stained floral bedspread at a Vermont roadside motel near Korean Kamp, my parents had told me that Daddy was moving away to live in Africa. I didn't fully understand what they were implying, thinking that Dad's leaving had more to do with his work than with his relationship with my mom. Fomenting my confusion, they assured me that we were still a family, only in a different way. It wasn't until I returned from camp that the full implications of my parents' divorce hit me. No more of Dad's Sunday morning chocolate chip pancakes; no more Monk, Mingus, or Morgan blasting from the stereo; no more staying up late to catch the end of the Orioles game. But by that time, I had Mindy, and I seized upon her to fill the void left by my father. My parents splitting into two halved me as well, and I saw in Mindy a mirror image that made me whole again. She was all light and sweetness, I dark and sour; she pure Korean, I two continents stuck together, blurred into one word: *Amerasian*. She was a classic beauty, with a high forehead, a sweetly rounded chin, and features that perfectly matched; I was befreckled, was large pored, and had a Frankenstein's monster nose that looked like it had been sewn onto my face from someone else's dead, discarded corpse. She was the star of her school's lacrosse team, class president, merit scholar, lead actor in local theater productions, and student member of the board of the Korean Cultural Society; I racked up suspensions at school, was arrested for shoplifting, filched liquor from my parents, and dabbled ambitiously in pharmaceutical and recreational drugs. She liked boys; I liked rebellion. She was fanatical about Korean culture, taking Korean language lessons, teaching herself how to cook Korean food, getting a black belt in tae kwon do, learning indigenous arts and crafts. I was interested in every culture but the Korean one and, thanks to my father, traveled to the dusty, downtrodden far reaches of the earth, where few Americans dared to venture.

But we fit together well, the two of us. I was pointed where she was soft; she was curvy where I was thin. We nestled into each other and made a perfect yin-yang circle.

When we were about twelve—that precarious time when the child starts to become aware of her place in the world and how she is not at the center of the universe but some insignificant spot way out in the cosmos, and the adoptee of ethnic origins realizes that the world does not accept what she takes for granted and that explanations have to be given over and over (*yes, they are indeed my parents; yes, my last name really is Pearl; yes, I am from here and speak English at home; well, OK, you may guess where I was born*)—Mindy and I decided we'd become famous. If we were famous, everyone would know our story, and we wouldn't be obliged to trot it out every time we met someone new. "But," Mindy said to me, her lips closed self-consciously over her newly installed braces, "can adopted people be famous? I've never heard of one famous adopted person."

We were lying on our stomachs in her family room, the hairy jute carpet scratching our bare thighs, weaving friendship bracelets, Mindy's fingers plucking the strings together with graceful dexterity, my bracelet (which would be her bracelet) a lumpy string of rough knots. I let the slippery threads fall from my fingers as I contemplated that shocking statement. "C'mon, there has to be someone! Think!"

We wrinkled our brows and racked our brains, but in the time it took Mindy to finish her (my) bracelet, we still couldn't come up with one person. Then, as she was tying it to my wrist, the tips of her hair brushing my arm as she bent seriously to her task, she raised her head so suddenly she almost smashed into my nose, which I was just being made to realize by the bullies at school was a preposterous nose for probably anyone, but especially a slant-eyed girl. She announced, "I know! Moses!"

"Moses? Is he a real person?"

"Of course he is, silly! Remember, he was sent down the river in a basket of bulrushes to save him from the slaughter of Jewish babies? C'mon, you're the Jew here."

It's true, my parents were Jewish, but more as a cultural heritage rather than as a religion. It was Mindy who went to church regularly. "All I remember about Moses is he was a grumpy old guy who brought the Ten Commandments down from the mountain." I shimmied my wrist, admiring the bracelet, woven in my favorite colors, yellow and black. Then I looked guiltily at the crooked, half-finished skein of knots that lay tangled among the prickly furrows of the rug.

"Well, baby Moses in his basket was found by an Egyptian princess, a daughter of the Pharaoh, the same one who ordered his death!"

Ever the skeptic, I muttered, "Real life doesn't happen like that."

"Why not?" she demanded. "We're living examples of strange coincidences. We came to America on the same plane. And now we're best friends. How freaky is that?"

"Yeah, I guess so..." I conceded. "What happened to Moses? I mean, did his family find out he was Jewish?"

"Um..." She bit her lip, dimple crumpling under her eye. "I dunno. But eventually *he* finds out he's Jewish and leads his people out of slavery by parting the Red Sea!"

"Wow!" We gazed at each other, her smile mirrored on my face. "That's so cool! We can be like Moses, so famous that we are remembered two thousand years later."

"And help our people," Mindy added earnestly.

"We know you'll be a famous actress." Mindy had just finished a stint as Annie in her school play. "But what about me?"

Tilting her head, Mindy looked at me through squinted eyes, as if it was just a matter of seeing me in the right focus. I chewed on the inside of my mouth, waiting for her verdict. "You like to read a lot..." she mused. "And you keep a diary. You always scribble in that thing before you go to bed, even when you come for a sleepover."

I looked away in embarrassment. So what? Any old fool could keep a diary.

"You're going to be a famous writer," Mindy decided, clapping her hands to make it final.

"I do like to read," I agreed with a small stirring of pride tickling my chest like a furry animal twisting in its lair. Mindy had revealed a truth that I hadn't been able to admit to myself. I *did* want to be a writer. Saying it made it so, and I felt like it was already an established fact, an integral part of my identity, my books already inside of me, to be produced with an effortless ripple of fingers over a keyboard. Feeling excited and full of energy, I leapt up and slipped on her checkered Vans. "Let's go outside and play on the trampoline. I'll finish your friendship bracelet at home."

Though I don't remember exactly, I'm pretty sure that the friendship bracelet never got finished.

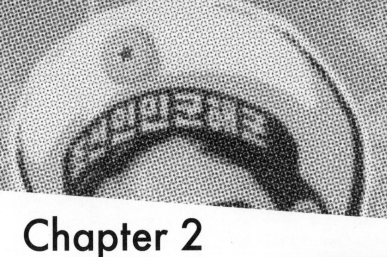

Chapter 2

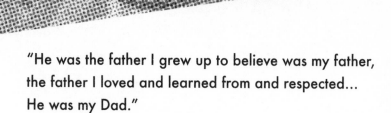

"He was the father I grew up to believe was my father, the father I loved and learned from and respected... He was my Dad."

–President Gerald R. Ford

I was halfway back to Spaghetti Kyu Bok's when my phone rang again. Wheeling my suitcase to a protected spot in the lee of a table piled high with coils of fake designer belts, I glanced at the number. It wasn't Mindy, who was no doubt happily sipping her umpteenth cup of tea with her new best friend, her birth mother, right now.

"Ah, hello, Lisa." A soft croon.

"Yes? Who is this?"

The softness sharpened into a hurt whine. "You don't know? It is I, Harrison."

"Oh, Harrison! What's up?" My head, just starting to settle down, began to throb again. Harrison was the person Mindy and I had met for a drink the night before.

"How are you feeling?"

"Well..." A laugh erupted from me like a sour burp. "Not too good, really."

"Why? What is wrong?" he asked with exquisite solicitude.

"First of all, that shit you gave me last night really fucked me up. It was like no cocaine that I've ever snorted. So then, to sober me up a little, I did too many shots, and now I'm really hungover."

"Oh, Lisa, I am so—"

"And this morning, my friend Mindy? The one who was with me last night? Yeah, well, she threw me out of my hotel room, and now..." Suddenly, the full enormity of the scene with Mindy hit me, and I felt as awful as I had felt that whole, entire shitty morning. "And now we're not friends anymore," I wailed, each word getting louder as the tears began to spurt from my eyes. The belt vendor spat out the toothpick he'd been shifting around in his mouth and squatted down on the flat of his feet, settling in for the show.

"Lisa, are you crying? Don't cry, Lisa. It's OK. I am your friend, and I can help you."

"Well, you haven't helped me very much so far," I sobbed, spraying my phone with tiny white bubbles of spit.

"No, you are right," he purred softly, like an affectionate kitten that wants to curl up in your lap. "It is all my fault. I feel terrible about it. Let me help you. Where are you?"

"I... I don't know the name of the alley. It's down Sogong-ro from the hotel about a mile and a half, and then... you know where that FamiMa is? Turn into the thin alleyway right after that, then turn left at the first, or maybe second, intersection, after a butcher shop. I'll be at the noodle shop on the right."

"OK, don't move. I'll be there soon."

"Really?" It seemed too good to be true. And then I remembered that he was probably operating under his role as a fixer rather than as the man he'd been last night at the bar. "You'll never be able to find it from those directions."

He laughed softly. "I am a man of many means."

Trudging back to Spaghetti Kyu Bok's, I stopped to peer at myself in the dusty window of a little stationery and candy shop to check just what state Harrison would find me in. I hadn't taken a shower that morning, thinking I'd do it after we returned from the Dunkin' Donuts, having no idea that Mindy had other plans for me, and I ran my fingers through greasy clumps of hair, thinking it was about time to change my hairstyle, which had basically stayed the same since eighth grade. In the fall of that year, Mindy's mother took us to her chichi hairdresser for matching haircuts for the Tweedledee and Tweedledum costumes we were to wear to a congressman's daughter's Halloween party. That Margaret would pay for me to get a $100 haircut for the sake of a Halloween costume (one she had dreamed up herself) indicated how badly she wanted Mindy and their neighboring congressman's daughter to be friends, but Mindy had hated the girl ever since she tried to give Mindy the nickname of Doll, short for China Doll, which was why she insisted her mother wangle an extra invitation to the party for me.

As I was stuffing a cushion into the waistband of a pair of Margaret's old stirrup leggings, I whispered to Mindy that we should have gone with my original idea of Mindy dressing up as Moses and me as Gerald Ford, who was also adopted, according to a *Life* magazine article I had just read. Mindy rolled her eyes as I yoked my shoulders with a pointy lapelled collar she had cut from construction paper. "Look at us," I hissed. "Could we possibly be more goofy looking?"

"You think you wouldn't look even goofier as Gerald Ford?" Mindy laughed, flicking at the floppy ribbon tied in a bow around my neck. "Anyway, no one would have a clue who you were."

"I'd just tell them I was a famous adopted person," I whispered. I wasn't sure why I was whispering, except Margaret was standing right outside the door, and the idea of famous adopted people was only for Mindy and me and most especially was not for Margaret, who viewed being adopted as some sort of special condition that had to be treated with therapy sessions, heritage camps, Korean cultural activities, and ersatz celebrations like "Homecoming Day," the anniversary of Mindy's adoption, which was marked by dinner out at a restaurant of Mindy's choosing and a lavish gift, usually jewelry, like the diamond stud earrings that were glimmering in her earlobes at that very moment.

"You could wear a sign around your neck, 'Gerald Ford, Famous Adopted Person,'" Mindy whispered back. "And then you'd gets lots of candy from people who felt sorry for somebody's fake child who didn't even know how to dress up properly for Halloween."

We laughed into our hands, because we weren't actually going trick-or-treating or to the Halloween party, really. We had other plans. But we had to be careful not to raise Margaret's suspicions. Margaret was CEO of Stormraker, a private security firm that, as Mindy described it to me, helped our government "fight the bad guys." There was a framed photograph prominently displayed on their living room wall of Margaret in full combat gear, blond hair spilling down from a camouflage helmet, leaning casually on a pickup truck filled with grinning men clutching machine guns and rocket launchers. Based on that photo, my youthful imagination endowed her with James Bond–like spy skills that Mindy and I had to very carefully evade.

Right on cue, Margaret asked, "What's going on in there?"

Mindy said, "Just about finished up here, Mom. We look awesome!"

We placed the striped beanies Margaret had found at Bruce Variety onto our heads and nodded at each other before marching out to Margaret's delighted shrieks.

She insisted on walking us the four blocks to the congressman's house, even though Mindy protested the whole way, making her promise not to pick us up. We stayed at the party for an hour, pure torture for me as the Georgetown girls completely ignored me while sharing inside jokes and obsessing over some guy called Fergus. As became her upbringing, Mindy politely thanked the congressman and his wife when we left, telling them we had to go to another party. Then we met up with the very same Fergus, the first in a long line of Mindy's rich white boyfriends with slicked-back hair, popped-up collars, and prep school jackets with gold-threaded insignias on the breast pocket. A sophomore at Landon, Fergus already had his driver's license and his own Volvo. His friend gave up shotgun to Mindy, hopping into the backseat with me. I was not good with boys, clamming up in their presence, excruciatingly self-conscious, doggedly trying to keep my crazy nose from being seen in profile. Mindy, on the other hand, was suddenly a burbling fountain of inanities, flicking her hair, flashing her chin dimples, squealing with delight at every fresh idiocy uttered by Fergus. We drove around for a while before finding the darkest corner of a public park parking lot. There, Fergus pulled a joint out of his glove box and lit it up, filling the car with a sweet, earthy aroma. He passed it to Mindy, but she shook her head. Fingers tightly pinching the end, he tried to insist, gesturing emphatically at her while he coughed inside his throat, keeping the smoke trapped in his lungs, until he gave up and passed the joint to his friend. The boy sucked earnestly at the twisted end and then slanted the joint over to me, smoke spilling out of the corners of his grimacing mouth. Without hesitation, I took it and put the tip, wet from the boys' saliva, to my lips, whistling smoke through pursed lips just as I'd seen them do. Immediately, my lungs spewed out what I had tried to force in. I coughed until I thought I would gag. Fergus smirked, "Can't get off without a cough," and took another deep drag. When the joint came around again, I was better prepared for it, lightly sipping the smoke, mixing in a lot of air. Nevertheless, to my acute embarrassment, I coughed again, but for the third round, I was able to inhale without causing a scene. Probably he and his friend had an agreement, because somehow the friend and I were out of the car. We found our way to a swing set, and I was pumping my legs, leaning my head back, and laughing. I could feel the beanie gently lift from the crown of my head as I swung forward; it seemed a minor miracle to me that it never flew off but landed in the same warm spot, again and again, on the upswing. Incoherent words dropped from my lips like stones into a placid pond, but the friend seemed to understand me, for he would drop his own stones as well. Giving up on the swings, we walked into the night, Halloween lights glazing the world orange. Costumed children paraded by at a reduced speed, so that I could follow every flutter of material, distinguish every sparkling sequin, see the glitter of eyes in the shadowed holes of masks. I was still laughing, but the sound seemed very far away. The friend told me to mellow out, but I couldn't, so he had me take the cushion from my pants and sit on it on a lonely curb near a dark house that got no trick-or-treat traffic. Long after I had forgotten his existence, he returned with pockets full of candy, and to ecstatic groans, we consumed it all. Candy has never tasted so good again.

Mindy lost her virginity that Halloween, and I my sobriety.

Of course, Margaret found out that we had left the party early, and naturally, she blamed it all on me because her sweet, smart, beautiful daughter would never think to deceive her best friend, which is how Margaret imagined her relationship with Mindy. We were not allowed to see each other for two months, the first in a long line of attempts by Mindy's parents to strangle our friendship, so we made up for it by talking on the phone for hours, driving everyone in our respective households crazy for tying up the phone lines. It was on one of those calls that Mindy informed me, "Gerald Ford doesn't count."

"What? Why not?!"

"Well, because you said he was a famous adopted person, I decided to write a biography on him for our presidents unit of US history, and it turns out that his mother left his biological father just days after giving birth, then remarried. And so even though Gerald Ford got the name of his mother's new husband, the guy *never* adopted him. Can you imagine, the kid names himself after you, and you can't even be bothered to adopt him?"

"But even if the new father had adopted Gerald Ford, he still couldn't be considered a famous adopted person because he was never separated from his birth mother."

"He's only half adopted," she agreed.

"Kind of like how I'm only half Asian."

"He's white on the outside and adopted on the inside," Mindy said, giggling.

Steam was still rising from my bowl when Harrison slid onto the stool next to me. "Wow, that was quick!" I marveled, dipping my head down to suck up another hank of noodles.

Chest rapidly rising and falling, he nodded breathlessly, perspiration blistering his forehead. "I was nearby," he panted.

Perhaps it was a cutthroat world of competition for adoptee fixers in Seoul. I was surprised at his eagerness and wondered what it would cost me.

Kyu Bok approached with a glass of water and metal chopsticks wrapped in a white paper sleeve, while his wife glared at us from the vapor clouds of the kitchen's boiling pots.

"Get what I'm having," I advised with a noisy slurp.

Harrison gave his order without a nod or a smile to Kyu Bok, who shouted the order without a "please" or a "thank you" at his wife before sauntering over to the cash register and ostentatiously shaking out his newspaper.

"OK, not to worry, I have everything figured out," Harrison assured me, leaning toward me with tender solicitude.

"Mmm?" I looked up at him while reeling in a long, thick noodle, the broth spattering my chin.

"A friend of mine is out of town, and he said you can use his apartment." He peered winsomely at me from behind a glossy fringe of hair. "You can relax, forget about your friend Mindy. Have a good time. I'll show you around Seoul."

Though no longer jelly-brained with a hangover, I was still slow on the uptake, and it took me a few seconds to become confused. "Is that in your job description?"

"My job...?" A dent appeared above each arched eyebrow as he looked at me with eyes the color of burnt sugar, his gaze sweet and sticky.

"Yeah, you work for MotherFinders, don't you? I thought they helped people look for their mothers. I wasn't aware they provided escorts for single female travelers."

He leaned in very close to me like he was confessing something, the soft pop of his lips tickling my ear. "My work for MotherFinders ended when I took you to the address in Itaewon. When I met you at the bar last night, that was as friends, friends hanging out."

I scooched back on my stool to put a little distance between us. "And so the use of this apartment and a few days' sightseeing will cost me just how much exactly...?"

"Lisa!" he rebuked me, lacing long ivory fingers protectively over his heart. Kyu Bok slipped a large bowl brimming with golden broth whorled with noodles before Harrison, veiling him in steam. "I come here as your friend. Because I like you, and I want to help you. And I feel very ashamed for offering you the drugs last night."

Dropping my voice, I hissed, "Yeah, what was that shit anyway? Didn't you say it was coke? Because I'm pretty sure that wasn't coke."

He hung his head, feathered locks flopping over his eyes. "I am very embarrassed. A friend of mine gave it me. I told him I wanted to impress you very much. He said American girls are liking this kind of a drugs." All of a sudden his English, which had been so perfect that I was sure he had an English-speaking parent, turned clumsy. "I was very bad for giving it to you. It must to be a dangerous something."

Two weary-looking men in workman's coveralls came in, and Kyu Bok's wife ran over, screeching and bowing, to settle them at one of the square tables wedged at the back of the tiny shop.

"Do you forgive me?" Harrison asked, gazing into my eyes with an earnestness guaranteed to make all the adopted girls go crazy, finely sculpted nostrils slightly flared, plump lips parted just a crack.

I picked up my long-handled spoon and started to scoop broth into my mouth. "You're making me nervous. I forgive you. Now eat your soup."

Harrison had been introduced to me by Miss Cho, my case manager at MotherFinders. For the simple fee of $500, plus incurred expenses, this organization, which also had branches in China, Russia, Romania, Ukraine, and Guatemala, would comb through archives and registries to find out the name and current address of an adoptee's birth mother. If it was successful in finding her (it advertised a 72 percent success rate in South Korea), it offered additional services, such as contacting the birth mother to arrange a meeting and organizing flights, hotels, itineraries, interpreters, drivers, and meeting rooms, as well as a whole array of seminars on how to build a relationship with your birth mother.

Even though I was ambivalent about finding my birth mother, I had filled out the forms for MotherFinders at Mindy's urging, and because she paid the exorbitant fee. I figured that if the service did unearth the woman who had cast me from her womb, I could always decide not to meet her. As if in answer to my lack of enthusiasm, my case languished while Mindy's moved forward. When Miss Cho had emailed me just a few days before I was to arrive in Seoul, asking me to meet with her, I figured it was just a courtesy on her part, since she knew I was going to be in Seoul anyway and since MotherFinders was making a mint off the Stamwells.

Miss Cho met me at the front desk with a sympathetic grimace. "Miss Pearl, I am afraid we have hit a dead end in our investigations. Yours is a most unusual case, for it seems that the information that should have been filed with the various agencies, both Korean and adoptive, are quite simply not there."

"Oh." I tried to crumple my face into the look of pained disappointment that Miss Cho clearly expected. "Are you sure?"

"Yes, quite sure. I have never seen anything like it before." She nervously fingered a delicate filigree cross that she wore around her neck. "About 18 percent of our adoptees have to be told that their mothers cannot be located, but we have never before encountered a situation where the paperwork is simply not there. The only thing we have—and please do not get your hopes up—is an address that your birth mother left as her place of residence. It is in Itaewon, an area that has gone through many changes since 1983." She handed over an envelope that she had been clutching in her hand. The paper was damp from her fingertips. "The address is written there, in both Korean and English."

Two women came into the office, the younger one with piercings studding her face like some sort of weird acne, a dagger tattooed on her neck, and ratty purple hair that might have been a wig. Miss Cho passed a critical eye over them as the older one announced who they were. The receptionist, with the bulging, sprung-out eyes of blepharoplasty, greeted them breathlessly, asking how their flight over was and if they were satisfied with their hotel.

I sighed. "Well, you did your best."

Clearly expecting a more dramatic reaction from me, Miss Cho blinked in surprise. Of a different generation, she had not had eye surgery. "Yes, we did. And your contract with us, I am sure you will recall, says that your fee is nonrefundable."

"I do recall," I agreed eagerly. It was worth $500 of Mindy's money to know that there was no way to trace my birth mother, that she'd remain the stranger that she always wanted to be to me. "Totally understood."

"Mmm, yes, but MotherFinders would like to offer you the complimentary services of one of our guides. He can take you to the address in Itaewon and tell you some of the history of the area—what kind of people lived there, what kind of a neighborhood it was." She flashed me a tight smile, meant to be sympathetic. "So you can get some idea of your roots."

"Oh, that is not necessary..." I protested, but Miss Cho was already beckoning someone over.

"Please meet Harrison," Miss Cho introduced him, speaking quickly now. "He will escort you to the address in Itaewon." She leaned back on her heels, as if anxious to retreat from the scene of a horrific accident. "Normally we charge extra for a guide, but in your case, there will be no fee." Extending an arm to the goggle-eyed receptionist, she hastily recited her final lines: "Please sign the final documents with Miss Ri. Thank you, Miss Pearl, and best of luck to you."

A swift double peck of a bow and then she was gone.

I turned to the man who stood with polite deference at my elbow. He was, quite simply, gorgeous. Every feature was perfectly chiseled and in complete harmony with the other features. His forehead was high but obscured by feathered bangs that were brushed forward; nose delicately molded; lips prominent, with pillowy contours and a slight, delicious upswirling at the ends; chin gently bifurcated with a hint of a dimple. His eyebrows were heavy, with a wild furring from the point of their arched apexes to the outer tips. He did not shave them, as other Korean pretty boys did, and it was this flaw that perfected the beauty.

"Hello, Miss Pearl, my name is Harrison." He smiled warmly at me, revealing perfectly aligned teeth, white as virgin snow. "It's nice to meet you." He held out a hand, fingers tapering delicately into squared tips, nails buffed to a shine. "I look forward to serving you."

I put my hand limply in his, and he squeezed it softly. He was looking carefully at me, and I felt his eyes lingering on my nose. More than my thin face, brown hair, or freckles, it's my nose that most betrays the miscegenation. It is long, but unlike the classic Korean nose, it has a crook high at the top, from which it is a precipitous drop down to the tip, which then curls inward, as if suddenly embarrassed by all the commotion it has caused.

"Uh, you know, I really don't need your assistance," I stammered, wishing I had thought to touch up my lipstick before coming in.

A small laugh like the tinkle of a wind chime in a light spring breeze blew softly from his lips. "Please, it is my pleasure." He put a hand at my back and directed me toward the receptionist. "Let's take care of that paperwork now."

The receptionist looked up at us, or rather at him, batting her false eyelashes with strobe-like rapidity. She pushed the paperwork my way while the two of them bantered in Korean. Without reading the text, I quickly signed my name.

"Look"—I turned to Harrison and then quickly averted my gaze from his luminous face to his earlobe, which was just as exquisitely formed as the rest of him—"I really appreciate this show of good faith by MotherFinders, but it's not necessary. I don't need to go to this address. I'm just here to support a friend, really, whose mother has been found. We're here for the reunion, and so I have plenty to do."

Directing me toward the door, he shone his movie-star smile full force on me. "Please, it's a free service. Just relax, and we'll have fun together. I've really been looking forward to it."

He drove his car, an Audi, with insolent aggressiveness through the clogged arteries of Gwanghwamun. Everything about Mother-Finders was plush, from the heavy linen weave of its stationery to the towering arrangements of tropical flowers that perfumed the air of the reception area, but I was surprised that mere factotums would apparently be sharing so freely in the profits. Not only was he driving a powerful sports car, but he also sported a chunky TAG Heuer watch, a pink Lacoste button-down, and Gucci loafers. Maybe they were all knockoffs, since we were in the land of the fake label, sidewalks lined with vendors offering Dunhill cigarette lighters, Chanel sunglasses, and Longines scarves. I myself had a new Louis Vuitton purse cradled in my lap. Still, I thought as I stroked the leather seat, as far as I knew the Koreans had not counterfeited luxury sports cars yet. *I guess no one ever went broke underestimating the need of adoptees to find their roots,* I thought as the glassy canyons of downtown gave way to squatter, more prosaic concrete buildings.

"Itaewon"—he nodded at the chaotic world outside the car—"is a favorite hangout of the army guys. And expats and tourists. It's like being in LA or something, not Seoul. Is that where you're from? LA?"

"No, I'm from the Washington, DC, area. Except actually I live in Japan now. So I guess I'm more of a nomad than anything." I almost asked him if he had ever lived in LA or the US, which would explain why he spoke English so well. But I didn't want him to think I was too interested. As it was, I was afraid that I'd have a hard time getting rid of him.

Inching into a tight parking space with expert twirls of the steering wheel, he announced, "Well, here we are. This is not the same building that was here in 1983."

We both peered up at an ugly concrete building that reared into the air like a dead tree trunk.

"OK, that's nice," I said cheerily. "I'm ready to go back now."

He giggled. "You are very funny, Lisa. I can call you Lisa, can't I? Now that we're here, we might as well take a look."

He hopped out of the car and came over to my side to open the door, offering me his hand to pull me out of the low-slung seat. His skin was soft, more sensuous even than the creaminess of the leather interior.

Still holding my hand, but lightly, as if cradling a chick that fell out of its nest, he turned to gaze upon the generic urban hulk of the building. "So, according to my research, this street was filled with wooden buildings that were mostly family-run businesses—tailors, restaurants, souvenir shops for the army boys." He let go of my hand to flick a pack of Marlboros from his shirt pocket. "Records show there were several businesses operating out of the address. It was likely a large building, taking up more ground space than this one, but only two stories high." He lit his cigarette with a slim gold lighter.

"And what were the businesses?" I don't know why I asked; I didn't really want to know the answer. Like asking the name of an unfaithful partner's lover: knowledge that would not uplift or improve me in any way.

"A souvenir shop and an antiques shop upstairs, and on the bottom a tailor and a"—he sharply inhaled—"bar."

I sucked on a cheek, chewing at the inside of my lip before sensing Harrison's interest in the gesture. I popped my cheek back out.

"Perhaps she worked there," he said, smoke streaming from his flared nostrils, the insides of which shone pink like the enameled lining of a seashell. "At the bar."

I nodded. Among the long ladder of placards advertising the building's occupants, I noticed one in katakana. From habit, I slowly deciphered it: *MA-SA-JI*.

"You know what, Harrison? I have to confess to you, I am kind of happy that they didn't find my birth mother, because I'm afraid she might not be a nice person. My friend Mindy, who's coming to meet her birth mother, she's a very nice person, so I'm sure her mother will be too. But me?" I shook my head skeptically.

He squinted at me through the smoke coiling from the cigarette that dangled from his mouth, then slapped his thigh and began to laugh with a mirth all out of proportion to the moment, shaking his head at me in amusement. "Oh, Lisa," he hooted, dropping his cigarette butt, "I am just coming to understand that you are a real joker." He waggled a finger at me as I crushed out his cigarette with my shoe. "Oh, I know your kind, you bet I do."

Still chuckling, he inspected the signs of the different businesses that occupied the building, so I did as well. Some were in hangul, some in English, some both. SOOKIE'S MODA FASHION SHOP. SLOPPYS BURGERS. KIM CHUNG-MIN, DDS. FAME LEATHER GOODS. HOLLYWOOD LOUNGE.

Harrison tapped a shiny fingernail on a discreet black sign that was etched in gold, HONEY DO GENTLEMEN'S BAR, gilded bubbles floating around the words. "I think I've been in this bar," he said wonderingly. "Yes. It was very nice. Nice atmosphere. Makes you feel relaxed. Even though it says 'gentlemen,' it's for ladies too."

As Harrison pushed his empty bowl away and softly burped into a loosely curled fist, I asked, "Your name isn't really Harrison, is it?"

"No," he admitted. "It's not."

I waited for him to volunteer his real name, but he didn't. So I asked, "What is your real name?" I was often asked the exact same question, and it annoyed the hell out of me, both because Lisa Pearl was my real name and because I was forced to admit that I did have another name, a foreign name given to me at birth.

I'm pretty sure it annoyed the hell out of him too. He paused before answering. "It's Ji Hoon."

I tried it out. "Ji Hoon. That's nice. Do you mind if I call you Ji Hoon?"

"No, not at all." He shrugged. "They ask us to use English names at MotherFinders, and so I picked Harrison."

"After Harrison Ford?" I hazarded.

He nodded glumly, staring past me at a poster of a man determinedly chugging a quart bottle of OB beer, sweat beading his brow from the effort. "I like movies."

Because I seemed to have offended him, I cast about for something complimentary that didn't involve his beauty. "Your English is excellent. Did you study in America?"

"Oh, really?" His bushy eyebrows perked up a little. "Thank you. I was fortunate enough to have a really good tutor, an American man, Mr. Smith."

Kyu Bok emerged from the kitchen to clear our bowls. "Min Hee?" he asked with a wistful tone.

I felt my cheeks splotch with heat. "Min Hee, she, uh, she and I, uh... She's busy today."

I looked helplessly at Ji Hoon, who obligingly said something in Korean to Kyu Bok. Kyu Bok grinned, looking at me with raised eyebrows as if we were sharing a good joke. His wife dropped some dishes in the sink with a loud clatter, and he disappeared into the steam, their barbed voices tangling together as they bickered at each other.

Groaning, I dropped my head in my hands. "I'm ready to go to your friend's apartment now, Ji Hoon."

Ji Hoon insisted on paying, and as he settled the bill with Kyu Bok, Kyu Bok's wife emerged from the misty recesses of the kitchen and, arms folded over a teddy bear picking daisies in a meadow, blinked belligerently at me through the fringe of permed hair that wilted over her forehead like a freshly used mop. Ji Hoon took hold of my rolling suitcase and preceded me toward the door.

"Go back to where you came from," Kyu Bok's wife spat at me. "Go home!"

"Wha...?" I stopped my weary drift toward the door. "Since when did you speak English?"

Waving her thin arms as if to waft me out the door like a pesky fly, she screamed, "Go home and don't come back."

I looked in shock at Kyu Bok, who was tucking Ji Hoon's money into the cash register. He did not meet my eyes, but intently began to stack coins into tidy columns in the money drawer.

Ji Hoon tugged at my arm, pulling me out the door. "Come on, let's go."

"Go home!" The wife's shrieking followed us down the street.

"What was that all about?" I asked.

"Don't pay her any attention. Some Korean people are crazy." Ji Hoon shook his head mournfully.

"I had no idea she spoke English!" I stammered. "This whole time, while Kyu Bok and I were trying to communicate, she could have translated! Fucking bitch!"

We rounded the corner onto the wide avenue, back in the other Seoul, where people with necks twisted to their cell phones rushed toward important business meetings, the subway shuddered underneath our feet, and shopgirls in neat uniforms waited at doors with hands folded precisely together in front of them. Ji Hoon seemed to relax a little. He pulled out a cigarette. "Some people are uncomfortable in the presence of Korean adoptees. They think of it as a national shame." He paused, his lighter poised in the air, cigarette waggling in his mouth as he finished his thought. "Especially women feel this way. Maybe she gave up a baby herself, who knows?"

That stopped me in my tracks. That woman could be my mother! Mindy's mother! Except no, Mindy's birth mother was right now dressed in her best *hanbok*, sipping tea with Mindy and her parents, holding Mindy's hand and tearfully explaining just why she had to give up her precious baby daughter.

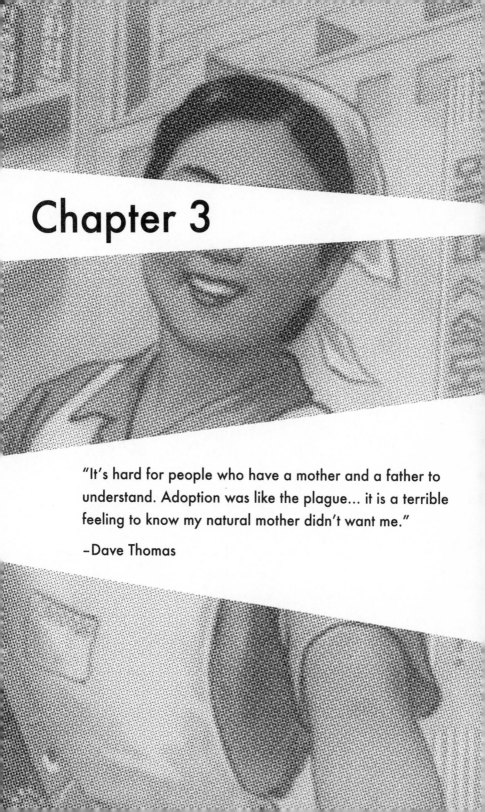

Chapter 3

"It's hard for people who have a mother and a father to understand. Adoption was like the plague... it is a terrible feeling to know my natural mother didn't want me."

–Dave Thomas

"Make yourself at home," Ji Hoon said, wheeling my suitcase into the cupboard-sized apartment that was bereft of furniture save for the kitchen cabinets, a tray table, and a three-legged stool. Nothing on the walls, no plants, no decoration of any kind.

"Here is the bedding." He slid open a closet door. "You know how to use Korean beds?" He squinted at me anxiously.

"Yeah." I began to pull the folded-up mattress off the shelf.

"No, no." He laughed softly. "Don't set it out until you are ready to go to sleep."

"I *am* ready to go to sleep," I said, nudging him out of the way so I could maneuver the mattress onto the floor. "Where are the sheets?"

Ji Hoon extracted a sheet from the bottom shelf and helped to tuck the mattress into the elasticized corners, allowing me a glimpse of his underwear, the elastic band of which declared in bold block letters JUICY FRUITS. I flopped facedown onto the mattress, mumbling as if already half asleep, "I'm exhausted. I promise I'll call as soon as I wake up." I closed my eyes and tried to fake a light snore. Finally, after much too long, he left, softly locking the door behind him. Just to be safe, I waited a few minutes before slithering silently across the floor to fish my phone out of my faux Louis Vuitton handbag, the zipper already giving me trouble. Checking the time, I saw that I was in danger of waking my mother but dialed the number anyway, hoping she was just coming in from catering a late-night event. To my relief, she answered on the second ring. "Hi, Mom," I said, trying to sound cheery. "Did I wake you?"

"Lisa! I was just thinking about you!" Her voice was like the bread she loved to bake, soft and warm, a little crackled at the surface. "No, you didn't wake me. I just got home from an over-the-top bar mitzvah party. You should have seen it! It was a Hawaiian beach theme, with real sand, potted palm trees, orchid leis, and a DJ who was flown in from Honolulu."

I cradled the phone against my ear, wishing it were my mom's cheek. "How's Scott?"

"Fine. Training for another marathon, so he's being really boring, not drinking wine and going to bed at nine so he can be up for five A.M. runs. But, Lisa, how did the meeting with Mindy's birth mother go? I've been thinking about it all day long."

My fingers crept to the hollow of my throat, where the yin-yang pendant nestled. I slid it back and forth along its short silver chain as I sputtered, "I don't know. We had a fight, Mom. She basically told me she was sick of me, that I was an embarrassment, and to go away and never come back. She pretty much broke up with me. Our friendship is over."

A staticky gap of intercontinental silence. "I can't believe that, Lisa. Twenty years of friendship shouldn't end because of one fight."

The tears that were forming deep in my sinuses fizzed painfully up to my eyes. "We said some pretty harsh things. She told me to take an early flight home. That I wasn't fit. To go with them. To meet her birth mother. It was so. Mean." My sentences were fractured by the sobs I sought to swallow.

"Do you want to tell me what happened?"

I sighed unsteadily. Not really. No. "This guy I met invited us to this bar last night. We went and I... I got drunk and behaved pretty badly, I guess."

"Give her a call. Apologize. She'll forgive you. I mean, it doesn't happen often, does it? That you get so drunk you embarrass yourself?"

"No," I lied.

"No, of course not! This must be a stressful time for Mindy, so she probably overreacted. What she needs is your love and support, so even if it was her fault, you should be the bigger person and apologize. Don't you think?"

This is why I called my mother. Even after all of my fuckups, the unending drama of my teenage years and the scare I gave her that time Mindy saved my life, she refused to even consider that I didn't always behave with the same noble rectitude that she and any other normal, whole, moral, good-hearted person did. "Yeah, Mom. You're right. We were both way stressed."

"She'll be so grateful to hear from you. She loves you, Lisa, and you love her."

"Oh, Mom." My sobs, which had faded, made a comeback. "I do love her, and I love you too. I miss you so much."

"We miss you too, sweetheart."

"I... I've been thinking," I murmured hesitantly, as if just struck by the thought. "Maybe I'll just come straight home from Korea. The news out of Fukushima is really freaking me out. They say the radiation is much worse than the Japanese government claims it is."

Did I feel bad about using a devastating natural disaster and its potentially much more horrifying man-made consequences to my advantage? I did, but at this point it was but a minor infraction compared with some of my more despicable, self-serving, cowardly, and possibly felonious trespasses.

"And besides, all of a sudden I feel so homesick."

"But, Lisa," she said, and laughed, "isn't your school expecting you back?" She thought it was just an offshoot of my spat with Mindy.

"Frankly, I don't think they'll care one way or the other. I was going to be a lame-duck instructor anyway, with only a couple months left on my contract."

"Yes, but what about your apartment?" I was confusing her, and I imagined her running a strand of hair through her fingertips, which she did when distracted. "What about all your stuff?"

"There's hardly anything there that I want or was going to bring home with me. Just my journals, which I'm getting mailed to your house. Let me know when they arrive?"

"You do what you feel best, Lisa," my mother said, after a very long pause. It was past two A.M. in her world, and I knew she was barely awake. "I must admit, I have been a little worried about the radiation, but everything I've read and heard has said that you're too far away to be affected. I still think..." Her words blurred with a yawn. "...that you should go back to Japan, but whatever you decide, we can't wait to see you."

"Mom?" I lay back on the mattress and pulled the comforter up to my nose. It smelled like it was fresh out of the plastic packaging, faintly reminiscent of a new Barbie or pleather upholstery in a car that's been baking for hours in the sun.

"Mmm?"

"Do you ever feel, like, disappointed in me? That I haven't made something of myself? That I've wasted the opportunities that you and Dad gave me?" I burrowed all the way under the comforter.

"Oh, Lisa, no! Your father and I, and Scott too—we understand. There are many different paths that people take through life. I mean, I did worry about you through those rough years." A little nibbling pause, I pictured her pinching a corner off a loaf of her home-baked bread. "Not worry so much as I felt bad for you and what you were going through. Teen years are tough for everyone, parents and kids alike. But we made it through, and we couldn't be happier with the adult that you've become."

I squeezed my eyes shut, trying to stanch the tears that once again welled up, in love, in sorrow, in guilt. "I love you, Mom. I can't wait to see you again. I really need one of your hugs."

"I love you too, Lisa," she croaked, voice scratchy with exhaustion. "You just tell me your flight information and Scott and I will be there at the airport to pick you up."

I reluctantly said good-bye. Why would I need another mother when the one that I had played the part so well?

Someone was in the room with me. I opened my eyes to see a pair of blistered and cracked hands reaching for my neck. Trying to cry out, I found I had no voice. The hands wrapped around my throat. And then my eyes opened to the very same room of my dream, but no murderous intruder. My head hurt, and I knew I had slept too long. Fumbling for my phone, I found it under my pillow, where I had dropped it after talking with my mother and crying myself to sleep. Seeing there was a text message, I quickly opened it, hoping it was from Mindy. It was from "Harrison," sent shortly after he had left the apartment yesterday: "Hello Sleepy-head! Call me as soon as you wake up!!!"

As I took a shower in the cramped bathroom, so small that there wasn't room for a shower curtain, the water splashing over the toilet and sink and onto my toothbrush and toilet kit, I wondered what Ji Hoon's angle was. The only conclusion I could reach was that he was helping me so I would help him. Not with money, because he seemed to be doing all right in that department. Not for language skills, like all the *pengyou* I picked up in China, since his English was damn near better than mine. The only other obvious answer was a visa.

I waited until seven to call him, and even then I didn't think he'd pick up, but he answered on the first ring. "Don't move, I'm just on my way there."

"Actually, can I meet you somewhere? I need to get online to send some emails and look for a plane ticket home. Is there a cyber café somewhere near?"

"Knock, knock!"

"What?"

"Knock, knock!"

"Uh, who's there?"

"Me! I'm at your door!"

And indeed, I could hear his voice, in stereo, over the phone and coming from behind the door of the apartment. I said, opening the door, "That's kind of creepy."

"Good morning!" he trilled, marching in with a carton tray holding two coffees, a McDonald's Happy Meal box dangling from a pinkie. "I thought you might want a little taste of home, so I got you some hot cakes."

Reaching eagerly for the coffee, I said, "You can have the hot cakes. The only fast food I eat is Wendy's." Which was a lie, told because I felt uncomfortable accepting any more favors from this guy who had apparently been lurking in the hallway, just waiting for my phone call.

"Wendy's?" Pursing his plump lips, he gently blew steam off his coffee. "What is that?"

"It's a fast-food restaurant founded by a guy named Dave Thomas, who was adopted."

His eyebrows wriggled in furry bemusement, as if he couldn't figure out what that had to do with anything.

"Mindy and I keep a list of famous adopted people. He's one of them." It sounded stupid when I said it. It was stupid. I opened the Happy Meal to see what the toy was and ended up eating the hot cakes, dribbling syrup on my last clean shirt.

Stuck in traffic opposite a blocky behemoth of a building that could only have been a government ministry, we watched a large crowd of people as they milled about clutching colorful signs in hangul, wearing headbands emblazoned with the red-and-blue yin-yang circle of the Korean flag; some brandished megaphones into which they were screaming so ardently that the cords on their necks looked ready to burst. My interest caught, I leaned closer to the window. Black-helmeted policemen in riot gear stood in rows between the crowd and the building, frenzied protesters, faces clenched in a rictus of hate and foam practically dripping down their jaws, pushing up against their shields.

"What is going on here?" I asked, checking to see if the doors were locked.

Ji Hoon had been tapping his fingers along to Katy Perry. "What? Oh that." He laughed. "Don't pay any attention. Demonstrations like that happen all the time here."

"What are they demonstrating against?"

One man was so enraged he was tearing his shirt off, rending the cloth with his bare hands. Another had wormed his way behind the line of plastic riot shields wedged together like a set of false teeth, and a knot of police was wrestling him to the ground.

Ji Hoon shook his head in mystification. "Who knows? US beef, the closing of an army base, the opening of an army base, a soccer match, Japan, China... you name it. We are a very passionate people, always looking for revenge." He chuckled at his countrymen's foibles and turned the radio up. "All I know is they are a nuisance. Everybody's slowing down to have a good look, causing this traffic jam."

The car in front of him started to crawl forward, and as I craned my neck to look back at the demonstration, a man dove into the police line headfirst with a powerful scissor kick, as if he would swim his way through the river of policemen. The last thing I saw was a wave of police surging toward the crowd, thumping their batons ominously against their plastic shields. And then they slipped from view and I looked out at a busy sidewalk swarming with industrious pedestrians, without a hint or a ripple of the violence that was happening a block away.

Ji Hoon laughed at me. "You have that Korean fire in you, don't deny it. I see it in your eyes." Behind his gold-rimmed aviator sunglasses, I imagined his eyes taking me in with a cool and appraising look. I imagined that he liked what he saw.

With a self-conscious laugh, I tucked a lock of hair behind my ears. "Curious that you would compare me with a Korean. Most Koreans, like Kyu Bok's wife, don't think of me as Korean. At least, that's the way it seems to me every time I'm in Korea."

"You've been to Korea before?" he asked in surprise, mercifully turning Taylor Swift down.

"This is my second time. Besides being born here, I mean. I spent a few weeks traveling around with Mindy after spending a year studying in China."

"A year in China?" he echoed wonderingly, as if presented with a perplexing set of puzzles pieces. "It is very curious, Lisa, that you have spent a lot of time in both Japan and China, but almost none in Korea."

"Mmm." I did not agree or disagree. "I really don't know much about this country at all. I think it's a little fucked up, though. But I guess it's only natural. It's in a tough neighborhood, the weedy, runty kid in a playground full of bullies." We had passed into a dreary section of apartment buildings and shops, and I let the streetscape blur by the window, no longer interested. "It's not even a whole country, but has been cut into two like Solomon's baby, or like a set of twins separated at birth." I fingered the yin-yang pendant at my throat. "Two halves that need to be made whole."

He nodded seriously. "Yes, we must reunite the two halves. That is the only way for peace and prosperity. We all feel it here"—he tapped a finger on the Tommy Hilfiger logo of his polo shirt—"a tear in our heart that can only be healed by reunification. Ah, finally we are here."

Ji Hoon drove the car up onto a litter-strewn sidewalk, almost completely obstructing it so that a pedestrian would have to inch past or else get off the pavement and walk in the street. "Are you sure it's OK to park here?" I asked.

"Oh, yes, perfectly all right here," Ji Hoon assured me, leading me into the lobby of a shabby building that emitted a dank chill. After stabbing at the elevator button for some minutes, we walked up an uneven stairway to the fifth floor. A door with no identifying placard was opened by a stunted, pale wraith, and we stepped into a room crammed with office equipment: fax machines, desktop computers, printers, modems, telephones, laptops, monitors, TVs, and some electronics I couldn't even identify. Two floor fans going full blast could not begin to mitigate the intense heat of the room. Yet the three office workers—as featureless and identical as button mushrooms, with the exact same blunt bowl haircut—wore thick, long-sleeved cotton shirts, collars and armpits stained with sweat, and heavy khaki pants. In unison, they bowed and bowed and bowed some more. We bowed back, Ji Hoon chatting amiably in Korean. One of them seemed to be the designated speaker and answered Ji Hoon's banter with nervous little outbursts, followed by dry little coughs of laughter on all sides.

After the small talk was over, Ji Hoon ushered me to a swivel chair, foam swelling out from the ripped and stained nylon cushions. "You may use this computer," he said. "The staff has made it ready for you."

"What for?" I hung back, eyeing the fat coils of electric wiring draped with furry centipedes of dust entangled beneath the desk.

He laughed, but it was kind of tense, like the laughs he had shared with the office workers. Which one, I wondered, was his friend? "To use the email! Didn't you tell me that is what you wanted to do?"

"Oh, yeah." I sat gingerly on the dirty foam stuffing of the chair and looked at the laptop. It was a sleek, late-model Asus, very fast. "There's a lot of equipment in this office," I muttered as I brought up my email account. "Who knew travel agents needed so many electronics?"

"Oh, yes," Ji Hoon explained knowledgeably. "International travel requires a lot of electronic equipment. While you do that, we will work on your ticket. When do you want to leave?"

"As soon as possible," I said, tapping in my password.

"To Washington, DC?"

"Yeah, any of the airports." There were thirty-seven new messages, but a quick scan showed that none of them was from Mindy. Fanning myself with my own shirt, I clicked through them. Most were from my friends in Fukuoka, writing to ask me if I was OK. Apparently the news about Kenji had gotten out.

"Miss? Miss?" a little voice was whispering in my ear.

Startled, I swung around to see one of the mushrooms offering me a cup of tea. Detecting small mounds under her shirt, I realized she was a woman, which would explain why they had sent her with the tea. I took the cup from the tray, wondering if one more heat-radiating thing would cause the whole room to melt into a pool of molten plastic and metal. "Thank you," I said, and lifted my cheeks in a forced smile. She nodded gravely and scurried away.

Somebody had sent a link to a Japanese newspaper article, but the only thing I could read was my name in katakana and the name of my high school. At least there were no photos.

Ji Hoon approached with a mournful face. "I have some bad news. The earliest available flight to Washington, DC, is not until Friday."

"Oh, that's OK," I mumbled, quickly exiting from the article. "What day is it today?"

"Monday."

"Monday?" I brought my shoulder up to my cheek to wipe away a trickle of sweat. "You're telling me there are no seats for four days? That's crazy."

"I know, right?" Ji Hoon shook his head in wonderment. "We don't know why. They even checked for New York, and that is five days. LA is three days, but then you have to get across the country."

Nibbling at the inside of my mouth, I looked up at a very faded and fly-specked poster of a girl in a white bikini frolicking in a smooth milky sea, with the word BAHAMAS smeared like dirty clouds on a sky of faintest blue. *How many Koreans go to the Bahamas?* I wondered distractedly.

"But I have some good news as well," Ji Hoon said with an encouraging nod. "They have told me that they can get us a free vacation to Jeju Island. Did you ever hear of it? It is the most beautiful place in all Korea. They"—he indicated the drab trio, standing in a row behind him like prisoners lined up to be shot—"received a free promotional offer, including all transportation, from the Jeju Island Tourism Board. We can go tomorrow and then be back in Seoul in time for your flight on Saturday. It's an almost perfect coincidence, no?"

"Uh..." My mind was stuck in neutral, still thinking about the emails from Fukuoka.

One of the travel agents cleared his throat. We all turned to look at him. "It is very ro-ro-romantic," he stuttered, his face flaring crimson. "Fa-fa-famous for natural beauty."

"Uh..." I took a contemplative sip of tea.

"It's for free!" Ji Hoon emphasized. "A luxury hotel on the beach. We can hang out and drink soju all day long."

Finally comprehending what was being proposed to me, I wondered, "Will it be all five of us?"

"Five?" Ji Hoon's beautiful brow contracted in puzzlement. I nodded slightly to indicate Wynken, Blynken, and Nod lined up behind him. "Oh, no." He laughed scornfully at the very idea of the travel agents traveling. "No, no. It is just for the two of us." And he gave me such a tender, seductive smile that the part of me that was still unsweaty sloshed with a hot wave of desire.

"And we'll be back in Seoul when?"

"Thursday. Then I will take you to the airport on Friday."

What the hell? Up until now, every action I had taken was the wrong one, getting me deeper and deeper into trouble. Perhaps if I just did nothing and left it all up to fate, everything would work itself out. Besides, an image of Ji Hoon tenderly running his sensitive fingers over my naked body flashed unbidden, but not unwelcome, in my brain. I shrugged. "Why not?"

"Yes, OK?" Ji Hoon insisted on a more affirmative answer.

With a self-conscious little snort, I complied. "Yes."

He turned triumphantly to the triumvirate and they all shuffled back to the other side of the room. I had just opened an email with the subject line "WTF Lisa?!?!" when Ji Hoon once again approached. "Sorry," he whispered apologetically, "but how will you pay?"

Leaning my head into the breeze of the fan, I fluffed my hair to release the heat trapped between the follicles. "I thought you said it was free," I accused him.

"No, no," he hastened to assure me. "For the plane ticket to Washington."

"Oh." I laughed embarrassedly. Digging through my purse, I came up with a credit card.

"They also need your passport."

I handed the stiff little blue booklet to him, our fingers brushing, sparking a blaze that exploded all the way down to my groin.

After I had deleted all the emails alluding to Kenji from my inbox, I sent my mother a note with my flight information, omitting the details on the trip to Jeju Island, because there was no way I could adequately explain to my mom why I was taking an impulsive trip with a handsome stranger. Finally, after much hesitation, I sent Mindy a two-liner: "Hope everything went OK with your birth mother without me there to embarrass you. My mom told me I should apologize, so sorry."

Then I quickly logged out before I could regret the defensive tone of my message. Closing the laptop, I turned to find the four of them looking at me. The travel agents seemed to blink in unison, like computer-programmed avatars.

"Ready?" Ji Hoon asked, handing me back my credit card and passport.

"Yeah." I stuffed them into my purse, wrestling with the faulty zipper to close it but quickly giving up, because my fingers were too sweaty to get a good grip on the metal pull tab.

The travel agents bent simultaneously into a low bow. "Thank you for your pa-pa-patronage," the designated speaker said solemnly.

Back in the car, with the air-conditioning blowing icily even though it would have been easier to open the windows to the cold early-spring air, Ji Hoon mentioned that a friend wanted to meet up at Honey Do. "I thought you might like to join us. He's a nice guy and likes to practice his English."

"Honey Do?" I echoed incredulously.

"Yes, well, actually, I suggested we meet there," Ji Hoon explained as he deftly slid through traffic. "I remembered what a pleasant place it is for just hanging out. The girls don't bother you if you tell them to leave you alone."

I thought to point out that there were plenty of bars about that weren't hostess bars, but instead asked, "Is his English good? Because I have to be honest with you, it's really boring having a conversation with someone who thinks their English is good, but it really sucks." In a grating falsetto, I mimicked an Asian accent: "Do you rike my shity? Can you eat lice?"

"Oh, his English is excellent," Ji Hoon declared, honking his horn at a Hyundai that was crawling along too slowly for his taste. "And he loves American culture. You'll see."

I shrugged. It wasn't as if I had anything better to do.

Though it was still full daylight when we entered Honey Do, inside it was Saturday-night dark, the backlit bar and tiny pinpoint lights embedded in the ceiling the only illumination. There were no customers, just two lacquer-faced hostesses and the mama-san owner. Mama-san, whose blaring blond hair was cut short in an early Princess Di pouf, brought us a bottle of Johnnie Walker Red Label, a wooden tag around its neck, and two glasses clinking with golf-ball-sized ice chunks, while her hostesses followed bearing shallow dishes filled with peanuts, rice crackers, dried squid, and popcorn. They tried to sit down on the low leather couch with us, but Ji Hoon shooed them away, muttering something to Mama-san that made her hurry off, patting worriedly at her hair.

"What's the little tag on the bottle mean?" I grimaced as the whisky blazed a fiery trail down to my stomach.

"It is my bottle. I pay for it and they bring it out whenever I come here."

"I thought you said you hadn't been here in a long time."

"I came last night, to make sure it hadn't changed since the last time I was here," he said, cocking his eyes sideways at me underneath the velvety swoop of his tousled bangs.

In the glum darkness, my thoughts turned to Mindy, wondering if she had read the email yet, wondering if she missed me like I missed her. I took another deep draft of whisky, and Ji Hoon promptly poured more into my glass. "I feel terrible about Mindy," I confessed, my tongue already sprung loose by the liquor. "I miss her like crazy."

"I think it's always best to let these things cool down a bit after an argument. Wait until we are back from Jeju Island to contact her. She will be so happy to hear from you by then," Ji Hoon advised. "We Koreans are hot tempered and need time for our emotions to cool before we can see things clearly."

"Do you really think we're Koreans?" I wondered, popping a salt-flecked peanut into my mouth.

"Oh, your friend is a classic Korean beauty!" Ji Hoon declared.

I took a dissatisfied swallow of whisky. Ji Hoon topped up my glass. "What about me?" I asked, pouting.

"You..." He slid his eyes sideways at me with a delicate, just-between-you-and-me smile. "You can be as Korean as you want to be. It is your choice."

Almost half the bottle and a few karaoke songs later, I asked where his friend was. "Oh"—Ji Hoon smiled apologetically—"he is famous for being late. He'll be here, though."

"Well, I think I better switch to beer," I slurred.

Ji Hoon snapped his fingers in the air and yelled out, *"Maekju."* A bumper-sized bottle of Cass materialized quickly. He poured beer for me and I reciprocated, clinking the bottle heavily against his glass and almost knocking it over.

"I feel really good right now," I suddenly decided. "I feel like things are looking up. I can't wait to go home and see my mom again. Working at MotherFinders, you probably think all adoptees want to meet their birth mothers, but not me. I think it was fate that my birth mother can never be traced. Many adoptees believe it's their destiny to find their birth mother; I believe it's my destiny not to."

There was a bit of a commotion at the door, but I continued to ramble on, barely even noticing when Ji Hoon stood. By the time I turned my bleary eyes up, Ji Hoon was bowing deeply to a chubby number wearing an oversized Chicago Bulls jersey, baggy nylon basketball shorts, bright yellow Jordans, unlaced, a leather baseball cap emblazoned with a gold skull skewed sideways on his head. From a thick rope of gold chain, a gigantic dollar-sign pendant glistening with rhinestones hung down to perch on the cushion of his paunch. I giggled. "Yo, bro! Whazzup?!"

Ji Hoon frowned seriously at me. "Lisa, it is my pleasure to introduce you to my friend Jonny."

"Hey, blood!" I held out a clenched hand for a fist bump.

The hip-hop wannabe looked angrily at Ji Hoon and they exchanged a few terse words. Sensing that I was maybe messing things up for Ji Hoon, I laughed. "I'm just kidding, Jonny. It's just, I love your outfit. You got a real sense of style. I dig it!"

Jonny nodded, chewing the inside of his lip, a little dimple quivering in the massive slab of his cheek, silken strands of a Fu Manchu hanging down like a beaded curtain over his little mouth. The hostesses were flitting about, stroking the air around him and making frightened little squeaking sounds. A few large men lurked in the background, sensed more than seen. He lowered himself next to me on the couch, and immediately Mama-san brought an overstuffed pillow to put behind his back and an ostentatious cut-glass decanter with a crystal stopper. A tray of bar foods also materialized: hamburger sliders, chicken wings, miniature hot dogs wrapped in puff pastry. After everything had been arranged just so, the women were dismissed with a shake of his meaty hand. Jonny held out to me a snifter that gleamed with an amber liquid poured from the sparkling decanter. I shook my head and held up my glass of beer. Ji Hoon snapped, "Take the glass, Lisa. It is rude not to accept it."

I shrugged, accepted the snifter.

Jonny raised his glass, pinkie extended, and proclaimed, "To mothers."

"To the motherland," Ji Hoon added with a hot exhalation.

"Motherfucker," I joyously rejoined, swooping my glass toward Jonny's, but he already had his at his lips.

"Harrison has told me about you, Lisa." His accent, like Ji Hoon's, was almost nonexistent. "I'm very pleased that you agreed to meet a nobody like me."

My loose laugh was cut short by his finger probing the bridge of my nose. "Hey!" I jerked my head back. "What the fuck do you think you're doing?"

Jonny regarded me with bemusement, as if he wasn't used to people talking back to him. "It is not often one sees a nose like yours," he said by way of apology.

I reached out to touch his nose, nestled unobtrusively between his massive cheeks. His skin felt rubbery. Ji Hoon leapt up as my finger skidded down the clean slope of Jonny's nose and two hulking men emerged from the shadows. Chuckling, Jonny said something in Korean. Ji Hoon sat down again, and the two men melted back into the gloomy periphery. Jonny stripped the flesh from a chicken wing before tossing the bones onto the floor.

Taking a pull off my drink, I asked, "What is this, cognac?"

"Yes," Jonny said, and took an appreciative sniff. "Hennessy X.O. The best."

"Just like Jay-Z likes, eh?" I teased him. Guessing what Jonny did for a living, I now knew where Ji Hoon got his drugs from. "You like Jay-Z?"

Popping a pig in a blanket into his mouth, he shrugged. "I prefer singing, you know? We Koreans love our folk songs."

"Oh, like *enka*?"

"*Enka* is Japanese," he growled sternly. "You must know that we Koreans hate the Japanese." He glared hard at me, gnawing at the inside of his lip. I ran my tongue over the ragged flesh of my own mouth.

"Oh, yeah, yeah," I agreed. "Goddamn Japanese."

"Monkey demon puppets," he muttered in answer. Then he grinned boyishly, and I thought maybe I had been wrong to assume we were about the same age—maybe he was just a teenager, which would explain his silly outfit. "But they make damn good sushi, am I right, Harrison?" The two of them laughed knowingly as if at some inside joke, slapping high fives. Sighing happily, he leaned back into the couch, slinging his arms across the top, where they lolled like beached whales. "Tell me about yourself, Lisa," he enjoined.

"Uh..." I blinked at him. "How about you tell me about yourself first? Looks like your story is much more interesting than mine."

"I don't know how my story could be more interesting than someone who was ripped from the bosom of her mother and her country, but OK. My story is not a remarkable one at all, for Korea. My father works very hard. As a child, I did not see him much but was always under his loving guidance, and it is for him that I strive to do my best. My mother sacrificed everything so that I could become successful. If I can prove myself, I can become head of the family business."

"And what is that business?" I asked, aware that Ji Hoon was rigid as a corpse by my side.

"Oh, it's complicated," Jonny said, snapping his fingers toward a gold cigarette case that lay easily within his reach. "A huge conglomeration of businesses, mostly in entertainment."

Mama-san placed a cigarette between his lips and worked the lighter.

"Now it's your turn." He squinted at me through a cloud of smoke.

"Well..." I took a fortifying gulp of cognac, emptying the glass. One of the hostesses immediately slithered up to pour more, but Jonny waved her away gruffly and personally filled my glass. "My name is Lisa Sarah Pearl, and I..."

A small smile played through the glossy threads of his mustache. "You don't look like a Lisa Sarah Pearl."

"Yeah, I know. Um, as you seem to already know, I was adopted. My parents divorced when I was eight—"

"Whoa, whoa." He held up a hand, small and bloated like a baby's hand, the knuckles dimpled, nails bitten down into little half-moons. "Where were you born? When?"

"I was born here..."

"Here? At Honey Do?" When he smiled, his chubby cheeks and long, curved front teeth gave him the spunky cuteness of a chipmunk.

"Here, in Seoul," I snapped. "In 1983."

"And what do you know of your real mother?"

"My real mother is on the other side of the Pacific," I told him. "As to my birth mother, I know nothing, but I presume she was some bar girl or prostitute. As Ji Hoon must have told you—"

"Ji Hoon?" he echoed.

"Yeah, Ji Hoon." I rolled my eyes toward Ji Hoon, who had barely blinked since Jonny had come on the scene. "Your pal here."

"Ah, Harrison." Jonny's glance at Ji Hoon was like a glare of a searchlight on an escaping prisoner.

"Lisa wanted to know what my Korean name was," Ji Hoon squeaked apologetically.

"Yeah, Jonny." I dripped sarcasm onto his name.

He fluttered two fingers through the wispy fringe of his chin hairs. "So, what is it that Ji Hoon has told me?"

"That the company he works for, MotherFinders, could not locate any records on my birth mother. Which just really reinforces what I thought all along: she was some downtrodden, two-bucks-a-pop whore—"

"Hey, hey, now," Jonny cautioned sternly.

"What?" I shrugged my shoulders, reached for another chicken wing. "No need to get offended. It's my mother, after all."

"Your language is unladylike," he said, pursing his lips prudishly.

My laughter crackled loudly amid the strange hush of the bar. "Whatevs, motherfucker. You sitting there in your ghetto outfit. Isn't that what you entertainment purveyors do? Sling filth?"

He glowered at me, his eyes thinning to dark crevices and his mouth puckering up into a little dot. I grimaced back, lifting my upper lip off my teeth.

"Can you sing?"

"What?" Just then a disco ball started to spin, flinging bright sparks through the empty room. A brief blast of music made us all jump, then was quickly silenced.

Jonny stood up, beckoning me to do the same. "Let's sing something together, shall we? Beatles? 'Yesterday'? 'Twist and Shout'? Abba? 'Dancing Queen'?"

"'Top of the World'?" Ji Hoon volunteered in a thin voice.

"Umm..."

"'Yesterday'!" Jonny decided. With a snap of his fingers, he directed Mama-san to cue the song. "Come on, Lisa, get up!"

I stumbled a little as I struggled to stand up. "Oopsie!"

Holding a microphone out to me, he instructed, "Now I really want you to belt it out."

Mama-san poked violently at the remote control, and then a disconsolate man buried his head into his hands on the screen as the guitar strummed and words began to skip across the bottom. "Yesterday, all my troubles seemed so far away..." we yowled asynchronously.

"No, no, no." Jonny waved his arms in the air. He barked at Mama-san, and she hurriedly clicked the remote control, starting the song over again. "Together now, Lisa, OK? Ready? And a one, and a two, and a three."

He chopped his arm through the air, and we sang again, together this time.

Chapter 4

"I grew up with a big hole inside of me. Most adoptees grow up sensing that same hole inside of them... Many people spend their whole lives searching for something to fill that hole."

–Michael Reagan

In the elevator, Ji Hoon said, "My girlfriend is driving us to the airport."

Sludgy-headed from the evening before, throat raspy from a night of karaoke, I croaked, "Your girlfriend?"

He nodded glumly. "She is angry with me. Just ignore her."

The elevator thudded to a stop and I stumbled out. He had a girl-friend for fuck's sake?

I ducked into the backseat of the Audi, singing, "Hello! I'm Lisa!"

The dark helmet of hair didn't turn around.

"Look, I'm sorry to inconvenience you like this..." I wanted to explain that I hadn't even known she existed until five seconds ago. But really, if I had, would it have changed my plans? A free vacation with an Adonis was a free vacation with an Adonis. Not that I really thought anything would happen between the two of us.

The car shuddered as Ji Hoon slammed the trunk. On his way to the driver's seat, he opened the back door. "Are you comfortable?"

"To be honest, I'm a little hungover. I'm going to try and get more sleep, if you don't mind."

"Here." He stripped off his leather jacket, turning it inside out to the soft quilted lining, warm from his body heat. "Use this as a pillow."

As he handed it to me, the girl turned around, following his gesture with angry eyes. I gave her a quick glance as I took the jacket. Plump face, pearly skin, long taut eyes, little button mouth. Tucking his jacket, which smelled of sickly-sweet cologne mixed with a more enticing muskiness that I imagined was his natural scent, under my cheek, I tried to make myself go to sleep. For a while, I listened to their hushed conversation that occasionally burst into sharp nips and out-raged growls, like tussling puppies who didn't know the strength of their own jaws. To be unconscious was really the kindest thing I could do to my body, and I finally managed a queasy state of suspended consciousness, the car like a space capsule, or a casket, cradling me in cushioned, hushed monotony.

Shaking me gently by the shoulder, Ji Hoon purred, "Lisa, we're here."

My eyes creaked open to see the two of them twisted around in the front seat to peer at me. Sitting up, I wiped the drool off my cheek, corrugated with the pattern of the quilted lining of his jacket. His girlfriend's lip rose in a hostile curl before she turned to get out of the car. She was beautiful, but not as beautiful as Ji Hoon, poor thing. It must be a constant aggravation to have such a gorgeous specimen of the human form for a boyfriend.

As he stuck his head through the driver's-side window to say good-bye, I imagined Ji Hoon soothing her: "See, just take a look at her. You don't have anything to worry about." He nuzzled his face toward her cheek, but she leaned away and began to nose out of the parking space before he'd pulled his head out the window. Cheekbones edged with crimson, he shouldered his MCM leather bag, grabbed the handle to my dingy rolling suitcase, and marched into the vast concrete bunker of the terminal.

While we shuffled forward in the check-in line, my attention was captured by a crowd of white people slowly advancing toward us like a thundercloud rolling across the prairie, identifiable as Americans by their NFL team caps, gum-snapping jaws, and cacophonous hooting. As they neared, I saw that some of them were cradling bundles in their arms, while others had baby carriers strapped to their chests. All eyes were turned down to the soft packages that they held, though occasionally they would roll their gibbous eyes at one another and squeal, "Oh, she just yawned!" or "Oh my god, I still can't believe I'm holding my baby. Oh my god."

"Come on, Lisa," Ji Hoon called, beckoning from the counter. The airline representative flicked her eyes away from him just long enough to give me a dismissive look. She kept us a long time, chatting and cooing at Ji Hoon. I turned to find the crowd of Americans again, but they had disappeared.

When we arrived at security, however, we squeezed in behind the group. There was some fuss as to how to get the babies through the scanners. "He's too little to get x-rayed," one of the new moms fumed. I stood behind a blond woman who already looked exhausted by motherhood, eyes pouchy and red rimmed, hair pulled back into a greasy ponytail, clumsily applied foundation streaking her face. Her baby was propped against her shoulder, looking blankly at me. "Does Bessie have a burpie?" the woman was babbling softly as she massaged the infant's back. "Widdle baby Bessie, sweetums." She began to jog the baby slightly, even though it had not squirmed or fussed. "Your mama loves Bessie, loves baby Bessie so much."

The woman's husband leaned close to the baby, taking a deep whiff of the top of its head. "Bessie baby smells so good! What a great smell, eh, Ava? Better than money!"

The baby's black eyes flickered toward the man but then settled back on me. I gave a wave, and the baby followed my fingers. I waved again, and her pudgy little cheeks convulsed, lips spreading open to reveal smooth gums. "She's smiling, she's smiling!" the man panted with a hint of hysteria.

"Oh my god, oh my god," his wife squealed, comically turning about in a little circle, trying to catch her new daughter's happy expression by chasing it as fast as she could.

"Her first smile," the husband explained apologetically to me. Then, unsure if I could understand him, he gave me a little bow.

A strange prickle ran down my body, and I doubled over to slowly unlace my Converses, trying to get ahold of myself. Straightening up, I looked at the accumulating crowd on the other side of security, everyone peering down at their black-haired, slant-eyed babies with concern to make sure they hadn't been unduly traumatized by their first encounter with airport security. Tears blurred my eyes as I walked through the metal detector. On the other side, I grabbed my handbag and muttered, "Gotta go to the bathroom," to Ji Hoon.

"Can't it wait?" he asked as I broke into a trot. When I didn't answer, he shouted after me, "It's Gate 4. Hurry up! The plane's about to leave!"

I ran blindly down the concourse, searching for a nook to hide myself in and pulling out my phone. I huddled behind an advertisement of a glamorous woman holding a bottle of skin whitener against her spectrally incandescent face. She answered almost immediately. "Li-li?"

"Min Hee."

"Lisa! Oh god, Lisa."

"Mindy..."

"No, before you say anything, Lisa, you were right. You were so, so right. I never should have come here to meet my mother. She's not my mother. Oh god, Lisa, she came to our meeting with her other kids."

"You have siblings?"

"Two older brothers." She started to sob. "She brought them to the meetings, both times. And all she does is talk about them; she doesn't have the slightest interest in me. She barely even looks at me."

"She's unsure how to act, Mindy. It's not every day that you meet your own daughter."

"I don't care!" It was a strangled scream. "The sons are the ones who do the talking. They are really interested in our financial situation, constantly taking note of our material possessions. When they found out I was a doctor, they almost started drooling, talking about how much money American doctors make. It's scary. I'm wondering what I got my parents into."

"Mindy, you didn't get them into anything. Stop freaking out. Asians talk a lot more openly about money and salaries and things like that. It's just a cultural difference."

"My mom and dad don't have a clue that things aren't going well. My mom thinks that my birth mother is a nice woman and has nothing but sympathy for her."

"Well, of course, Mindy," I started, but then bit my tongue. Mindy didn't want to hear that her mother was relieved that her chief rival, Mindy's biological mother, was cold and unlovable. "Margaret is eager to be friends with the woman who gave you to her."

"Oh, Lisa," Mindy sobbed. "Where are you? Why did you leave me?"

"Why didn't you call?" I countered. "Didn't you get my email?"

"Email? No. There was nothing from you in my inbox."

"That's strange. I emailed you yesterday, early afternoon."

"I've been checking, there was nothing from you. Lisa, I am so sorry for the horrible things I said to you. Can you ever forgive me?"

"Only if you forgive me first," I said, my voice shuddering against a hot wave of tears. "It was my fault, all of it, entirely. As usual. You were completely right, I was acting like an ass, like I always do. But listen, I don't have much time—"

"Where are you?"

"At the airport. We're catching a flight and I—"

"Who's we? Where are you going?"

A shadow fell across me, and I looked up to see Ji Hoon, his beautiful face a little less beautiful as he glared angrily down at me, chest heaving with panic. "What the hell are you doing, Lisa? The plane is boarding!"

"I've got to go."

"Lisa..." Her voice held a warning, telling me to stop.

"I'll call you as soon as I get there..."

"Get where?" Mindy demanded. "What's going on, Lisa?"

"We have to go! Now!" Ji Hoon violently tapped a shaking finger on the oversized face of his TAG Heuer.

"OK, bye for now, Mindy. I'll call you soon! I love you!"

"Lisa, wait!"

Ji Hoon grabbed hold of my arm and pulled me to my feet, voice pitched high in alarm: "If we've missed the plane..."

"Come on, Ji Hoon, let's run," I whooped, wrenching my arm from his clammy fingers and sprinting off toward our gate.

We just made it, the flight attendant leading us on a perp walk down the aisle to the disapproving stares of the other passengers, the plane pulling out as soon as we had buckled up. Ji Hoon sat with arms tightly folded, staring out the window, refusing to look at me, both of us still breathing hard from our dash through the airport. That sudden burst of activity had unleashed the throbbing queasiness of the hangover that I had been trying to keep at bay ever since Ji Hoon had roused me from my drunken slumber that morning, when he came to pick me up for the airport, and I closed my eyes as the plane lifted creakily into the air. Soon, the monotonous throb of the engines and the peculiar serenity that comes with hurtling through the sky at 500 miles per hour 3,200 feet up in the air lulled me into sleep, until Ji Hoon roused me to ask if I would like a beverage. "I got myself a beer." Ji Hoon pointed to a can of Hite on his tray table. "Do you want one too?"

Yawning into my hands, still treading the borderlands between sleep and consciousness, I nodded. The flight attendant passed me a can of beer and a plastic cup with a superior sneer. If she didn't want me to drink beer at nine o'clock in the morning, then she shouldn't offer it, I thought, sneering back. But I didn't actually want the beer, I wanted more sleep, so I closed my eyes, trying to recapture the dream that I had inhabited just moments ago. But Ji Hoon, who seemed to have recaptured his high spirits, jostled my arm as he gallantly poured beer into my cup. "Cheers, Lisa!"

The familiar, yeasty aroma wafted into my nose, promising me something—whether it was a cure for my hangover or a full barf bag, I couldn't be sure, but I decided to find out. I felt the beer flood to the back of my throat, through my chest, and into my empty stomach, and since I didn't gag, I decided I had made the right choice. "Breakfast of champions," I said, grinning at Ji Hoon, who was back to attending to me with his usual flirtatious solicitousness, declaring I was prettier than the girl on the cover of the airplane magazine he was leafing through. I asked how old she was, and he said sixteen.

"You must have been a very sweet sweet sixteen," Ji Hoon teased a moment later.

"I was never sweet sixteen, I was toxic sixteen," I snorted. "I was zitty and sullen and really insufferable. Nothing like I am now." Which I wished were true but knew wasn't. "The only thing that remains of me at sixteen is this." I touched the yin-yang pendant.

He leaned close to inspect the dime-sized medallion of interlocking silver and gold commas, murmuring, "That's very nice metalwork. Is it Korean?"

"Yes. My friend Mindy brought it back from a heritage tour. A gift for my sixteenth birthday. It's kind of symbolic of our relationship."

Ji Hoon exclaimed, "I get it! So, which one are you? Yin or yang?" He gently stroked the pendant, his finger brushing the tender skin at the hollow of my throat.

"I'm the yin, obviously," I said, my skin tingling from his graz-ing touch. "Especially that year. I got into a lot of trouble when I was sixteen, doing drugs, skipping school, getting arrested for shoplift-ing. After that, my mom made me go see a shrink." Technically, Mrs. Frank wasn't a shrink, but it was more dramatic to say "shrink" than "licensed clinical professional counselor specializing in Asperger's syndrome, gay and lesbian, and adopted teens." Oh, how I hated her, with her too-bright shade of cherry-red lipstick, her impertinent, probing questions, and the stupid lists she made me write: "Five Things I Can Do to Have a Good Day," "Six Literary Characters I Admire" (because she knew I liked to read), and "My Seven Worst Fears." And then she would go through my lists and explain to me that the fact that I wasn't taking them seriously, writing things like "Fear of Math" and "Fear of Cheerleaders," was evidence that real-ly my greatest fear was of rejection. That's what it all came back to with Mrs. Frank, the original sin of all adopted people, Fear of Being Rejected.

"What did your shrink tell you?" Ji Hoon inquired, obligingly pouring more beer into my cup.

I obligingly drank what he poured. "She told me that I was act-ing upon my environment by internalizing the locus of control."

He tilted his head to show that he didn't understand.

"I know, right?" I laughed roughly into my glass. "Basically, it means that my life was shaped by forces outside of my control—my birth mother giving me up, my parents adopting me and bringing me to another country—leaving me to feel like I needed to take con-trol of my own life by behaving in a way that people wouldn't ex-pect. So by being bad, I was changing the narrative that other people had made for me, thereby seizing control of my own story."

Pinching his lips between his teeth, he nodded as though he fol-lowed the tangled idea that I was so inarticulately expressing. And maybe he did understand.

"You must hear this from all the adopted girls you squire around town," I joked.

He shook his head, remaining serious. "So what did she suggest you do?"

"She suggested I find my birth mother, actually." I poured the last of my beer into the cup. "She said I wouldn't become a fully developed person until I did, and by finding her, I'd return the locus of control to me, but in a positive way, instead of a negative way. She said it was a rite of passage that all adopted people should go through."

"That was very wise of her," Ji Hoon declared, wagging his head in emphatic approval. "I feel very sorry that MotherFinders failed you. I am sure that your mother is a very beautiful and intelligent person, just like you. You must not give up hope. Maybe one day she will come to you."

I shrugged, shook the last few drops of beer from my glass onto my waiting tongue.

Ji Hoon drove us straight from the airport to the famous Dragon Head Rock in a tiny Hyundai hatchback that was a tin can compared with his Audi. It was as if we were in another country, a different season, a previous era. Palm trees fringed the roads, the traffic was calm and orderly, and the air warm and sun-kissed. Lush green pastures speckled with yellow and pink blooms rolled by like unfurling bolts of silk on one side of the road, while dramatic volcanic coastline plunged into the opalescent swell of the sea on the other. At Dragon Head Rock, we made a dutiful pilgrimage down to the viewing platform, dodging newlyweds frozen in artificial poses as they had their pictures snapped and an unceasing tide of tour groups marching with smiling determination behind their perky guides, who held the company flag aloft like it was a beacon of justice. We stopped at an ocean-side restaurant for a lunch of seafood so fresh it was still moving, Ji Hoon cautioning me not to eat too much because that evening we would have a spectacular meal of island delicacies. Hypnotized by the metronomic rhythm of glassy waves crashing against the craggy, tidal-pool-pocked shoreline, I dutifully drank the glasses of soju he poured for me. Occasionally, Ji Hoon's cheerfulness would recede, and he'd fidget anxiously, his unruly eyebrows descending to shade his eyes, so he'd be looking right at me but clearly not seeing me at all, and I could only assume that he was thinking of the sticky situation with his girlfriend.

Promising to blow my mind, he nosed the Hyundai into a long line of idling cars and tour buses at Mysterious Road. "Now you can see, we are at the bottom of the hill, yes?" Ji Hoon asked, looking at me out of the side of his eyes with delight.

"Uh-huh," I agreed.

"Now, see, I put the car in neutral and release the brake."

The car started to roll. "Whoa!" I snorted through my nose. "No way! We're rolling uphill!"

He nodded at me triumphantly. As the car defied gravity, he had to be careful to avoid the thronging tourists who were let loose from their vehicles to pour water and drop pencils on the tarmac. "But of course, Lisa," he explained seriously as he started the engine again and put the car into drive, "it is just an optical illusion. You must not be so gullible."

But then the very next place he took me made me wonder how gullible he wanted me to be. Called Jeju Love Land, the first clue that it was not your usual theme park was a sign in the shape of a penis pointing the way to the ticket booth. As we entered, we were greeted by penis and vagina mascots, each wearing mittens and a hat, perhaps to make them seem more cuddly and adorable. Underneath a Möbius strip of ecstasy—three people performing fellatio on each other—a gaggle of grandmothers flashed the victory sign as they mugged for a group photo. A path took us on a meandering walk around a large lake, past erotic statues, engorged phalluses, pornographic fountains, lewd dioramas, mounds of earth that were shaped like breasts, and other strange sexual decorations.

"This seems like the kind of place that Jonny would like," I said for no particular reason, except that we were looking at a chubby man in a mask being bounced upon by a woman who was held up, apparently, just by the stiffness of his dick.

"Yes, he would," Ji Hoon agreed smilingly. "Did you like him?" He strolled on toward a fat woman who seemed to be sucking a scrawny, much smaller man into her vagina.

"You mean 'like' like this...?" I wondered, as I leaned close to see what was going on.

"No, no, no!" Ji Hoon vehemently disavowed the misunderstanding. "No, I mean 'like' as a person, a friend. Like a cousin, say, or a brother."

"How come the fat men look like they are satisfying their sex partners, but the fat women look like they are sapping the very life blood out of theirs?"

"So, did you like him or not?" Ji Hoon insisted.

"Uh, yeah, I guess so." I shrugged. "He seemed kind of yakuza."

"Oh, no, no." Ji Hoon gazed at me with a worried wrinkle mussing the smooth perfection of his forehead. Naked, he would not be like the statue I was staring at, the man extremely well muscled, with thick thighs, a chunky taut ass, and bulging biceps. He'd be more like the woman who was clinging to his hips, delicately wrought, exquisitely shaped. "No, he is an honorable and upstanding man. A real leader, very smart, very strong, with a big heart. His family is chaebol, you understand what that means?"

"Sure, it's like zaibatsu." I nodded, watching as a tour group gathered around a woman arched in ecstasy as she pleasured herself with her fingers, some of the cheekier men grabbing up the side of her breast.

"Why do you always use the Japanese word for everything?" he snapped. "Are you not Korean? Why do you love everybody else's culture but your own?" He sat down abruptly on a bench next to a half-dressed statue who looked yearningly in his direction.

I gave him what I hoped was a withering what-the-fuck look. "So what is he? Hyundai? Daewoo? Samsung?"

He buried his face in his hands, his fingers digging into the silky plumage of his hair. "No, you wouldn't recognize it. It's something that only real Koreans know."

With an exasperated laugh, I stalked onward. The sexual ecstasy was beginning to bore me, and I had no idea why intertwined upside-down legs sticking up from a lake would be considered erotic. But then I saw a figurine of two mounted turtles perched on a rock at the pond's edge. Kenji had two pet turtles, named Orihime and Hikoboshi after star-crossed lovers of Japanese folklore who could meet only once a year on July 7. "Aww..." I sighed and took out my phone to snap a picture for Kenji.

"You want a photo?" Ji Hoon asked, suddenly by my side. "Let me take one with you in it."

Annoyed with Ji Hoon and his ticktocking between snappish critic and obsequious tour guide, I said, "No, really..." But then it seemed like a cute idea. I'd send the photo to Kenji with a funny little note about me being his Orihime and he my Hikoboshi, along with a gentle reminder to mail my journals. "All right then." I passed him the phone and crouched by the turtles with fingers in a V.

He ducked and bobbed, turning my phone this way and that. "Crouch lower!"

"I'm as low as I can go," I groaned. "Just take the damn photo."

"OK, OK, let me just hop over here. It will give me a better angle." He made a quick leap onto a boulder that poked from the algae-clotted surface of the lake. But his foot slipped, and for a second he was comically windmilling his arms in the air before he lost his balance and fell into the water with a theatrical splash. "Oh, no, oh no!" he howled, frantically dipping his hands into the green water, coming up with soggy plastic wrappers and squashed drink bottles.

I laughed at him until I realized what he was looking for. "Fuck! My phone!"

He brought up fistful after fistful of slime and glop and plastic. When he saw that I was rolling up my pants to join him, he cried, "It's no use, Lisa. There is too much mud at the bottom." He lifted up a foot to show me the muck that encased it. "I've lost my other shoe to it. It's... I'm afraid it's gone. Your phone is gone."

Even though the water came up only to his knees, he was completely soaked from all his frantic splashing. Distracted from the erotica, tour groups and young couples flocked about to gawk. Several started to applaud as he emerged from the pond. "I'm so sorry, Lisa."

"Let's just go," I snapped. "This place is really beginning to creep me out."

He waddled after me, trailing greasy splotches of mud, legs spread to mitigate the chafing of wet cloth on his tender parts.

After settling me at a snack stand with a bottle of beer, Ji Hoon went to change his clothes, and by the time he returned, I was on my second bottle. The gentle alcoholic buzz, the drained aftermath of the surge of energy that had swept through me with the loss of my phone, and the rocking of the car as it snaked around the peak of Hallasan lulled me to sleep. Next thing I knew, he was gently stroking my shoulder. "We're here, Lisa."

For the second time that day, I wiped drool from my wrinkled cheek. Squinting into an interstellar explosion of sunlight off metal and glass, I saw we were in a sea of cars, a huge parking lot that seemed to stretch for miles. "Where's here?" I asked, my voice phlegmy from sleep.

"At the resort," he said. "I've already checked us in." He stepped away to light a cigarette. "You can freshen up, and then we'll go to the restaurant in time for sunset."

I ran my tongue over my fuzzy teeth. "Yeah, OK."

As we made the long trek across the parking lot, Ji Hoon confessed, "I probably should've told you this earlier. I haven't been totally honest with you."

"Mmm?" I wiped a small nugget of crust from the corner of my eye.

"Well, because this is a free trip... Well, I'm sorry to say... It's just that..."

"Oh my god, Ji Hoon, just spill it." I sighed, exasperated. "They've put us in a linen closet? We have to wash dishes? What?"

"No, it's just..." With a nervous gesture, he brushed his hair forward with his fingers to hang in a veil over his eyes. "We are sharing a room."

About to say something lewd, I realized that he was intensely embarrassed and took pity on him. The hotel reared over us, a concrete monstrosity built to look like a cruise ship, with a jutting prow, circular porthole windows, and funnels poking up from the roof. "Wow! This place is hideous."

"No, no, inside you will see it is very nice, very luxurious," Ji Hoon hastened to assure me. "And the view is spectacular. You will see. It looks different from the other side, the side that faces the ocean."

Emerging from a choking fog of exhaust spewing from the tailpipes of a long line of coach buses idling in the front driveway, we plodded through doors held open by men dressed like Edwardian fops in velvet suits with frilly shirtfronts. The lobby was a churning mass of holiday-making humanity: elderly women dressed in identical track suits and floppy hats; young couples with the strained look of people at a dinner party who were exhausted from being bright and bubbly and were ready to go home; haggard mothers chasing chubby children who were demanding more, more, more; meticulously groomed matrons in Chanel suits and Kate Spade kitten heels clutching the chains of their Dior handbags; stylish twentysomethings smoking cigarettes and flirting furiously. Ji Hoon ushered me into an elevator, which we shared with two doll-like women who turned to the mirrored walls to rearrange gingery locks of hair while surreptitiously checking out Ji Hoon, who also looked in the mirror, not to check out the girls, but to check himself out, running his fingers sideways through his floppy bangs as he looked with seductive earnestness at his own reflection. It wasn't that he was vain; he was merely checking his equipment, like a soldier cleaning his rifle or a cook sharpening his knives, making sure everything was in good working order.

Our room was all but filled by two queen-sized beds with ridiculously froufrou headboards of tufted satin framed by gilded cherubs. A picture window looked out on the parking lot. "Mountain view," he said, and lamely waved his hand at the distant peak of Hallasan that hung over the carpet of cars.

"I guess this is the suite for honeymooners who don't get along," I said, giggling and bouncing on one of the beds.

"It is true, not all honeymooners get along," he said, throwing his bag onto the other bed. "We still have arranged marriages here in Korea, through professional matchmakers."

Flopping back against the headboard, I asked, "What about you and your girlfriend?"

"What about me and my girlfriend?" he echoed, his voice prickly and churlish.

"Are you getting married?"

He sat down on his bed with a heavy sigh. "Yes, we will get married."

"You don't sound very happy about it!" I teased him.

"Happy?" He groped the outline of his cigarette packet in his shirt pocket. "It is our duty. We have known each other since we were born.

Our families are very close, and it has always been understood that she was for me and I was for her."

"Eww." I grimaced, turning my bottom lip inside out. "It's kind of like marrying your sister."

He stuck a cigarette wearily between his lips. "No, no, nothing like that. It's more like... marrying the daughter of my father's business partner."

"Hey," I gasped, "are you a member of the same chaebol as Jonny?"

A rough laugh that I had never heard before. "My family is very midlevel compared with Jonny's." He lit his cigarette, blew out a massive cloud of smoke that curled and writhed in the late-afternoon sunlight. "Better hurry up and get ready. It would be a great pity if we missed the sunset."

Driving to the restaurant along a curvy road that hugged the coast, Ji Hoon seemed agitated, going too fast at times, then at others, trailing slowly along, as if lost in thought. I imagined he was thinking about his girlfriend. "What's her name?"

He jumped slightly, the car swerving over the double line. "Who?"

"Your girlfriend."

His jaw clenched, muscle rippling under flawless skin. "Never mind."

"I'm just trying to make conversation!" I laughed.

"Never mind," he repeated menacingly.

I shrugged and turned up the radio, but that only made the static crackle more loudly over the faint undercurrent of pop music. He lurched a little too quickly around a curve, and I slammed into the hard molded plastic of the passenger door. "Ouch," I murmured, rubbing my arm. "I miss the Audi."

Throwing his head back, he began to howl with laughter, banging the heels of his hands on the steering wheel.

"Hey, watch it!" I cautioned, as he drove perilously close to the edge of the road, from where it was a sharp, jagged drop into the sea.

Veering off the paved road onto a rough trail of two bald lines worn into a downward-sloping field of grass, he whooped, "An Audi is a good thing, isn't it?"

Stones spat up from the wheels as we descended, the car bouncing wildly.

"You know what else is good?" His voice dipped low as the car heaved over a big hole. "A Rolex. A Rolex is mighty fine. As is a sushi banquet and a bottle of Johnnie Walker Black Label."

We pulled up in front of a traditional wooden-framed house with mud-daubed walls, rice-paper windows, and a thatched roof. As he cut the engine, Ji Hoon reverted back to tour guide mode, explaining in a plangent croon, "This place is a hidden treasure that most tourists don't know about. They only serve local specialties, like *obunjagi ttukbaegi*, which we will have tonight. The *obunjagi* is like a clam, found only in the waters of Jeju-do."

He directed me inside and we passed through what looked like someone's living room, a short-legged table with cushions scattered around it squatting in the center, a glass-fronted cabinet crowded with porcelain figurines in the far corner, a gigantic flat-screen TV dominating one wall. A woman scurried across the dark shine of the wood floor, bent low in greeting, and led us through a large room, the smell of garlic and red chili paste mingling with the salt-rimmed sea air, past a group noisily enjoying dinner, their table a mosaic of little dishes and large platters, and onto a porch that seemed to be suspended over the water, where ours was the only table.

"You don't mind sitting Korean style, do you?" Ji Hoon asked apologetically.

"I think I'll manage," I grunted, collapsing on the floor, grateful that I had passed over a tight, short skirt for an ankle-length dress.

Settling next to me, Ji Hoon flashed me a teasing smile. "You always think you can manage. But we'll see how Korean you really are with this meal." As the woman poured soju for us, he explained, "We don't order from a menu. They just bring us whatever they have prepared today."

The fragile rims of our shallow cups kissed lightly before meeting with our pursed lips. The woman, moving silently and discreetly, started placing dishes on the table.

"*Bingtteok*," Ji Hoon explained, pointing to pillows of rolled-up white pancake, ends draping over the edge of the plate. "Like a daikon crepe. And this one is called *hanchi mulhoe*. It is"—he pulsated his hand in the air—"a sea creature. Like a squid."

"Jellyfish, perhaps?" I nibbled on it, red pepper sauce dripping from the sliver of milky, translucent flesh. "Mmm, not bad. Tender."

"It is also good for hangovers," Ji Hoon mumbled as he stuffed *bingtteok* into his mouth.

"Oh, well, we'll have to come back in the morning." I laughed, tipping another cup of soju empty. "What's that, steak tartare? I love raw beef!"

A wicked smile hovered on his face. "It's raw, yeah. Try it!"

Tweezing a slice of the marbled meat between my chopsticks, I brought it to my mouth. "It's really gamey," I said as I chewed. "Definitely not beef. Oh god, please don't tell me it's dog."

He snickered at my squeamishness. "It is horse."

"Oh, Flicka!" I gagged, taking a hasty swig of soju.

The woman did not stop bringing food until the table was covered with plates, making it difficult to find a place to put our tiny cups of soju. Meanwhile, the sun sank to its knees right in front of us, as if humbly paying tribute, flaming the wispy clouds to a neon tangerine, which deepened into a golden bronze threaded with mauve and violet before bruising to an eggplant purple. The breeze turned cooler, bringing a hint of the darkness that was creeping across the sea. Ji Hoon was very attentive to my soju glass and ordered bottles of beer as well, and we inched closer and closer as we leaned across each other to reach the various dishes, until we were hip against hip, the soft swell of my upper arm nestled against the warm crook of his armpit. Leaning against him, I sighed. "It's really beautiful here. I must say, I was a little skeptical about this trip; that travel agency was kinda weird and I half expected to wind up in a dingy dormitory with a bathroom down the hall. But so far, it's just been great. Even losing my phone." I began to giggle, butting him gently with my shoulder. "You looked so funny, splashing about in the water."

Plucking an *obunjagi* from its earthenware pot to scoop the flesh, which looked like curdled snot, from the shell with his bare fingers, he murmured, "I am so sorry about that. I mean, it's your *phone*! All those numbers, lost." He extended the jellied meat toward me, and I ate it from his fingers.

"It doesn't really matter," I mumbled, mouth full of the surprisingly supple flesh, thinking more about his fingers, and how they'd feel stroking my belly and breasts, than my phone. "I know how to get in touch with all the people who really matter to me. Except for Kenji."

This time it was he who was nudging me with his shoulder. "Who's Kennnjiiii?" He drew the name out with a schoolyard playfulness.

"He's a guy I know in Fukuoka."

"Boyfriend?" he teased with a sideways smile.

"I wouldn't call him that," I hedged. What would I call him? What would he call me?

"But you like him?"

I took a swallow of soju and then washed it down with beer. "I like him well enough, but a relationship is out of the question. But I did say I'd call him, and now..." There was no way for me to get in touch with him. I didn't know if he had an email address or a Facebook page or a Twitter account. I couldn't even really remember his last name. Hasawa? Hasagawa? Higawa? "Shit," I mumbled, and dipped a pheasant dumpling in vermilion chili sauce before sucking it into my mouth.

"It'll be OK, Lisa." Ji Hoon patted my knee, then let his hand stay there, warm and moist through the thin fabric of my dress. "If it's meant to be, you'll find a way to get in touch with him again."

Kenji who? I could barely remember what he looked like as Ji Hoon's face hovered so close to mine, his smile intimate and possessive. His face came closer and closer until his lips just brushed the tip of my nose, then he must have thought of his girlfriend because he quickly jerked his body back. He poured more soju, snipped up a morsel with his chopsticks, stared moodily out into the night. The last hint of color had been blotted from the heavens, and now the horizon between water and sky was almost indistinguishable.

"It is supposed to be a moonless night, so we should get a good view of the stars," he murmured. Then, to my surprise, he dropped his head forward onto his chest, and his shoulders began to heave.

"Ji Hoon?" I uncrossed my legs and knelt beside him. "Are you OK?"

He must have been more attached to his girlfriend than he let on. His back muscles tensed beneath my kneading fingers. His skin was soft, just a bit sticky.

He stroked his face hard with his open palms, fuzzing his eyebrows into wild peaks. "I guess I just had too much to drink." His voice was soft and dry, like an autumn wind whispering through desiccated cornstalks. "Why don't you and I go for a walk? There is a pier that we can walk out on. You can see phosphorescent creatures swimming about, like stars trapped under the water."

"OK," I murmured. "I just need to make a quick stop into the ladies' room first."

I held on to his shoulder to balance myself as I wobbled onto my feet. Our server scurried over to personally escort me to the bathroom. The dining room was mostly empty now; there was only one other couple, who ate in stony silence in the dimly lit room. It surprised me that a place with such delicious food had so few customers, but the tourists probably ate at their gaudy, gargantuan resorts. The toilet was a squatter, so I carefully gathered up the hem of my dress, having learned the hard way how much spatter a really full bladder can make. My escort startled me when I exited, waiting to solemnly lead me back to our table.

"Here." Ji Hoon handed me a glass of soju. "One for the road."

I lurched forward for the glass and polished it off without a second thought, wiping my arm across my mouth, the drink more bitter than I had remembered.

"You better take your sweater, it will be cold on the pier," he advised, holding it by the shoulders for me to slip into.

The woman handed Ji Hoon a flashlight and we stepped out into the darkness. The flashlight beam carved a tunnel of light that ended with a splat on the path. "Hold on to me. It's a bit rocky."

"And I'm drunk." I giggled as I eagerly grabbed on to his arm.

"Careful, careful," he cautioned.

A giant bullfrog hopped sluggishly across our path. The breeze slurred through the space between our bodies, wafting away some of the soju fumes. It was cold out in the full wind, and I shivered closer to him. My toes knocked against wood. "Step up," he said, and we were on the pier. It went a long way out over the sea, our footsteps thudding with a hollow, forlorn cadence, the two of us hooding our shoulders forward against the onslaught of the wind. Ji Hoon shone the light on a decrepit motorboat tied to one of the posts of the pier. "The family catches much of the seafood for the restaurant themselves," he noted in his formal tour-guide voice.

When we reached the end, he waved the flashlight in sweeping arcs over the water, the beam probing a silvery finger into the night's depthless void. "Water looks fairly calm despite the wind," Ji Hoon observed, grazing the light over the tufted waves, back and forth, back and forth. "That's good."

Then he shut off the flashlight and we stood in silence. At first it was like being blind, black on black, but then I caught the onyx gleam of restless water and the glinting coil of the Milky Way rolling like barbed wire over us. "It's beautiful," I whispered. My hand sought his, or his mine, and they fit together in a warm knot.

"Lisa," he whispered, his other hand cupping my neck and then sliding down my back, drawing me closer to him.

"Yes, Ji Hoon," I murmured, pushing my lips out.

But not yet. He leaned away from me a little, let go of my hand. "Lisa..." A tremulous finger traced my hairline, then down my nose, brushing my lips and slowly stroking the shallow cleft of my chin. Was it his touch making my legs feel rubbery? All of a sudden, my whole body felt deboned. "I always knew I would find you, Lisa. I knew you were out there and would come to me. I just had to be patient."

His hand gripped the back of my head. I closed my eyes, waiting for the kiss, but it didn't come. A dull drone that had been tickling the back of my mind seemed to be getting louder, coming closer, becoming the sputter of an engine, carrying with it a whiff of gasoline. Suddenly, a piercing light flooded on, illuminating Ji Hoon's face, carved marble, hard and implacable, the eyes bald of human tenderness or emotion. I struggled to turn around to see where the light was coming from, but Ji Hoon held me tight, cradling my body against his. "I'm sorry, Lisa."

And I saw his hand, which one moment ago had been clutching at my ass, come toward my face, a white handkerchief nestled in the palm. Instinctively, I jerked my head away, but my muscles no longer seemed to be working properly. Tightening his grip on the back of my head, he covered my mouth and nose with the damp cloth, which smelled faintly sweet, like an empty box of candy. The motor throbbed louder and then softer in my ears; my vision blurred. Then the night swallowed me up.

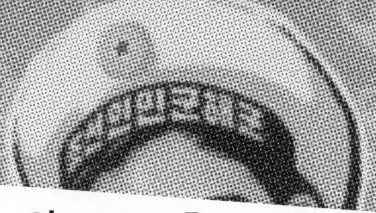

Chapter 5

"I was adopted into this incredible home, a loving, positive environment, yet I had this yearning, this kind of darkness that was also inside me."

–Faith Hill

I had swallowed the universe, and it was churning, in constant motion, ballooning against my insides with a gentle but inexorable pressure. Stars spun slowly, striking sparks as they bumped into the jellied skin of my organs. Planets were cold, hard pits, burning through the heat of my body like ulcers. Comets ricocheted like pinballs, knocking against the hard blades of my ribs and hips, blazing through my skull, jolting me back to consciousness.

At first, I couldn't focus, everything was a blur. Slowly my vision sharpened. My eyes wandered, not recognizing the bamboo-patterned silk curtains, the lemon-yellow walls, the painting of a windswept mountain peak, or the stitched ecru linen coverlet on the bed. My mouth felt as if it were coated in glue, and I could not unstick my tongue from the roof of my mouth nor tear open the seal on my lips. There were no memories in my brain, just a sickening gray mist, cold and frightening. I didn't know who I was or where I was: I was a blank slate.

I closed my eyes. *Think, Lisa, think.* OK, there was my name, Lisa. And hadn't this happened to Lisa before, awakening somewhere without knowing how she had come to be there? Hungover on a cigarette-burned couch, waking up still high in a stranger's apartment, or regaining consciousness in a hospital room... Shame flared through me, and with the shame came my memory of that hospital room, everything flooding back, scenes flashing before my eyes like they do, supposedly, before you die, or before you're reborn.

The last scene was Mindy and me at the Dunkin' Donuts. Mindy, cheeks flushed poinsettia red, eyes curved like samurai blades. I groaned aloud, the force of my misery somehow tearing the two slabs of my lips apart and ripping the cured leather strip of my tongue from the baked and droughty bed of my mouth. My whole body felt parched and stiff. Beef jerky. A block of salt. A cone of ashes. Another throaty excrescence gurgled in my ears.

A door, bamboo green to match the curtains, opened with a strange hiss, and in slipped a small girl. She approached tentatively on tiptoes, her lollipop-shaped head tilted inquisitively to one side. When she saw that my eyes were open, she stopped short, still tipped up on her toes.

"Waa," I croaked. I could taste the blood from my cracked lips smearing my teeth.

She stared, every muscle frozen.

"Waaaa." My voice broke and shattered.

She backed away with tiny little ballerina steps, crescent eyes trained unblinkingly on me.

"Waaadaa," I whimpered as she slipped out of the room. One dark eye glimmered at me for what seemed like an eternity before she finally shut the door.

Tears rolled into my hair before darkness descended upon me once again, and the universe began to churn and heave in my belly.

I didn't notice her at first when I woke up next. Carefully inching my throbbing head up from the pillow, I glimpsed the shining black dome that was the crown of her hair and let out an involuntary scream. She leapt up with the furtive movement of a half-wild animal. Her face, Charlie Brown round, came within inches of mine, so I could see a light zipper of a scar across the small bump of her nose and the soft bristle of her eyelashes that peeked from under her lids. She helped me sit up before bringing a cut-crystal tumbler of water to my mouth. When I tried to grab at the glass with my hands, she gently but firmly put them back in my lap. My tongue lifted up like a wizened claw to drag the liquid to the back of my throat. Blissful relief! But all too soon she was pulling away the glass. With a deft skip backward, she bowed deeply and then scurried out of the room, carrying with her the precious glass of water.

"Waaii," I rasped into the empty room. "C'baaaak."

Thinking I might follow her, I swung my legs out of the bed but became distracted by a strange crinkling sensation around my crotch.

I realized I was wearing a hospital gown. Trying to look under the thin blue fabric, I tipped backward and banged my head against the headboard. Luckily, it was tufted leather, and my head just slid down it like a gob of spit. Finally managing to sit up, I lifted up the gown to see that I was wearing a diaper. For the first time, it occurred to me that I should be afraid.

The door opened again, and then a cherubic face with small blue eyes drilled deep into blanched flesh, topped by a thin thatch of blond hair, hovered over me. "Ah, Lisa, you are in the land of the living. Finally." He grabbed my wrist with icy fingers and took my pulse before threading a stethoscope into his ears and poking about my chest and back.

It was all so sudden, his gestures so forcefully authoritative, that I didn't think to protest or ask him who he was, but wordlessly and obediently submitted to his ministrations.

The little girl materialized from behind his back and rudely thrust a thermometer between my lips, the glass tip knocking against my teeth.

"Open up for the thermometer," the man said impatiently, nodding at the girl to jigger it in there. Using his thumb, he pulled up a lid and shone a bright light into my eye. "Look over my shoulder at the painting," he instructed. He had a heavy accent, with abrupt vowels and rolled r's, like the villain from a 1980s action movie. "Now look over my other shoulder at Ting."

My eyeballs faltered, rolling around in a circle as they wondered what "ting" was.

"The servant. Look at the servant."

My eyes found the black-haired girl, who surprised me with a shy smile that made her cheeks bloom like two peonies. With a decisive nod, the man clicked off the light and stepped back and stared at me. A fingertip guiding my chin, he turned my head to present in profile. He and Ting exchanged significant glances. Then he extracted the thermometer from my mouth and read it with another satisfied nod. "Good, good. You are doing fine, my dear." He gave me a congratulatory pat on the shoulders.

"Water," I creaked, my tongue a wooden clapper.

Ting dutifully brought the crystal tumbler up to my lips and I gulped thirstily. She took it away too soon.

"More."

"Moderation in all things," the man said. "You've been getting your nutrients from an IV drip. We don't want to shock your body with too much too quickly."

"Where am I?" I cawed, my speech a blare of voice that only loosely approximated words.

Squinting one eye closed, he asked jovially, "What is the last thing you remember?"

"The fight," I muttered, running my fingers over the crinkly material of the diaper.

"Fight? I don't think there was much of a struggle." The man frowned, his pallid eyebrows arching up toward his ebbing hairline.

"The fight with Mindy," I insisted. "At Dunkin' Donuts. In... in..." What was the city called? "S-s-s-s..."

"S-s-s-s?" the man hissed along with me.

"S-s-s..."

The servant, Ting, nodded her head encouragingly.

"Sow..."

The doctor held me with his pale, clinical gaze, neither encouraging nor discouraging.

"Sow... Soul, Seoul!" I found the word triumphantly. "Seoul, Korea."

"South Korea," the doctor clarified.

"Republic of Korea," I concurred with satisfaction, settling back on my pillows, which Ting had plumped up for me.

But the doctor ruined my brief moment of complacency. "The last thing you remember is a fight in Dunkin' Donuts in Seoul?"

"Yes. No." I put a hand up to my forehead and rubbed hard. My brain was a tiny piece of fruit, a plum or apricot, swaddled in straw and cotton, packed in a wooden crate. "Can I have more water, please? I can't think, I'm so thirsty!"

The doctor gave a curt nod, and Ting held the glass to my lips again. This time, I was allowed consecutive gulps, and I erupted with a belch so enormous it ruffled the silky black hair that framed Ting's clock-dial face. "Oh god, excuse me."

"It is to be expected, your stomach is completely empty," the doctor intoned. He pronounced *stomach* phonetically. "As you were saying...?"

Clutching at my head, I couldn't quite dredge up those most recent memories that I knew where there, shadowy figures in an occluding haze. "I can't!" I wailed. Looking up at the two of them, I pleaded, "Where am I? Who are you? Is this still Seoul?"

"Does it feel like Seoul?" the doctor asked cryptically.

"What?"

"You may finish the glass of water," he said with an insincere smile. "You are doing fine. All your vital signs are good. You should remember soon enough."

The fake smile lingered as he watched me guzzle the cool, sweet water. Ting gently took the empty glass from my weak grip, and the two of them filed out the door, which closed with a soft sucking that made my ears pop. Exhausted, I fell back against the pillows, trying hard to free my brain from its swaddling, but the swaddling bound me ever tighter until I slipped into unconsciousness again.

Sometime later, I was roused from my sleep by a gentle shaking. Dragging my heavy eyelids apart, I saw a pale circle set with delicate features and fish-shaped eyes, a little scar like a caterpillar crawling across her nose. "Ting."

The ends of her lips crept up in a tentative smile. With a gentle wipe, she pulled a lock of hair out of my eyes and then helped me to sit up. Working with quiet efficiency, she smoothed the covers and then straddled my lap with a little tray with fold-out legs. On it was a steaming lacquer bowl of broth and a glass of water. When I rushed the soup to my mouth, she fluttered her hands in alarm, then blew softly on the golden liquid shining in the well of the spoon. A single star-shaped noodle spun lazily as she blew. Then she nodded her approval. The broth was incredibly rich and delicious, and a small moan escaped me as it trickled down to my entrails.

"This tastes so good," I whispered as she blew on the next spoonful. "Did you make it?"

Though she nodded, it was to tell me that the liquid was sufficiently cooled to be sopped up by my eager lips.

"Do you speak English?"

She smiled sweetly and nodded encouragingly again, making happy slurping noises.

"Yes? No?"

She nodded in answer to both questions. Maybe she was a deaf mute. Up close, I saw that she was not the little girl I had thought she was. Small lines creased the tapered ends of her eyes and parenthesized her mouth.

After I finished the soup, I realized simultaneously that I had to urinate and that I was still wearing a diaper, which was swollen and damp against my skin. I wanted that diaper off and started to pull at the elasticized waistband through my gown. Ting understood and led me to the bathroom, which, like the bedroom, was interior decorating gone wild, Martha Stewart on steroids, with a claw-footed bathtub sheathed in sheer drapes that were swooped back like drawing-room curtains, a glass-bowled sink with a sleek parabola of polished chrome for a faucet, a massive beveled mirror trimmed with lights like at a professional salon, and pastel pink granite tiles and counters. While Ting began drawing a bath, the smell of lavender wafting out upon curling fingers of steam, I dropped the diaper with a heavy thud on the floor. Gently, she untied the hospital gown and slipped it from my shoulders, then gestured at the bath. I sank my body into the cloud of softly popping bubbles, groaning gratefully as the hot water enveloped me. She pointed to the back of the door, where a pair of pumpkin-colored satin pajamas hung from a hook, then placed a wicker table with a *People* magazine on it within easy arm's reach of the tub before exiting the bathroom. I picked up the magazine to see the date, March 28, 2011. That was two days before I was going to return to Japan. Kenji.

Oh god. Kenji. Bubbles nibbling at my skin, I sank down until the water closed over the top of my head, lifting my hair up in a cloud. I lay submerged until my breath ran out. The sloshing water unlodged a memory: the slap of restless waves against pier pilings, a motorboat approaching... As I surfaced, my eyes popped open, and I exclaimed,

"Ji Hoon!" He was the missing link between Seoul and wherever I was. It was blindingly clear to me now, as it should have been clear to me from the first, that he was something much more sinister than a tour guide for adopted girls. He was a honey trap, and I, with my ravenous craving for fun, distraction, and attention, fell for it like the simple, feckless fool that I was.

"Ting! I need to talk to Ji Hoon!" I called as I stepped out of the bathroom, hair wrapped in a meringue of Turkish towel, the satin of my new pajamas caressing my skin, but the room was empty. "Ting!"

I rushed to pull on the doorknob, which was cool to the touch. The door did not budge. I tried pushing against it; it didn't yield a millimeter. I banged against it with the heels of my hands; it neither rattled in the frame nor creaked. It was made of steel. Stomach tightening, I scurried over to the window, which was placed so high up that I had to climb on a chair to look out of it onto a tiny strip of rocky ground bordered by an impenetrable thicket of bamboo. With no hinges or crank, it was unopenable. When I knocked on the glass, it had the dull solidity of a wall. A metal taste of fear flooding my tongue, I crept back into bed and watched the light drain from the window, straining to hear ambient noise that would give me a clue as to where I was. But there was nothing. No traffic, no barking dogs, no distant sirens. The only sound was the thrum of my blood being pushed through my brain by my pounding heart. I could no longer deny that I was being held captive, and I was pretty sure I knew by whom. After all, who had long wished me out of their lives? Who had motive and means? Who had paid for me to come to Korea in the first place?

Margaret and Howard Stamwell.

How did they hate me? I counted the ways.

There was the shoplifting arrest at Macy's that forever cemented my reputation as every adoptive parent's worst nightmare: the bad seed, genetically incapable of nurture, hopelessly corrupt by nature. There was the time that Margaret caught me and my one-hitter in flagrante in their laundry room, and the other time when she found a three-inch cap of ice floating in the Stoli bottle they kept in the freezer. There was my slovenly appearance, my bad posture, my wardrobe of ripped jeans, thrift-store T-shirts, and clunky-soled shoes. My mediocre academic performance, my mediocre college, my English major, my lack of postgraduation accomplishments. My directionless wandering. My unrealistic dreams. But more than anything else, there was my deep-seated conviction that Mindy was destined to become a great actor.

It culminated the fall of our junior year with a late-night dinner at the Four Seasons to celebrate Mindy's opening night performance as Maria in a local production of *West Side Story*. The audience had given Mindy a standing ovation, Margaret clapping so hard I thought the diamonds in her rings would fall out, which was why I felt emboldened to say, only half joking, "Mindy should skip college and just go straight to Broadway."

A discreet hum of conversation lapped around us, the light tinkling of the piano drifting in from the bar. Mindy twiddled with her lobster ravioli. Gave me a furtive glance. She still had her stage make-up on, her skin bronzed to a deep Puerto Rican tan, eyeliner applied under her lashes to make her eyes look rounder, mouth a delectable cherry-red heart. Looking down at her plate, Mindy said, "This is going to be my last play."

I laughed. "What, you mean, like, ever?"

"Well, ever is a very long time," Margaret answered for her daughter, the soft light of the pewter table lamp gleaming off the lustrous sheen of her skin and the amber waves of grain of her hair. "But for the foreseeable future. At least until she gets into college. What with all the rehearsals, Mindy's grades have been slipping, and at such an important time! Colleges look very carefully at the eleventh grade GPA!" She waved an emphatic finger in the air, urgently alerting me to this very important fact.

"But, Min Hee." I leaned in close to Mindy in order to exclude Margaret from the conversation. "Acting credits will increase your chances of getting into Juilliard and Bennington. This is your first professional production! You're actually getting paid to be onstage! You can't stop now!"

The dimple under Mindy's eye was a flickering star, appearing and disappearing, flashing at me in warning.

"She's not applying to Juilliard and Bennington," Margaret said firmly.

"Of course she's applying to Juilliard. She's been talking about it forever! It's what she wants to do, Mrs. Stamwell." I glanced at Howard to see if he could give me some support. He couldn't, sitting there with his habitual Mona Lisa smile, content to just bask in the incandescence of his wife and daughter.

"Tell her what Candy Bronson, the girl who plays Velma, said," Margaret prompted Mindy.

Mindy stirred the ice cubes around in her glass with a bendy straw, still not looking at me. "She told the director that no one was going to believe that I was Maria, since I was obviously Asian. In front of everyone. While I was standing right there."

A hot flush spiked over my skin, and I blinked fast to clear away a sudden prickling of angry tears, hating Candy Bronson, hating Margaret. "She's just jealous! You got a standing ovation! Anyway, Natalie Wood was white! Why does that make her any more believable as a Puerto Rican?"

"Unfortunately, Lisa"—Margaret tilted her head sympathetically, grimacing at the painful news she had to deliver—"the acting business isn't very welcoming to Asians. It's just not realistic to think that Mindy could support herself as an actor. There are no roles for Asian Americans, except for Miss Saigon, and only one girl can play her at a time. And there would be so much rejection, so many hurtful comments, much worse than what Candy said."

Angry at Mindy for sitting there like a cipher, furious at the blond goddess Margaret for broaching the topic of race, and sick of Howard and the dumb, meaningless smile that creased his big marshmallow face, I stabbed my fork accusingly in Margaret's direction. "You're being racist by telling Mindy she can't be an actress. You've always been obsessed with Mindy's race, so worried about how it was going to affect her life, affect her future prospects. You should have adopted a white baby instead."

Gasping, Margaret clapped both hands over her mouth, tears glittering like diamond chips on the lush ledges of her lower lashes.

"I think you owe Mrs. Stamwell an apology," Howard intoned sternly, sandy eyebrows drawn in consternation, white peaks of skin ridging his furrowed brow. Mindy studiously rearranged the ravioli on her plate, hiding behind her poufed-up Maria hair.

I didn't believe Margaret's tears. Margaret was hard as nuts, CEO of Stormraker, which profited handsomely from dispatching guns-for-hire to terrorize brown people in blighted, war-ravaged countries. I had seen her bully any number of people, from sales clerks to other parents—some to tears—to get her way. She had Mindy's future gridded out when Mindy was but an application to an adoption agency, and she would stop at nothing to ensure that her daughter was the success that her parents deserved, ruthlessly taking down those who got in her way.

Nevertheless, I apologized, mostly to put Mindy, who was nervously slicing a ravioli into tiny little pieces, out of her misery. Margaret wasn't above a gloating smile, which she tried to cloak as a gracious acknowledgment of my apology.

Then Mindy muttered, "I still might be a theater major."

Margaret's satisfied smile shriveled into a tight scowl as she directed the angry glare that was meant for her daughter at me. Perhaps it was at that very moment that Margaret decided to get me out of her daughter's life for good, waiting patiently all these years for the perfect opportunity, which finally presented itself with this trip to Korea. With her security connections, Margaret could easily hire someone like Ji Hoon to kidnap me and arrange a safe house in which to hide me while paying some doctor of fortune to keep me sedated and, presumably, alive. After Mindy was safely back in America, they would release me. I had to hand it to them, it was a brilliant plan, guaranteed to succeed precisely because it was so bold. It would be my word against theirs if I accused them of kidnapping me, and Mindy would never believe her parents capable of such malfeasance. It would cause a rift between us that could not be bridged. They'd finally be rid of me.

The worst part of the whole sad scenario was not that my best friend's parents hated me so much they would go to such extreme measures to separate me from their daughter; it was that I had played my own part so well, behaving just as badly as they expected me to, walking right into their trap.

The following morning, Ting brought me a breakfast of real food: two soft-boiled eggs, toast, a tiny pitcher of cream, a little pot of jam, a ramekin of butter. A French press awaited plunging. At least Margaret and Howard weren't going to let me starve to death. As I fell upon the food, Ting laid out on my bed fresh underwear, a pair of stockings, and a wrap-around jersey knit dress, placing a pair of open-toed spectator pumps with precipitously high heels next to the floor-length mirror. She handed me a note written in loopy cursive on thick, creamy paper.

> *Dear Lisa,*
> *Please put these clothes on. Don't worry about doing your hair or*
> *makeup—that is up to me.*
> *Yours,*
> [incomprehensible squiggles]

The signature didn't look like Margaret's and the handwriting wasn't hers, but I presumed Margaret was a pro who would never write a note in her own handwriting that could later be used as evidence against her.

The dress looked like something that Margaret would pick, and no surprise that it fit me perfectly, for throughout the years Margaret had given me Christmas and birthday gifts of the fashionable, preppy clothes—fuzzy cashmere sweaters, pleated tartan miniskirts, pastel linen blazers—that she wished I'd wear when I came over to their house.

I waited impatiently in my new dress for my mysterious correspondent to come. At last, the door opened, and in slipped a slim figure impeccably attired in a form-fitted tweed suit and patent leather stilettos.

"Lisa, I am so pleased to meet you. My name is Yolanda," she declared, strutting toward me with a hand extended. Strawberry-blond hair smoothly coiled into a French twist. Skin so pale, it was almost translucent, and a face so strikingly strange that I at first looked away, as one does from the stump of an amputee or a hideously disfiguring scar, not wanting to seem rude by gawking. She gave a very limp handshake while slowly running her eyes up and down my body, taking care not to miss a detail.

"Where's Ji Hoon?" I demanded. "I must speak to him."

"All your questions will be answered in just a moment," she murmured, stepping to the side to view my profile. "Mmm, yes," she commented approvingly. Her eyes were unnaturally angled, one tighter and more slanted than the other, the glassy irises a weird yellow-green color. "Didn't Ting bring the stockings? Why aren't you wearing them? Don't tell me the shoes didn't fit! They are just your size." Her vowels pulled long and sticky like taffy. Australian?

"They're here." I waved the stockings at her. "And of course the shoes fit, but Margaret already knows that I don't like high heels."

"You will wear them and the stockings as well, yeah?" she pronounced severely, the question at the end menacing.

"Does this mean they are sending me home?" I sat down on the bed, folding my arms and crossing my legs to show her I meant business. "I'm not going anywhere until I get an apology from Margaret. I'm pretty sure that getting someone to go on a trip under false pretenses and then drugging and locking them up against their will is illegal. Ji Hoon's going to be in a lot of trouble too, and MotherFinders..." I faltered as I followed the logic of what I was saying. Would MotherFinders have collaborated with the Stamwells? Would the Stamwells really put themselves in legal jeopardy for me?

We stared defiantly at each other for a few moments, but she had the distinct advantage of her weird face. The more I looked at it, the more unsettling it became. Incredibly prominent cheeks, the skin stretched taut and shiny over the swollen ridges. Wide mouth creeping upward in a perpetual half smile. The mismatched crookedness of her eyes. It must have been a pretty horrific accident to require so much face work. Finally, I looked away to grab the stockings and work them onto my feet, pulling them up my legs, parting the fabric of the wrap-around dress to bring the waistband over my hips, her eyes closely following my every movement.

Shoving my feet into the shoes, I teetered over to her. "There, voilà! Now, do I get to leave?"

"Not yet, we've got to do something about your face."

Taking my hand, she led me to the bathroom. As she ran a soft sponge saturated with foundation over my cheeks, she said, "I don't want us to get off on the wrong foot, Lisa. I want you to remember that I am here to help you. You can trust me." I opened my mouth to speak, but she hushed me. "Wait until I'm done, you don't want to spoil your face." Coming from her, it was a funny line, but I obeyed. "You are a lucky girl." The sponge passed delicately over the bridge of my nose, and then again, and then again. "Somebody loved you enough to find you and bring you here. You'll have a lovely life here. You'll learn the rules soon enough. There aren't that many of them really. The most important one is to always obey her." She patted gently at my face with a fist-sized powder puff.

This charade of Margaret's was going a little far. "Always obey her?! What has Margaret been smoking?"

"Uh-uh! Don't move!" she admonished me, daubing at my cheekbones.

Despite myself, I watched the transformation of my face, mesmerized. When she slicked on the mascara, it tickled. "Mascara doesn't work on me," I warned her. "My lashes are too stubby or my eyelids too chubby, but the black just ends up getting smudged onto my skin."

"I was afraid of that." Yolanda sighed. "This is special smudgeproof, so let's cross our fingers. We might have to resort to falsies."

Then she went to work on my mouth, first drawing an outline with a fat pencil and then filling it in with a bloodred lipstick that she daubed onto the end of her index finger. "Make an O with your mouth," she had to remind me more than once. Finally, she ran her fingers through my hair with a sigh, head cocked to one side. "She'll have to decide what needs to be done with your hair, but in the meantime, I'll just put some sparkly combs in it."

As she pulled and fussed with my hair, I stared at the stranger in the mirror. My eyes looked bigger and more dramatic, my cheekbones sharper, my lips more delicate, freckles and moles and big pores smoothed into oblivion by a drywall of foundation and powder.

"Here, put these on," Yolanda instructed, handing me a pair of dangly turquoise earrings. "Then take your necklace off, and this will complete your look." She held up a chunky silver-and-turquoise necklace.

"I'll put that necklace on, but I won't take this one off," I said, hooking in an earring.

"She won't like it. You'll have to take it off," Yolanda insisted.

I shook my head so that the earrings jangled. "I know what Margaret is doing, and it won't work." My fingers closed protectively around the yin-yang pendant. "She knows I haven't taken this off since Mindy gave it to me."

"Lisa!" Her voice curdled into a harsh growl. "I don't know who this Margaret person is you keep talking about, but whoever she is, forget her. You're not here for her, you're here for Honey, and Honey wants that necklace off!"

"Honey?" I laughed scornfully in her fun-house mirror face. "Is that what she told you her name was? Her name is Margaret Stamwell, and you have made yourself an accomplice to kidnapping."

Wiping a fleck of my spittle from the swollen blister of a cheekbone, Yolanda said, "Her name is Honey LeBaron, and the charge of kidnapping is absurd."

"Honey LeBaron?" I sneered in disbelief. "Who the hell is Honey LeBaron?"

"Honey," Yolanda said, the tight bow of her lips bending ever upward until I was afraid that her whole face would crack, "is your mother."

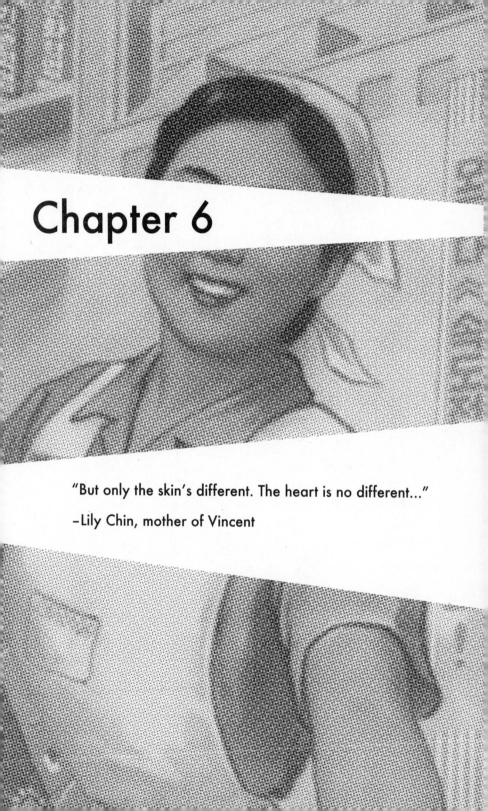

Chapter 6

"But only the skin's different. The heart is no different..."

–Lily Chin, mother of Vincent

As I followed Yolanda down a long, dark, twisting hallway, I wondered in confusion if MotherFinders had located my mother after all. But surely this was not its usual method of managing a reunion. Maybe Mindy, worried that I would refuse to meet my birth mother, had set up this surprise first encounter with her. But that didn't make any sense either. She was too busy getting through residency, planning her wedding, and meeting her own birth mother to think up such an elaborate, melodramatic ruse. Besides, she knew I hated surprises.

We entered a room that was straight out of *Garden & Gun*: gleaming wood-paneled walls crowded with mounted animal heads, a scattering of overstuffed brown leather club chairs, a mammoth slate fireplace, a glass coffee table supported by curving tusks of ivory, the floor a patchwork of animal skins, most strikingly a tiger with black markings like long, sad eyes, head rearing up openmouthed to show fangs lacquered to gleam as if wet. A woman in a peach peignoir of lace and satin lay recumbent upon a cowhide sofa absently paging through a copy of *Vogue*, looking like a 1930s screen goddess waiting for the director to call "Action!" She did not in the least fit any scenario that I had conceived, and all thoughts of Margaret or Mindy orchestrating this meeting vanished.

Yolanda knelt down to whisper something in her ear. The young and stunningly beautiful woman's burnt-butter-blond hair was swept into an updo with stray wisps hanging in delicate corkscrews about her diamond-shaped face: wide forehead, chiseled cheekbones, thin but widely curving lips, and a sweet, diminutive elfin chin, all dominated by enormous eyes of electric blue. She glowed as if spotlighted, her eyes shimmering as they flicked up and down the length of me.

"Come closer," she commanded with a breathy, Marilyn Monroe–like sigh.

I took a tentative step toward her. Yolanda, who was standing respectfully to one side, waved me forward with a spastic yet subtle clenching of her hand. I traversed the tiger skin and stepped onto a thick fox pelt that lay directly in front of the couch.

"There must be some mistake," my putative mother murmured, narrowing her bush baby eyes. "There is nothing me about her!"

"Wait, Madam, wait!" Yolanda reassured her soothingly. "May I turn on the light?"

The woman gave a slight, enervated nod.

Yolanda strode across the cavernous room and adjusted a switch so that light blazed from the central chandelier, intricately fashioned from interlocking pronged antelope horns. The woman put a hand up to her eyes with a wince, squinted at me, and softly groaned, "Doesn't help."

"One moment, Madam," Yolanda cooed as she skirted the tiger's jutting head. "All right now, here we go." Directing my chin with an insistent finger, she swiveled my head so I was looking away from the woman.

I heard a sharp intake of breath. A long silence, and then, "Has it ever been broken?"

"Dr. Panzov says not. It's the nose she was born with."

"All right, Yolanda. Bring her something to sit on." Her voice had changed from bored and cold into a sudden softness. She gave me a warm smile. "Yolanda has told you who I am?"

"Not really. I mean, other than the fact that your name is Honey."

"Nothing else?"

Yolanda placed a snakeskin ottoman flush to the sofa and forcefully nudged me down onto it. "She made the absurd claim that you were my mother."

"Absurd?" the woman echoed, as if the word were unfamiliar to her. "Why absurd?"

I laughed harshly. "My mother is Korean. You are clearly not Korean. And as you just so astutely pointed out, we look nothing alike." I looked at Yolanda for agreement on this obvious fact, but she was only staring with rapt adoration at the woman.

"How do you know your mother is Korean?" she asked, a finger placed artfully on her chin as she struck a pose of disinterested inquiry.

"I was born in Seoul. The adoption agency said my mother was Korean. Look at my eyes, my face. It doesn't take a genius. So, please. Clearly MotherFinders made a mistake and I am not the person you are looking for. Please just let me go and I won't say anything to anyone about this, I swear." I zipped my mouth shut and turned an imaginary key.

"All right, Lisa," she drawled in her breathy little-girl voice. "It is Lisa, isn't it? Let me just show you one thing, and then you can decide for yourself what you want to do. Does that sound reasonable to you?"

"I already know what I want to do, I want to go home," I retorted.

Yolanda clamped my shoulder with a distinctly threatening grip, while the woman ate me up with her neon eyes.

"OK, go ahead. Let me see what you got."

But all she did was look away from me toward the same spot that Yolanda had forced me to look, at the yawning pit of the stone fireplace. I saw it instantly and felt as if someone had punched me in the gut, knocking the wind out of me. Her nose was the very replica of mine: long, thin, with a high bridge that swelled out like a knuckle and then plunged downward to end with a hint of an undercurl.

"You see, Lisa, don't you?" she said with triumphant glee, opening her arms wide, bell sleeves softly shimmering like bird plumage. "Come give your mother a hug."

When foundational myths crumble and history is rewritten before your eyes, it takes more than a single moment to understand what is happening, and I stared in stunned incomprehension at her.

"Come now, baby, I've been waiting so long to hug you," the golden-haired stranger wheedled, reaching for me. "Come to mama."

Despite myself, I rose up from the ottoman and leaned down toward her. She turned her cheek to me, I suppose for a kiss. And I kissed it, god help me, I did, leaving the waxy imprint of my mouth on her smooth, marmoreal cheek. Then her arms closed around me and, bringing me down to my knees, she pulled me to her lacy bosom, her breasts a generous pillow to my spinning head. I heard Yolanda sigh happily, murmuring, "Oh, Madam!" And then her arms slipped away and she shimmied me off her chest.

"We have a lot of catching up to do, Lisa." For a moment, a lacquered nail touched the yin-yang pendant that was cupped in the notch of my collarbone. "Yolanda will take you back to your room for now, so you can rest up and get refreshed for lunch."

In a stupor, I rose from my knees. "Maybe Ji Hoon can explain this to me," I said slowly, ripping at the inside of my lip with my teeth as I tried to make sense of things. "Can I speak to Ji Hoon, please?"

"Who's Ji Hoon?" the woman asked, glancing at Yolanda for an answer.

"I don't know, Madam, but she has been talking about him and someone called Margaret. I think she must still be confused from the sedatives."

"Yes, it's been an awful shock," the woman commiserated as she languidly reclaimed her magazine. "Rest now, Lisa. We've got the rest of our lives to catch up."

Yolanda touched me sympathetically on the elbow and tipped me a slow, satisfied wink. The wink, I realized, was the only way that her face could communicate subtle emotions. I looked back at the woman reclining on the couch like Cleopatra in her litter. She sensed my glance and blew me a coquettish kiss. I turned away just in time to stumble over the tiger's head.

Yolanda deposited me back at my room, the door sealing shut with a soft sucking sound as my thoughts clamored and squirmed over each other, trying to comprehend my present reality. In just one week, I had broken up with my best friend, had become a fugitive from Japanese justice, and now found myself who knows where, the captive of a lunatic who claimed she had given birth to me.

But that nose. I rushed into the bathroom and turned my head as far as I could while looking at it out of the corner of my eyes. It was the exact same nose. What were the odds? I had occasionally encountered people, always Caucasian, with noses similar to mine, though the noses in question either had the bump or else the hook, never both together.

I shook my head in refusal. The world cannot change in a moment. I had always and forever known that my mother was Korean. It was an entrenched part of my history, the story I had created of my origins: my mother was a poverty-stricken, helpless Korean girl, perhaps an alcoholic or a drug addict, or perhaps she saved up all her illicitly earned pennies to support a blind father and a crippled mother and her five younger siblings. Maybe a prostitute, maybe a bar girl, maybe a hapless local, she was impregnated by a Caucasian American, one of the tens of thousands of American troop members stationed in the country, who used her up and threw her away. She was black haired and slant eyed, with the flat face and strong bone structure of a Korean. She ate rice with metal chopsticks, slept on a thin mattress on the floor, and honored her ancestors. She was not ever a beautiful blond woman in a peignoir named Honey who lived in a hidden lair that was decorated like a soap opera set.

Fingering my yin-yang pendant, I stared at myself in the mirror. With the heavy mask of makeup, I did not look like anyone I knew. Who was I? Was I, all along, someone else?

I was used to being the only one of my kind in a room, the raisin in the oatmeal, as one tipsy dinner guest of my parents once put it. Even though there were a number of other Asians at my school—FOB ESL kids, first-generation overachievers, and a sprinkling of diplomat brats—I hung around with the white kids who were on the fringes: slackers, dirtbags, hippies, skater punks, emo kids, and all-around oddballs. I was the only Asian, and the only minority, among them. It didn't feel weird to me, because all my life I had been the only person of color in a sea of white, whether at family reunions, on a summer home-stay program in Spain, or at a raging kegger down the street from my house.

In a psych class during my senior year, I learned about the Kübler-Ross model, otherwise known as the five stages of grief. At the time I took it literally, useful only for the terminally ill and victims of tragedy; but if I'd had the acumen to apply it to my own situation as a transracial adoptee, I would have recognized that at age seventeen, I was three steps into the process.

For the first decade or so of my life, I was swaddled in denial. Though I looked different on the outside, I blithely presumed that everyone—my family, neighbors, and classmates—knew I was just the same as they were on the inside, so I tuned out the lady in line at the grocery store who asked my mom where she got me from, the business associate of Scott's who got all weepy-eyed over how my mom had rescued me, the young mother at the playground who squealed how she wanted one just like me. I ignored the strangers who oozed their unctuous blessings all over me, telling me how fortunate I was and how grateful I should be; blocked out the compliments on how well I spoke English; earnestly answered the snickering inquiries from my classmates about what I ate for dinner at home and how come I didn't eat my lunch with chopsticks. I thought that when Kirk Hobson pulled his eyes at me on the playground, it was no different from him making fun of the fat kid, the bucktoothed kid, and the ginger. But then Tommy Feinstein took to yelling "Ching chong!" whenever he saw me, Wayne Goddard liked to follow me around chanting about dirty knees, and Jane Hahn, who I thought was my friend, asked me where my real parents came from. And it wasn't just white people. When I visited my father in Gaborone, kids would make karate kick moves at me, screeching "Hai-yaaa!" and growling like cats in heat. Eventually, I could no longer ignore that my race was the first, and sometimes only, thing people saw about me, and that it was not I who was in control of my identity, but they.

During my tweens, I moved on to the anger stage. Why should the shape of my eyes make Kirk, Tommy, and Wayne think they were better than I? I was obviously smarter than they were, and yet they got to make fun of me? But any insult I lobbed back at them was answered with a slur, which immediately won the argument according to the playground crowd. As I entered my teen years, boys began to tell me I was ugly because of my squinty eyes. They were only slightly worse than the boys who flirted by trying to guess which strain of Asian I was or waxed ecstatic about how hot Asian girls were. The eye shadow and mascara that the other girls applied looked frightful on me, drawing attention toward the narrowness of my eyes and their epicanthic fold. I began to parry the dreaded "Where are you from?" with "America," but that just delayed the inevitable, for the inquisitor would not be denied an explanation: "No, I mean where are you from *originally*?" And then I'd have to admit that I wasn't really an American like they were, I was "from" Korea. Sometimes they'd ask how I came to America, and I'd have to confess to being adopted. I hated having to tell complete strangers the intimate details of my life as if I were some one-person exhibit in a freak show. I started to deliberately rebel against the stereotypes. Because I was supposed to be good at math, I failed geometry. Instead of being docile and obedient, I was troublesome and disruptive. Where I should have been strait-laced and demure, I was sloppy drunk and in-your-face outrageous. Though I was an indiscriminate consumer of illicit substances, it was alcohol that brought out the best (as I saw it then) in me, because nothing says "I don't give a fuck" like puking into a storm drain in broad daylight on a school day.

My final years of high school, I seized on all things Asian, grabbing indiscriminately, turning my ethnicity into a parody of an identity. I bedecked myself with jade rings, Buddhist prayer bracelets, good luck Chinese coin earrings, dragon-embroidered Mary Jane slippers, padded silk jackets, bright satin brocade cheongsam blouses, and a Mao cap emblazoned with a red star. I dyed my auburn hair black, sharpened the angles of my pageboy cut, used eyeliner to emphasize the slittiness of my eyes, and whitened my face with rice powder. When I found out that Vincent Chin, a Chinese immigrant whose murder by two white men galvanized the birth of the Asian American civil rights movement, was adopted, I built a small shrine to him in my bedroom before which I burned incense every day (which also helped to cover up the pot smoke). I dropped Spanish for beginning Chinese, briefly joined the Manga Club but couldn't give two fucks about *Naruto* and *Dragon Ball*, and then tried the Asian Student Union but felt embarrassed and out of place among the "real" Asians. I scoured libraries and bookstores for Asian literature, reading Yasunari Kawabata, Yukio Mishima, Lu Xun, Mao Dun, Amy Tan, and Maxine Hong Kingston. I rented videos of films by Kurosawa, Ozu, and Zhang Yimou. I didn't consciously avoid Korean culture; it was just that Chinese and Japanese cultures were much more prominent and accessible, and anyway, it wasn't about exploring my roots but about exploiting them, an inside joke, a sarcastic sneer. Call it my bargaining stage.

Yolanda's heels detonated loudly on the marble tiles, *crack, crack, crack,* like rifle shots, as she led me through the twisting corridor, feebly lit by widely spaced lamps that looked like phosphorescent toadstools, with long stretches of dark between the pale puddlings of light. We stopped in front of a door, which Yolanda opened by affixing an eye to a small glowing panel, similar to the device that controlled the door to my room. The room we entered was dominated by an extremely long table of glossy dark wood, one end laid with four formal place settings, a whole arsenal of silver cutlery flanking gilt-rimmed plates. A short but well-built man with gossamer hair spiderwebbed carefully over his skull sprang up to greet us, the same man who had taken my vitals shortly after I regained consciousness. Rubbing his hands together to make a noise like crinkling paper, he exclaimed, "Lisa! You look the very picture of health!"

"Who *are* you?" I demanded to know.

"Ah, yes, forgive me. I never properly introduced myself." He took my hand, bending over it so that I could see the careful arrangement of his comb-over. "Dr. Vladimir Panzov, at your service."

"Panzov?" I echoed with an incredulous laugh, reclaiming my hand. "Can that really be your name?"

"As really as Lisa Pearl can be yours," he said, his thin upper lip curled against salmon-colored gums in a not so convincing approximation of a smile.

Yolanda icily indicated I should take the seat next to hers. In my room, we had argued again about the necklace. She had seemed almost desperate to get it off me, and I thought tears would leak from her crooked eyes when I refused.

A three-tiered crystal chandelier caught the sunlight streaming through windows that, like the one in my bedroom, were set high in the wall, revealing only a narrow strip of sky. Two doors—the one we had entered through and a swinging door inset with a diamond pane—were separated by a six-legged mahogany sideboard tastefully arranged with silver candlesticks, gleaming showpiece china objects, and tulips bowing from crystal vases.

"So, Lisa," Dr. Panzov said jovially. "How are you feeling? Hmm?"

"I feel like I need to get out of here," I answered, before gulping down some water so violently that I almost choked on an ice cube.

"You do?" His blond brows came down in concern, his small eyes disappearing into blue dots.

"I need to contact the closest US consulate. I know my rights! Your lunatic boss can't just keep me captive against my will."

His ingratiating smile contracted into a shocked pucker and then spread out again in a smile, this time nakedly malicious.

Yolanda hissed, "Don't you dare hurt Madam's feelings or you'll have hell to pay from the rest of us."

"The rest of who?" I wondered as Yolanda jumped to her feet, grabbing me by the arm and pulling me up as well, a split second before Honey swept in wearing a grass-green linen pantsuit and a pomegranate silk chemise, hair spilling down her shoulders in a golden cascade.

"Ah, here we are!" she trilled happily.

Dr. Panzov deftly pulled out an intricately carved, throne-like chair from the head of the table, and she floated down onto its thickly padded leather seat with a satisfied sigh. She nodded, and Yolanda primly seated herself. After pushing Honey snug to the table, Dr. Panzov followed suit.

"Lisa?" Honey looked at me, her hands suspended in midair in the act of shaking out her napkin.

"I'm not sitting until I get some answers," I declared, leaning on the table with my knuckles. "I want to know why I am here. Where here even is! Who are you? What do you want from me?"

"Lisa, dear," she cooed, "sit down. Let's be civilized about this. There is plenty of time to talk. Cookie has made a wonderful lunch." Her lips, just the same fruity shade as her chemise, curved into a disarming smile. "We'll talk about it if you'll just sit down. Please, baby."

I clung to my defiance for a few seconds more and then crashed angrily down into my seat, whereupon she gave a careless shake to a little silver bell. Immediately, Ting swung through the door with the diamond-shaped pane. So now I knew that she wasn't deaf, which meant that she probably wasn't mute either. She removed the gilt-edged plate that was at each setting, replacing it with a delicate double-handled bowl brimming with pale green soup. "Cream of asparagus," Honey announced to appreciative murmurs. The other two waited with hands in laps until Honey had taken a first taste before they picked up their soupspoons.

"Mmm," Yolanda purred, licking her lips. "Cookie has really outdone himself today."

Dr. Panzov grunted in agreement, quickly ladling the contents of his bowl into his mouth.

It *was* good, and I found myself bending my head to my bowl instead of glaring defiantly at the others, as I wanted to be doing.

"So, Lisa," Honey said after a few moments of soft sipping. "You want answers."

Quickly swallowing a rich dollop of soup, I eagerly gurgled, "Yes. Yes, I do."

"Who am I?" She brought her napkin up to dab at the corners of her mouth. "My friends call me Honey. I would like you to as well, because, well, 'Mom' would just be awkward for the time being." A grimace that was halfway between a smile and a frown trembled on her lips. "About twenty-eight years ago, I gave birth to a baby girl. But it was a difficult time for me. I was a stranger in a strange land, without a friend, all alone. There was a man who fell in love with me and said he'd take care of me, but he made me understand that the baby—who was not his—could not be included in his offer. I had no choice. Much as it grieved me to give the baby up, if I wanted to be with the man I loved, a great and honorable man whose favor I treasure above all else, I had to give her up."

"What about the father?" I asked.

"What father?" she asked, soup glimmering in the spoon she had just dipped into her bowl.

"The baby's father. My father."

"Oh!" She shook her head dismissively. "Some university student with toothpaste under his eyes to combat the tear gas, no doubt. No one important. No use thinking about him."

Maybe because he had nothing better to do now that he had finished his soup, Dr. Panzov chortled. But it died a quick death in his throat when Honey dealt him a sharp look.

"Did you give the baby a name?" I was surprised to hear that my voice was shaking.

"Vladimir, do be a dear and pour us some wine," Honey murmured. Barely had the words escaped her before Dr. Panzov was on his feet. "No, Lisa, I did not." She gave a rueful shrug of her shoulders. "I knew it would only make our parting much more difficult. But I have always liked the name Felicia."

"Oh, Felicia," Yolanda agreed softly.

"Thank god I didn't have to go through life with the name Felicia." I rolled my eyes as Dr. Panzov came back to the table cradling a decanter of wine.

Honey froze for a moment, as did Dr. Panzov, who was about to pour her some wine. Then she threw back her head and laughed with breathy gasps. "It will be so refreshing to have a little American wit around here. The others can be such toadies." She shook her gold bangles at Yolanda and Dr. Panzov, who grinned ingratiatingly at her. "I think I'm going to like being your mother. Your spunkiness reminds me of a younger me."

"I already have a mother!" I protested, dashing my spoon down into my empty bowl. "One who I am sure is very worried about me."

"Ha!" Honey softly breathed into her wineglass. "That is one thing that cannot be undone. They can change your name, but they can't change who gave birth to you!"

Making a split-second, and rather surprising, decision to hang on as hard as I could to my sobriety, I put my hand over my glass when Dr. Panzov approached. Drinking was what got me into this mess, and I made a hasty vow to myself that I wouldn't drink until I was out of it. Dr. Panzov almost couldn't believe it and bumped my fingers with the decanter, before he gave me a have-it-your-way shrug, poured his own glass up to the brim, and, after a quick glance at Honey, took a long, deep swallow. Honey snapped, "Oh, for god's sake, Vladimir, get drunk off the cheap stuff, not my cellar wines."

"Why were you in Korea?" I asked.

Tinkling the silver bell again, she said, "I was like a shipwreck victim, washed up on its shores."

In a slow choreography of china, Ting replaced the soup bowls with scallop-edged salad plates arranged with tender green Bibb lettuce and cherry tomatoes sprinkled with chives and pine nuts.

"So we're still in Korea?" I demanded.

"Mmm." She nibbled a tomato that was dripping seeds from the gash made by the tines of her fork.

"Yes or no?"

Her eyelids parted, and she stared at me. The color of her eyes was mesmerizing, a dark blue that rippled and changed with the light and the angle, like an opal. "Yes, we are in Korea."

"Where?"

"About seventy-five miles away from Pyongyang."

"Pyongyang." I crinkled my brow. "So just this side of the DMZ?"

"Eat your salad, Lisa. Look, Dr. Panzov has already finished his."

Dr. Panzov lifted his wineglass, clouded with greasy fingerprints, to me.

Loading salad onto my fork, I persisted. "So, like, we're near Incheon, near the airport?"

"Wrong direction," Yolanda chimed in, an eye scrunching closed in a slow-moving, exaggerated wink to let me in on the joke.

Macerated lettuce fell from my mouth.

Honey batted her eyes at me innocently. "Do you see now what trouble I had to go through to bring you here?"

I looked from Honey to Dr. Panzov, baring the frill of his white teeth at me in what he must have thought was a smile, to Yolanda, who was winking gaily.

"No," I whispered, the fork clattering from my fingers. "No! That's crazy!"

Obviously, she was just teasing me, getting me back for my insubordination, for my less than joyful reaction to the revelation that she was my mother.

Honey reached over to pat my hand reassuringly. "There, there, dear. Once the shock wears off, you will quickly get used to life here. Soon enough, you'll come to cherish the privileged way we live."

My stomach felt like it had just swallowed my blood-glutted heart. "I... I feel sick."

"Here, Lisa, drink a little wine, it will make you feel better." Dr. Panzov leaned over with the carafe. "Come, come, doctor's orders."

I pushed the carafe away, sloshing wine onto his sleeve. With a good-natured shrug, he refilled his own glass.

"All right, Vladimir," Honey murmured, ringing the little silver bell. Again, the laborious ritual of the clearing and the serving of plates.

"I think I better go back to my room." I tried to push my chair away from the table but my legs weren't working.

"Nonsense," Honey protested. "Cookie went to great lengths to prepare this welcome luncheon for you. He and I spent a long time planning the menu."

Goose bumps hardened my skin, my muscles starting to shiver from a chill that swept down my spine and wouldn't let go. "So, Ji Hoon is North Korean?" I stammered, trying to tease some sense from this latest unfathomable development.

"Ji Hoon? I don't know any Ji Hoon." Honey shook her head.

Pressing my palms hard into my face, I said between clenched teeth, "That extraordinarily handsome guy you hired to kidnap me. The one who took me on a long walk off a short pier."

"You weren't kidnapped," Honey said, her voice frothy with laughter. "How can a mother kidnap her own child?"

Gently nudging my elbows off the table, Ting laid in front of me a plate laden with rosy slices of meat, fat coins of glazed carrots, and baby red potatoes glistening with butter.

Honey looked down incredulously at her plate. "What is this?" she muttered. "Cookie!" she screamed. "Cookie, come out here at once!"

Dr. Panzov, who had his utensils at the ready, placed them gently back on the table.

The door swung open and out shuffled a stocky, grizzled man in a soiled chef's jacket, bowing low as he approached.

"What is the meaning of this?!"

His stubbled jowls trembling, the man groveled in heavily accented English. "So sorry, Madam, so sorry. I try to send message before, but Ting say you not available. Vegetable delivery was not good today. So I take carrots from the garden." Eyes turned down, he cringed and cowered, back stooped and knees bent practically to the ground.

Shrieking, Honey raised a hand and delivered a resounding smack on the man's head. "You should have called me before the delivery boy left! I would have cleared up the whole mess! Now you have ruined the entire meal! Don't you know anything? I would have changed the carrots for the canned peas and saved the carrots for tonight's dinner with the roasted duck. Now it will have to be the other way around, so then you have ruined two meals for today!" *Smack, smack,* her hand came down two more times on the man's head, which looked like he was bowing it the better to be slapped.

Dr. Panzov eyed his wineglass mournfully while Yolanda squirmed with either glee or fear. For a moment, I was distracted from my own anguish by this bizarre scene, but then the primacy of my own situation reasserted itself and a deep, painful lowing welled up from my chest, and all eyes, even Cookie's, squinting up in anticipation of another blow, turned to me. With one more deliberate *thwack* of her hand, Honey pushed the chef away from her. He scampered off without a backward glance.

"Let's eat," Honey said, picking up her knife and fork. Dr. Panzov and Yolanda quickly followed suit. "Come on, Lisa. You don't want your food to get cold."

Clutching my stomach, I swung my head dumbly.

After staring at me with narrowed eyes, Honey ostentatiously turned away and sunnily inquired, "So, Vladimir, any news on the arrival of our guests?"

"Yes," he answered, straining to swallow an enormous chunk of beef that he'd just troweled into his mouth. "I have been assured that they will arrive tomorrow morning."

Scrunching up her shoulders, Yolanda clapped her hands together in a dumb show of ecstasy.

"Wonderful," Honey proclaimed. "You'll really enjoy meeting the Gang, Lisa. We have such fun together. They will cheer you up."

Wrapping my arms tightly over my chest, I just shook my head. My teeth were beginning to chatter.

With a small sigh, Honey put down her knife and fork and, blotting at the corners of her lovely mouth, said, "I suppose it's all been a bit of a shock. I should have given you more time to adjust to your new circumstances."

"Oh, no, Madam," Yolanda murmured in protest.

Honey waved away her objection, nodding bravely, her lips thinned into a stoic grimace. "We need to give her time. She doesn't understand yet what big plans we have for her, what a wonderful life awaits. But she's smart. After all, she has my brains." Yolanda and Dr. Panzov chuckled appreciatively. "I think it's best that we let her rest up for a little bit." She leaned over to tenderly chuck at my chin with a manicured fingernail. "Vladimir will take you back to your room now. Take a bubble bath, have a good night's sleep, rest up. Tomorrow we'll have a big welcome party for you, and you'll see then how good life is here."

With a clownish smile, Dr. Panzov pulled my chair back and helped me to stand. "After you," he said, hand at the small of my back gently propelling me through the door, the hard slap of his flat-footed gait sounding behind me down the hallway. When we arrived at my room, he hustled in front of me to lean his eyeball into the scanner, releasing the door. Just before I stepped through, he crooned, "Just one thing, Lisa..."

I turned toward him, and he had his hand at my throat. I felt a sharp tug at the back of my neck that seemed to cut through to my cervical vertebrae. "Thanks, Lisa," he said, waving the yin-yang pendant in the air. "Rest well, for tomorrow we party." Then he pushed me through the door and quickly slammed it shut.

Chapter 7

"I don't think you can be adopted without being a little bit screwed up."

–Liz Phair

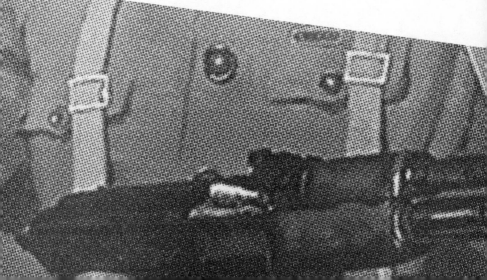

When Ting came in the following morning, I pleaded with her to bring me a phone, putting my hand with pinkie and thumb extended up to my ear in the universal sign for a phone, even though North Korea wasn't really a part of the universe and I doubted that most citizens even had a phone. But I had to at least try, after a night of my brain running itself round and round like a tweaked-out hamster on a rust-ruined wheel, trying to find a way out of whatever it was I had stumbled into. Ting sidestepped me and hurried across the room on the balls of her feet, placing a breakfast tray on the small table that sat under the window. As she brushed by me on her way toward the door, I begged, "Won't you help me, Ting?"

When I said her name, her eyes shifted toward me, the look gliding along the floor like marbles. Then she pleadingly scooped her hand toward her mouth, urging me to eat, before slipping out the door. I was strangely moved that she cared about me at all. I ate the breakfast and the lunch that she brought too. It was, at least, something to do, a way to distract me from the sick vortex of thoughts that whirled in ever tighter circles in my brain.

When next the door opened with a hiss like the unscrewing of a soda bottle cap, Yolanda strode in, bearing a dress on a hanger, a pair of strappy, rhinestone-studded heels dangling from one hand.

"Yolanda! I need to use a phone to get in touch with my parents! Please bring me a phone or at least let me send an email! This is insane!" I had meant to be ingratiating, but the pent-up fear and anger came spewing out in a hot, unstoppable torrent. "My family must be frantic about me. I need to tell them I'm OK."

"*Laat my met rus,*" she snapped, flinging the dress on the bed. "Oh, you are funny! It is going to be a joy having you around, livening things up."

"People are worried about me!" I insisted weakly. "No doubt the authorities are on alert, looking for me. Don't you have a family, Yolanda? Can't you understand what I'm feeling?"

A derisive snort erupted from her squashed nostrils. "Shower and then put on this dress. Don't forget the pantyhose! I'll be back to do your hair and makeup." She spun on her stilettos and was out the door.

For a brief moment, I thought about defying her orders, but the promise of an end to the monotony was too much and I dutifully climbed into the shower. The dress was an elegant black silk Prada sheath with a scoop neck, three-quarter sleeves, a drop waist, and an accordion-pleated skirt. Except for being a little too big at the bust, it fit perfectly.

Yolanda reappeared and carefully assessed me with her crooked green eyes, pinching at the extra material at my bosom with an impatient click of her tongue. Not in her usual business suit, she was wearing a seafoam chiffon number with floaty sleeves and a low back, a sparkly crystal bead necklace triple-stranded around her neck, which was surprisingly smooth and youthful for someone with as much face work as she had. If it was a car crash that had made her face into what it was, it must have been a really bad one. "It needs augmentation," she muttered.

"I'm already wearing a ridiculously padded bra," I protested. "Unless you want me to stuff socks in there."

Her puffy lips stretched a few millimeters into what I now recognized as her smile. "Not socks, dear. I think it is some kind of silicone gel that they put in there."

I clutched at my breasts or, more accurately, at the foam of the bra cups.

"Everyone does it nowadays," she informed me as she led me into the bathroom. "From what I hear, plastic surgery is normal in America."

"Is that what happened to your face, Yolanda?" I asked, wincing as she dragged a comb ruthlessly through my hair. "Plastic surgery?"

The hair dryer began to roar. After styling my hair into an artfully mussed mop, she set to work on my face. "Pay attention now," she instructed. "Soon you're going to have to do this yourself. I've got better things to do than make you look presentable."

When she was done, I inspected my new face in the mirror, skin freakishly smooth, blemishes almost, but not quite, invisible. Eyes somehow larger, false eyelashes scratchy against the sliver of my inner lid. Lips thinner but with a more exaggerated dip to the Cupid's bow. Cheekbones shadowed with blush so I looked lean and hungry like a model. She encircled my neck with cool, smooth pearls and handed me matching double-dropped earrings.

"Nice to see you finally agreed to ditch the tacky necklace," she taunted, fluffing my hair with her fingers. "Now Madam needs to decide what to do with this rat's nest. Maybe a pixie cut?" She glanced at her tiny wristwatch. "Right on schedule. Let's put your shoes on, yeah? Then we'll go have some fun. You are lucky to have a party so early in your stay here. Sometimes we go ages without one."

The shoes were stilettos adorned with four different glittery buckles. As I laboriously notched each buckle into place, I warned her, "I'm not going to be able to walk in these."

"Nonsense. Just takes a little practice."

"Heels kill my feet. See how high my arches are?"

"Lisa," she said sternly, "you cannot be stylish in flats. You just cannot."

As I wobbled to my feet, I said doubtfully, "Well, as long as I don't have to stand up very much. Or walk very far." I took a tentative step and then another.

"You'll get used to it. We all do." She flitted over to the mirror to double-check her makeup. "All ready then?"

Teetering forward, I asked, "How did you guys know what size shoe I wear?"

"Oh, Lisa." Yolanda's eye shuttered in a slow wink. "We know everything about you."

As I followed her out the door, I sputtered, "How is that possible? Have you been watching me all these years? How did you even find me in the first place?"

"I have no knowledge of how you came here," Yolanda declared loudly, marching ahead, the distance between us growing as I hobbled carefully down the hallway, the smooth soles of my new shoes slipping precariously on the slick surface of the marble floor.

A current of air ran through the hallway, like the hot whoosh of wind that announces the arrival of a train in a subway tunnel, whistling eerily past my ears. "Where's that wind coming from?" I called ahead to Yolanda, but she didn't answer, perhaps because I was downwind from her and my words were blown in the wrong direction.

I heard the chatter as we approached the blaze of light flooding from an open door into the shadowed corridor. Yolanda indicated I should wait just outside as she announced, "Ladies and gentlemen, it is my great privilege to introduce Miss Lisa LeBaron."

I stepped into the room to a soft smattering of applause. To my surprise, it was not the tiger-skin room, nor was it the dining room, but a Versailles-style salon, replete with marble columns crowned with gilt capitals, stone-inlaid walls, wedding-cake chandeliers, a ceiling frescoed with Bacchanalian scenes, and a parquet floor inset with an elaborate geometric pattern. Besides Honey and Dr. Panzov, there were four others, devouring me with hungry stares as they gently tapped their hands together. Not sure what to do, I lowered my head and shrugged my shoulders with a stupid, apologetic smile. Yolanda took my hand and led me with a fashion-runway strut to Honey, who was standing alone, resplendent in a clingy floor-length aqua dress with a long slit up the middle, hair sculpted into a towering bouffant, sparkling blue gems dripping from her ears and neck and flashing from her fingers.

"Lisa, dear," she said, taking my hand in hers and turning a dazzling smile on the little group clustered around us. "It is my pleasure to introduce you to the Gang, starting with Harvey Cockburn."

She passed my hand to a large man with a bloated face and the empurpled, engorged, and pitted nose of a chronic drinker, and he pressed his flabby lips to it before passing it on to a woman with a kind smile that revealed a sweet little gap between two front teeth, her hair braided into an elaborate crown. "His wife, Patience," Honey explained as the woman brushed her lips against my skin before very gently lowering my hand and bowing as she stepped away from me. Filling the void that Patience left was a very tall, very thin man with gangling insect-like limbs, who grabbed my hand with extreme enthusiasm and rushed it up to his lips, damp with spittle.

"I am your most humble servant, Wendell Squibbly." Just as I began to fear that he would take out his tongue and start licking my hand, he placed it in the waiting embrace of a woman with wide-set cinnamon eyes, doe-like in their innocence. "And this is my wife, Lahela, whose greatest honor it is to greet you."

She did not kiss my hand, but I felt the hot moistness of her breath upon it. Her grip dissolved like sugar in hot water and my hand slipped away. Ting, outfitted like a manor maid in mobcap and white frilly apron, glided up with a tray of champagne flutes. Honey took one and then so did I. The rest of the guests swarmed around, grabbing up glasses. Honey cleared her throat, and they reverently lowered their heads.

"All of you know what trouble we've had to bring Lisa home. I thank you all for your support and comfort. Now that she is finally here, I beseech you to take her into your hearts and to be patient with her. Think back to your first days here and the challenges that had to be overcome. In the meantime, please join me in a warm welcome."

The others raised their glasses and responded heartily. "Hear, hear!"

"Welcome, Lisa!"

"*Dobro pozhalovat!*"

"*Nyinditonhab!*"

"*Welkom!*"

And then the champagne was sipped, or gulped, or, in Dr. Panzov's and Harvey Cockburn's cases, entirely polished off. I too automatically lifted the glass to my lips and drank. And then I remembered that I was on the wagon because I needed to keep my wits about me. But that first sip had felt so good going down, so I took another. And then, because everyone was looking expectantly at me, another. It was too late then; I could already feel the happy effects of the alcohol, tingling down my gullet, making me less tense and more willing to be embraced by this motley group of strangers. "Do I make a speech?" I asked Honey.

Placing a reassuring hand, each finger laden with a cocktail ring blazing with a different type of blue gemstone, on my arm, she said, "No, no, you'll get to know them one-on-one."

Harvey Cockburn waddled up to us, mopping his forehead with a handkerchief.

"Harvey is one of my oldest and most stalwart friends," Honey purred.

"Oh, ma'am, you do me too much honor," he brayed, shoving the handkerchief in the pocket of his dingy safari jacket, a telltale shadow of grime on the pocket flaps indicating years of hard use.

"Were you kidnapped as well?" I asked, bringing my glass up to my lips.

His head snapped back, the hammock of flesh that hung from his lower jaw quivering. "Who's been kidnapped?"

Honey attempted to pinch my arm but scratched me instead.

"And what's with introducing me as Lisa LeBaron? My last name is Pearl."

"It is a great privilege to be a LeBaron. It's a surname of the highest distinction. Pearl is so very... not you," Honey cooed, indicating to Harvey with a flick of the fingers that he should wander off.

"It's Jewish." I'd always had trouble with my last name. Strangers expected me to be called Lee, Chung, or Park. On the first day of class, teachers would scan the classroom for a clean-cut white girl, perhaps with curly hair and a Semitic nose. Sometimes, upon introduction, people would come right out and challenge me, as if I did not correctly remember my own name.

Honey's eyes flew open in alarm. Either the dress matched her eyes, or her eyes changed color, like a mood ring. "I can assure you that there is not a drop of Jewish blood in you."

"Judaism is a religion, not an ethnicity," I corrected her primly. I did not feel the need to let her know that I had been raised secularly, or that Judaism was matrilineal and some rabbis thought that adopted children didn't qualify.

"Well, you should forget all that." Honey patted unnecessarily at the lacquered spire of her hair. "LeBaron is your rightful last name, and with it, you join a very elite family. We're American aristocracy, if you will. Haven't you heard of the New York LeBarons?"

"I've heard of the Chrysler LeBaron," I snickered.

She bathed me in the cold glow of her aqua eyes for a second before whinnying with laughter. "Oh, Lisa, your wit is so refreshing.

Usually I must suffer the fawning truckle of this lot." She wafted her hand toward the others, who were working very hard to pretend like they weren't following every word of our conversation.

"That seems an unkind thing to say," I replied loudly for their benefit. My glass was empty, and I felt an urgent need for more. Spying Ting across the room with a fresh tray of drinks, I moved toward her, an ankle wobbling from its precarious perch atop the ridiculously attenuated four-inch heel, then folding at a sickening angle that made me drop to my knees.

"Oh, poor dear," Honey murmured, voice dripping with maternal concern. "Here, hold on to my arm. Let's get you over to the couch." She rubbed my back. "Harvey! We could use your help over here."

Harvey stopped pretending to be engrossed in conversation with Wendell and hurried over.

"Help poor Lisa to the couch. She twisted her ankle."

Hooking my arm across his shoulders, Harvey half dragged me to a nearby green moiré divan. Honey came twittering after with a few stiff tapestry cushions. Kneeling by my side, her fingers scrabbled ineffectually at the buckles of my shoes, long nails getting in the way of such intricate finger work. "There, there, you'll feel better in a moment. Aren't these darling shoes? But oh dear, what tiny buckles."

Yolanda came to her rescue, quickly undoing each buckle. With a tender pat to my cheek, Honey murmured, "Put your legs up, baby. We'll be back soon to check on you."

Then she and Yolanda left me to Harvey's care. "Here you go, young lady," Harvey bellowed cheerfully, tucking the cushions behind my back. Leaning in close, he gasped sotto voce into my ear, "Every one of us here knows what you're going through, Lisa. We are your friends, and you'd be wise to let us help you. I came here in 1974, defected really, just crossed the demilitarized zone to the North Korean side and declared my intentions. I had no idea what I was getting into, just wanted to escape from some stupid decisions. At first, I thought I'd made a mistake. Life was hard here, and there were lots of strange things to get used to. But lucky you, you won't have to go through the things I went through. With Honey, you have nothing but a life of ease ahead of you. Don't believe all the crazy things you've read about North Korea. We're not like that at all here, as you have seen."

"Actually, besides Ting, I haven't seen a real live North Korean yet," I muttered, gesturing at Ting, her ridiculous mobcap slipping down her forehead. "Maybe that's why it's so hard for me to comprehend that I'm really in North Korea."

"Oh, there's no doubt about it, you're in North Korea," he assured me, fussing again with the pillows, the woolen thread scratchy against my neck. "My advice as an old-timer is for you to take it easy on yourself and go with the flow. Honey is a wonderful woman and she only has your best interests at heart. Join our happy family."

And then he struggled to his feet, pulling himself up slowly with a low groan.

Reaching down to massage my ankle, I closed my eyes, and when I opened them again, the oval face of Harvey's wife was looming over me, the light burnishing her sable skin with a bronze patina.

"Are you feeling better then, Lisa?" The opposite of her husband—dark where he was pale, beautiful where he was repulsive, youthful to his decrepitude—she spoke in a vaguely British accent with extremely precise enunciation and a slight shivering of the r's.

"Mmm, yes, thank you, Patience," I murmured with an embarrassed little laugh. "I'm so clumsy."

"Oh, no, Lisa, there are no such things as accidents." She smiled. "Your body is reacting to the shock of the news you've received recently." She arranged the hem of my dress more decorously over my knees and, in that one simple gesture, imparted a motherly care that made my eyes prickle in requital. "I too was taken from my mother at an early age. I never met my mother again, but you have. I can imagine the depth of your emotions." A little quiver trembled through her wide cheeks. "Then, on top of that, to find yourself in a strange country, far from your homeland." She grimaced sympathetically. "I am from Zimbabwe, which is faaar away in Africa."

"Oh! I know where that is," I exclaimed, staring at her face because it comforted me. "My father is married to a Motswana woman. Your accent reminds me of hers."

"Really?" She was startled by this news, eyes widening to reveal freckles of brown flecking the whites.

"Yes. I've been to Botswana several times. In fact, I've been to Zimbabwe, to see Victoria Falls."

Her hand went up to her mouth. "Oh," she gasped, blinking hard once, twice. "Oh, what I wouldn't give for just a glimpse..." she whispered, clutching my hand. "We are sisters, we are African sisters." Then she shook her head, and raising her voice again, she said, "And North Korean sisters too. I have been a citizen now for five years, after I married Harvey and started working for the propaganda department."

"He must be twenty years older than you," I said sympathetically.

"Oh, he is a good man, a good man," she averred. "They are all good here. These people are your friends, all of them. And your mother!" Her smile was wide and trembling, revealing the soft pink inside of her bottom lip. "She is a wonderful woman. You are so fortunate she has brought you here to live."

I could see why she worked for the propaganda department, for I almost believed her. "Where do you live, Patience? Nearby?"

"We live in Pyongyang, in a place not nearly as nice as this. It is always a great treat for us to come here." Her eyes rolled about as she took in the gilt molding, richly upholstered furniture, and glittering chandeliers. Then, as if remembering herself, she clapped her hands and said, "Now, how does your ankle feel? Better, doesn't it?"

I had to admit that it did feel better and allowed her to help me to sit up. Yolanda scurried over to rebuckle my feet into the shoes. "The chef has announced that dinner is served."

Perched on the edge of the divan, I tried to maneuver my feet to evade Yolanda's grasping hands, but she was too quick for me and, gesturing for Patience to help her, managed to get the torturous shoes back on.

"I'm only going to trip and hurt myself again," I complained, pouting.

"Nonsense," Yolanda said jovially, as if we were best friends. "Most girls would die to own a pair of Jimmy Choos like these. Isn't that right, Patience?"

"Ehh." Patience nodded gravely in agreement. She was wearing a pair of flat sandals, the straps cracked and scuffed, to go with a drab long-sleeved brown sack dress with a Peter Pan collar that was a little frayed at the edges.

Yolanda grabbed my arm. "Mustn't keep your mum waiting, now. Up, up."

Wedged in between the two of them—Patience round and soft, Yolanda tough and bony—I was escorted into the dining room, where the table was draped in damask, twinkling with crystal, and shining with silver, shallow vases tumbling with roses placed in mathematical precision down the center. Honey sighed and whispered conspiratorially to me, "There are too many girls. Five to three makes for a dreadful imbalance at a dinner table."

Wendell, seated across from me, leaned eagerly into view, nodding enthusiastically. "Us guys aren't complaining!" he asserted, waggling his eyebrows.

"I wasn't talking to you, Wendell," Honey said severely, hitting him between the eyes with a laser glare.

"No, of course not, Honey. Please excuse me." He shrank back, folding up his long body to take up as little space as possible.

"How about inviting the cook to dine with us?" I suggested.

"The chef? He's not fit for normal society," Honey assured me.

Ting came marching into the dining room, followed by another person who looked like her twin, short and slight, with a blunt bowl cut of black hair encircling a round face. But when the other person came around to put a plate in exactly the same place where Ting had just removed one, I saw that she did not look like Ting at all. She was older, with a face like a weathered fence post, stooped shoulders, and a creamy blot over the iris of one eye.

"A toast!" Honey sang out, holding her glass up. "To our hosts, who treat us with such kindness that we never want to leave."

"Hear, hear," Wendell and Harvey intoned.

"*Gesondheid*," Yolanda whispered in my ear, tipping her glass toward me.

Feeling the rush of goodwill that always came just before a drink hit my lips, I clinked the rim of my glass to hers.

"No, no, Lisa!" Honey screamed. Wendell had just put his glass up to his lips but slowly lowered it, shooting a dark glance first at me and then at Yolanda. "One never, ever touches glasses at a toast. Just raise your glass and extend it slightly in the direction of the person being toasted. Never make contact with another glass."

"Why not?" I squeaked, the glass frozen just inches from my lips, still puckered expectantly to receive it.

"Why not? Because it's vulgar," Honey declared, breathy voice suddenly hard and low. She took a deep breath, buoying the already buoyant breasts that strained against the stretchy fabric of her dress, then lifted her wineglass to her lips and drank. Everyone else followed suit. Then she did the same with a spoonful of soup, and again, everyone followed.

While Honey and Wendell murmured inanities to each other, I muttered to Yolanda, "You could have just told me."

"Ah, but one learns best from one's mum," Yolanda observed, before delicately sipping from her spoon. "Mmm. Life is not so nice elsewhere. Eat, go on. Eat!"

I kissed my lips to the spoon. The soup was delicious, creamy with a hint of sherry and shallots. Already buzzed from the champagne, I decided to take Harvey's advice to take it easy on myself and just go with the flow. I took an appreciative sip of wine and felt the warmth spread from my stomach to my head. "So, Wendell, what's your story?" I asked, my voice thick with soup. "How did you end up on Gilligan's Island?"

He grinned his fat grin. "Like you, I thought I was going on a three-hour tour."

"Oh, oh," Honey interjected in her high-pitched baby voice. "I know that one." Putting a hand on her bosom, she quavered, "Now sit right back..."

From down the table, Harvey joined in when Honey got to the part about the mate. And then Wendell piped up for the line about the skipper. What could I do? I joined in at the three-hour tour.

Patience, Dr. Panzov, Yolanda, and Lahela applauded wildly when we were done. With a triumphant flourish, Honey waved her silver bell in the air, and Ting and not-Ting came through the door.

"Well?" I prompted Wendell, who was sticking his long nose in his empty glass wistfully.

"Well? Well, what?" He put the glass down guiltily. "Oh, yes. Well, I was bumming around China and somehow ended up in Liaoyang, married and teaching English at a cram school."

Everyone leaned in, as if hearing a favorite campfire tale.

Noticing he had an audience, Wendell began to play it up, gesturing dramatically and stretching his rubbery face into exaggerated expressions. "I got to be friends with a guy there. My wife didn't like me hanging around with this guy..."

"Why didn't your wife like him?" Harvey prompted.

"He was, well, to put it plainly, a pimp." The table laughed appreciatively. "So, one night when the two of us were carousing, she locked me out of the house. I rejoined my friend and told him I was sick of my wife and wanted to divorce her. He suggested killing her instead. We were both fall-down drunk, so I thought he was joking."

"But did you *really*, Wendell?" Yolanda stage-whispered, shaking her head affectionately.

"I did, Yolanda, I did!" Wendell averred, to giggles all around. "In jest, I replied, 'Yeah, yeah, let's kill her,' and then we drank another bottle of *baijiu*. Finally, I stumbled home to find my door smashed in and my wife lying in a pool of blood, her throat slit."

"I bet that sobered you up," interjected Honey merrily.

"It most certainly did, Madam. I went screaming back to my friend, and he had it all figured out. With the ATM password to my bank account as his payment..."

Fish lipped, Harvey whistled appreciatively. "That friend set you up but good."

"...we drove in my car to the Yalu River. I left a suicide note in the car, and then in the wee hours of the night, he rowed me across the river and I defected to the first soldier I could find."

The fork wilted from my hand as I stared at him, my mouth stretching and closing like some sort of sea creature's. Finally, I managed to ask, "Was your wife Chinese?"

He nodded, one cheek bulging with food. Bringing the napkin up to his greased lips, he wiped them carefully. One loud swallow, and I could practically see the food traveling down his long, thin neck. "Yes. I married her because she said she was pregnant. Also, my visa would soon expire, and I wasn't ready to go home yet."

"Was she?" I nibbled on poached langoustine, tender and succulent, drenched in butter.

"Was she what?" He was getting annoyed that I was asking all the wrong questions.

"Pregnant!"

"Oh. Yeah." He began to drum with his fingers on the table, as if he were bored with the conversation.

"So... what about the kid?"

He shrugged and shot a long arm out to move a candlestick a half a millimeter to the right. "I imagine he lives with his grandparents in their hovel in Liaoyang."

"Lisa, dear, don't hold up the table," Honey whispered at me.

"Huh?"

"Everyone has finished but you."

"Wendell's story made me lose my appetite."

"Nonsense," she trilled. "It's a happy story. Without Wendell, we would probably die of boredom here. Why, he introduced the whole internet thing to me, for which I am forever grateful!"

"You guys have internet here?" I asked, probably too quickly.

"I do, Lisa. But for you"—a small apologetic smile—"you have to earn the privilege. Like you'll have to earn all privileges. By proving your loyalty."

"Proving my loyalty...?" The langoustine flesh turned into a hard mass in my throat. "How does one do that?"

Harvey chortled. "With years and years of service. I'm still not allowed to go on this internet thing, even though I dedicate myself to Madam's every wish and command."

"Years and years," I gasped to myself, leaning past not-Ting's little form as she whisked away my plate.

"Years and years," Honey affirmed with finality. Fixing me with a hypnotic stare that sucked me into the cold cobalt whirlpool of her eyes, she proclaimed, "We were separated once, but now that we've found each other again, I am never going to let you go."

In retrospect, this was the moment that I should have flung myself on the floor with a scream and beat my head against the marble tiles. That I should have smashed my china plate and declared that I was going on a hunger strike until they let me go. That I should have taken one of the knives from the table and sunk it into my heart or into hers. But I didn't. I finished the rest of the meal, all the way through to the poached pear and the snifter of brandy. Then I followed meekly along with everyone else as we retired to the Versailles room for karaoke and more drinking.

Sometime deep in the night, while Honey was channeling Rick Astley, singing "Never Gonna Give You Up" while pointing at me as she slithered her hips to the beat, Yolanda leaned toward me, my eyes crossing as I tried to squint away the contours of her face to see what lay underneath, and advised, "The sooner you begin to play Honey's game, the better it will be for all of us. Take it from me, resistance is useless."

Far later, after Honey had sung herself hoarse and Harvey had passed out on the Louis XVI chaise longue, Wendell was assigned to lead me back to my room. We stumbled along the corridor, me holding on to the wall, he reeling ahead as he babbled about what he missed most from home: slutty girls, fast food, cable TV, regular TV, pornography, hot showers, short shorts, reliable electricity, big cars, big breasts, Big Gulps... At one point he wavered in front of a door, trying to get the retina scanner to release the lock, propping his lids wide with his fingers for the machine to read his eyeball, evoking a violent red flash. "Fuck!" he shouted, digging the heel of his hand into his eye. "Must be the wrong door."

"Don't you have access to all the doors?" I inquired as we waited for him to recover.

"Not even Madam has access to all the doors," he growled. "Jesus Christ, I can't see a damn thing. Let that be a lesson to you, Lisa. Don't try to open doors willy-nilly. They say that the locks to the doors that lead outside can permanently blind you if you try to open them without authorization." Leaning heavily into the wall, he shuffled forward, blinking furiously. "That sure sobered me up."

Trailing after him, I lamented, "So there's absolutely no way to escape this hellhole!" Then I slapped my hand over my mouth, fearing

Wendell would report my treasonous statement to Honey. But Wendell continued to grope his way down the hall as if he hadn't heard me.

Our progress was so slow that I began to worry that Wendell was lost. It wasn't inconceivable—we had passed at least two other corridors that spider-legged into dark obscurity—but finally we stopped in front of a door, Wendell peering closely at the scanner to make sure it was labeled for the right room before submitting his naked eyeball. As I stepped past him to push open the door, he clutched my arm and leaned so close toward my face I was scared he was going to kiss me. Instead he whispered, "I can help you."

"How?" I squeaked, breath catching in my throat.

Touching the side of his nose, he winked. "By you helping me. We aren't all as lucky as you, sitting here in the lap of luxury just stroking Honey's ego all day. Some of us have to earn a living, you know. But all in good time, my dear. It's still early days for you. In the meanwhile, get to know your way around. Work on earning Honey's trust so you can access other rooms. And don't forget to enjoy yourself. I miss the States, but to be honest, my life there would never be as good as it is here."

Chapter 8

"They [My biological parents] were my sperm and egg bank. That's not harsh, it's just the way it was, a sperm bank thing, nothing more."

–Steve Jobs

No one came for me the next day, but that wasn't unexpected as the Gang was returning to Pyongyang and Honey had mentioned she wouldn't be seeing me for a few days because of "prior appointments." Apparently when I was out of Honey's sight, I was out of her mind, left in my room to endure the tortuously slow progress of the day, with no books, no TV, not even a pair of knitting needles, just the constant churning of my mind, knotting tighter and tighter around Wendell's offer to help me. In a crowd of sniveling toadies, he was the one whose belly slunk the lowest, and I strongly suspected that whatever he proposed would be more to his advantage than to mine. But if he approached me again, what choice did I have but to take the bait? No one else was clamoring to help me, and it was clear that I could not escape on my own. I couldn't make it out of my room, much less find my way through the labyrinth of corridors to an exit, much less flee North Korea—a country about which I knew next to nothing, except that its leader was often a punch line to morbid jokes.

One day turned into two and then into three.

The only person to visit my room was Ting, whose response to my incessant chatter was an occasional blank stare. Once I tried to slip out the door with her, and she shoved me back with surprising ferocity, pausing to make sure I wasn't hurt before slamming the door shut.

On the fourth day, Ting brought me a simple cotton frock and ballerina flats. Elated at the prospect of release, I encircled her tightly in my arms, causing her to briefly flutter against me in panic, before relaxing and enduring my hug, even flashing me a shy smile that revealed ivoried corn-niblet teeth.

After another confusing odyssey through the serpentine corridor, Wendell's advice to learn my way around ringing in my ears like a cruel joke, Ting delivered me to a door that required not only an eye scan but also a numeric code to open. Entering through a dark vestibule, I walked toward the light into a vast kitchen, where I was greeted with a deep bow by a stocky man in a white chef's uniform, shoulder-length hair slicked back into a ponytail, face composed solemnly into cascading pleats of skin. "Welcome, Lisa."

"Hello, Cookie." I bowed back. "It is nice to finally be formally introduced to you."

"Yes," he intoned, bowing to my bow. "But no. My name is Miura Masaaki."

"Miura-san." Crooking forward at the waist, I quavered, *"Hajime-mashite. Lisa Pearl desu. Yoroshiku onegaishimasu."*

"Waa! Nihongo wo dekimasu ka?" he yelped in surprise.

"Sukoshi dake," I admitted. "Your English is much better than my Japanese."

"Nihongo ga jouzu desu ne?" he marveled, politely giving me much more credit than I deserved, as was the Japanese way. Showing me a stack of books—*The Joy of Cooking, Mastering the Art of French Cooking,* and *The James Beard Cookbook*—still in their cellophane wrapping, he said, "Madam asks you show me new dishes for cooking."

"She thinks I can teach you?" I laughed. "That's absurd. You're an excellent cook."

"Maybe not teach," he said. "Maybe advise. Lisa knows the foods Madam was eating in America. Together we choose new foods for Miura-san to cook."

"Will Madam be joining us today?" I flicked at an enormous copper-bottomed pot that dangled from a ceiling hook, the reverberation shimmering in the air.

Pulling back his ponytail, he smoothed the tight cap of his hair, blazed down the middle by a streak of white. "No, Madam rests after surgery."

"Surgery? What for?"

He must have thought my voice conveyed alarm rather than surprise. "Nothing serious," he assured me with a crazed giggle. "To take fat away from tummy." He darted a finger at his own paunch and made little sucking sounds.

"Liposuction?!" I gasped.

With a wicked smile, he flashed a finger to his lips and gave a nervous shrug, signaling that we should change the subject.

Light and airy, the kitchen sparkled with stainless steel and copper: counters, sinks, an industrial-sized fridge, an eight-burner gas stove, exhaust hoods, a double-tiered oven, and racks of shining pots, pans, and utensils. But I had eyes for only one thing, a large window through which real light poured. Here, finally, was the outdoors! Peering out, I saw that it wasn't really the outdoors but a neatly furrowed greenhouse teeming with edible plants in various stages of growth, the glass ceiling revealing the blue, blue sky, blotted by a few unraveling cotton-ball clouds. "Can we go out there?"

"*Sou.*" He scurried over to a door tucked behind wire shelves stocked with jars of dried beans and sacks of grains. "Come, come," he urged me, pawing at the air with an underhanded motion.

It was like stepping from a flat drawing into 3-D, the air hot and moist against my skin, eyes squinting shut against the painful glare of the sun, nose twitching in olfactory overdrive, picking up the umami bass notes of damp soil, the muscular scent of onions, the sweet trill of sun-warmed glucose. An overhead fretwork of pipes and wires cast a delicate gridded shadow over the straight green furrows and raised vegetable beds. Parting a curtain of oregano trailing from a hanging pot, I peered through the glass at a tidy swath of lawn bordered by an outcropping of mossy rock that blocked any further view. "Can we go outside?"

"No," he replied mournfully. "Only Madam can take you outside." Tapping me on the arm, he extended his upturned palm to me, a cherry tomato cupped inside. It dissolved like sugar on my tongue.

Seeing him now in full sunlight, I couldn't tell if he was a young-looking old man or an old-looking young man. A silver stripe slashed through his thick midnight-black hair. His skin was smooth and uncreased, but his face was heavy with folds of flesh, nose emerging in a long, clean curve like a hawk's beak.

Brushing at a gnat that was hovering in front of my face, I asked, "How long have you been here, Miura-san?"

He stilled, lidding his eyes in contemplation. "Eight, nine years."

"Were you kidnapped as well?"

"Kidnapped?" he wondered, probing a finger into the soil of a raised bed of tender seedlings, emerald leaves just beginning to unfurl, then wiping the dirt off on his pants. "I don't think so. I worked in Thailand, in very luxury resort in Phi Phi Islands. I was number one sushi chef, one hundred pounds of fish a day. One day a young man ask me to work for him for a lot of money. I say no. But he comes back again next year, with same question. Many things happen in a year, and so I say yes. And"—he spread his arms wide, knocking into a hanging basket of thyme—"here I am."

"You're a sushi chef?" I asked, following him to a thick pipe studded with a series of taps, each one a different color. "Why haven't you served any sushi since I've been here?"

His thick, square-tipped fingers unscrewed a yellow tap, and a gentle mist hissed from the overhead pipes. "Madam is tired of sushi. She wants only Western foods."

"Why does Madam have a sushi chef if she only likes Western food?"

"You know they are like that, those guys. They like things the same."

"What do you mean?" I turned my face up to be tickled by the settling droplets of water vapor.

"The father had sushi chef, so the son gets sushi chef, to show respect for the father."

"What father? What son? What are you talking about?"

"Don't you know?" he demanded, the thin aperture of his eyes dilating in surprise.

"I assure you, Miura-san, I know nothing."

Tiny beads of water turned his black hair gray. "The father is the Dear Leader."

"Kim Jong Il?" I whispered.

"Dear Leader," he said, nodding and picking a few dead leaves off a stalk drooping with slender scimitars of purple-skinned eggplants.

"Is he your boss?" I asked.

"No, the son is."

I shook my head. "I'm sorry, I don't know who his son is."

Slowly turning the tap closed, Miura-san said, "Kim Jong Un."

I put out a hand to catch the last few microdrops of water; they sparkled like diamond chips on my skin. "What does Honey have to do with Kim Jong Il and Kim Jong Un?"

Kneeling by a row of verdant feathery stalks bowing in the sun, he said, "These are carrots," his fingers caressing the lacy crowns. "Pick up one." As I hesitated, he insisted, "We want to show we are talking to each other about the foods."

"Why, are they watching us?" I turned to look over my shoulder.

"Lisa-san," he said solemnly, "the cameras are always watching. Do not forget. Cameras are everywhere. Pick up a carrot."

Gingerly, I grabbed a lacy clump and started to pull, thinking a lot more about the cameras than the carrots. *"Dame, dame,"* he scolded me. "Down at the bottom, you pull from there. You have two, three carrots you pick up now. Don't be lazy. Find before you pull."

I did as he directed. As the vegetable was torn from its cradle of dirt, he said, "She is his mother."

Clots of dirt pinged against the stiff white front of his chef's jacket. "What? Honey is what?" I began to snicker. "Stop it. You're freaking me out!"

The ridges of his face settled into the armor plating of a rhinoceros. "I am not saying a joke."

"So," I said, my brain slowly processing what Miura-san was telling me, "Honey is the mother of Kim Jong Un, and Kim Jong Il is his father?"

Still clutching the carrot, I wobbled away from him, fleeing past frilly heads of lettuce, effulgent stalks of broccoli, sinewy vines heavy with pregnant pea pods, until I arrived at the far end of the greenhouse. Beyond the glass was a narrow strip of jumbled boulders bordered by a dense grove of bamboo. I leaned my forehead against the glass, expecting it to be cool upon my suddenly flushed brow, and was surprised that it was as warm as a human cheek. Miura-san followed me, busying himself with a coil of hose that snaked at my feet.

"Remember, they are always watching. No one is your friend. Not even I am."

When I returned to my room that afternoon, I found a paperback propped against my pillow, the title emblazoned in red: *Guiding Light:*

General Kim Jong Il. It felt like a reward, for what I wasn't sure, and I was grateful for it and then alarmed at my gratitude, at how quickly I was adjusting to my new circumstances, how soon the unacceptable was becoming the normal. Nevertheless, when I wasn't working in the kitchen with Cookie, I hungrily devoured the adulatory text, savoring each hyperbolic word, treasuring each outlandish assertion, and marveling over each overwrought exclamation point. The Jong Il in the book was a selfless, benevolent humanitarian of superhuman proportions who bore little resemblance to the stunted, cold-blooded asshole that the rest of the world knew him to be.

Two weeks after I arrived in Boston to attend college, airplanes hurtled from the sky like thunderbolts, and I watched the endless replay of the Twin Towers collapsing, the Pentagon burning, and people running for their lives from a smothering cloud of rubble that pursued them with nightmarish intent on my crappy portable TV, sitting on my narrow bed in a cinder-block-walled dorm room with a boy named Nigel, whom I had met my very first night at a dorm mixer. Never before had a boy pursued me with such ardor. Without a trace of self-consciousness or hesitation, he offered himself up to me, hanging on to my every word, staring at me with eyes that fairly smoldered with adoration. He was smart, frighteningly so, wielding his wit like a leather whip. He was also beautiful in a delicate-boned, long-haired kind of way.

About a week later, we were sitting on his bed, listening to the Replacements and talking about *Heart of Darkness,* when he blurted out, "Can I kiss you?" We leaned toward each other, and his lips were warm and pliant, his tongue gently insistent. When we finally broke away, I murmured, "I'm sorry about my nose," because it had knocked into his several times, requiring some neck-cricking maneuvers.

Gently cradling my face in his hands, he brushed his lips over the bridge of my nose, slid his silken tongue down the ridge, and sucked softly on the tip. "I've been wanting to do that ever since I met you, Lisa Pearl," he said breathlessly. I was in love.

There was only one point of incompatibility: Nigel did not drink. He'd do the occasional bong hit, and one wintry day we took some mushrooms and went to the Boston Aquarium, but he said he didn't like how out of control he got when he drank. So, at first, I stayed sober for him, not because he asked me to, but because I feared he wouldn't like the drunk me very much. But as time went on, I began to cheat, not with booze, because he'd be sure to smell it on my breath, but with pills, usually a Percocet or Vicodin, something to give me a nice, discreet buzz.

One night I took two OxyContins and blabbed to him about the famous adopted people list, which I had never told anyone else about, feeling it was a sacred secret just between Mindy and me. He gave me another name to add: Steve Jobs. Nigel was an Apple acolyte, but in a doubting Thomas sort of way, believing Jobs to be a genius, a revolutionary, and an asshole, and it became a favorite debate of ours whether being an asshole was a prerequisite to being a genius. Nigel wanted to be a writer too, and most of his favorite authors—Ernest Hemingway, William S. Burroughs, Patricia Highsmith—we decided were assholes; mine, an ever-evolving list of mostly female authors that he called the "clit club," which at that moment included Margaret Atwood, Toni Morrison, and Ursula Le Guin, were not, or if they were, we hadn't heard about it. I also told him about the pact between Mindy and me to become famous and that wrenching moment of betrayal when she put aside her dream to become an actor in order to please her mother, leaving it to me to become the famous one. He teased me that I needed to be more of an asshole to become famous. Little did he know.

Mindy was just across town, at Harvard, but whenever either one of them suggested that they meet the other, I put them off, afraid that the two people I liked the most in this world would like each other more than they liked me when they finally met. Just the fact that they wanted to meet each other raised my suspicions. Jealousy wasn't a new emotion for me—according to Mrs. Frank it was common in adoptees—but it had never so completely possessed me the way it did when I was with Nigel. A joke shared with another girl, an admiring comment, and it would come for me out of a perfectly blue sky: a seething black cloud like the one that roared down the streets around the World Trade Center on that calamitous September day, and instead of running, I let it come, and I let it envelop me in hot, smothering ash.

Having recovered from liposuction, Honey summoned me for a hike in the woods, providing me with a tracksuit that matched hers, only mine was jade green to her hot pink, and telling Yolanda to do our hair in sporty-looking pigtails. Tremulously, I stepped from the gloomy portal of the compound out into the naked sunlight, savoring the delicious stroke of the gentle breeze on my skin, the satisfying crunch of dirt beneath my feet, the ambient noise of insects and birds and stirring leaves. Drawing pure, unadulterated fresh air deeply into my lungs, I welcomed the chilliness of the spring day after being cosseted for so long in a temperature controlled to a Goldilocks perfection, the air so sere it crackled. Honey started off at a brisk pace, arms working like pistons, stabbing her walking stick into the ground with each step, and we headed into the bamboo, where the air glowed green and shed husks and leaves rustled beneath our feet, a bodyguard following closely on our heels. When we emerged from the grove, Honey paused in the full sunlight, eyes closed as she soaked up the sun.

I spoiled her moment of tranquility by asking, "Can you tell me a little about my father?"

She sighed and resumed walking, leading us into the woods, sunlight splotching through tall pines in scrappy patches, needles crackling underneath our feet, the air sticky with the aromatic pungency of pine resin. "I've already told you that I'm not exactly sure who your father is, probably one of the earnest young university students who visited Honey Do, talking revolution as an aphrodisiac. I really can't remember a thing about any of those men who came before Jon."

"Does Jon know I'm here?"

"Not exactly." She bent to pick a creamy white flower, tucking it behind her ear. "It leaves you vulnerable, but you are fortunate to have the protection of the second most powerful man in this country, my son, Jonny." The flower fell out, but she didn't notice.

"Are you talking about Kim Jong Un?"

Her face softened, the varnished mask dropping away, briefly exposing a tremulous vulnerability that I had not glimpsed before. "Yes. My boy. Your half brother. After many years of indecision, Jon has finally named my child his successor. He would have done it sooner, only there were certain risks, for even though our son looks fully Korean and was raised by Jon's wife, the secret of his true heritage had to be fully erased."

"You didn't raise your own son?" I asked.

Our climb suddenly turned steeper, and her words rode in on galloping puffs of air. "It is not uncommon in Asia, taking a baby away from his mother to be raised by the father's wife, in his house and under his watchful eye. When my son turned thirteen, Jon allowed me an occasional visit with him. Korean children have a very special bond with their mothers, and little Jonny was no different. He loved me with a fierceness that was almost frightening and hated the woman whom he had to call 'Mother.' I suppose she was not very nice to him, as he was a rival to her own children. And she had a lot to worry about." A small, bloodless smile split her chin like a paper cut. "Her oldest son is a sissy, and the other one a big fat slob. The only one of her children with any gumption is the girl, and in this society there's no way that *she* will come out on top. When it became evident that the wife's sons were just as stupid as she was, his father began to take more interest in my boy. He liked the way he rode a horse, the way he managed his friends, the way he didn't back down for anyone. He liked the dimple in his chin, which was just like his own." She dreamily placed a finger at the tip of her own pointed and dimpleless chin.

"How could your son ever be the leader of North Korea? Don't his looks reveal that he has 'American imperialist bastard' blood, as that fascinating biography of Jong Il so insistently puts it?"

She came to a sudden stop, knocking her walking stick against the stout base of a towering pine tree, startling a flock of doves to spiral off into the sky like roman candles, wings whistling through the air. "You don't know what he looks like?"

"No, why should I?"

With a little laugh she said, "I thought everyone in the world knew what he looked like!"

"Well, I know what Kim Jong Il looks like," I said. "And I think you have crap taste in men."

Jaw clacking open and shut like a marionette's, she laughed in high-pitched, staccato bursts. "Oh, Lisa, you can get away with saying that out here"—her hands flowered underneath the perfect blue sky—"but you must learn to control your tongue if you are to be of any use." Resuming our climb, she said, "To be perfectly honest, I didn't choose him. He chose me. When a powerful world leader says he wants you, well, that makes a girl feel really special. He gave me all this." Her beringed fingers fanned wide to indicate the trees, the sky, the earth, her bodyguard, who dogged us like a grotesque shadow, and me. "He loves me so much that he keeps me locked away, at some peril to himself."

"What, even you can't leave here?"

She jangled her head back and forth, making her pigtails dance. "I don't think that would be advisable, no. For many reasons. The most important of which is my son. Ah, here we are!"

We had crested a ridge to arrive at a vermilion-roofed pagoda that was perched in front of a rocky outcropping tufted with hummocks of pale green moss and feather-finned ferns, argent trickles of water lacing between them. Waiting as the burly guard laid the table with a surprisingly deft delicacy, I peered down into a wild valley that stretched far below us, a distant roar telling me that the thread of silver that could be glimpsed stitching the thick tapestry of lush foliage was a river. I took careful note of that, for in the accounts of people lost in the wilderness that I'd read, they always followed the river to civilization.

Honey eagerly heaped her plate with food. "It's such a relief to once again satisfy my appetite." Gingerly patting her midriff, she said, "Still a little puffy from the lipo. But in a few weeks my tummy will be flat as this table."

"Did Dr. Panzov do your liposuction?"

Crunching on a drumstick of fried chicken, she nodded. "He is indispensable to me."

"Is he the one who did that to Yolanda's face? Because she is not exactly a convincing advertisement for the benefits of plastic surgery."

"Ah, Yolanda. She is a true friend. She has sacrificed much for me. She is not happy about your arrival, though," Honey noted with spiteful satisfaction. "She sees you, quite rightly, as a rival for my affections."

No stranger myself to jealousy, I felt a brief pang of sympathy for Yolanda, who seemed to have sacrificed so much for Honey and received so little in return. "What happened to Yolanda? Was she in some sort of accident?"

The high cry of a hawk skittered like a stone skipping across the lake of the sky.

"She did it for my son. For little Jonny."

Another hawk's cry, a mournful warning that sent a shiver down my back. "Jonny had his face redone? So that he would look like a full-blooded Korean?"

Tipping her eyes up at me with a coquettish glance, she exclaimed gleefully, "See, you are smart! You can figure things out for yourself, if you will only think. I know as an American, you are not used to having to think to survive, but you'll have to get used to doing that as a North Korean."

She made it sound as if being North Korean was merely a state of mind, like being in love or achieving nirvana. "Is Yolanda supposed to look Korean?"

"She kindly consented to being a guinea pig, especially for the eyes, which was tricky. Making an Asian eye Western is a well-researched field, but making an eye look more Asian? It had never been done before! She also helped with the cheek and jaw implants, which made Jonny's face look rounder and much more like his grandfather's. Vladimir didn't have to do anything to the chin, though. That chin, with the dimple, is pure genetics."

"And the nose?" I asked, my fingers wandering up to my own.

"Yes, of course. The nose." She also passed a quick stroke of a red-glossed nail over the cubist angles of her nose. "Vlad didn't need any training with that. That was his specialty, and how he came to my attention. He was on a visiting delegation of medical professionals from the Soviet Union, which had just become Russia. I was assigned to translate during a demonstration Vlad gave of his, at the time, cutting-edge technique. With Jonny in mind, I begged Jon to hire him."

"At the fall of the Soviet Union? But Jonny would have just been a kid."

"A mother must plan ahead. Which brings me to why we have brought you here..."

She placed a hand on mine, and I could feel the desire like a heat off her body. It scared me. To forestall her, I pulled my hand away to reach for the foil-wrapped tip of a drumstick. "How did you end up in North Korea? Were you kidnapped too?"

"I wish you would stop talking about kidnapping, baby, OK?" The incandescent glow of her eyes held my gaze until I slowly nodded. She *pat, pat, pat* my cheek in approval, then launched upon a meandering and sometimes inconsistent story that started with a round-the-world trip after graduating from her posh boarding school, which took her and a boyfriend to Thailand where they became addicted to heroin, which led to her parents cutting off her funds, forcing her to work in Patpong luring American customers into the Puss N Buss nightclub, where she met an American man who persuaded her to go with him to Korea, where he was based as a something or other in the army. There was no heroin in Korea, so she became clean and, bored with life with the soldier, reconciled with her parents and had them buy her a bar in Seoul, which she called Honey Do. Unbeknownst to her, the bar was a secret rendezvous point for North Korean agents, and one of them proposed she take a trip with him to China. Lured by the chance to get a glimpse inside a country that few westerners had visited, she flew to Shanghai, where she checked into the Peace Hotel. It was not the man who had arranged for her to go to China who came to her room that night, but a man with an Elvis quiff, square gold-rimmed glasses, and adorable baby cheeks. Three days later, having seen nothing at all of China, she returned to Seoul with the promise that Jon would send for her once he had arranged things with his dad. But after returning to Seoul, she found out she was pregnant and feared he would drop her when he got news of her condition, but he asked her only to give up the baby. A few days after giving birth, she returned to China, from where it was a simple trip over the border into North Korea. Soon, she was pregnant again. The day after she gave birth to her son, she again had her newborn baby taken away from her, this time against her will. She didn't see him for another thirteen years.

She paused at this point in her story for a second helping of food, and I found my throat parched, as if it were I who had spent the last hour talking nonstop, and shakily brought a glass of lemonade up to my lips, each swallow detonating in my ears. We sat in primitive silence, which was really just the absence of human-made noise: no distant whine of traffic or hammering of construction, no footsteps or muted conversation, no bicycle bells or barking dogs. Not even the silver flash of a jet passing way up in the sky. Eventually, a lone fly arrived to drift around the unfinished food, landing on the fruit salad to rub its front legs together like a money-grubbing millionaire. With a shudder, it occurred to me that Honey had brought me out here to reveal the full extent of our splendid isolation, showing me that escape was impossible.

Daintily nibbling at an almond lace cookie, she continued. "Jon's older children were sent to schools in Russia and China, but with the collapse of the Soviet Union, our entire country was thrown into turmoil. The highest cadres of China were beginning to send their children to American schools, and I used all of my wiles to persuade Jon to do the same with our Jonny. It was a hard-fought battle, but in the end I triumphed. Registered as a Chinese student, Jonny spent three years at St. Paul's, the alma mater of a long line of LeBaron males." Her mouth curled at the irony. "His father, extremely pleased with his progress, consented to allow Dr. Panzov to operate on him upon his return. After Jonny graduated from Kim Il Sung University—the first student ever to pass all his exams with perfect marks—his father bestowed upon him his very own country retreat. He called it Villa Umma in my honor, and ever since, it has been my home. And now it is yours." She snapped her fingers at the bodyguard to indicate that lunch was over.

The man quickly cleared the table while Honey and I started down the path. She linked her arm in mine, squeezing me close. "So,

Lisa, I hope you are satisfied now that I've answered your questions. And I hope you realize that all those secrets I have just told you mean you can never leave this country again. You simply know too much. I've trusted you with the truth, and now you must trust me with your future."

I stumbled over a root, my knees bending precariously beneath me as if they were made of paper, Honey's grip on me tightening to hold me upright. My brain clicking uselessly like a gun firing on an empty chamber, I stammered, "What do you want from me?"

She paused, waiting for the bodyguard to catch up, his boots smacking the ground as he hurried toward us. "I'm glad you asked."

The bodyguard huffed up behind us, and she started into the trees. I realized that the bodyguard was there not to protect us from intruders, as I had first presumed, but to protect Honey from me.

"Jon understood that when you strip away centuries of tradition, you must offer the masses something in its place, and he has given them films, mass spectacles, traveling acrobats, and other quaint entertainments. But times are changing, and the people want something new. Now, this is a secret that I'm sharing just between you and me." She rattled at my arm, hugging me to her side. "I've mentioned it to Jonny a few times, just to plant the seed, but haven't yet revealed to him the full extent of my plan. That's the way you handle powerful men, Lisa, by planting seeds so they think the ideas that eventually bloom in their head are their own."

I murmured my appreciation of her handy gardening tip for the Machiavellian helpmeet.

"Jon doesn't like the internet; he doesn't understand it and thinks he can just throw a wall up around it, pfft." She raised a hand like a stop sign. "The irony of it is he's *huge* on the internet. There are whole websites dedicated just to him! So, what if we did that for Jonny, make a website with lots of fun stories and flashy photos that subtly promote Jonny as the natural, inevitable heir to his father? There would be news stories, cultural pieces, human-interest stories, uplifting and a little sappy, all with the underlying message that Kim Jong Un is making life better for all North Koreans. You can do that, right?" Her eyes, like halogen headlights on bright, blinded me. "Create a website."

"Uh..." Of course I couldn't, but I wasn't about to tell her that when she was offering me access to the internet. After all, there was more than one way to escape. I modestly shrugged. "Yeah, probably."

"Of course you can." She sighed happily, planting a tender kiss on my cheek. "Now, not a word to Jonny yet," she whispered conspiratorially. "Let me sell him on the idea first, make him think he was the one who thought of it. For now, it will just be our little secret."

"How could I say anything to Jonny? Is he coming here?"

But Honey didn't answer, dropping my arm as we entered the bamboo grove, the light murky and thick. We walked the rest of the way in silence, and soon we were at the entrance of the compound, which yawned suddenly from the earth like the mouth of a serpent, waiting to swallow us whole.

In retrospect, maybe a romance that started in the shadow of 9/11 was destined to end in disaster. I cheated on Nigel during winter break with an old boyfriend of Mindy's, a lacrosse player at St. Albans, who now, a mere two years after high school, had already begun to spread, the rugby shirt with the flipped-up collar just a little too tight across his stomach and chest. He recognized me at a party and asked me out, taking me to a swank steak place of a type that proliferates near the hallowed halls of power in Washington, DC, serving expensive red meat to expense account lobbyists and their politician guests. Without consulting me, he ordered us both Cokes, which I thought mulishly sexist, and when the waiter brought the drinks, he scooped the ice into his water glass, urging me to do the same and tapping on his hip. Then, with a practiced grace, he pretended to show me something on his phone while pouring rum into my Coke from a hip flask. I relaxed a little. My kind of guy. A rummy who knew a rummy.

Promising a well-stocked bar and absent parents, he took me to his house, a large stone mansion on a bluff overlooking the Potomac River. After more than a year of playing it sober for Nigel, it felt liberating to drink and flirt with a guy. This was really who I was, I told myself, the party girl who could drink any of her dates under the table. Soon, he was nuzzling my neck. His desire for me stirred my desire, and when he slid his hand under my shirt, I arched my back in invitation. It wasn't that I was more attracted to him than to Nigel. In fact I found him kind of sad. I just wanted him to want me and was gratified when he did.

"Just confess to Nigel," Mindy advised me later. "He'll forgive you and then you can move on."

But I couldn't. I was the serpent eating my own tail, my jealousy a self-fulfilling prophecy: terrified that Nigel would find someone worthier of him, I made myself unworthy. It really hurt me to break up with him, but I thought my unhappiness a small price to pay to keep Nigel from finding out just how much of an asshole I really was.

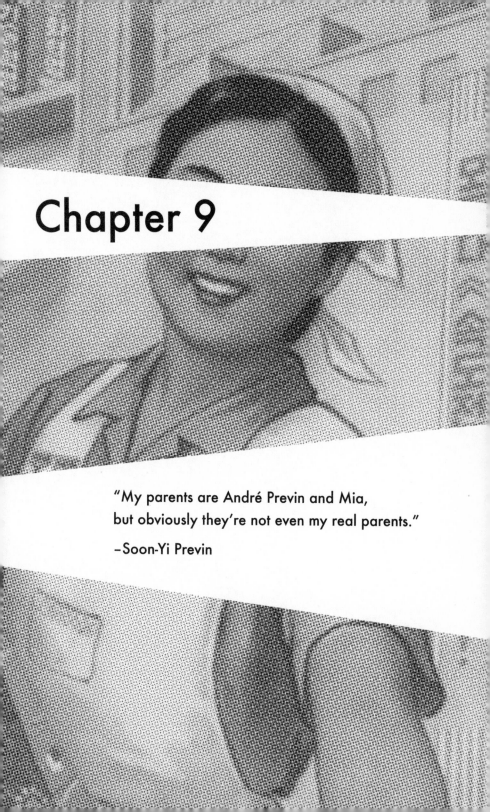

Chapter 9

"My parents are André Previn and Mia,
but obviously they're not even my real parents."

–Soon-Yi Previn

When the door of my room locked shut with a slow exhalation, I stood with my forehead pressed against the cold steel for a long time. Was it better to have tasted freedom and lost it than to never have had it? The very real prospect of months passing before I could once again savor the simple joys of the outdoors sent a numbing haze of despondency stealing through my body. I wished I had been more forceful about pressing Wendell on how exactly he could help me escape, because that was now the only thing I had to hold on to.

In the ensuing days of solitude, the enigma of Honey—the anti-mother who had reached across the years and the continents to drag me back to her stonehearted bosom—consumed me. I spent hours staring at my face in the mirror, searching for any trace of Honey there other than the nose. She was nowhere to be found in the close canthi of my brown eyes, the lowness of my brow, the roughness of my skin, the generous swell of my lips. But what about intangible characteristics? Along with her nose, did I inherit that big lacuna inside her, that dark cavern where a heart was supposed to be? Was her legacy to me her wanton cruelty, her narcissism, her utter disinterest in anything but herself? After all, what was it but cruelty, narcissism, and blind self-interest that led me to sleep with Kenji? To upset Mindy right before her big reunion with her birth mother? To go with Ji Hoon to Jeju-do? Behind every mistake I had made, I now saw the shadow of Honey. I was but a chip off the old block, a sapling off the mother root.

But maybe I could turn that to my advantage. Above all, Honey was a survivor. Scheming to advance her son's fortunes, she took the long view, hatching a plan to do the impossible and working ruthlessly toward that goal over the decades. That was a legacy of hers that I could fully embrace: the will to survive. For whatever mess I had made of my life, I knew that I didn't want to give it up. If this nightmarish twist of fate had taught me anything, it was that I wanted to return to the wreckage of my old life to put things right, to complete the journey toward self-actualization that I had started, even if I did stumble right out of the gate and had wandered so completely off track. I resolved to do whatever it took to get out of North Korea alive. I would not succumb to despair; I'd wait patiently and feel my way forward. I'd turn my inherited character flaws into my most potent weapons and practice the dark arts of cruelty, narcissism, and monomaniacal self-interest. And I'd do so at my mother's knee, following by example and, at the same time, earning her favor. I'd play the game by her rules and win.

To pass the time, I stood on the chair to look out the window at the lonely view of rocks and bamboo, the only change the waxing and waning of the light, the wind rustling through the daggered leaves, the occasional sweep of rain. Once, Ting caught me on my perch, and I thought I saw an expression of pity quickly pass over her face. She was my only companion, my only diversion, and I'd babble at her as soon as she came in the door. "How are you doing this morning, Ting? You look very sporty in that zebra-striped chiffon blouse. And those pants, for once you don't have to cuff them. Though they sag on you, they would have been very tight capri pants on Honey. I'm guessing that you are the lucky recipient of all the clothes that turn out to be too small for her. Am I right, hmm, Ting?" Every time I said her name, she would flinch just a little without looking my way. I wondered if maybe they had cut her tongue out, as I had yet to hear her utter a word.

Then one day, she brought me dumplings for lunch, and I exclaimed, "*Jiaozi!* Oh, yum!"

She had been deftly karate chopping the sheets as she made my bed, but stopped and looked straight at me out of her wary, fishshaped eyes. What had I said to elicit this unprecedented reaction? The next moment, though, she was back to hospital corners. Eyes on her, I put a dumpling in my mouth, the thin skin tearing to release an oleaginous explosion of minced pork and chives. Chewing loudly, I exclaimed, "*Haochi!*" She paused for an infinitesimal beat and then finished smoothing the bedspread over perfectly fluffed pillows. I stood up and confronted her. *"Ni yao bu yao chi jaozi ma?"*

Flattening herself paper-thin, she gave a little shake of her head and slid by me. I smelled blood in the water.

"Wo jiao Pao Li Jia," I exclaimed, using my Chinese name. *"Ni jiao shenme mingzi?"*

It was a stupid question to ask—I already knew her name, or her first name at least—but it was all I could think of in the heat of the moment; my Chinese was very rusty. As she slipped out the door, I pleaded, *"Wo yao shi ni de pengyou."* As an answer, the door closed with that awful, vacuum-seal *whoosh.*

Heart hammering, I was proud of myself for finally figuring something out on my own. Ting was not North Korean. Ting was Chinese. Somewhere within me, a rag of hope fluttered like a plastic bag caught upon a bush. That afternoon, I paced my room like the caged animal that I was: ten steps long and fourteen wide.

Shortly after the breakup, eager to escape an environment that was suddenly claustrophobic and stultifying as I huddled in my cramped dorm room hoping to avoid Nigel, whose wounded eyes would accuse me whenever we crossed paths, I applied for a yearlong study program in Xi'an, crafting a writing project with my adviser in order to fulfill credits toward my English major. The project was simple: keep a detailed daily journal, which I would have done anyway, and write a final paper using my journal as source material.

I loved and hated China, not simultaneously, but often in lightning-quick succession. Love, hate, love, hate—all in the space of a short stroll down a city block. At first, there was a lot of love, or at least wonderment. It thrilled me to see flat-faced, single-lidded, dark-haired people everywhere I looked, and I felt instinctively at home in a sea of similar faces, one among a billion people, all who looked like me. But the reality of living with a billion people quickly broke the spell. There was simply no such thing as being alone. People were everywhere, in every nook and cranny, every bush and bench, crowding around the stalls at the market, squeezing onto the bus, elbowing to the front of the line, threatening to run you over on the streets, exhaling pungent garlic breath, and spitting everywhere—in restaurants, on the bus, in class—the streets of China were paved with sputum. As soon as they heard me talk in a loose, sloppy accent, the Chinese would become very friendly and claim me for one of their own, as an overseas Chinese, even after I explained that I was actually born in Korea. *Korean, Chinese, we're all the same,* they'd happily assure me. Being American accorded me an immediate respect, as well as constant requests: changing yuan for dollars, language exchanges, TOEFL study sessions, help with applications to American universities, lectures to cultural clubs, even sponsoring visas. Relationships in China were all about scratching backs, and the Chinese were not shy about asking for favors. Soon, I had so many *zhongguo pengyou* that I had no spare time for myself. Life was a slog of classes, language exchanges, lectures, and excursions. But that was the life of a Chinese student, who lived as if in a beehive, always part of a group, always working toward something. Even drinking was hard work, a communal event where people gathered with the explicit intent of getting shit-faced and doing crazy stuff, like dancing around with a bottle between their legs like it was a penis, or doing a striptease to a traditional folk tune, or simply weeping uncontrollably into a glass of *baijiu.* If you were a man (and as a foreigner I was an honorary male), there was no shame in drinking to excess, and whatever you did at the drinking party stayed at the drinking party, with nary a mention of your transgressions the next day. It was as if you were two entirely separate people, sober you and drunk you, and sober you was never blamed for what drunk you did. You might say I went native with my drinking habits.

As the winter wore on, I became disenchanted with life in China, weary of battling the unceasing tide of humanity; irritated with the constant blaring of the school loudspeakers, which announced the new day at seven A.M. and imparted important reminders on how to comport yourself as a good citizen throughout the day; tired of shivering in the unheated classrooms; and appalled at the relentless obliteration of the old for the new, downtown Xi'an a forest of cranes and scaffolding, the air cloudy with concrete dust and factory smoke.

Each day there were fewer bicycles on the street and more cars, fewer sidewalk restaurants serving the local specialty of flatbread soaked in mutton broth and more KFCs, fewer Mao suits and more business suits. All my *pengyou* wanted to talk about was how to get an American visa and money: how to make it, how much of it my family had, how much I would make after college, how much they could expect to make if they were able to go to the US on a work visa. I knew it was ridiculous for me to be nostalgic about a China that I had never experienced, and it was unfair to expect the Chinese to stay in their Mao suits and their shabby Communist poverty—that they had just as much right to enjoy private transportation, cable TV, and status consumerism as I did. I was also aware that it was horribly colonialist of me to want the Middle Kingdom to stay frozen in time, a relic of tile hip-and-gable roofs, stone arch bridges, and tiered pagodas rising from the mist. Nevertheless, the relentless paving over of the past depressed me, and by the spring I couldn't wait for the school year to end, when I would meet Mindy in Korea for a two-week visit, my first return to the country of our birth.

I had never been so happy to see Yolanda as when she strutted into my room late the next afternoon, vacuum-packed into yet another fashionable business suit, not a strawberry-blond hair of her French twist out of place, eyes gleaming like glass in the ravaged contours of her face.

She, however, was not happy to see me. "Change into these clothes. Quickly," she commanded, throwing a zipped-up garment bag on my bed. "And this is the last time I'm doing your face, you hear? From here on after, you will do your own bloody makeup!"

Unzipping the bag, I suggested, "Maybe you can supervise me while I try to do it myself? Does that...?" My voice died in my throat when I saw that inside the garment bag were my own clothes: the leopard-print underwear and bra that I had bought at the Canal City mall in Fukuoka, black skinny jeans, a pink long-sleeved T-shirt emblazoned with Hello Kitty in a kimono, and a pair of high-top Chuck Taylors in neon green and orange. "Uh, does that sound all right?"

She grunted in angry agreement, gesturing for me to hurry up and get on with it.

"Why these clothes, Yolanda?" I tried to keep my voice even, my first thought being that they were going to dress me in my own clothes and murder me, throwing my body into the ocean to wash up on some distant shore.

She didn't know what was in the bag and poked a finger through the folds of cloth. "What the hell are these?" she wondered.

"They're mine. They were in my suitcase when I got kid— when I was in Jeju-do."

"Are those really your clothes?" she sneered. "You never grew up, did you? Christ!" Then she snapped her fingers at me as I had seen Honey snap her fingers at her. "Come on, girlie, get on with it!"

"Aren't you going to at least turn around?" I asked as I unbuttoned my pajama top.

"Ag, I've seen it all." Her head waved from side to side, reeling from all the things she had seen. "Dead babies, machete wounds, starved corpses, rabies... Nothing can shock me."

"How old are you, Yolanda?" I inquired brightly, hoping that she would take it as a friendly stab at conversation rather than a challenge.

"We don't have time for your stupid questions. We've got a schedule to keep. You don't mess around with the schedule."

"All right, if you won't tell me how old you are, I'll guess. You're thirty-five."

Maybe because I was standing in front of her stark naked, she replied, "Thirty-eight."

"Really? That's only about ten years older than I am." I sniffed my shirt before putting it on. It smelled like chilly concrete with an under-whiff of gasoline.

She laughed harshly, a guttural clearing of her throat. "I was never as young as you, domkop."

"I was thinking Australia," I said, zipping up my jeans, which cradled my hips familiarly with the warm embrace of an old friend. "But I knew it wasn't right. You just called me domkop. You're South African."

Shrugging, she sauntered into the bathroom. "Hurry up. Madam is expecting us soon."

Before I joined her, I checked the pockets of my pants and shook out my shoes. Empty. I looked at my reflection in the mirror and smiled at the old me there. The me before Honey.

The marquee lights blazed around the mirror, gleaming off the various jars, pots, and compacts she was arranging on the shelf. "I've been through the Jo'burg Airport six times. My father lives in Gabs and he has loads of South African friends." I started to sing: "Ag, man, Deddy won't you take us to the bioscope?"

Despite herself, a giggle escaped her. "Those aren't the right words." Handing me a foam wedge soaked in BECCA Aqua Luminous Perfecting Foundation #2, she began to sing: "Popcorn, chewing gum, peanuts and bubble gum..." Her voice was pretty good, strong with a little bit of wobble.

Carefully slathering on the foundation, I cried, "You got a set of pipes on you, Yolanda! Madam should let you sing more often at karaoke."

Taking that as a criticism of Madam, she set her lips primly together. "You need more under the eyes."

Obediently, I swabbed the hollows under my eyes. "Why did you leave South Africa?"

"Oh, the crime was awful," she said, her accent all of a sudden getting as thick as blood, the c and r sounds cracking out like a leather whip. "After the blacks took over, we weren't safe in our own neighborhoods."

I presented my face for her inspection and she leaned close, so I could see the strange cottage cheese clotting just underneath her skin. Nodding her approval, she handed me a glossy clamshell compact of face powder.

As I dusted my skin with the silky powder, I inquired, "So how was it you got to North Korea?"

"Oh, no, Lisa, I won't be telling you that story," she murmured almost tenderly. "That's not your business."

Sucking in my cheeks as she had showed me, I brushed on a shimmery plum rouge before tilting my face toward her for her inspection. "Look, Yolanda, I'm sorry if you're upset by my arrival here. As you know, I was a little upset by it too. I apologize if anything I did offended you in my first days, but I was just trying to make sense of things. I realize now that I'm here to stay, and I think we should both make the best of it. Do you think we can be friends?"

She stared at me without saying a word, which I took as a no. Carefully, I extruded my lips to stain them a matte blackberry, her face leering over my shoulder in the mirror. Trying to dredge up some sort of pity for her, I imagined what it must be like to see such a frightful kabuki mask looking back every time you glimpsed your own reflection. As I carefully drew a thick black line under my lower lid, I tried another tack, "I know that you and Honey have an extremely close relationship, and I respect that. I don't want to come between the two of you. She told me that she hopes we'll become friends." A lie, but one that I thought I had little chance of being caught in.

She said nothing, handing me a set of false eyelashes pinched between her long red fingernails, then folding her arms tightly across her chest to watch me put them on. As I ripped off the adhesive back and wedged the quilled strip onto my upper lid, I felt like I had only succeeded in making her hate me more.

As we made our way to the trophy room, hot air eddied through the hallway with a high-pitched scream. The occasional tunnel wind was one of the mysteries of the compound, a weather pattern without any discernible source, always bringing with it a keening that sounded eerily human.

A young man with a retro haircut was recumbent on the cowhide sofa, bowling-ball head propped on Honey's thigh, frowning down at something that he held in his lap. He did not look up as Honey exclaimed, "Here she is!"

"One sec," he grunted, "almost done annihilating you."

Honey giggled, jiggling his head with her thigh so that his capacious cheeks quaked. She was dressed in a pair of tight white jeans and a short-sleeved white cashmere sweater, an unusual departure from her customary formal evening wear. With the young man in a T-shirt and track bottoms and I in my own clothes, it was casual Friday at Villa Umma.

"Mom, stop it! Seriously!" he growled, thumbs punching at the black box cradled in his plump hands. With an upward jerk, he finished the game off. *"Whoa! Yeah! In your face!"*

With mock sorrow, she sighed. "Do you have to win every time?"

Chuckling, he raised his stockinged feet in the air to seesaw upright, tousled hair spiked into two unruly horns before Honey smoothed them down. "I always start out telling myself Imma let my moms win, but something happens while I'm playing..."

"You don't know how to lose," she crowed triumphantly.

"Oh, hello, Lisa," he said, as if just noticing me.

Honey purred, "Lisa. Darling. Finally, you get to meet your brother—"

"Half brother," he corrected her.

"Half brother, Jonny."

Without standing up, he held out a hand for me to shake. His hand was soft, but the grip was painful, and he pulled me so violently toward him I almost dropped to my knees, our noses coming within inches of each other before he gave me back my hand. He seemed very familiar to me, and I was thinking that was the power of our shared genetics, that this complete stranger would look like someone I already knew, when he smiled teasingly at me and I noticed the Mindy-like winking dimple under his eye. But of course. I should have realized it when Honey had first told me about Jonny, but with all that had happened to me recently, I had almost forgotten about the evening Ji Hoon and I had spent at Honey Do. "I think we've met already, haven't we?"

"Whaaat?" Honey screeched, looking from him to me and back again. "Is that right, Jonny?"

His small mouth expanded into a full-teeth smile, eyes slivering into mirthful crescents. "That's right, Moms. I made one of my stealth trips to Seoul to see for myself if Harrison had the right girl this time."

"You did that? For me? Oh, Jonny!" Honey swooned, rubbing her cheek fervently against the padded hump of his shoulder.

"Nothing's too good for Moms," Jonny assured her, tipping me a conspiratorial wink. "How have you been getting along here at Villa Umma, Lisa? Settling in all right?"

Both sets of eyes burned at me, his onyx and cold, hers a depthless blue and unfathomable. I said, "Yes. Learning the ropes. I'm afraid I've been a bit slow at first, but Honey is a patient and astute teacher."

His hand slapped onto her knee and began to stroke it, pinkie delicately curled. "You have nothing to fear with Moms on your side. Just do as she says, and you'll be all right. Sit down, sit down. No need to stand on ceremony. You're part of the family now."

I didn't dare sit on the couch with the two of them, so I settled into a club chair.

"Yolanda!" he shouted unnecessarily, as she was standing right there. "What about some drinks, eh, old gal?"

Yolanda bustled to the bar, returning with shallow crystal glasses clinking on a tray. Expertly wrapping a napkin over a champagne bottle, she popped the cork and poured three glasses full. Jonny raised his glass in the air, declaring, "To Moms!"

"Here, here." Honey tilted her glass first at him, then at me.

"To Honey," I chirped. After we drained our glasses, I asked, "How's Ji Hoon doing?"

"Who *is* this Ji Hoon guy she's always talking about?" Honey asked, waggling her empty champagne glass at Yolanda.

Chin dimpling with a frown, Jonny shook his head in bewilderment.

"You know, the guy who brought me to Honey Do to meet you?" I also waggled my glass at Yolanda.

"Oh." The boy laughed. "Is that what he told you his name was? She's talking about Harrison," he told Honey.

Honey sputtered, "Ji Hoon? Where did he get that name?"

"From Ju Ji Hoon, most likely," Jonny guffawed. "Or maybe Kim Ji Hoon. Or could be Lee Ji Hoon. They're all popular actors who make the girls go crazy."

"What was wrong with the name Harrison? I thought it suited him very well." Honey seemed pissed off.

"No, it's just that I asked him what his Korean name was," I explained. "Since Harrison was obviously not his real name."

Small mouth pushing out into a pout, Jonny whined at Honey: "Where are my snacks? You know I have to constantly feed this." With his thumb, he flicked the surge of flesh that hung below his chin.

Clapping hands, Honey called, "Snacks! Snacks!" Then she said to me confidentially, "Jonny is naturally svelte and must work very hard to keep his shape."

"In leadership shape," he concurred. "In the image of my grand-father."

"Luckily," Honey simpered, "he has his father's appetites."

"In all things!" Jonny roared, poking at his mother's belly. "Ah!" He rubbed his hands in delight at the array of delicacies that Yolanda placed before him. "That Cookie! How's he doing, hey? Satisfied with his perks?"

"For the time being at least," Honey said, rolling her eyes. "Lisa is helping Cookie expand his repertoire," she explained, teasing a strip of dried squid free and lowering it into Jonny's waiting mouth. "He's getting gourmet."

"You should try the stuffed mushrooms," I suggested, grabbing one myself. "Mmm. He's a quick study, that Miura-san."

"Who?" Honey asked sharply. Then shaking her head so force-fully that the tassels of her freshwater pearl earrings whipped her cheeks, she said, "What is it with you and names? Why can't you just use the names that are given to people?"

"That name was given to him," I protested. "It's his real name."

"Well, here his name is Cookie," Honey insisted, biting into a mini-quiche.

Jonny began to laugh at me, his mouth opened wide to show the chewed-over squid coating his tongue. "His real name isn't even Mi-ura-san. Same thing with Ji Hoon. You are so gullible."

"What? Why would he lie to me?" I asked, feeling my cheeks redden.

"Men like him are born liars. It's the only way they can survive in society."

"What do you mean, 'men like him'?"

The two of them shared a private smirk. "Since you are such good friends, ask him. See if he tells you."

Annoyed, I nibbled on a mini-quiche. Spinach and bacon. Very nice.

Unable to keep it in any longer, Jonny tittered and said, "He likes little girls. As part of his contract, I have to provide him with a new one every year. But he's become very demanding lately, complaining that he can see them aging before his eyes, and insists on a fresh one every six months. I think he's getting restless." He and his mother exchanged a meaningful look.

The quiche turned mealy in my mouth, sticking in my throat like sand. "I don't believe you!" I protested. "Miura-san is a really nice guy!"

Jonny's eyes bugged out to Honey-like dimensions and he fixed me with a cold stare. "It is foolish not to believe me. My word is truth."

"His word is law," Honey berated me, petting the bulging roll of flesh that was Jonny's neck consolingly.

I hung my head to show proper remorse. "Yes, of course, I'm sorry for contradicting you. It was just the shock of hearing that about Miura-san."

"Pedophiles are often charming, that's how they keep on getting away with it," Honey declared as if she had some authority on the subject.

After pouring the last of the champagne, Yolanda minced over to the bar and plinked ice cubes into tumblers, bringing them to us with a bottle of Chivas Regal.

"Ah, Yolanda, now you're a treasure," Jonny exclaimed, smacking her on the butt as she poured him a hefty drink. "You make Cookie seem like a coward and a traitor."

Yolanda actually blushed, which I never would have believed if I hadn't seen it with my own eyes, tiny starbursts of scarlet mottling her pale cheeks. After she had distributed drinks all around, he flicked a finger peremptorily at her. "Now run along."

She obediently retreated to the far reaches of the room, stationing herself beneath the mournful head of an Isis-horned buffalo. "So, Lisa." Jonny propped his elbows on his knees, leaning toward me, his belly straining against his Mickey Mouse T-shirt. "I believe that my mother had a little talk with you earlier."

"Yes, she did," I agreed, smiling sweetly. "She explained everything."

"Quite a story, huh?" he asked, chewing on the inside of his lip as he watched me closely.

"Oh, yeah." I laughed. "Unbelievable!"

"Moms explained that we brought you here to help me, right?"

Biting my lip to show that I understood the gravity of the situation, I nodded. "She explained everything but how, specifically, I might help you." I hoped Honey took note that I was loyally guarding the secret of the website.

He struck a ruminative pose, one arm folded across the hillock of his belly and propping up the elbow of the other arm, a loose fist cupping his chin. "Some people are born lucky, others have to make their own luck. I am somewhere in between the two. If I were the oldest son of my father's wife, life would be easier, but my destiny was not handed to me on a velvet cushion, as it is to some. I must make it come true myself."

"You decimated your closest competitors," Honey purred, stroking a thick curl of hair that hung over his forehead.

"Ha, my half siblings were easy prey. Now I face real warriors, experienced men—tough, wily, battle hardened, and allied against me. They are just waiting for my father to die to stick their knives into my back."

"If only he could last another year." Honey laced her fingers together in prayer. "That would be time enough to settle everything, and then the generals wouldn't dare to lift a finger against you."

"Mother, you saw how frail he is. It's a matter of months."

Burying her face in her hands, she leaned heavily against him, whimpering, as he patted her perfunctorily on her back.

"Moms will need your help in this crucial period as we prepare for my regime. Smart as she is, she cannot do it all alone."

Dropping her hands to reveal a face that bore no trace of the anguish that had seemed to torment her just a moment ago, she proclaimed, "If I had stayed in the US, I'd be the one running the family interests now, not that idiot Eric, who didn't even learn to tie his shoes until he was ten!"

Trying not to overplay my eagerness to ingratiate myself to them, I mused, "I am flattered that you think I can help, but how? I don't imagine I would be joining the politburo or the central committee, or whatever it's called, and I know very little about governance or politics."

Honey waved her hand in the air, ivory bracelets clicking. "So what? Great leaders are not made; they are born. It's a matter of native intelligence and killer instincts. Bill Gates was a college dropout."

"So was Steve Jobs," I added brightly, touched that she thought I had the native intelligence to survive in the cutthroat world of North Korean politics, even though I knew that her confidence was based on self-regard rather than on any cold, hard evidence.

"Yes!" she exclaimed like a hallelujah. "You have people like Angelina Jolie and Bono representing the UN, advising politicians on refugees, and eliminating poverty. What does Bono, a fabulously wealthy Irishman, know about poverty in Africa? Nothing, but people listen to him anyway. It's all about confidence and charisma."

"But what exactly is it that you want me to do?" I insisted, looking at Jonny, who was sorting through a bowl of Oriental mix for the wasabi peas and already seemed bored with the conversation.

"Whatever Honey asks of you," Jonny replied with a shrug. "She'll guide you every step of the way."

Because I knew I would not earn their respect unless I tried to bargain a little, I asked, "What do I get in return?"

Nudging her son in his well-padded side, she exulted, "See, Jonny? She's already learning! Didn't I tell you that she had the instincts?"

Crunching a mouthful of peas between his powerful, well-exercised jaws, he looked at me thoughtfully. "You get your life."

"Not just any life," Honey said breathlessly, "but all this!" She scooped outstretched hands through the air, like a game-show hostess showing off the prizes that could be won.

"Could I ever leave the compound, say for excursions into Pyongyang?"

Honey brushed some crumbs off Mickey Mouse's smiling face. "It is imperative that we not be seen. No one must ever guess that I am his mother."

Jonny shrugged his shoulders and raised his carefully groomed eyebrows, as if to say he didn't agree but would defer to the wisdom of his mother.

"OK, then can I have access to pen and paper? I've always kept a journal, and it would help me to adjust to my new life here if I could maintain some of my old habits."

"I wouldn't advise that, no," Jonny said, licking the residue of a stuffed mushroom from his fingers. "Writing is a dangerous activity here. But as for other habits..." He raised his glass at me suggestively.

I raised mine back and we matched slug for slug. There was one last request, and if they refused it, I feared I'd break down and cry in front of them, losing what little respect I had managed to gain so far. "What about books? I mean, real books, not propaganda."

"Why, Lisa," Honey exclaimed, "all books are propaganda." She clapped her hands for Yolanda, who came bounding across the room. "Show Lisa the books."

Yolanda stood on tippy-toes to pull down the notched horn of a mounted antelope head. The wall began to move with a whir, a whole herd of small, delicate deer heads disappearing, replaced by bookshelves. I leapt up to see what was there, my fingers hungrily running over the spines. *Kim Il Sung Works*, volumes 1 through 44, packed two shelves; another shelf was dedicated to Kim biographies, the one below filled with books on Juche. Lots of Marx, Lenin, Trotsky, Mao. But also the collected works of Shakespeare, Dickens, Austen, Melville, and, bizarrely, Philip K. Dick. *Alice's Adventures in Wonderland, Frankenstein, Animal Farm, The Catcher in the Rye, The Metamorphosis, Fahrenheit 451, Light in August, The Bell Jar...*

"There are more," Honey purred. "Two huge vaults crammed with books."

Finally, clutching *Great Expectations* under an arm, I wandered back to the two of them leaning crookedly against each other on the couch, Honey watching me with a small smile playing at the end of her lips. "I was a nobody in America, just a spoiled rich kid. If I'd stayed there, I'd be wasting my talents organizing charity galas and chairing vanity foundations. But my destiny was different. It brought me here, to the highest echelons of power. That same destiny is now yours, Lisa. Just think about it: the whole world trembles before North Korea. Billions of dollars are spent monitoring and negotiating with us. We have China eating out of our hand, South Korea and Japan quaking at our every move, the United States allocating huge sums and some of their most formidable minds to containing and managing us. You will be a part of world history. You will help affect the course of the human race."

I tilted my head, as if considering their offer. What was there to consider, though? What answer could I give them, except for the one they wanted? It was an offer I literally could not refuse. And the way that Honey put it, why would I want to? Who didn't want to leave her mark on humanity? Fame didn't always come through talent or brave deeds. Look at famous adopted person Soon-Yi Previn, who gained worldwide notoriety through salacious scandal, or poor, martyred Vincent Chin. I nodded slowly. "OK. I'm all in for Team Jonny."

Throwing her arms exuberantly around Jonny's neck, Honey screamed, "That's my girl!" Her sweater rode up to reveal the soft, milky swell of belly hanging over the tight band of her jeans, white on white.

Jonny stared inscrutably at me with flat, dark eyes, lips pushed out as he chewed on the inside of his cheek.

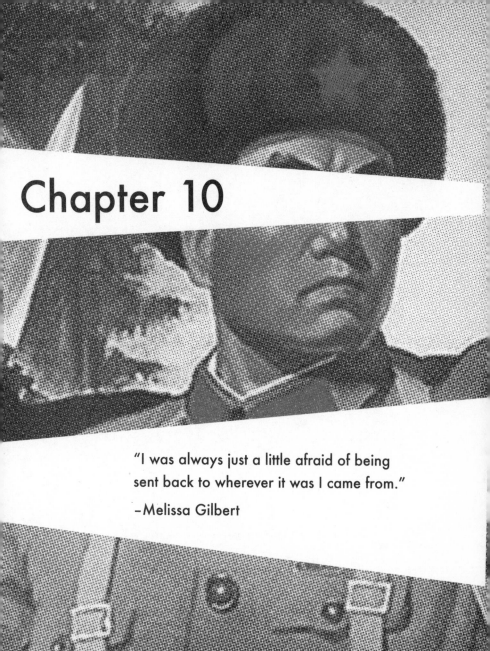

Chapter 10

"I was always just a little afraid of being sent back to wherever it was I came from."

–Melissa Gilbert

When Ting brought my breakfast the next morning, I was dry heaving into the toilet. She came into the bathroom and knelt beside me, pulling my hair back from my face. "Go away!" I rasped.

Last night's bottle of champagne had been just the beginning of our bacchanalia. There were tumblers of Chivas Regal and then sake, soju, and wine with Cookie's sushi dinner. The meal was a revelation in sea flesh, platter after sumptuous platter emerging from the kitchen, each one a jeweled mosaic accented with the perfect garnish: diaphanous slivers of fugu arranged into the shape of a flying crane, strips of eggplant for the legs, neck, and beak; marbled rectangles of rosy whale meat artfully fanned over shiso leaves and dotted with tiny yellow blossoms; vermilion fatty tuna, alabaster squid, and creamy blue suckered octopus tentacles arranged to resemble the North Korean flag; a massive lobster spilling snowy flesh from its tail while its tentacles yet waved. The evening culminated with Hennessey X.O, sipped and then gulped as we reviewed the audition clips of the finalists for this year's crop of the Joy Brigade, which Honey explained was the ultimate dream of all North Korean girls and their families, securing their position in the "core class," with all the privileges and opportunities that came with that coveted designation. As we watched an endless parade of teenaged girls disrobe, I learned that Jonny had recently been married to the daughter of a powerful general, a political arrangement that Honey assured me would soon blossom into a love match, because "Sally" was beautiful, graceful, and charismatic. "And none of this hiding the woman at home," Honey chided Jonny. "You need Sally to be your Jackie O, an inspiration for all the commoners and a trendsetter for the women to model themselves after."

Honey took her Joy Brigade obligations very seriously, keeping a careful evaluation of each girl, rating her on beauty, figure, breasts, legs, sex appeal, comportment, talent, and patriotism. Oddly, a 1 was the highest rating, a 5 the lowest, so the girls with the least points won. Each candidate gave an impassioned speech on her warm feelings for the Dear Leader, a few words of which Jonny would translate before collapsing into giggles at their clumsy metaphors or scoffing indignantly at their lack of ardor. Then she had to walk back and forth, bow, clap, wave, perform—the accordion was especially popular—and, finally, disrobe. Honey and Jonny favored full-figured girls with apple cheeks, a strong jaw that tapered to a softly rounded chin, and big, plump wonton-shaped eyes.

It seemed as if we auditioned every pubescent schoolgirl in North Korea, and I quickly found it depressing, but then Yolanda brought in a second bottle of Hennessey, and I decided to go with the flow, shouting out whatever free-association thing floated in my brain—*Teacher's pet! Banana tits! Wants it hard! Likes to kick puppies!*—until Honey told Yolanda to take me back to my room.

Finally, I turned to look at Ting, a strand of saliva wobbling from my lips. Solemnly, she presented me with a note, which rested on her upturned palms. The notecard, monogrammed with Honey's initials, was blank. "What the fuck, Ting?" I whined. My brain felt like there was an ax wedged into it, and I wasn't in the mood for Honey's weird games. Ting gracefully lifted herself up from her subservient crouch and beckoned for me to follow her out the bathroom door. She guided my hand to hold the stationery over the steam curling from the lip of the coffee press. A wild, childish scrawl began to appear.

Dear Lisa,
Let's have fun together! We'll leave tomorrow morning. I'll show you my town. Shh!!! Don't tell __anyone__!!
Your bro,
Jon-Jon

P.S. Dress for a day of thrills, chills, and laughter, because you're going to the happiest place on earth!

P.P.S. Rip this note up and flush it down the toilet so that you-know-who doesn't see it.

During her noontime visit, Ting delivered two white pills with my lunch, scrunching up her face and pointing to her head to tell me that they were for my headache. I seized her hand and covered it with kisses, until I remembered that my lips were probably still flecked with vomit. I was pretty sure I saw her lips briefly circumflex into a small smile. On the lunch tray was another missive, this one also on Honey's personal stationery, the words elegantly transcribed as if by a calligrapher.

> *Baby,*
> *You won't be seeing Jonny before he leaves. He wants to spend some alone time with his mother. But I haven't forgotten about you and have sent you some books to help you pass the time.*
> *Kisses,*
> *Honey*

One by one, I picked up the books that Ting had piled on the bed-side table: *The Koreans*, *The Two Koreas*, and two volumes of *The Origins of the Korean War*. They were heavy, forbidding tomes, and I almost wept in gratitude for them.

When I disembarked the Qingdao ferry in Incheon, there was no thrill of recognition or homecoming as I returned to the land of my birth, just a weariness with travel, with Asia, and with myself. I spent the days before Mindy's arrival huddled in the common room of my cheap youth hostel, poring over my journals for a theme that I could expand into a witty and poignant essay on how my year in China led to life-changing insights into the nature of my own character or some such shit. The problem was my journals were an inco-herent mess, filled with petty and inconsequential observations with nary a profound thought in sight. Though I had been keeping a diary since Santa gave me my first one when I was six, this was the first time I actually read through what I had written, and I was shocked at the laziness of the prose, the artlessness of the descriptions, the trivial things that preoccupied me, and my sneering, negative attitude. Time was running out, though, and the paper was due the day Mindy arrived, so I rushed through a sloppy essay on the system of *guanxi*—the reciprocity of favors between individuals—and how it had shaped my relationships with my Chinese friends, emailing it off just before leaving for the airport to pick up Mindy, queasy with the knowledge that I had submitted a disappointing, disorganized, and fatuous paper.

When Mindy came through the international passengers exit, juggling a ridiculous amount of luggage and looking impossibly fresh and dewy-skinned after a fifteen-hour flight, she dramatically dropped all her bags and ran to me with open arms, the eyes of about fifty Koreans following her. "Liiiiisaaaa! Don't ever leave me for so long again!" she yowled as she threw herself into my arms.

"Oh my god," I snickered. "You're such a diva."

She frantically kissed me, leaving butterflies of lipstick all over my face. I tried to fend her off with small slaps. More people stared at the commotion.

"Let me kiss your scruffy face. Oh, who couldn't love your scruffy little face? You know who you remind me of right now?" She leaned away from me, squinting critically.

"A dancing bear? The sad clown in the circus?"

"Noooo. Though we could try a frilly tutu on you. But no. Melissa Gilbert, when she was Laura on *Little House on the Prairie*."

"The fuck...?"

Brushing my face to accentuate where I resembled Melissa Gilbert, she crooned, "She had these cute little almond-shaped eyes that crinkled up when she smiled. Freckles across her nose. That crazy smile that showed all her teeth. The frizzy hair." She flicked at the two stubby braids I had put my hair in to keep it off my neck in the sultry summer heat. "The braids."

"You are such a bitch," I said, laughing and picking up the handle of one of her rolling suitcases. "Come on, let's go. It's a long ride into Seoul."

"My dad booked us a room at the Hyatt Regency airport hotel. He knew I'd be exhausted after the trip."

"The worst kind of bitch, a rich bitch," I grumbled, hitching my ratty, towering pack higher on my back.

"You know you love it!" She laughed.

Walking out of the terminal into the heat and fumes, we shuffled up to the hotel shuttle bus stop. "So, Melissa Gilbert—who you so adorably resemble right at this moment—is adopted!" She shook a bright smile at me, playing up how cute she was to both annoy and cheer me up. "Another one for the list."

"The list is dumb," I grumbled, squinting into the traffic for our bus. "What's the point of it if you're not going to become a famous actress?"

"Don't say that about the list," she gasped, rummaging in her handbag for her sunglasses. "You're going to be the famous one, remember? It's all up to you now."

"Melissa Gilbert, Scott Hamilton, Dave who-the-fuck-even-knows-who-he-is Thomas. They suck. Adopted people suck," I moaned. "I'm never going to be anything. I just wrote a really shitty paper, and it's painfully obvious that I don't have an original or worthwhile thought in my head. I can't write, my observations are boring and petty, I'm shit at expressing myself."

"Li-li!" Mindy admonished me. "That's not true. I've saved all your letters, and I read them over and over. They're raw and sometimes rambling, yeah, but you definitely have a talent for writing. You just need to practice more. I thought that was what your journal was for, sort of like daily exercises to strengthen your writing muscles. That's why I always give you one for your birthday, so you can practice your lines for your big debut."

I had never thought about why I kept a journal; it was just a daily compulsion, like eating and sleeping. I did it because I had to, because the day was incomplete if I didn't. As usual, Mindy was right. As usual, I was going about things all wrong. Writing was as much discipline as anything else, and instead of using my journal as a random repository of the words that rolled around in my head, I should have been using it to hone my narrative skills, a sketch pad on which I made the preliminary studies for a larger work. Instead of feeling invigorated by this insight, though, I only felt aggrieved with myself. Five minutes with Mindy, and she was straightening out my life for me. Why couldn't I straighten out my life on my own? Gazing into the brown penumbra of exhaust that overhung the road, I said, "I don't like Korea. It depresses me. I've felt like shit ever since I got here."

A well-dressed man joined us, smoking a cigarette and fiddling with his phone. He paused to ogle Mindy.

"No, no, no, Korea is the bomb," she chirped, stroking a lumpy braid. "You've just been missing me. You have MAD, which is like SAD: Mindy Affective Disorder. Now I'm here and you'll feel all better soon."

"Have you ever looked in the mirror and been surprised by what you saw?" I demanded through clenched teeth. "I mean shocked at your own face, like who *is* that?"

"Yeah," she said, grazing my cheek with her fingers. The man stared even harder. "It's called cognitive dissonance. If you'd been paying attention at Korean Kamp, or stuck it out with that adoption therapist, you'd know about it."

"I thought coming to Asia would tell me something about myself, uplift me, the way you were when you came back from your first trip to Korea. Instead, it's just made me sad. Like nowhere is home. Like I don't fit in anywhere. Like I'm a stranger in a strange land no matter where I am."

"You're just homesick. You've been away from your family and friends for too long, and it's time for you to go home."

"No, I'm just sick of myself," I spat, stepping back to avoid the cloud of smoke that drifted downwind from the businessman. "I've always hated that everyone made assumptions about me that were wrong. But you know what? I'm just beginning to realize that I'm wrong about the assumptions I've made about me as well."

"Lisa," she said, laughing. "You know who you are! You're my best friend."

"Sadly, that used to be enough for me, but it isn't anymore." Most unexpectedly, I began to cry.

"Oh, Li-li." Mindy nudged her luggage out of the way and enveloped me in her arms. I could smell the stale air of the plane in her hair. "It's OK. I'm here. You're right where you belong, with me. We're going to have fun in Korea. Look! Here comes the hotel bus!"

The knock at my door came earlier than expected, but I was ready after a sleepless night chasing feverish ideas of how I could escape without needing to rely on Wendell after all, slipping away into the crowd, just another Korean on the streets of Pyongyang.

The man who had come to fetch me was a Frankenstein's monster-type with a square head, thick neck, and huge, murderous hands. He led me for what seemed like miles through the twisting corridors, then onto an elevator that took us to a steel door that required a complicated series of codes. The door opened up like a ship's hatch, fuddling my concept of spatial relations so that I felt like I was stepping into another dimension as I emerged like a rabbit from its hole into the pastel wash of early-morning light. A gleaming silver vehicle awaited, and though I was no expert on cars, I immediately recognized the boxy, long-nosed silhouette and the winged silver hood ornament of a Rolls-Royce. The windows were mirrored, and when Frankenstein's monster opened the door for me, I saw that Jonny was already inside.

"Morning, Lisa!" he greeted me with hearty bonhomie. "Ready for Jonny and Lisa's big adventure?"

"Wow," I exclaimed. "What happened to you? You look totally different!"

His hair was sculpted into a stiff meringue atop his head, bordered by a freshly shaved swath of skin that stretched from temple to temple in one of the weirdest hairstyles I'd ever seen. His eyebrows were plucked to short parabolas, and his double chin spilled over the lapels of a boxy black jacket buttoned to the very top, a red flag-shaped pin decorated with the smiling faces of his grandfather and father pinned over his heart.

As I settled into the backseat, pants squealing loudly against the leather seats, he said, "Hold up! Hold up! What're you wearing?"

Looking down at my ensemble of leather rock-star pants and sheer silk shirt heavily embroidered with gold thread, I sheepishly explained, "I had to work with what Honey allows me to wear, and these were the only pants that were in the closet, besides pj bottoms and a pair of sweatpants."

"Better you wear the sweatpants!"

"I'm sorry. Should I go back and change?"

He glanced impatiently at the chunky Rolex on his wrist. "No, we don't have time. We'll just have to make a stop at the Paradise. I mean, you look good"—he raked his eyes over me in a way that was not quite brotherly—"but the noble masses are not ready for such, um, provocative fashion."

He knocked his knuckles on the smoked glass that divided the backseat from the front, and the car thrummed forward.

"Here." He motioned to the burl-paneled console that divided our seats, travel mugs snug in the cupholders, two wax-paper packets laid out on a shallow lacquer tray. "Cookie made us some takeout, bacon and egg sandwiches. Be careful with the coffee. The beginning of the ride is a bit bumpy."

The driver maneuvered carefully over the heavily eroded road, swerving to avoid the ruts when he could, easing the car through them when he had no other choice.

"I'd love to pave this road," Jonny explained apologetically, "but that would be like a huge arrow pointing spy satellites to the compound, so it has to seem like any other country road. Otherwise, it would be a quick ninety-minute drive to Pyongyang."

I dipped my face to take a bite of Cookie's egg sandwich so that he wouldn't see the eagerness in my eyes. Pyongyang. The big city. My chance to escape.

But as if he could read my thoughts, he advised, "You have no idea the number of eyes that will be on you at all times. One word from me, and you'll be torn apart, limb from limb." He gave me a gleeful openmouthed smile that featured all his teeth except for the very back molars.

"What?" I smiled back. "I wouldn't dream of it. I'm just ready for that day of fun you promised me."

Picking up what looked like a walkie-talkie with a baton for an antenna, he said, "Excuse me, I have a few phone calls to make."

I was glad for the chance to stare out the window, wishing I could inscribe the landscape onto my brain to replay on endless loop when I was locked up in my room. The car was nosing down the crenellated, flower-starred flank of a mountain, other peaks rising about us into eternity in the sun-hazed distance. There was no evidence of human activity, no other cars, no pedestrians, no houses. It was as if we were the only life for light-years around.

When Jonny finally stopped barking into his phone, we were suddenly enveloped in an eerie cocoon of silence. We couldn't even hear the sound of the wheels on the dirt road. But Jonny didn't like too much time to go by without hearing the sound of his own voice. He asked, "Did you destroy the note I sent you?"

"Of course," I averred. "Just like you asked me to. Why did I need to do that?"

"I didn't want *her* spoiling our fun day together. If she'd found out about our plans, she'd've tried to stop you from coming."

"Why would she do that?" I had slipped out of my Swarovski-encrusted black velvet Louboutin mules to brush the soles of my feet over the Rolls's plush sheepskin carpeting.

He shrugged. "Jealousy. She wants me all to herself. Lucky for you, she got word that Pops is arriving today, so she'll probably be too busy to check up on you. But if she finds out..." Catching his lower lip under his hypsodontic front teeth, he rolled his eyes. "She wants to believe that she's in total control of you. You're her little project."

"What do you mean, 'her little project'?"

"Look, Lisa, I'm going to be straight with you. I brought you here to keep Honey distracted during this very, very dangerous time. My father is going to die soon. Like a dumbass, he waited too long to appoint me his successor, and now I'm in a life-and-death battle against the bad guys to take control once the old man finally kicks it. Your job is to keep Moms occupied, keep her out of my hair, and manage her when she starts to lose her shit about my dad. That's why I rescued you from your sad little existence and brought you here for this life of fabulousness. If you fail, well, then, I'm sorry but I'll probably have to kill you."

"You'd kill your own sister?" I gulped, the words sticking glutinously in my throat.

His cannonball head bobbled about for a few seconds as if it were a tough call, before he raised his sculpted eyebrows, nodding decisively. "You're just a half sister, and not the important half."

"I'll handle Honey for you, I promise," I gabbled, a cold sweat breaking out down my back and all thoughts of escaping into the streets of Pyongyang vanishing like street-corner drug dealers when the cops roll by. "I'll do whatever I can to keep Honey happy, to keep her busy. She wants me to build a North Korean website. Even though I don't know anything about that. But I'll pretend I do."

"Relax, Lisa." He patted my knee, his hand lingering there as he appreciated the buttery quality of the leather. "She really likes you. As long as you play the dutiful daughter, it'll all be good."

"But," I said, confused, "you just said she'd be unhappy if she finds out I left the villa without her permission."

"*If* she finds out." He grinned. "You better hope she doesn't." Humming a little tune to himself, he turned away to look out the window.

I too turned to my window, glad to hide the shocked realization— no doubt evident on my ashen face—that he was setting me up to fail. We had descended the mountains to the plains, and suddenly here was the evidence of humanity that I'd been searching for: a man walking behind a yoked ox—the early-morning sun picking out the ribs of the lumbering beast—and guiding a primitive wooden plow as it tore up the field. My first real North Korean. I craned out the window to get a better look.

"Yeah, I'm going to have a lot of cleaning up to do," Jonny announced to the air.

The car slithered by two farmers working a flooded rice paddy, pants rolled up, mud slicking their calves and arms. When they beheld our shining chariot, they quickly dropped to their knees, foreheads touching the glinting water.

Did he want me to respond to what he'd just said? I'd better, just to be safe. "How much cleaning up?" I quavered.

He gave me a coquettish, sidelong glance. "I haven't decided yet. But there are going to be some real surprises. None of those fuckers are safe."

A lone child watched raptly as we flew by. I did a double-take, sure that he had been wearing nothing but a plastic bag, the handles serving as straps over wizened shoulders, skeletal legs that knobbed out at the knees sticking out from the bottom.

Jonny reassured me: "Don't worry about the website. We have the best computer geeks in the world. I'll send one of them to the villa to help you set up a prototype, not that it's ever going to become a reality, but at least it'll keep Moms happy. Ah"—he clapped softly—"finally. The paved road."

The Rolls-Royce shuddered onto a wide stripe of glossy tarmac and then accelerated until the land was but a smear of green fields interrupted by occasional huddles of blocky concrete buildings. There were no other cars on the road but more people, on bikes and walking, some of them riding wooden carts, others harnessed to them. All who were quick enough to react dropped to their knees and bowed as we streaked by.

"So much love," Jonny murmured, nibbling on his fingernails, and I couldn't tell if he was being facetious.

Pyongyang announced itself with tall cookie-cutter apartment buildings that loomed abruptly upon the landscape. Soon, we were speeding down a vast, empty avenue, past a sudden sprouting of curvy modern towers, catching glimpses of a shining *Wizard of Oz* rocket-ship-shaped building in the interstices of the crossroads. Despite the thickening congestion of the streets, the car didn't slow down, and everyone—drivers, bicyclists, and pedestrians—knew to get the hell out of its way.

A svelte young woman in a snug navy-blue uniform cinched tightly at the waist, a plastic-brimmed hat with an enormous white crown perched atop her head, pursed her lovely lips around a whistle while repeatedly thrusting a red-and-white-striped stick in the air, waving our only road companions—two packed buses and a single car—to a dead stop as we blew by them. Two off-duty traffic cops clutched at each other with white-gloved hands as we passed, their faces stretched in distraught rapture. People on the sidewalks, too, would stop to wave and scream as we rolled by, some wiping tears from their cheeks.

We came to a stop in front of a squat building paneled in reflective glass. Picking up his phone, Jonny announced, "You go in. I'll wait here."

I swept through the revolving door into complete darkness. "Hello?" I called.

A scuffling came from somewhere deep in the shadows, and then the lights flooded on, bouncing off the spit-shiny glaze of the marble entrance and flashing off mirrored columns and the glass and chrome of display cases. The soft leather soles of my Louboutins slipped against gray-veined marble as I wandered past shelves stocked with plastic buckets, hot water thermoses, shiny metal pots, and rice cookers. I had just discovered the liquor—Dragon Heart Dry Gin, Soleil Banana Liqueur, Amitié Brandy—when a woman came running up behind me, still buttoning the form-hugging jacket of her uniform.

"Please, please, can I help you?" she panted, wriggling her hand in her sleeve to straighten an errant cuff. When she noticed my outfit, her brow crinkled in astonishment before she managed to subdue her features into an impassive mask.

"I'm looking for women's clothes."

"Please," she said uncertainly.

"Women's clothes," I said, plucking at my shirt.

"Ah, clothes," she echoed, literally wiping her brow with relief before marching off at a brisk, businesslike pace. I hustled to keep up with her as she led me up a wide staircase banked with vitrines offering a random selection of luxury goodies, then past a counter displaying timepieces that would have proudly graced the wrists of westerners forty years ago and into the women's clothing section, where she began to aggressively rattle clothes at me.

"I need pants," I said, not seeing any. I waved my hand up and down my legs, but her brain seemed to comprehend only the leather and not the pants.

"No have, no have," she repeated with aghast vehemence.

I spied some shirts and unfolded one. It was shiny and slippery, the material slimy against my fingers. Pointing at her shirt, I said, "I want one like yours. Do you have that?"

Her fingers crept apprehensively up to her collar.

"Something like that? A long-sleeved button-up?"

She began to undo the buttons of her jacket.

"No, no, don't do that."

She worked faster, flinging off the jacket and then picking open the buttons of her blouse.

"Oh for god's sake," I pleaded. "No."

But she peeled off her shirt, proffering it to me with a stiff-armed gesture, as if she were thrusting something into a fiery furnace. Her undershirt was frayed, the cotton flossy from washing, brown crescents darkening the armpits, and she made such a pathetic picture that there was nothing for it but to put her out of her misery. I took off my shirt and offered it to her in exchange. She pinched it between two fingers as if it were a used tissue before stuffing it into her suit jacket pocket, which she had buttoned all the way to the top so only a small triangle of her undershirt was visible.

"Now for pants," I said, not even daring to look toward her skirt.

She trailed me, touching the very same clothes I touched to show me she was searching hard for whatever it was that I was looking for. It turned out there were no pants, only skirts. I randomly picked a pleated black polyester number with an elastic waistband. "Can I try it on?" I asked, aping the motions.

The salesgirl led me at a brisk trot to the changing room, where it took me a while to rip the leather pants off my legs. The skirt fell like a bell from my waist to my calves, and I smiled at my reflection, thinking how horrified Honey would be. The salesgirl would not even take the leather pants that I extended to her, pretending not to see them as she bowed me toward the cash register.

"Oh, but I don't have any money," I said, patting my nonexistent pockets in dumb show as she gaped at me. "I have to wait here for my, er, friend to come. He'll pay for me."

But she kept ushering me on, past the cash register, down the stairs, and toward the door.

"But the money," I insisted, rubbing my fingertips together in the universal sign language for cash. Unsure how to react to my dancing fingers, she decided to go the safe route and assume it was the strange way my culture had of saying good-bye. She rubbed her fingers back at me and practically pushed me through the revolving door.

"They don't have any women's pants in that store," I announced indignantly to Jonny.

"Nah. Pops doesn't like pants on women. He thinks it's unfeminine."

I bit off the sarcastic retort that quivered at the tip of my tongue, turning to look out the window at a fashionable gaggle of young women, all in flattering pencil skirts, walking in lockstep down the broad sidewalk. People walked at one speed, I noticed, a brisk, purposeful gait that was just short of a full gallop.

As he settled a pair of horn-rimmed glasses onto his nose, Jonny said, "Our first stop is the Kaeson Youth Park, a pet project of mine. I must warn you, shit's gonna get a little crazy when we get out of the car. Try not to get trampled."

We pulled up in front of a twinkling arch from which hung a metal banner inscribed with gold writing, the chauffer rushing to open the door for Jonny and me and bow us out of the car. It was almost as quiet on the street as it had been in the car, without the honking traffic, jackhammers, blaring sirens, and other typical ambient noises of a city; the loudest sound was that of the wind whooshing down empty streets. The first blush of spring had passed; the trees were minty green with fresh foliage, and the air held a sticky foretaste of the humidity that would come with the summer. The small crowd that awaited us on the other side of the arch began to churn with excitement, and a rhythmic clapping hailed our arrival.

Out in the sunlight, I could see powder clinging to the chub of Jonny's cheeks, a hint of eyeliner tightening the corners of his eyes. "Jonny"—I leaned close to look at his face—"are you wearing makeup?"

"Lisa," he explained in a joyful, sunny tone, smiling widely for the crowd, their faces set to pained euphoria as they watched our approach. "Out here, in front of my people, I am the sun and the moon, the oceans and the rivers, the green mountains and the fertile fields. I am a deity and you must treat me with the reverence that is my due."

We passed under the arch, whereupon a throng of comely young women in chaste but figure-flattering clothes rushed him with squeals and moans, trying to grab ahold of his arms, jostling me, but lightly, as they squirmed around me to get to Jonny. A smattering of older men in drab green military uniforms milled about at the fringes, shouldering each other out of the way. As the women pulled Jonny forward, he twisted his head around to shout to me as I was swept along in the tide: "These are the members of the all-girl band that I am forming. We will get a sneak preview of their act later tonight."

Though the women did not grab ahold of me as they did Jonny, they pushed me along gently, a few of the bolder ones darting curious looks my way, but mostly they seemed fascinated by the crystals on my shoes, which caught the sun in bedazzling flashes. They all seemed to know where they were going, rushing by the brightly colored metal girders that formed the familiar architecture of amusement, the same here as in the American heartland: brightly painted metal molded into serpentine coils, arced swoops, laddered pylons, and octopus-like tentacles.

We came to an abrupt stop in front of the vertiginous helix of a roller coaster, where Jonny asked me with a maniacal giggle, "Are you ready for the most thrilling ride of your life?"

"I don't really like roller coasters." I grimaced apologetically.

Slapping me hard on the back, Jonny cackled like I had just told a good joke, and a man firmly guided me toward the torpedo-shaped car, indicating I should use the metal rungs that extended from the bottom to stand belly-up to its hollowed-out plastic shell. I nervously gripped the handles that were at face-level as the man strapped me in, then lowered a metal shield to screen my face and that of the woman next to me, who had been chosen at random from the crowd and was already whimpering in terror. The car levitated with an electric hiss until we were suspended facedown over the platform. My mules fell off and the man obligingly picked them up, rubbing the velvet in wonder as he tucked them under an arm for safekeeping. Jonny waved at me from below.

"I thought you were going to ride with me!" I yelled.

Ho-ho-ho-ing like a jolly Santa Claus in a Mao suit, he said, "I would never be allowed to ride on such a dangerous machine. What if it malfunctions? It's been known to happen."

The ride shot off, twisting quickly around a corner, then climbing at an agonizing pace up, up, up, before plummeting down so fast I could feel my lips being blown back from my teeth. My companion was weeping hysterically, screaming the same phrase over and over. A whiplash turn, and then another, and I thought my head would dislocate from my neck. A few more stomach-churning flips and turns and then we were back at the beginning. As we disembarked, my neighbor threw up to the delighted cheers of the crowd.

"I was just joking about the safety of the ride, Lisa." Jonny giggled as he led us on to the next ride. "Just like any world-class amusement park, we are deadly serious about safety at Kaeson. Now, you simply have to experience the Spinning Wall of Death!" He rolled out an arm, presenting the ride with a jazz-hand wave.

I shook my head no but was already being spirited away by the same guy who had strapped me into the first ride, a muscular automaton programmed not to take no for an answer. There were many seats to fill on this ride, and most of the crowd was recruited, just a lucky few women left to cling gratefully to Jonny as they trilled encouraging words to their colleagues. The city of Pyongyang whirled like a kaleidoscope on fast-forward as the centrifugal force of the ride pinned my spine to the seat.

After I was made to go on the Spinning Saucer, Jonny announced it was lunchtime. He and I were the only ones to descend to the restaurant, where alluring photos of fast-food fare hung over the counter. Our meal was already waiting for us, double cheeseburgers nestled inside cardboard containers with a side of French fries in grease-blotted paper sleeves. A young beauty scampered up with a big bottle of beer, which she ceremoniously uncapped and lovingly poured into two small glasses. When I thanked her in my best Korean, Jonny laughed and admonished, "Please don't thank her. She has been told not to look us in the face, and by speaking to her, you might get her in trouble."

He tore into his burger, using his impressive front chompers to shear off chunks of meat, cheeks pouched with food as he chewed with openmouthed satisfaction, his fat tongue licking the ketchup off his lips. The wet sucking sounds of his mastication, combined with the sight of the macerated meat and the smell of griddle grease, did nothing to settle my stomach, still queasy from the rides. Breathing slowly and deliberately through my mouth, I stared at the pin on his chest, finding a small comfort in the airbrushed benevolence of the two elder Kims. After he had gobbled down his burger, he boomed, "Eat up, Lisa. Don't you know there are starving kids in Alabama?"

Feeling a little better, I took a sip of beer, thinking that the bubbles might be soothing to my stomach. He reached for my burger, lifting his upper lip to free his two front teeth to do their job.

"People say these are the best burgers in Asia," he declared, quickly scooping back a chunk of meat that threatened to escape his lips with a flip of his tongue. "I came up with the recipe myself."

He put the burger back in its little box, and not even thinking about it, more from reflex than anything else, I pulled the container back over to its rightful place in front of me.

His eyes goggled with astonishment, his small mouth rounded to a Cheerio, and I immediately realized my mistake.

"Oh god, I'm sorry, here, here, you finish it." I hastened to correct the situation, and then the angel of a serving girl swooped in to my rescue with a fresh, piping-hot cheeseburger.

He unleashed his signature full-toothed smile on me, which I recognized from the pin as the very copy of his grandfather's. "You know, Lisa," he said, warmly patting my arm, "I feel like you're the sister I've always deserved. Someone I can joke around with; someone who is my equal, almost; someone who will love me unconditionally."

Ever a whore for approval, I actually felt a twinge of pride that this overindulged man who had a whole nation of people vying for his affections liked me. As he sunk his teeth into the virgin burger, grease spurted down his jacket and onto his pin, blurring the smiles of his illustrious forefathers.

The server swayed gracefully between us, pouring glasses of beer with a perfect cap of foam, before retreating with tiny, mincing backward steps.

"I've liked you from the moment we met at Honey Do. You tell it like it is. I'm surrounded by people who tell me what they think I want to hear. The only person who is honest with me is Pops, but he can be a real asshole about it because he's jealous of me, of my youth, of the fact that he has to die soon while I will live on. It's what made him wait so long to announce me as his heir. His years of silence have emboldened the hyenas who cringe on their bellies before me, drowning me in flattery, all the while dreaming of the day when they gather to feast upon my carcass." He pawed gently at my shoulder. "To show you how much I trust you, I'll answer any of your questions about North Korea. Ask me about the prison camps, the drug running, the nuclear program, that goddamned satellite photo of the Korean peninsula at night, anything. Go on. I know you want to."

"Um..." I stalled by taking a bite of the cheeseburger. It was actually pretty good, a real taste of home. Chewing slowly, I formulated a question that was impertinent but not offensive. "Uh, well, Kaeson was pretty amazing, but wouldn't it be better to spend the money it took to build Kaeson on feeding your people?"

"Have you seen any starving people in Pyongyang?" he asked, fingers scuffling in the paper bag for the last few stubs of French fries.

"Not Pyongyang, no. But some of the people we passed on the way..."

The serving girl materialized like some sort of kitchen genie with another serving of fries.

"Your country's propaganda department loves to go on about famine in our country. Sometimes, not often, but yes, I admit it does happen here in North Korea, we have drought or we have floods. Then the people must make do with less. They are happy to do that. They know that is the price of freedom from the American imperialist bastards."

"Do you make do with less at those times?" I oh-so-gently mused.

"Now, Lisa." He wagged a finger at my sophomoric logic. "Do you ask your president to go without breakfast because there are American children whose parents can't afford to feed them? Do you expect your politicians to go homeless until everyone in the country has a roof over their heads? Do you not go to the doctor because the poor in your country are denied access to health care?"

"Jonny, I saw a little boy wearing a plastic bag," I whispered.

He shrugged, belched, and then shrugged again. "And I've seen the homeless wearing plastic bags for shoes in your country. You Americans think, because you outsource your human exploitation to foreign shores, that you are blameless in the misery that you wreak upon this earth. While you talk about your lofty principles of democracy and equality, people are worked to death and their homelands poisoned for your ease and comfort. Ask the tantalum miners of the Congo, the gold prospectors of Peru, the seamstresses of Bangladesh, or the oil pirates of the Niger Delta. Instead of examining your own role in exploiting the masses and raping the earth, you westerners like to point fingers at other countries, like ours, that they have deemed their enemies based on some arbitrary classification that serves their political interests. Are we really more of a threat to your country than China, with its billion people, nuclear arsenal, and aggressive territorial moves in the South China Sea? No, but it serves the propagandistic purposes of your leaders to pretend as if we were." Satisfied that he had schooled me, he leaned over to refill my glass, much to the distress of the serving girl, who fluttered up to take the bottle from his hands so that he might not debase himself any further. "Any other questions?"

Since he seemed to be in such a good mood, I asked a question whose answer I really did want to know. "Did you ever consider that I had a pretty good life before you brought me here?"

His laughter rattled like machine-gun fire. "You weren't doing anything with your life. *Now* you'll do something with your life."

When Jonny waved away a fourth cheeseburger, the serving girl brought out a tray of hot towels and carefully wiped him down, lovingly patting his chin and mouth clean, swabbing off each fat finger, and cleaning the congealed grease from his pin with a careful reverence.

The entourage was waiting for us outside, and once again the ladies skirmished among themselves to link arms with Jonny as we quick-time marched to the bumper cars, where to the relief of everyone with a vagina, it was men only, Jonny himself wedging his rotundness into one of the tiny vehicles and gleefully ramming any officer who was hapless enough to get in his way. I couldn't get out of the Drop Tower, but compared with the Spinning Wall of Death, it was as tame as a Ferris wheel. The excursion culminated with Jonny riding the carousel as the rest of us cheered him on with adoring applause.

The women pushed and shoved one another to get in a last touch to his sleeve as they escorted us back to the Rolls-Royce. Some gained the courage to walk side by side with me, bending their faces down to my shoes with the same yearning expression with which they looked at Jonny, hypnotized by the bling. As we pulled away, I looked through the rear window to see the women bursting into nervous laughter, their pretty faces stamped with abject relief and the men lighting each other's cigarettes with shaking hands.

Jonny consulted his Rolex. "We have some time to kill. What about a driving tour of Pyongyang?"

"I'd rather meet Sally, if I could?" I suggested.

"Who?"

"Sally, your bride."

"Oh, no, no, no." He waggled his hand as if chasing the idea away. "You will never meet my real family."

The sedate pace of the Rolls told me we were in no hurry to go anywhere. As we passed an electric tram crammed with people, some of the more alert passengers noticed the car and pressed their anguished faces ardently to the window, mouths and noses smashed flat against the glass. "How do they know it's you?"

"They know it is either me or Pops. We are the only ones who ride in the silver car with the winged lady."

"Do you and your father share this Rolls?" I asked, stroking the creamy leather of the seat.

"No. Pops's car is even more fly than this. It's got a bar built into the front here and the seats have footrests that fold out with a press of a button. How sick is that?"

We drove by muscular, grandiose monuments: the Arch of Triumph of Ideals, the Chollima Statue, and the Mansudae Grand Monument, where I got out to pay my respects to Il Sung. "Buy flowers to lay at the foot of the statue," Jonny advised. I didn't have any money, and neither did he, so his chauffer had to cough up a few limp, well-worn won.

"Pretty impressive, huh?" Jonny demanded when I returned to the car. "Pops will get his own statue when he goes to the great Mount Paektu in the sky. The craftsmen have already finished it."

"Someday you'll get your own statue," I gushed fawningly.

"Yeah." He nodded, jowls trembling with satisfaction. "I already know how it's gonna look. I'll be brandishing a model of a nuclear bomb like a big middle finger to the world."

"I thought North Korea was in talks to end its nuclear weapons program," I said as we cruised slowly by Sungryong Hall, remembering the heavy coverage of the issue on NHK News.

"That's just a little bit of harmless flirtation to make the imperialist bastards think we're ready to spread our legs for them. Meanwhile, we're this close"—he held up his chubby fist, thumb and forefinger almost kissing—"to developing a ballistic missile that can deliver our bombs all the way to the Pacific shores of the American bastards." When he saw the shocked look on my face, he patted my knee reassuringly. "Don't worry, Lisa, we'll try not to use them. Ah, here we are!"

He knocked against the window, and the car came to a stop in front of a gray ship tethered like a forgotten old burro to a concrete dock.

"Proof that we kicked the imperialist bastards' ass once and we can do it again."

"What is it?" I squinted at the small vessel, a troupe of schoolchildren filing up the gangplank.

"The USS *Pueblo*. Captured in 'sixty-eight spying in our waters. I'm surprised you didn't learn about it in school. Every North Korean schoolchild knows the story. We humiliated the American bastards, making them eat shit for eleven months, only releasing the crew after your government signed a written apology for spying on North Korea and promising not to spy on us again. But once we had honored our part of the agreement, your country retracted the apology, the admission, and the promise. It was a valuable lesson to my grandfather, which he passed down to his son, who passed it down to me. All Americans are lying scum, and any agreement they make isn't worth the paper it's written on because it won't be honored by the US and therefore doesn't have to be honored by us." He rapped angrily on the driver's window before flopping back into his seat, chewing at the inside of his lip with a disgusted expression on his face.

The tour seemed to be over, the car accelerating to motorcade speed, leaving the downtown behind and winding up into the hills, in whose crevices were hidden large buildings that bore a startling similarity to McMansions. I thought perhaps Jonny had grown tired of me, for he lit a cigarette and didn't speak until he had smoked it down to its gold-tipped filter. Finally, he growled ominously, "Wonder if Moms has noticed if you're missing yet. I hope not. For your sake, I really, really hope not." But then he turned back into good dictator, bestowing me with one of his grandfather's openmouthed smiles to declare, "Now you'll see how we party Pyongyang style. Tonight I debut my all-girl band. It's gonna blow the generals' little minds."

We entered a long, curving driveway to stop in front of a colonnaded hall, where a man in military uniform hastened to open our door. I trailed Jonny as we made our way through a cavernous banquet room, the assembled cadres and military brass standing to greet us, hands blurring in frenetic applause, eyes pinned with fanatical adoration on their leader, then fastening on me as soon as he had passed by, staring with frank curiosity. Jonny, it seemed, was the only person in North Korea who was allowed to walk slowly, and though he didn't stop to shake anyone's hand, he did slap some of his favorites on the back as we strolled to the front of the room, leaving whispers of speculation about me in our wake.

"These are my inner circle, the allies who I will rely upon to fight off the traitorous jackals. It is for perks such as this that they are loyal to me," Jonny confided.

We sat alone at a table close to the stage, far enough from the other tables that we could not be overheard, each with our own pretty server to pour our drinks, serve our food, and, occasionally, wipe our mouths.

The musicians, youthful beauties in slinky black dresses, began to take their places onstage to thunderous applause that stuttered into a bewildered silence as the singers followed them. "They have never seen so much leg before," Jonny squealed with delight to me, his hands describing an hourglass to approximate the way the singers' sequined dresses clung to their every curve, the hems just barely covering the globes of their rear ends.

While the generals gaped with drop-jawed fascination as the singers wiggled and gyrated through their first song, Jonny kept looking back at them, aping their shocked expressions and roaring with laughter. Dead silence followed the last notes of the song, the girls giving one final titty shake. Jonny leapt to his feet, clapping so that his cheeks quaked, and then all hell broke loose as the men rose up with a sex-fevered howl.

"No one in this room is ever going to forget tonight as the moment that they realized it's no longer their father's North Korea," Jonny crowed.

As the performers continued to bump and grind and the liquor flowed, the banqueters began to spin their servers onto their laps and put their hands up their skirts.

Jonny gazed happily at the scene, taking obvious delight in the revelry of his men, and I felt a surge of affection for him, my only known blood sibling. Sure, he was a bloodthirsty half-blood sibling, but he was flesh of my flesh, and most important, he really seemed to like me. I knew that because he had his arm slung about my shoulders, gently hugging me to him as he said, "You and I are as close to each other as teeth and lips, Lisa. You know, I too was raised by a woman who was not my own mother. I understand that about you, how it has wounded your heart and warped your mind. But I see it has also made you strong, because you realize you only have yourself to rely upon. It's you against the world. They've taken away your mother, and nothing that happens after that will ever hurt as much. It either destroys you or makes you invincible."

Chapter 11

"I think that is the fear and why I didn't search [for my birth parents] earlier. I was afraid that I'd find somebody or something worse than what I knew."

-Christina Crawford

I was Cinderella fleeing the ball at the stroke of midnight, my elegant coach turned into a humble Toyota sedan, a crochet doily covering the headrest and grubby curtains hanging over the rear passenger seat windows, the air tinged with stale cigarette smoke and midlevel cadre flop sweat, but in my inebriation I barely noticed, the soft hum of the engine and the gentle undulations of the vehicle rocking me to sleep before we had even left Pyongyang. Next thing I knew, Frankenstein's monster was ushering me down the rabbit hole and back to my room, where I toppled into bed and didn't open my eyes again until Ting brought in my breakfast, the same two soft-boiled eggs, buttered toast cut into strips, and French press pot of coffee as always. Hopeful that this meant that Honey had not noticed my absence, I tried to get an answer from Ting, asking, "All good here, yes or no?" in my broken Chinese. Normally, she would have continued picking up my clothes from the floor as if she hadn't heard me, but this time she paused, clutching the black polyester Paradise skirt to her chest, and gave me a wide-eyed glance of... warning? Fear? Disgust? I couldn't tell. The egg I had just scooped up turned into a slimy gob of spit at the back of my throat.

During the days of lockdown that ensued, Ting retreated into cringing servant mode, looking down at all times, black wings of hair falling over her face like blinders. When I tried to confront her by standing in her path or putting my foot in the way of the vacuum nozzle, she merely cleaned around me, like a worker ant with an instinctual compulsion to complete the task at hand. One day, I grabbed her arm and shook her, but still she refused to look at me, her thin arm slippery like steel, glissading from my grasp.

To get my mind off its did-she-or-didn't-she-notice-I-was-gone merry-go-round, I devoured the modern Korean history books that Honey had sent me, which read like the goriest of Shakespeare's tragedies, the kind where everybody dies in the end. What a blighted and hard-used country I had been born in, a tonsil off the immense and voracious gullet of Asia, a tiny pawn to the imperialistic ambitions of its neighbors, each one harboring its own crazed dreams of total world domination. There were no heroes, only villains. The Kims were the mirror image of their corrupt and despotic South Korean counterparts—one left and the other right, one serving a red master and the other a red, white, and blue one—each the very profile in greed, arrogance, and bloodlust. The Americans, Stalin, and Mao just trying to add points to the scoreboard, splitting the country like an atom, into the yin and the yang, the East and the West, until never the twain can meet.

The day after I started reading *The Two Koreas* for a second time, Ting brought me a missive from Honey. My fingers trembled as I struggled to remove the thick linen paper from the envelope.

Baby,
I've missed you sooo much! But finally I am free to spend time
with you. The Gang is here, and we have an afternoon of fun and games
planned. Dress accordingly. Ting will bring you after lunch.
XOXO,
Honey

Clutching the note to my lips, I crumpled jelly-spined onto my bed. All was well. She wasn't punishing me; she had just been completely consumed with tending to Jong Il, and then maybe after he left she got a celebratory nip-tuck from Dr. Panzov. She was blissfully ignorant about my short visit—less than twenty-four hours!—to Pyongyang. The bit about the Gang niggled at me—how long had they been here?—but I got busy making myself into the spackle-faced, blow-dried, poreless me that Honey wanted me to be, pushing all doubt from my mind.

Eyebrows freshly plucked, moles hidden under a plaster mask of foundation and powder, my hair in a high ponytail with artful wisps framing my face, I bounced after Ting as she guided me through a series of corridors into a gently declining tunnel that ended in a bright emerald field of fake grass, which permeated the air with the synthetic smell of plastic. Under the blare of stadium-bright LED lights that hung from the ceiling, we walked across the field toward a swimming pool, the reflection of the lights off the water glinting and swirling across the ceiling, which was painted the same blue as the pool. The walls were also painted blue, giving the arena the aura of an undersea aquarium, we the creatures on display. A gentle, constant stream of air wafted across the cavernous room, filling my nostrils and pushing air into my lungs as if to do my breathing for me.

Bobbing like a melting iceberg in the pool, the pale crown of his belly poking out of the water, Harvey shouted, "Look who it is everyone! Lisa's back!"

As the others shouted their greetings, Patience, wearing a muumuu that looked like it was sewn from bedsheets, greeted me with a hug.

Wendell sidled up to slap me on the back. "We've missed you!" he shouted. Then, leaning in close so that his sharp nose prodded my ear, he whispered, "Find a moment to talk with me before Madam arrives."

Lahela, in a pair of saggy bloomer-like shorts that looked like they had been excavated from the 1850s, took my hand in hers and touched it to her forehead. They all scattered like backyard birds the moment Yolanda swooped in.

"Hello, Lisa," Yolanda greeted me coolly, taking me in from head to toe before delivering a curt nod of approval, her ponytails, sprouting from the top of her head like horns, sparking red in the light. "Not bad."

This was the first time I had seen her out of business or cocktail attire, and in sports bra and capri leggings, she looked like a cover girl for a hard-body health magazine, sinewy shoulders rippling, stomach flat and plated with muscle, legs shapely and well defined. Until you got to her face, the warped rictus of her features and the lumpiness of her skin delivering a shock that any horror-movie auteur would envy. "Madam wishes me to inform everyone that she will join us poolside this afternoon. She said she feels like a bit of volleyball."

"Ooh," everyone said, turning to look at Patience. ·

"Volleyball? Oh, no, Mma!" she wailed, to general laughter.

Her husband stretched his neck out of the water to yell over the mound of his stomach, "I'm rooting for ya, baby!'

"What, do Patience and Honey have a rivalry?" I asked Yolanda.

"Let's just say Patience is scared of the ball." Yolanda winked. I pictured her in the dead of night somewhere deep in the bowels of the compound ruthlessly working the StairMaster, spinning the miles away on the Exercycle, pushing past the pain for that one extra sit-up, giving herself to Madam mind, body, and soul.

Joining Patience and Lahela, who were stretched out on plastic-slatted chaise longues, I casually inquired of them how long they had been at the villa, relieved when Patience answered that they had arrived only the day before. Alert for any hint of change in their attitude toward me, I chatted them up and was further mollified when they responded with their customary shy, or maybe reticent, friendliness, Patience doing the talking for the two of them, as Lahela was slow and halting with her English. I learned that she had never heard a word of English spoken until she met and married Wendell. When I asked how she had come to North Korea from Laos, she blushed and looked down at her lap, whispering, "Sec."

Reaching a hand to place it over Lahela's, Patience explained, "She entertained officers in the army."

"Oh, Lahela!" I murmured, taking up her other hand. Startled, she glanced at me with her velvety brown doe eyes, and when she saw the tears limning my lower lids, let me hold her hand.

"What's up, ladies?" Wendell interrupted us. Noticing that Lahela and I were holding hands—Patience had heard him coming and yanked hers away—his wet lips spread like a grease slick over teeth that were one size too big for his mouth. "Hey, Lisa, no one gets to hold Lahela's hand unless I can watch."

"We were just having some girl talk, Wendell. Don't worry, it wasn't about you," I said, giving Lahela's hand a squeeze before I let go.

"Oh, darn, I love it when the ladies talk about me," Wendell brayed, before bending to press his spitty lips to the top of Lahela's head. "OK, girls, I'm going to set up the volleyball net. Would you like to help me, Lisa?"

Though my skin crawled at being on the receiving end of his leering attention, I went with him, Harvey lifting his menhir head from the water to follow our progress around the pool. As we crossed the field, Wendell pointed out the sockets that were set into the turf, explaining at full volume that they were for poles, goal posts, and croquet hoops, before ushering me inside the equipment shed, where he asked sotto voce, "Do you still want my help?"

Looking around to see if there was something I could knock him over the head with if he tried anything on me, I nodded.

"Good. I've got a plan. You want to hear it?"

Edging toward the croquet mallets, I nodded again.

"Where are those damn volleyballs?" he suddenly yelled in my face, lips exuding into a smile when I startled backward into the croquet mallets, knocking the stand over. As I scrabbled around for the scattered mallets, he described his plan, words hissing from his mouth like air escaping a punctured tire. "The fellow who's in charge of delivering the food and supplies here was a student of mine, and now he's a fishing buddy. I've done plenty of favors for him, and so he's agreed to personally drive the supply truck here and smuggle you back to Pyongyang hidden in one of the garbage bins." He began to rummage among the equipment. "Look for the net, will you?"

"What'll happen to me in Pyongyang?"

"He'll give you a change of clothes and a disguise, a wig and maybe a pair of glasses, something like that, and you'll walk out of the warehouse and I'll meet you, take you somewhere safe." Then he screeched, "Come on, Lisa, find the damn net!"

"Stop screaming, you're just making it more obvious! Where will you take me?"

"I can't tell you, but I swear you'll be safe." His eyes goggled about, not meeting my own.

"Why can't you tell me?"

"Because it wouldn't be safe!" he snapped. "Come on, find that net unless you want Yolanda coming in here."

"This?" I grabbed up some webbed nylon.

"No, that's the tennis net. The blue one below it. We can carry it off, Lisa, but I'm going to need five thousand dollars."

"Five thousand dollars? Are you crazy? Where the fuck would I get five thousand dollars? I haven't seen a single greenback since I've been here."

"This guy's not going to do it for free, Lisa. And I'll need another thousand for Cookie."

"Cookie?!"

"Yeah, all deliveries come in through the kitchen, and all the garbage goes out from there. You need his buy-in. I can help you raise money by selling things you swipe from the villa—small trinkets, clothes, and whatnot."

I shook my head skeptically. "That would never work. Honey would be sure to notice."

He shrugged as if that was a minor and unimportant detail. "It's been working for years now."

"You've been stealing from Honey for years?"

"I haven't. Other people do the stealing. I am merely the person who turns the goods into money. You just have to be careful to take the things that she won't miss. For instance, never try to steal the booze; she and Yolanda keep a pretty sharp eye over the cellar. But maybe a silver candlestick here, a crystal tumbler there. Fancy ashtrays are in high demand, as are drugs, if you ever happen to be able to get your hands on any."

"You're a fence!" I accused him.

But to him it was not an accusation, just simple reality. "We all have to get by, Lisa. I'm only trying to help you. I help you, you help me—that's the way things work here. Think about it and give me an answer tomorrow. Or the next day. Or next month. There's no hurry. We've got the rest of our lives." He put the poles under his arm and shouldered a bag of volleyballs before stepping out of the shed.

We were just about done setting up the net when Honey floated in. "Wheeeere's my baaaaby?" she shrieked.

"Hi, Honey." I gave her an embarrassed little wave.

Folding me in her arms, she pressed my face down to her chest. "I've missed you, Lisa! Did you miss me?"

"Of course, Honey." I rubbed a cheek on the soft valley of her cleavage.

She held me at arm's length, pretending to get a good look at me but, of course, wanting me to get a good look at her, to notice how radiant she looked, how the low-cut sports shirt hugged her fabulous curves, how her arms were toned, the skin taut and smooth. I gushed, "Oh my god, Honey, you look amazing!"

"You look..." She bathed me with her aquamarine gaze. "...a little different. I can't put my finger on it." She reached out and briefly cupped my breast, but before I could pull away, she lifted the hand to cradle my chin. "Oh, Lisa, you're growing into a beautiful woman before my eyes. Yolanda tells me you're putting your makeup on all by yourself. If only you'd agree to a little..." She curved her hand in a generous arc over her own generous bosom.

As if summoned by her thoughts, there was Dr. Panzov behind her, surprisingly trim and muscular in a tight tank top and short shorts, striped tube socks sheathing rock-hard calves. "Lisa! You are looking well."

"Isn't she, Vlad? I was just telling her she could look even more fabulous with a little help from you. Imagine how much more flattering that adorable Fendi T-shirt would look if it had more to cling to!"

Dr. Panzov trained the small blue dots of his eyes on my chest, and I quickly zipped up my hoodie. Honey summoned Yolanda to stand with us on our side of the net, before quavering to the others, "Let's play ball!"

It was the four of us versus Wendell, Harvey, Patience, and Lahela. And though Wendell and Harvey had a definite height advantage, Lahela batted ineffectually at the ball with open-handed slaps, and Patience ran away from the ball instead of toward it. Whenever she got the layup, Honey drove the ball as hard as she could at Patience, whooping with delight when the ball found its target with a painful smack. I was no star on the volleyball court, but buoyed by my teammates, I managed to make a few good shots as well as a lot of lousy ones, some of which Honey insisted were in bounds when they were out, which caused Wendell's sunken cheeks to redden with rage, though he dared say nothing in protest. We beat them 32–18.

The activities that ensued seemed designed as an exercise in humiliation for one or the other of the Gang. There was a men's swimming competition, with Dr. Panzov thrashing through the water, beating Harvey handily while practically drowning Wendell, who sputtered and choked on his churning wake. Then followed a round robin of badminton, during which Yolanda made Lahela chase the birdie so much that she slipped and scraped up her knee, and a croquet match, where Honey continually ruled Yolanda's ball out of bounds while looking the other way for me. The Gang would obediently taunt and belittle the weakest player, alliances and enmities eddying and pooling, unceasing and changeable as the tides. Because I enjoyed Honey's favor, no one dared heckle me, even when I really sucked, like in horseshoes, where I almost clocked Harvey when a shoe slipped from my hand prematurely. Bathing in the warm glow of Honey's favor, beholden to her for either ignoring or being ignorant of my Pyongyang field trip, I enthusiastically played my part as jeerer in chief, peanut in her gallery, sharp-toothed cog in her machine.

At the end of the afternoon, Honey herself accompanied me back to my room, her arm around my waist as she and I exchanged compliments in elated tones, Yolanda trailing us disconsolately. "I had Ting deliver some fabulous dresses to your room today. I can't wait to see which one you pick for tonight," she said, before she left me at my door with air kisses and a sharp pinch to the cheek.

There were three dresses, and I had to try them all on, for though they fit me beautifully everywhere else, they all had expectations for my bust that my bust couldn't fill. I chose a shimmering silver cowled slip dress, pulling the shoulders back so the neck scooped higher, knowing that it was inevitable that after a cocktail or two, the dress would slip down. Honey was delighted with my look, which I had paired with dangling silver earrings and a silver mesh lariat, though she made a point to tut-tut over my hair and pull at the soft folds of the cowl, proclaiming, "Just think how much better this dress would look draped over a pair of beautiful C-cup breasts."

At dinner, where I occupied the coveted seat to the right of Honey, she asked, "Who wants to watch a movie tonight? Lisa?"

"Great idea!" I cheered, sinking my knife into the weeping flesh of a perfectly crusted lamb chop.

A fork clattered from Lahela's grip. "Oh, pardon, pardon," she muttered in a shaky voice, her coppery skin suddenly tarnishing green.

"The movie's still in theaters in the States," Honey gushed. "We're seeing it even before it's available on DVD!"

"Ooh!" I warbled, impressed.

"What movie is it?" Wendell asked, sounding as if he were choking on his Adam's apple.

"*The Green Hornet*. Starring your favorite movie star, Vlad!"

Dr. Panzov forced a dry chuckle. "Oh? Eh-heh-heh-heh? Which one is that?" He took a showy bite of scalloped potato, swallowing it down with a taut, sinewy jerk of his neck.

"Cameron Diaz, of course!"

"Oh, yes, of course!" His thin lips jerked into an unconvincing grin.

No one contributed much to the banter after that besides Honey and me, but who could blame them? After a long afternoon of physical activity, we were tired. Still, it hadn't happened before, a lag in the conversation. Usually at least Harvey and Wendell could be counted on to vie with each other with the more dipshit observation or wandering, pointless story.

When Honey announced it was time to retire to the theater, I poured myself a hefty glass of cognac and was up and ready while the others dithered at the table, Patience searching ostentatiously for her shawl, Wendell folding his napkin meticulously back into shape, Lahela just sitting there, staring helplessly in front of her. Finally, Dr. Panzov led the way, me right on his heels, thinking how nice it would be to sit and stare at a screen and not have to interact with the others, whose company I was already sick of. Pleasantly surprised to see Miura-san already seated in the back row of the theater, I collapsed into the seat next to him. "What's up, my man?"

Shoulders rounded in on themselves as if he were trying to take up as little space as possible, he giggled nervously in response.

"Hey"—I patted him warmly on the arm—"great job with the rack of lamb! Honey was really pleased. That must be why she invited you to watch the movie tonight."

He ducked and squirmed in acknowledgment. Taking a handkerchief out of the front pocket of his frayed suit jacket, he passed it over the sweat beading his plated brow.

Harvey blundered into my chair on his way in. In a group of problem drinkers, Harvey was by far the most problematic. "Hey, Harvey, you're pissed! Drink a coffee!" I hectored. When I turned back to Miura-san, I was surprised to see him violently rubbing his palms over his thighs, face stretched into an anguished grimace.

"What's wrong, Miura-san?" I asked.

A small groan escaped Miura-san, and he patted his upper lip with his handkerchief.

"Lisa, you're up front with me," Honey commanded as she swept by, the gauzy hem of her dress fluttering after her. "Lights!" she called out as I slipped into the seat next to her. "Roll the preview!"

She leaned over and tapped me affectionately on the knee. I grinned and raised my cognac glass at her before nestling into the plush embrace of the chair, ready to enjoy the show.

A collective sigh of relief whooshed up into the air as a close-up of a familiar face filled the screen. It took me a moment to realize that the face was mine, and I was kissing Honey's note of this morning, my face slack with relief. In a blink, that image was gone, replaced by me asleep, my eyes twitching with dreams, jaw flexing as I ground my teeth.

What the fuck? I wondered at my sleeping self, who groaned and gnashed away.

Cutaway to me taking my pajamas off and then my underpants, pausing to scratch at my belly.

"You have a tattoo? What is it of?" Wendell asked as I headed naked into the bathroom. A quick cut and there I was, sitting on the toilet, an intense look of concentration on my face. I was taking a shit.

"Oh my god," I whispered. "Honey, what is this?"

Another shot of me, wearing only underpants, rubbing at my clitoris as I writhed on my bed. A close-up as my jaw waggled back and forth and my eyes squeezed shut. "Orgasm!" Harvey shouted, as if announcing a touchdown.

Next I was in the shower, washing the crack of my ass. Then I was puking into the toilet. An extended shot of me compulsively chewing the inside of my mouth as I read. "That repulsive habit she has of biting the inside of her lip is just another form of masturbation," Yolanda pronounced in a stage whisper, and Dr. Panzov tittered in agreement.

Followed by a shot of me actually masturbating, this time in the shower. Then me standing in a stream of sunlight, shaking the dandruff from my hair. Gouging a finger deep into a nostril. Another close-up shot of me in the throes of sexual self-satisfaction, a thread of saliva trickling from my gaping mouth. Wiping my ass. Picking at a zit. In deep conversation with my reflection in the mirror. Rolled up in a tight ball on my bed, crying. Standing in front of the full-length mirror with my hands in my underpants.

I heard the soft tones of Lahela chime in with the general catcalls and abuse that came from the men. "She is insatiable."

"Total horndog!" her husband happily agreed.

I put my hands over my eyes. "Make it stop!"

"That's not a giant mole on her ass, it's a yin-yang tattoo!" Harvey announced triumphantly.

"Gives new meaning to up the yin-yang, eh?" Wendell crowed.

"Is one breast larger than the other, I wonder?" Dr. Panzov asked. "What do you think, Cookie? You are an expert on child-sized breasts. Is she uneven?"

"Most definitely," Miura-san readily answered. With a chuckle.

"Why are you doing this to me?" I screamed, jumping out of the chair. "Stop it!"

"Sit down!" Honey grabbed a handful of my skirt and tugged at it with some violence, handling it rather roughly for a Tory Burch. "You're blocking the view of the people behind."

"Why does she always look at the toilet paper after she's wiped her bum? Is that an American thing?" Patience inquired.

"Sit down, Lisa! You don't want me to have the men subdue you, do you?" Honey warned from between clenched teeth.

"Why are you doing this to me?" I implored.

"She does touch her privates a lot, doesn't she?" Lahela noted loudly. "Even more than you, Wendell."

Laughter erupted throughout the room.

"You're being ridiculous, Lisa!" Honey hissed, releasing the crumpled fabric of my dress with a spiteful swat at my thighs. "This is your last chance to behave yourself."

Whirling about, I caught a glimpse of myself drunkenly humping a pillow, eyes lidded and glazed, body rocking in an animal motion that expressed neither pleasure nor excitement but just vacuous compulsion. Of course I had been warned about the cameras, but I didn't know they could see in the dark or in the shower. And I certainly didn't know that what they recorded would be broadcast for public consumption. "Fuck you!" I screamed, and lunged up the dark aisle toward the door. The lights blazed on, revealing Miura-san at the switch.

As I clawed at the doorknob, I heard Dr. Panzov's soft voice behind me. "You've really done it now, Lisa."

His hand gripped my shoulder and jerked me around, his face glowing phosphorescent with joy, a wide, sadistic grin pushing his cheeks into doughy dumplings. Then a fast approaching fist eclipsed his grin, until the last thing I saw was an enormous gold ring glittering with a cabochon-cut bloodred ruby that got closer and closer until the whole world went red and then black.

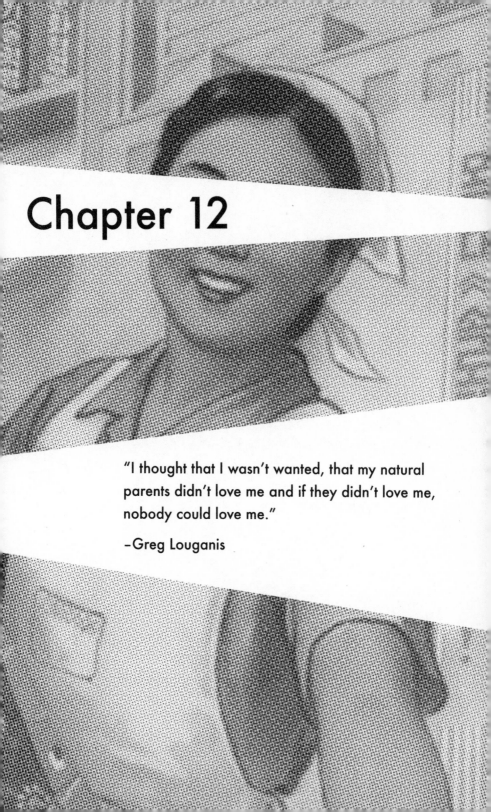

Chapter 12

"I thought that I wasn't wanted, that my natural parents didn't love me and if they didn't love me, nobody could love me."

–Greg Louganis

Chapter 12

When I finally unloosed myself from the sticky, insistent embrace of the unconsciousness that was holding me too tightly, too dearly, I was in a windowless, dimly lit cubicle. From somewhere inside my body, pain pulsated like a second sickening heartbeat. Was I in a hospital? An insane asylum? I felt pretty insane, like I was trapped in some sort of psychotic delusion. I concentrated on my pain, tracking it to its volcanic core, the trail of molten lava leading to my head. I tried to bring my hands up to my face to explore further, but they wouldn't move. The inside of my left arm ached, and when I looked down I saw needle bruises blooming like night flowers on the white flesh, some creeping in long snail trails up the veins, and brown leather tightly circling my wrists. The portal for an IV was buried into the back of a hand, but there was nothing attached to it. Panic mounting, I yanked desperately at the straps, but they held tight.

Returning to Boston for my last year of college, I started dabbling in pharmaceuticals, particularly depressants, particularly OxyContin. Mindy was all about getting into medical school in New York, where she'd live with Trip while he attended law school, and what little free time she had was parceled out between me and Trip. When graduation finally came, the rules of inertia kept me in Boston, working as a receptionist in a law firm that specialized in asbestos litigation. Mindy, of course, had been accepted to Columbia, and in July she and Trip moved into a floor-through, one-bedroom starter apartment in a prewar brownstone on East Seventy-Fifth Street.

Eight months later, I moved to New York City, ostensibly to get a job in publishing, but really because where Mindy was, so went I, as helpless to her gravitational pull as Earth to the sun. But I hated the city, seeing only ugliness wherever I looked: rats creeping along the subway rails, dog shit smearing the pavement, trash clotted against the curbs, people shouting abuse at each other, beggars baring their stumps for loose change. My heart broke every time I ventured out the door of my tiny Flatbush studio until it was so cracked that it could hold nothing but loneliness and loathing. Though I couldn't find anyone to employ me, I could find a drug dealer, and, swaddled in a dark veil of opioids, I hid away in my apartment, emerging only for takeout, job interviews, scoring more drugs, and dates with Mindy. After one particularly embarrassing dinner where I knocked over not one but two wineglasses and dipped the ends of my hair in my soup as I sloppily tried to drink it up, she told me not to come and see her high anymore. Taking umbrage, I reared up from the table and slammed into a waiter, running out the door as china, cutlery, and glass hit the floor with a symphonic crash. Back in my tiny mouse hole, I crushed three 80 mg OxyContins, tipped the fine powder into my mouth, and washed it down with a PBR. Bliss rolled in to seal me in a glaze of unconsciousness, whose enchantment was broken when a tube was shoved down my throat. Crowned by a golden halo, a half-shrouded face dominated by spiky-lashed eyes peered down at me. Dead. I was dead and the God that I had never believed in had eyes like silverfish that were sizing me up, judging me, getting ready to consign me to the hungry maw of hell. But then he said, "What's her name again?" the tissue flesh of his blue mouth caving in, and I knew it wasn't the God that I didn't believe in because the God I didn't believe in knew everyone's name, all the people who ever were and all the people who would ever be. "You're a lucky girl, Lisa," the not-God told me. "A few more minutes and it would have been too late." I didn't have to ask what "it" was.

Maybe I was still at Brooklyn Hospital, and any moment Mindy would come in, tears streaming down flushed cheeks to hug me tightly. But no, I already had that memory of Mindy grabbing fistfuls of my hair as she sobbed, arms enfolding me tightly, heedlessly pulling the IV needle that was buried in my hand. And this room was too dark and narrow to be the room at the Brooklyn Hospital, which had fluorescent lights zizzing from the ceiling and a window that showed a patch of dirty sky. The same shame that I felt then infected me now, and I seized upon that shame, hugged it close, following its slinking trail until it led me to myself, or the image of myself, on the screen of a private theater in North Korea. I tried to scream but could manage only a brittle croak, like a stalk crunching underfoot. "Help! Please, somebody help!" I waited for a moment but knew that nobody would come. After a minor eternity, the gray light of the room melded with the gray twilight behind my eyelids, and I regained unconsciousness.

When next I came to, I was all alone behind a curtain, a soft, steady electronic blip sounding regularly, like a heartbeat. It was a heartbeat, I realized. Mine. My throat ached, bruised and violated, and my chest felt like a turtle with a cracked shell, vulnerable and broken. Shame filled me to overflowing, and I wished that I had never woken up. I, who had endeavored my whole life not to appear vulnerable or weak, was now exposed for all to see as a fraud and a failure. A heavy nurse with the dewlap of an ox pushed back the curtain.

"Oh, you awake?" she asked approvingly. "How you feeling, baby? Throat burn a little?"

My answer came out as an old man's wheeze, frightening in its impotence. I meant to say, "It hurts like hell." But while my lips formed the whole sentence, the only word that was audible, in a high, whistling whisper, was the last one. The nurse mistook my meaning.

"Oh, baby," she said, stroking my brow as she inserted a thermometer in my ear, "it's OK. Don't worry. You didn't die. You got another chance. Things are going to be fine with you." She had an accent that hinted at the sweet sea breezes and sweaty lassitude of the tropics. "The waiting room is full up with people anxious for your recovery. When they hear you are conscious, they're going to holler hallelujah like shouter Baptists. Your mama will be in as soon as we're done here." As she spoke, she checked my blood pressure, reviewed the recent history of my heartbeat, and hooked another bag of fluids to the tube that burrowed into the back of my hand.

"It hurts," I croaked.

"I know it does, baby, I know." Her stubby fingers, plump like hand-rolled cigars, stroked my forehead. "That hurt means you are healing. No pain, no gain."

Under her reassuring caress, I closed my eyes. When I opened them again, she was gone. Yet I could still feel her touch.

A moment later, the baby-blue curtain billowed and my mother tentatively stepped from behind it. "Lisa, oh, my daughter, oh, Lisa," she gasped, sinking to her knees by my bed and taking my hand in hers. "You gave us such a scare. Oh, Lisa, I promised myself I wouldn't cry." And then she bowed her head and started to bawl. Quickly getting to her feet, she wiped at her eyes and nose with the back of her hand. "These are not tears of recrimination," she hiccupped, "just tears of happiness."

"It was an accident, Mom," I rasped, every word like giving birth to a ten-pound baby through my windpipe. "I didn't try to kill myself. Only wanted to get high."

She tried to rearrange her face; everything shut, mouth, eyes, nostrils pinching in as she took a deep breath.

"For a little while, I was floating in the upper ether and everything felt so gooood." That electric rush and the sensation of falling weightless through space. Gone... gone... gone. "That's all it was, Mom. Really."

She nodded vigorously, her whole face writhing and jumping. "Scott and Mindy are out there, but they can't come in because they aren't blood relatives..."

"You neither," I croaked.

"What?"

"You're not a blood relative either," I pointed out.

Normally, my mother would have reacted with a laugh and a hug. But this time she hesitated, unsure what to do with my comment: Was it said in belligerence, shame, inadequacy? Or was it just a truthful observation, the kind that we made to each other regularly, openly acknowledging the peculiar circumstance of our relationship?

This was the legacy of my pursuit of the highest high. My own mother would now question the motivation for every comment I made, wondering if it was a veiled cry for help or a confession of pain. I had officially outted myself as "damaged" and deprived myself of the right to be ironic. "Because I'm adopted, Mom. Get it?" I forced the words out in as lighthearted manner as I could. I sounded like a bird caught in a snare.

With a fluttery giggle, my mother patted at her nose with a sodden tissue. "Yes, Lisa, I get it." A shuddering, deep intake of breath. "I feel so, oh, I don't know, negligent for not knowing how unhappy you have been lately."

Shame swelled big as a pumpkin inside my chest, squeezing everything else out. "This is not your fault, Mom. Please don't blame yourself." Hot tears slid from my eyes, plopping off my cheeks onto the hospital bed, staining into a wider and wider circle, until the circle of my tears intersected with the circle of my mother's.

"But, Lisa, I should have known something wasn't right. Mindy noticed—she said you had been, well, a little depressed since coming back from China and thinks you started to self-medicate then. She was the one who found you, you know. If she hadn't arrived when she did..." My mother clenched her fist in front of her mouth to stopper a fresh round of sobs.

"Mindy found me?" I asked, trying to keep up with my mother's racing, breathy narrative.

Hand wrapped protectively around her throat, my mother nodded rapidly. "She... she said that you two had an argument and you stormed out of the restaurant, already 'messed up,' as she called it. She tried to call, but you wouldn't pick up. Suddenly, an intuition took hold of her, and she jumped in a cab. She banged on your door, but there was no answer. So she called your cell and heard it ringing inside. Thank god you had given her a key to the apartment. She found you..." Fresh sobs. "...on the floor..." Silvery strands of saliva threaded her open mouth like cobwebs. "...lips blue..." Her limp little tissue was a soggy lump of uselessness in the palm of her hand. "...totally unresponsive. She gave you CPR until the ambulance arrived."

The change in pressure as the door opened woke me. My eyes didn't seem to be working right, as if I were wearing glasses whose lenses were too strong, and it took me a moment to recognize Yolanda, hair crackling with red, green Tilt-A-Whirl eyes ablaze. "Bloody hell, it stinks in here," she muttered to herself, patting the pockets of her power jacket, bringing out a silk handkerchief to place over her nose and mouth before stepping into the thin slot of space between my bed and the wall. "You look a fright, Lisa."

"I don't feel so good either," I groaned, suddenly aware of how my scalp crawled and my skin itched, of the thick carpet of scum on my teeth and the cheesy feeling in the folds of my skin. "Will you let me out of these straps?" I strained weakly against the leather.

The glassy gleam of her eyes told me she was enjoying herself. "Is that any way to ask for a favor?"

"Please, Yolanda, goddamn it. Please."

"It was for your own good," Yolanda said as she unbuckled the straps. "Dr. Panzov didn't want you ruining his handiwork."

"How long have I been here?" I asked as I rubbed at the chafed flesh of my wrists.

"You've been out for a few days. Madam thought it best to sedate you after the operation."

"Operation? What operation?"

"A Dr. Panzov operation. You are very lucky, you know. He's a leader in his field, and most people have to pay out the nose for what you got for free."

"Oh my fucking god," I gasped, my hands flying to my chest, relieved to find that my breasts fit snugly into my cupped palms, just as they always had.

"Not there," Yolanda cackled.

"Then where?" I asked, my fingers tentatively wandering to my face. The flesh around my eyes was swollen and sticky, narrowing my field of vision to a peephole, and it hurt to even lightly stroke the air around them. "My eyes?"

Yolanda blew softly on my face and something tickled my upper lip. When I tried to brush it away, I followed the filament to my nostrils and discovered that they were filled with something. I plucked at the strings with horror—another life-form had colonized my body, a moth maybe, crawling up my nose to spin its cocoon. A little wisp broke free, floating off my finger: cotton gauze. My gentle probing caused a lightning flash of pain, conjuring in its garish glare Dr. Panzov's fist flying toward my face. He must have broken my nose. Trying to keep my voice calm, I asked, "May I see a mirror? Please?"

"I've got something better," she said, unfolding the laptop she had been cradling in the crook of an arm. Angling the screen toward me, she pressed the power button and the machine started up with a hot exhalation and a whir. For a moment all I could see was the ghostly shimmer of my face reflected in the black screen, eyes puffed to slits and a swath of white straddling my nose; then the screen illuminated with me laid out on a gurney under a papery blue surgical drape, eyes shut, nose a swollen crescent, body limp. A figure in a blue scrub cap stepped into the frame. He looked at the camera with a grin. It was Dr. Panzov. Immediately, dread gripped me like a vise. "Noooo," I moaned. "Nooo, nooo."

"Oh, come on, Lisa, it hasn't even started yet," Yolanda purred, staring transfixed at the screen.

Someone else entered the camera's eye, swabbing at my cheeks and nose with a sponge, oily liquid clinging to my skin. The camera caught a glimpse of mismatched eyes as she bent to place a gauze mask over my mouth

"Is that you?" I slurred, my tongue thick and useless in my mouth.

"Yes." Yolanda snapped her fingers jubilantly. "I used to be the best damn OR nurse in Port Elizabeth. Shh, now." She nodded seriously at the computer screen, where Dr. Panzov was needling into my nostrils with a scalpel and slicing through the septum flap. Blood oozed languidly down my cheeks, and Dr. Panzov dabbed it away with an almost tender regard.

"My nose?" I wheezed, my hand flying up to stroke the bandage that covered it, sending staticky crackles of pain through my body.

Offscreen, Yolanda winked hard at me, while on-screen, she handed Dr. Panzov a hook, which he used to lift the skin off my nose, exposing the glistening red underflesh. Yolanda held the hook in place as he began to snip away at the cartilage, sometimes pressing so hard that my whole face sank in. He extracted a bloody shard, small as a baby's tooth, and set it on a tray that lay just outside the camera's eye.

"I think I'm going to be sick," I said, bile washing up the back of my throat.

"Oh, don't be a nuisance," Yolanda groaned, leaning over to pick up an enamel pot from under the bed.

Hot saliva began to foam out of my mouth, and I curved over the enamel bowl, expelling little clouds of spit.

"Shall I pause it?" Yolanda asked impatiently, the smooth vermilion hook of her fingernail hovering over the keyboard.

I shook my head. "It's almost over," I said, more to myself than to her.

But it wasn't almost over. When I looked back at the screen, Yolanda was hammering a flat chisel deep into my nose. "I'm breaking up that knot of bone that forms the bridge. That is, that formed the bridge," she helpfully explained. Then Dr. Panzov was going at me with two hands, wrestling as if with the devil, pulling his shoulders high, jiggering his instruments this way and that, scraping and gouging until I thought he would tear off his gloves and burrow his bare hands in there. Finally, he extracted a glistening, gore-flecked hunk of bone, turning it this way and that like a trophy for the camera. And it was a trophy of sorts, one that Honey could nail up in the hunting room between the bristly snout of the tusked wild boar and the spiraling horns of the mountain sheep, for it was as if Dr. Panzov had tunneled his cruel instruments into my body to extract my very soul, or the closest thing that I had to a soul. My eyes were the eyes of every Korean adoptee, but my nose was mine alone, never found on the face of another human being until I met Honey. It had taken me the first two decades of my life to rise to the challenge of my nose and become worthy of it, to embrace it as my own true birthright, to wield it proudly as the flagship feature of the one and only Kim Jae-Lisa Sarah Pearl, sui generis.

"Where're you going, *bokkie*?" Yolanda asked as I slumped down onto the mattress. "Come on, sit up. Show's not over yet."

"All I did was go with Jonny when he invited me! How could I say no to him?!"

"Don't try and blame this on the Young Master. You should know better than to play his games. If you had bothered to ask any one of us, Wendell, Dr. Panzov"—she gestured at the screen, where he was delving deep into my skull with a curved pair of scissors—"even Lahela for fuck's sake, we would have told you you were heading toward trouble." Realizing that she was getting off topic, she redirected her attention to the screen. "Now, here, Dr. Panzov is inserting a graft strut made of a sliver of your own cartilage to give the tip of your nose an adorable perk."

Separating the gelatinous flaps of my septum with tweezers, Dr. Panzov tucked in the strut before skewering the flaps and the cartilage with a steel pin, using curved scissors to guide a tiny comma of a needle through the skin as he sewed it all in place.

On-screen, Yolanda was gently prodding a two-pronged fork up my nostrils, while offscreen, Yolanda narrated in the hushed, soothing tones of a nature documentary. "Here, I'm shaping the nose, making the passages straight and free of obstruction. And now for the hard part, getting rid of that hook at the end of your nose. This is delicate work—you have to admire the good doctor's skill."

Indeed, as I watched Dr. Panzov's gloved hands do the fine work of snipping and sewing, I had trouble imagining that on the other end of them was the booze-swilling, sadistic henchman who had punched me unconscious. After carefully enmeshing the loose meat at the tip of the nose into a net of surgical thread, Dr. Panzov trimmed the excess skin around my nostrils with a few deft swipes of a scalpel before lowering the hood of my nose back onto my face, turning each nostril inside out as he pulled the needle through, leaving as the only visible evidence of the operation a tiny track of knotted thread like barbed wire across the skin of my septum. The video abruptly stopped, and Yolanda snapped the laptop shut.

"At least it's over with," I whispered, knowing, actually, that it wasn't over with, and it would never be.

"Not a bad show, hey, Lisa?" She sprang up from the bed, running finicky fingers over her skirt to straighten it out. "Ting will be in soon with your dinner and some tablets for the pain. Better eat something first before you take them."

As she pivoted toward the door, I clutched the frilled hem of her peplum jacket. "Can I see a mirror?"

She pulled her jacket from my grasping fingers. "You don't want to see a mirror yet, *bokkie*. Wait until the splint comes off."

"What did I do that was so wrong, Yolanda?" I importuned. "Why did she do this to me?"

Bringing the laptop up to her chest, Yolanda sighed, pinioning me with the laser gaze of her glowing green eyes. I stared back, willing myself not to look away, staring first into the eye that was stretched at a precipitous angle, the skin pulled so tight that her eyelid could not fully close, then into the other eye, the one that she winked with, less sharply angled but with a hard overhanging ridge of flesh where the filler that had been injected to create the illusion of a single lid had settled.

"You have no idea how hard it was to watch you preen and strut and act like you were better than us. The way you took advantage of Madam's love for you. But then you went too far, as posers and strivers always do. Poor Madam was so upset when she discovered your perfidy. She cried on my shoulder and wondered what she had done wrong. I assured her that her only sin was to love you too much. I advised her to be a good mother and discipline you, no matter how much it hurt her, or you would never learn your lesson. No, no, *meisie*, you don't get to look at me like that. I warned you many times not to fuck it up. But did you listen to me? Last time I'm going to tell you this, *dumkop*: obey Madam. To the letter."

She flicked a fingernail against my nose splint, leaving me writhing in pain as she strode out the door, heels clattering triumphantly down the corridor.

Ting must have been waiting outside with my dinner, because she suddenly materialized at the foot of the bed, placing a covered tray and a pitcher of water on the small table that was wedged into the corner. Balled up tightly in a sickening vise of pain, I followed her with my eyes but did not, could not, speak to her. She assiduously avoided my stare as she replaced the chamber pot I had wretched into with a fresh one, pausing only as she was getting ready to leave the room for a quick glance at me, maybe to make sure that I was alive. Eyes like two black bars, face completely immobile; she was unreadable. "Ting," I whispered. And then she was gone.

It was the water that finally beckoned me to the table, the promise of wet relief for the burned crisp of my tongue, the brittle crust of my palate, the splintered rind of my lips. But when I took a sip, the swirl of water against the roof of my mouth rekindled the cooling ardor of my pain.

In a saucer next to the pitcher were the two pain pills that Yolanda had advised me to take. I picked one up. It was big, about the size of a penny, a smooth circle with beveled edges that caught the dim light in a glossy flash. Etched diagonally across one face was a slash, like the groove in a screw head. The other side was featureless. It could have been anything: acetylsalicylic acid, paracetamol, codeine, hydrocodone. I put it down next to its mate.

Lifting the dome off the tray, I found a simple meal of Japanese comfort food: cubes of tofu bobbing in miso soup freckled with thin slices of green onion, a triangle of rice wrapped in seaweed, a small array of homemade pickles, four snow-white slices of *nashi*. I pictured Miura-san expertly skimming the golden skin from the dewy pear flesh, and then I saw Dr. Panzov trimming the skin from my nose, and the tears that I had been trying so hard to suppress spilled forth from the bruised portholes of my eyes, and it hurt because I cried and I cried because it hurt.

When Mindy brought me home from the hospital, she combed through my apartment, throwing out all the pills I had hoarded like loose change: a pastel blue Valium, two salmon-colored Xanax, a red-and-white capsule of phenobarbital, a small collection of snow-white Ativan. "Look, Lisa, I am not going to ask you to promise to never take pills again," she said, her plump lips uncharacteristically pressed into a hard, straight line. "I know that's not realistic. But I do want you to know that finding you comatose here was one of the worst moments of my life, and if you really cared about me, you wouldn't put me through that again."

"Oh, come on," I cajoled. "It's what a medical student lives for! The chance to save someone's life. I did you a real favor."

"OK, I won't lie to you." She flashed a wicked grin. "It was kind of a thrill. But you know how they say a doctor shouldn't operate on her loved ones? Well, now I know why. Panic at the thought of losing you definitely wobbled that laser-like focus I needed. I just wanted to go straight to the CPR without wasting time calling 911."

"So you actually did CPR on me?" I asked, hugging my knees and rocking forward. "You, like, put your lips to mine?"

She nodded seriously.

"Eww!" I tried to play it off with a joke.

"Your lips were blue and cold, your skin was clammy. You were completely gone. There was nothing left of you but the pod of your flesh. You were a stranger to me." She narrowed her eyes into spearheads. "I'm not going to joke about it, Lisa. You almost died."

I reached out to grab an arm that was angrily folded over her chest. "And you saved my life. Just like you've always done. I know it must get tiresome." I finally pried the arm loose and clutched at her hand. "No more pills, Min Hee, I promise."

She squeezed my hand so tightly that I could feel the bones grinding against each other. "I'm depending on you, Lisa. You're gonna be my maid of honor when I get married, you're gonna be there when I give birth, you're gonna make the speech at my retirement party..."

"...help you pick out your gown when you win the Nobel Prize in Medicine..."

She let my hand go, flashing a pleased smile. "The same year that you get the prize in literature."

"One usually needs to have written something to win that prize, so I hear," I quipped, grinning so she'd know I was just joking.

But she wasn't ready to joke. "Well, then write, Lisa. You've been talking about it all your life. Stop talking about it and do it! What are you waiting for? Are you afraid of failing? Are you scared of the rejection? Are you worried you're not good enough?"

"No!" I protested, taken aback at her vehemence, wavering between being insulted and being honest. "I do write! Look!" I grabbed up a spiral notebook and flipped the ink-filled pages at her. "See?"

"OK, that's great. But that's not a novel, Lisa." She grabbed my face in her hands, thumbs stroking my jaw, the dimple under her right eye trembling. I knew it was as painful for her to say what she said as it was for me to hear it. "You're twenty-three, Li-li, and it's time for you to put up or shut up. Write your goddamned Great Adoption Novel or never, ever say anything again about me and medical school. Do you really want to be a writer?"

She stared deep into my eyes. I don't know what she saw there, but I saw a pale smudge that was the reflection of my face on her dark pupils.

I nodded slowly.

"Then fucking write."

Chapter 13

"She was an entertainer, but she was looking for approval. It was: 'If you like me, maybe you'll keep me.'"

–Lionel Richie on his daughter Nicole

I held out for as long as I could, though it was not very long. Time was measured by meals; each meal arrived with two white tablets, which I immediately hid under my napkin, not out of defiance, but to fulfill my promise to Mindy.

But the pain was incredible. Agony surged in waves from my violated nose, circulating through my trembling body, passing through my exhausted heart, which insisted on hammering too hard and too fast for someone who did nothing but lie in bed. Even eating was painful, and I could force only a few bites before hurt won over hunger. Physical pain melded with mental anguish, and I wasn't sure where one ended and the other began. Honey had played me like the fool I was, puffing me up until I got so swollen that I popped of my own accord. She wasn't a mother, she was a monster, and she had me firmly in her grip, squeezing and squeezing until... Until what? Until I became like her? Until I was a shattered shell of a human, like the other members of the Gang? Until the physical manifestation of her ownership of me was written all over my face, as it was on Yolanda's? One thing was certain: by breaking my nose, Honey had also broken the spell that had, I realized with not a little shame, so easily charmed me, the cowering optimism that if I played her game, she'd let me win. I played by her rules, and she changed them. The whole point of the game was that I would never win. But so eager was I to gain her approval, to be liked by her, even to be *loved* by her, that I blinded myself to the warning storm clouds that hung darkly on the horizon.

Soon the time came when I let those two snow-white pills sit on the rim of the plastic plate (nothing breakable for me, nor did I merit sharp cutlery, every meal eaten either by hand or with a spoon).

Exhausted and undernourished, I had begun to hallucinate: tongues and tails curling and whipping just on the periphery of my vision, undulating frills of light, small scuttling creatures with long, filamented legs that quivered menacingly as they dashed out of view. The white pills proliferated and disappeared around my plate, two becoming four becoming eight becoming two again. My heart galloped along. My palms were damp. Dr. Panzov's grin hung in the air like the Cheshire cat's. I was unable to turn my mind off, obsessively reliving the trauma, thinking of my violation to the exclusion of all else. I looked down to see a blinding white dot on the tip of my finger. If I swallowed it, then maybe I would get a few hours' peace. The white dot was getting closer to my face, and my mouth had somehow opened up to receive it. But then, just as the brittle leather strap of my tongue was emerging from the fetid cavern of my mouth, I put the dot of pure light back on the plate. My skin crawled, thin sheets of muscle twitching just below the surface. My thoughts began to break up and fuzz around the edges, becoming a deafening cacophony of static. A long black bug with feathery legs crept just past my defiled nose and slipped into my pillowcase. My heart continued to rocket along, my whole body gently reverberating with its percussive thuds. My nose, the seat of my universe, throbbed with each heartbeat.

The next meal arrived—a tuna salad sandwich with the bread still warm from the oven. I took a bite, mayonnaise dripping onto the plate. And then another bite and another, in quick succession, powering through the pain. I sucked on a few grapes, which slipped easily down my throat. Then I nibbled another corner off the sandwich and stopped, fearing my stomach would rebel if I ate more and all my effort would be for naught. I hoped it would be enough for what was coming next. I crushed the dots of light under the bottom of the plastic cup and then licked up the powder with my tongue before hastily scouring my mouth clean with water. As I laid my thrumming head down to await sleep, the static faded into a distant hum, my heart slowed, and I knew I had done the right thing. "Sorry, Mindy," I whispered. She understood; she forgave me. Euphoria lapped gently up and down the byways of my veins, and a sweet blankness built into a crescendo of numbness. I embraced the emptiness tightly, fervently.

My last legible thought was *I. Will. Never. Let. Go.* before I succumbed full body into the sweet lacuna of nothingness.

The blank fog from which I emerged blended seamlessly with the walls, and it took me a few moments to realize that the *sub* had been sundered from the *conscious*. Almost as soon as I finished squatting over the chamber pot, the door opened and Ting whisked in with breakfast and a book. The sight of the book made me forget to try to exchange meaningful looks with Ting, who at any rate kept her gaze turned down. Honey had been waiting for me to take the pills and was rewarding me. My fingertips traced the title: *The Aquariums of Pyongyang: Ten Years in the North Korean Gulag,* by Kang Chol-Hwan.

Reverently, I opened the book and read the dust jacket flap copy, lingering over the title page, the copyright page, and the table of contents before finally allowing myself to start on the text proper. I read s-l-o-w-l-y, savoring each letter, chewing over every word before swallowing the entire sentence. Ting came in on the second day with a steak, accompanied by a sharp knife with which to eat it. For one second, when I grabbed the wooden handle, I considered driving the blade hard into my chest; I'd probably have time to stab myself at least twice before the person monitoring the video alerted a body-guard to get into the room. I thrust the knife deep into the moist pink meat instead.

It took me three days and six pills to finish the book. I went back to this passage and read it over and over again: "My life was absorbed entirely in my efforts to get by and obey orders. I was, fortunately, able to accept my condition as fated. A clear-eyed view of the hell I had landed in certainly would have thrown me deeper into despair. There is nothing like thought to deepen one's gloom."

Kang Chol-Hwan couldn't control his dreams, though, and in them he would relive the horror of what he had seen during the day in Yodok and once again taste the sweetness of his previous life in Pyongyang. There were no dreams that stuck with me once I came out from behind the black veil of the pills; it was all blankness. So, in a way, I was the negative to Chol-Hwan. With nothing to do but think and remember all day long, my brutalization was covered by amnesia, my dreams blanked out by pills.

I awoke to find Yolanda bent over me, doing something to my face, her duck lips zipped into as tight of a pucker as her poor, molded face would allow. I thrashed my arms to ward her off, but they were once again restrained by the leather straps, and something was encasing my head, keeping it still. Rolling my eyes up, I glimpsed the white curve of flesh under Ting's chin, a blue vein swelling like an electrical wire as she held my head in the vise of her hands. Wielding a pair of tweezers and a cotton swab, Yolanda was prying the bandage off my nose. I couldn't tell if it didn't hurt because the pills were still in effect or if it just didn't hurt. Without a word, Yolanda stared down at Dr. Panzov's workmanship, Ting turning my head this way and that for her inspection.

"How does it look?" I croaked, but she declined to answer, marching out without a word, leaving Ting to help me up from bed. I caught Ting looking at my nose and tried to read from her expression what she saw there, but as usual she was unknowable, a sphinx behind whose implacable mask I suspected nothing resided. With the bandage off, my skin felt vulnerable, exposed, the soft defenseless viscera of a snail without its shell.

To my surprise, Ting herded me out the door and led me back to what I now thought of as my bedroom. She ran the bath while I stood in the doorway of the bathroom like a dumb beast, my head hanging, my shoulders slumped forward, eyes avoiding the mirror. When the bath was ready, Ting scurried by me for the door. The scanner would not read her eye at first, and she had to blot at it with the hem of her shirt before the door gave way.

The bathroom was clouded in steam, the mirror blanked with fog. I flipped on the vanity lights and wiped away the condensation with an open palm, my face emerging from the misted surface. Head on, the change wasn't too noticeable, though my nose now took up less space, shorter and slimmer, especially at the base, which had once been a sturdy pedestal but was now just a slight flaring, a delicate blooming of the nose stem. When I tilted my head, though, the damage was evident. Where once my nose had been assertive and muscular, now it was demure and petite. Boring. The knob was gone, and it was a straight, gentle slope from the bridge to the slightly rounded tip, which was almost, but not quite, snubbed. The nostrils, once dark tunnels that scooped up the sides of my nose, were discreet, well-camouflaged apertures. Its perfection looked out of place and lonely in my face. Remarkably, it did not bear the slightest hint of the violence that had so recently been visited upon it. My eyes, on the other hand, were embedded in puffy flesh, the bruising rusting into an autumnal russet with amethyst highlights that stained nicotine yellow at the edges. Beads of condensation slipped down the smooth surface of the mirror, silvery tracks rolling down my steam-blurred cheeks.

Emerging from my bath, wrapped in a fuzzy bathrobe monogrammed with my new initials, L.L., I discovered a beautiful gilt-tooled, leather-bound edition of *Great Expectations*—the very book I had chosen the night Honey showed me the hidden bookcase—propped on the pillow of my bed. In the drunkenness that had ensued that night, which seemed a lifetime away but was only a few weeks ago, I had lost track of the book, and now it had found its way back to me. My little treat for enduring Honey's punishment. But just as I settled onto the bed to start reading, Yolanda entered to stand before me, hip popped out, magnificently muscled leg on full display in a short-skirted tweed suit, green eyes lingering appraisingly on my face. "The swelling will go down in one to two weeks. Same with the black eyes. Man, but Dr. Panzov smacked you good."

"What swelling? You mean my nose is swollen? It's going to get even tinier?"

"Yes. You have a nose modeled on that cute Chinese actress. Zhang Ching Chong or something like that. Madam picked it out for you herself."

I wasn't ready for Yolanda yet, my skin too thin, my defenses eroded. "Thanks for dropping by, Yolanda," I said, opening the book across my lap. "Oh, and I don't need any more pain pills, thank you. I haven't had one in twenty-four hours and I feel OK."

But Yolanda stayed where she was, one leg jiggling just a little to tell me to stop wasting her time. "Look in the armoire."

Reluctantly, I put the book down and crossed the room to fling open the intricately carved doors of the mahogany armoire, revealing garments of shimmering silk, crisp linen, filmy gauze, prickly wool, stiff tulle, soft cotton, versatile rayon, clingy spandex, and shiny satin, immaculately arranged in color groups that went from darkest to lightest. Shoes lined the floor of the armoire in order of height, from ballet flats to spiked-heel boots. "Madam thinks you are ready to pick out your own outfits. It's a big step for you."

Ting entered, pushing a rolling cart rattling with scissors, a comb, a hair dryer, and a glass jar filled with a thick paste that flooded the room with a harsh chemical scent that made my eyes water. With a shove, Yolanda directed me toward the bathroom.

"Madam has finally settled on a hairstyle for you. First we cut, then we color."

As scissors snipped off hanks of my hair, I kept my eyes tightly closed, refusing to be witness to the persecution. When she slathered on the dye, my scalp stung as if attacked by a swarm of bees, my eyes secreting defensive tears against the fumes, and when she paused to let the dye work its way in, I steadfastly stared into my lap, carefully avoiding even a glimpse of myself in the mirror. Finally, she told me to bend over the tub, and I was surprised at the gentle way she massaged the caustic dye from my scalp, until I realized it was not Yolanda but Ting. After Yolanda blasted my hair dry and sculpted it into place with gel, she said, "Go ahead, take a look."

I was now a platinum blonde, my hair shorn to a shaggy, asymmetrical pixie cut, the left side mowed to a fuzz from my ear to the side part, hair sweeping over the crown of my head like Dr. Panzov's comb-over, bangs spiking down my forehead. The hair matched my nose but not the rest of my face, my eyes peering forlornly from the raccoon mask of bruises, my mouth confused.

"Very nice," I mumbled, turning away.

Flicking her wrist to consult her tiny watch, Yolanda strutted toward the door, throwing each long leg out with martial exuberance.

"Madam would like you to report for work tomorrow. I'll fetch you when she's ready."

"Will that be in the morning or afternoon?" I asked.

"What?" She spun back to face me, voice broadcasting the irritation that her face couldn't.

"When will she be ready?"

Rolling her face up to the heavens, or at least to the camera, she let out an exasperated sigh. "Your job is to be ready for Madam whenever she summons you to her presence. She doesn't accommodate your schedule, you accommodate hers."

Finally she was gone, but still I waited a few minutes to make sure she didn't pop back in like the scary clown in a slasher flick before picking up *Great Expectations*, eager to lose myself in Pip's upside-down, inside-out adoption story, wherein an anonymous benefactor has Pip searching for his identity in all the wrong places. I loved this book. It was, in fact, the book that I based my own novel on, with an A. S. Byatt *Possession*-like twist in the form of a Victorian poet named Evander Cadamon in the place of Pip.

Despite my mom's pleas to return home, I stayed in New York, determined to meet Mindy's challenge and fucking write. I signed up with a temp agency, and when there was no work, I wrote. To make things a little easier for myself, I used *Great Expectations*, a childhood favorite, as my template, but in an attempt to mask my purloined plot, I made my protagonist a tortured poet who wrote in haiku, both to bring an Asian element into the story and because haiku was much less difficult to write than Victorian poetry. Evander Cadamon was a mishmash of Pip (an orphan in search of himself), Nigel (brilliant and pale), my Victorian poetry professor Dr. Evander (British and enigmatic), and myself (vague and unformed), and each chapter opened with one of his haikus that foreshadowed the next plot twist, an authorial artifice of which I was particularly proud.

For the first time in my life, I woke up every morning with a clear purpose, which summoned in me some hidden strength that I'd never even suspected I had. I cherished that purpose, held it close, and it became my protector, my accomplice, and my sanctuary. As the word count of my manuscript grew and the story took shape, I found some sort of redemption from the mess I had made of my life so far. Writing required all those things that I had, until now, avoided: self-discipline, dedication, organization, insight, and thoughtfulness. Though I sometimes missed the companionship of the pills and the booze, I told myself that writing was a lonely endeavor, and if I was no good at being lonely then I was no good at being a writer, embracing the loneliness as proof that I was succeeding at my craft. I didn't need friends, I didn't need fun; all I needed was to write. I stumbled occasionally—the worst was when I finished the first draft and celebrated with an entire bottle of Stoli, waking the next morning severely hungover and ashamed, the day wrecked for writing.

After a year, my novel was a living, breathing thing, still a jungle of words, sure, but one that I had willed into existence, the evidence there in the computer files, hundreds of pages that told a story I had spun out of thin air. Every single word was one that I had birthed onto the page, every character my own creation, every action brought to life by me. I labored over every sentence, again and again, fashioning and refashioning the same scene, the same character, the same gesture, replacing the clumsy with the mediocre, the mediocre with the good, the good with the inspired. Another year, and the jungle of words became an overgrown weedy patch, the weedy patch a cultivated garden. Each polishing made the story shine just a little more, until I deemed it a brilliant gem ready to be shared with the world. Two years after Mindy issued her directive, I emailed the first chapter to her. It was not a well-chosen time: Mindy was in the midst of grueling clinical rotations and running on a serious sleep deficit, but I didn't think about that; I could only think of my manuscript, I could only think of myself.

One agonizing day later with no response, I sent her a text: "Have you read it yet?"

Silence. Doubt set in. What if she thought it was so bad she was avoiding me? Maybe she realized that after all these years of encouraging me to write, I just didn't have the talent, and she felt too guilty to face me. Maybe she didn't want to hurt me by giving her honest opinion.

I sent another text: "That bad huh?"

Nothing. Anger prickled my fingers into typing: "I can take the truth."

Another day went by. I called her from the dental office where I was on a two-week assignment, just to see if she was screening my calls, but her phone went straight to voice mail again, and I left another passive-aggressive, borderline nasty message. My anger congealed like a cannonball in the pit of my stomach, and I dragged it everywhere I went, exhausted by its adamantine weight. I stopped trying to contact her, returning home from the dentist's office to continue revising the manuscript, losing myself in what had once again become a jungle of words, trying to make order of the teeming growth, becoming tangled in my own vines, suddenly seeing only flaws where previously I had seen perfection. It was that *quick*, like waking from an enchantment: my confidence evaporated, the rose-colored glasses through which I read my own words shattered, and suddenly everything I'd written didn't make any sense to me anymore, and what I thought was treasure was revealed to be trash. A few short days of silence from Mindy, and it was all gone. I bought a bottle of vodka (Popov, because there was nothing to celebrate this time) and continued revising my novel, because I wasn't yet ready to admit to the world, and to myself, that it was no good, but now I was drinking and writing, waking up the next morning to delete everything I had done the day before, a loop-the-loop of writing and drinking and deleting.

When she finally called, Mindy's voice was flat and scratchy from exhaustion. She apologized perfunctorily for not being in contact sooner, but she had just had the rotation from hell and began to describe the boorish male attending physician who talked over her whenever she opened her mouth, when I cut her off. "You hated it, didn't you?"

"Yeah, I just said I hated it," she responded, yawning. "The guy was an asshole."

"Not the rotation, Mindy. The first chapter of my novel that I sent you."

"Oh. I haven't read it yet."

"Seriously? You couldn't bother to read forty pages? They're even double-spaced, so that's like twenty pages! You couldn't do that for your best friend?"

"Lisa, I've just explained to you what I was doing. I've slept about six hours in the last four days. I'm totally exhausted."

"You're the one who told me to fucking write, remember that? So I fucking wrote, and you didn't even bother to fucking read it!"

"Oh my god, Lisa, are you really yelling at me?" Her words began to bubble wetly over the phone. She was crying. "I haven't had a good night's sleep in months, I hardly ever see Trip, and now you're yelling at me? I think you might possibly be the most selfish person in the whole world."

And then the line went dead. Mindy had hung up on me.

Yolanda fetched me the next morning as promised, taking me for the first time into Honey's inner sanctum, where a version of Honey that I hadn't met yet awaited me behind a sleek, minimalist white desk with gleaming steel legs. Hair swirled into a severe, Hitchcockian bun, she was trussed into a pinch-waisted cream business suit, chunky tortoiseshell glasses perched on the end of her nose, slashing her way through a pile of papers with a mother-of-pearl fountain pen. As I walked across the vast room, the kitten heels of my leopard-print slingbacks sinking into the plush pile of the long-haired silk carpet, she put down the pen, propped the glasses up on her golden crown, and rose from her seat. "Come closer, let's get a good look at you," she said in her breathy baby voice.

Obediently, I approached, eyes lowered, afraid that they would betray the loathing for her that was eating me from the inside out. But when she cupped my chin with a soft, warm hand and cooed, "Poor baby, Mother is sorry that she had to hurt you," my eyes silvered with tears. She sounded so sincere, and I yearned for a gentle touch, a sympathetic word. As I began to sob, she tenderly directed my head toward her shoulder until she saw the pink bubbles coming out my nose.

"Oh, be careful of my Nina Ricci," she said, abruptly stepping away from me just as I was reaching my arms out to clutch at her.

I put a hand up to my nose and wiped away a stream of mucus threaded with blood. She pulled a clump of tissues out of a box sitting on her desk, handing them to me in a wad, while standing far enough away that a stray glob of mucus wouldn't splatter on her.

"My nose has been doing that since..." I let my sentence hang as I sopped up the snot.

"Careful, careful, you don't want to ruin Dr. Panzov's handiwork," she cautioned. "And watch your blouse!"

I looked down to see little pinprick dots of pink spotting the raw yellow silk. Rushing to the tissue box to tuck a few into the neckline, I squeaked, "I'm sorry, Honey."

"Oh, well," she said bravely, "that's what Ting's for. She's no stranger to getting blood out."

She seated herself in a chrome swivel chair padded in white leather and motioned for me to join her. There was no other chair behind the desk, and the ones scattered around the room were too cumbersome to move, so I stood behind her, staring down into the vertiginous eye of her shimmering bun. She settled the glasses—the first evidence I had that Honey was actually aging like a normal person—onto the knuckle of her nose.

"This," she said with a wave of her manicured fingers, "is the master schedule." It was a large desk calendar, each date crammed with annotations written in a rainbow of different-colored inks. "And this"—she tapped a leather appointment book—"is my daily programmer. You have one of your own. Now, where is it?" With an annoyed click of her tongue, she stabbed a button on an old-fashioned intercom with her mother-of-pearl pen.

"Yes, Madam?" Yolanda's tinny voice blared in answer.

"Where is Lisa's daily planner?" Honey shrieked.

"Right away, Madam," Yolanda responded, and in another moment came through one of the many doors that paneled the room.

"Didn't I tell you I wanted the appointment book waiting here for Lisa?" Honey harangued Yolanda.

"Sorry, Madam," Yolanda apologized, handing me a daily planner. "I have also brought the vitamins that the Young Master has recommended for your health." She placed an enameled pillbox in front of Honey.

"And how are we supposed to swallow them down? Honestly, Yolanda!"

As Yolanda bustled away, I called after her: "I think you made a mistake. This is a 2010 diary."

"It's not a mistake," Honey said with a sigh. "It's the best we could do at such short notice."

"But how am I to coordinate with you when you have a 2011 calendar?" I asked, not unreasonably.

"Oh, Lisa, what does it matter?" she snapped. "Every month has the same number of days no matter the year. Monday, Tuesday, Wednesday, what difference does it make to you? Here, there are no days of the week, just dates." However, the very next instant, she said, "Now, you and I are going to dine together every Sunday, Wednesday, and Friday evening, so you can start by filling in those days in your daily planner."

"But..." I meekly protested, offering my opened planner as evidence of the impossibility of the task.

"Oh, really!" Honey erupted in a strangled scream. "Must I do all your thinking for you?" Drilling a long nail onto the page of her own planner, she instructed in a voice boiling with impatience, "Start with tomorrow, which is Wednesday. As you can see by my planner, tomorrow is June 27. Now, in your planner put 'Dinner with Mother at 7:00 p.m.' Then count two more days, that's Friday, so again at seven, 'Dinner with Mother.' Then two more days, that's Sunday. Now on Sunday we eat dinner at six, so write 'Dinner with Mother at 6:00.' Now three more days, we're back to Wednesday."

I mechanically began to fill in the lines as she instructed, adding the initial of the day in a little circle next to each date just to be safe, but my mind was mostly preoccupied with the fact that it was the end of June already. Meaning I had been in captivity for three months. And that tomorrow was my birthday.

Meanwhile, Yolanda came mincing in with two glasses of orange juice, the pulp still swirling in the glass, as if she had just finished squeezing the juice from the fruit with her bare hands. She placed the glasses next to the pillbox.

I continued to scribble in my book, hoping that the extra glass of juice was for Yolanda and not me, that I would somehow escape

Jonny's vitamins. But it was not to be, as Honey flipped open the pill-box and tapped out two blue capsules. Throwing her head back, she popped one into her mouth, chasing it with the juice, and then held her hand out to me, her long nails curved like bamboo rain gutters, a blue capsule nestled in the center of her palm. I put the glass of orange juice up to my lips defensively.

"Take it. On Jonny's recommendation. He says it's like a health supplement, you know, essence of kale, green tea, and gingko, or something like that. We have a very sophisticated pharmaceutical industry, and Jonny is always bringing me new wonder drugs to try." She batted her aquamarine eyes at me, not caring if I believed her or not. "Go on and try it. You'll be amazed at how quickly you feel its benefits."

I took another stalling sip of juice. A ripple of annoyance fractured the glossy line of her lips. I pinched the pill from her palm. She watched as I slipped the pill between my lips, gagging briefly as it stuck at the back of my throat before flushing it down with a gulp of juice. She rewarded me with a dazzling smile.

"Good girl. Now"—she resettled the glasses on her nose and peered down at her desk calendar—"where were we? Oh, yes, Monday, Thursday, and Saturday afternoons you will spend with Cookie. I feel he has made so much progress under your tutelage. You should both be proud."

Another tender smile. I found the date after the Wednesday dinner, writing in Cookie in large letters in the P.M. hours, skipping the next day to write the same thing on what was supposed to be Saturday.

"Don't worry, you can fill in the rest of the planner during your office hours, which are to be Monday through Friday, nine to five, with an hour break for lunch, which will be taken in your room, from twelve to one. That is, when you are not here with me or in the kitchen with Cookie."

"Where will my office be?" I inquired, shifting from foot to foot, my calves tired from balancing my heels in the sinking softness of the carpet.

"Don't interrupt." She lifted a warning finger in the air. "You and I will meet every Tuesday and Thursday from ten to noon, after which we will eat lunch together, just the two of us." Her nails scratched against the paper of the desk planner, a dry, grating sound that irritated my ears. "If there is a lot of business to go over, we may extend our meetings after lunch."

"Except I can't on Thursdays," I muttered as I scribbled away. "Because that's when I help..." The look she gave me strangled the words in my throat. "Of course, if that happens, Cookie will understand why I can't be there," I hastily noted.

"All right, now as to your office," Honey said, tenting her fingers together as she leaned back in her chair. "Yolanda will take you there when we are done. This is a big step for you, as you will get your first clearance to use the ocular scanner. Mind you, it is only for entrance to two doors and not to exit, but I thought it was appropriate to give you a taste of the freedom that your loyalty will earn you."

"Oh, thank you, Honey," I said breathlessly, moved that she trusted me, a feeling of warmth and goodwill stealing over my body, along with an outbreak of goose bumps. My palms were sweaty, and my fingers kept slipping down the smooth casing of the pen. I paused to wipe my hands on my skirt. Looking down, I noticed the bib of tissues still tucked into my neckline and plucked them free. "Forgot about these," I tittered. My heart began to pirouette in my rib cage like a ballerina. Jonny's vitamin was beginning to take effect. "I must have looked pretty silly."

"You still look silly with that pink mustache under your nose," Honey teased me.

Gasping, I flitted over to the large gilt-framed mirror that she had hanging from a wall, to see that I did indeed have a lopsided mustache of dried pink mucus smearing up one cheek.

"Come here, baby," Honey called, spitting on a tissue and wiping it daintily across my upper lip. Her fingers hummed with a fine vibration, and I held out my hand to see it humming in answer to hers. "There, all better." She gave me an affectionate pat to my cheek.

"Except for my eyes," I reminded her, grinning goofily.

"Yes, they do look pretty awful," she admitted. "But it was worth it, wasn't it, baby?"

"Of course it was," I assured her, not because I agreed, but because I suddenly understood my mother on an elemental level, almost as if my nerve endings had jumped into her body and I was feeling what she felt, which was lightness, affection, a great, glowing, expanding love. She was me and I was her, and we were joined together as one organism by a pulsing, all-encompassing love.

Reaching into her cleavage to retrieve a small golden key, Honey exulted, "Now for the fun part." Fitting the key into the desk drawer, she slid it open to reveal a laptop computer. I was so excited to see that computer that I bunched my hands into fists and did a little jig, which fortunately Honey did not see, as she was flipping open the laptop and staring entranced as it sprang into life with a dramatic crashing chord. Scooping it up, she beckoned me to follow her as we went through a door into a cubbyhole of a room that was scattered with brightly colored cushions and what looked like harem furniture: divans and ottomans covered in lush gold-flocked silks of magenta and crimson. She settled onto a divan and patted the space next to her. I sank into the deep cushions, and we leaned against each other, the crown of my head nestling into the crook of her neck, as she began to navigate her clumsy way on to the internet, having to go through a number of sign-ins on blank gray pages, the text displayed in blocky letters like the WordPerfect programs of my extreme youth. Several times she typed in the wrong thing and was taken back to the beginning, and I bit my lip to hold myself back from taking control of the machine, which she approached like an uneasy lion tamer, keyboard strokes hesitant and uncertain, muttering instructions to herself under her breath. But then, all of a sudden, there she was, on the internet, YouTube her homepage.

"Oh, wait, wait, before we go any further let me show you this," she squealed, and called up a video of two red-cheeked babies in diapers *goo-goo-ga-ga*-ing at each other as if they were having a real conversation. Oh, we found that hilarious, clutching at each other until I gasped, "My nose, my nose," and we both tried to quell our giggles. That led to another video of a computer-animated cat with a Pop-Tart body flying through the air, trailing a rainbow, to the sound track of *Nya-na-na-nya-nya-na*.

"Oh god," I moaned, gently dabbing at my puffed-wheat eyes with the tassel of one of her harem cushions, "I love the internet!" Then we watched a fat guy in a tight Speedo do a belly flop, five guys in monkey masks do a dance, and a mother cat and her kitten hug each other in their sleep.

"Oh, I discovered the funniest thing the other day," Honey shrieked, pecking a new address into the browser with two fingers. After a few tries, she came up with the proper page and then had to find what she was looking for, me all the while rubbing my sweaty palms on my lap, using every ounce of self-discipline I had to keep from seizing the softly humming machine so that we could get on with it. "This is hilarious! Photos of Lindsay Lohan falling down in front of a club in LA. If you click on the photos quickly, it's like a movie clip." As she tapped quickly with a vermilion nail, I watched an obviously inebriated young woman, eyes lidded, mouth slack, ricochet among some bystanders, take a few lurching steps into empty space, and then whoopsy-daisy to the ground.

I felt bad for her, imagining what the paparazzi would have captured of me on a night out on the town, but following Honey's lead, I chortled gleefully. "Poor LiLo. It's sad."

"Lilo!" Honey screeched. "Yes, it's perfect!" *Boff-boff-boff,* she lightly slapped me with both sides of her hand on my upper arm.

"What's perfect?" I tried to stretch my eyes in imitation of her wide-eyed girlish delight.

"As a nickname! For you!" Her eyes grew and grew until they threatened to swallow up her whole face.

It seemed like a bad omen to share a nickname with a young woman rumored to suffer from substance abuse problems. "Yeah, but isn't a nickname supposed to be a shortening of the name? Lilo just substitutes one syllable of my name for another."

"No, no! Nicknames are affectionate names that are some sort of a corruption of the person's original name. Or, as in my case, illustrate a person's character or most striking physical feature. Honey is just as long as Mary, but Honey radiates more warmth and intimacy. It notes that I am blond and sweet. It's a sign of a special bond between me and the person who calls me Honey." She snapped my elbow with her nails. I was quickly discovering that to be Honey's pal was to be her human punching bag.

I opened my mouth to protest, but just then Yolanda came sweeping into the room. She pretended not to see the cozy couple we made on the couch, our arms intertwined, our sides heaving with hilarity, our skirts riding up to our thighs. "Lunchtime, Madam," she announced.

Seized by inspiration, I announced, "Well, if I'm to be Lilo, then Yolanda must be Yoyo."

"Yoyo!" Honey screamed. "I love it!" Skidding thumb and finger over the corners of her mouth to wipe away the webbing of dry-mouth gunk that had accumulated there, Honey said to me, "I'm not hungry. Are you hungry?"

I groped around at my stomach as if feeling whether I was hungry. My esophagus felt tight, closed, like something was crawling up it, blocking the passageway for anything trying to go down. "No," I said, my words clicking from my dry throat. "I am not at all hungry."

Ignoring me, Yolanda said in a surprisingly bossy tone, "Cookie has made you a wonderful lunch, Madam. Please come to the table to eat it."

"Oh, all right, Yoyo," Honey groaned, extricating her limbs from mine and wriggling into a standing position.

We moved deeper into the sanctum, to a conservatory with a big picture window that looked out upon a Japanese-style rock garden, the room itself bright with white wicker furniture and highly burnished copper shelves from which arched an array of orchids, their sumptuous scent sugaring the air. The table was laid with lunch already: a small bowl of thick white soup dotted with chives, a pear and walnut salad, and crustless white bread tea sandwiches. "It's all so white," I marveled, holding a hand up to shield my eyes.

"I like white!" Honey exclaimed, settling into a wicker chair. "This is new!" She dipped her spoon into the soup. "What is it?" Her tongue, as white as the soup, flicked out. "It's cold!" she shrieked. "Yoyo, what's the meaning of this?"

"Wait, wait, I think I know!" I said, anxious to save Miura-san from a berating. "It's vichyssoise. We looked up the recipe, thinking it an elegant way to beat the heat of summer."

My teeth began to chatter, my muscles contracting with a quick shiver that was gone almost as soon as it came upon me. We dabbed our tongues into the soup, took tiny bites from the sandwiches, ate a slice of pear or two, but that was all we could manage.

My office was a small, windowless cubicle much like the room where I had awoken to a new nose. In fact, I thought it might be the same room, as I recognized a tiny patch of air-bubbled paint in the far right corner, which would have been right across from where my head lay when there was a cot in the room. Instead of the cot, there was a simple wooden desk, no drawers, with a single ballpoint pen and my daily planner on it. Yolanda showed me how to look into the glowing panel of the scanner to release the door, instructing me to raise my eyebrows in order to expose more of my eyeball. She explained that I now had access to enter both my office and bedroom, but not to get out, and that I'd need to remember to leave the door propped open if I didn't want to get trapped in my cubicle all day. Through the open door, I could hear the occasional gust of wind that swept through the hallway with a whooshing, haunted howl, the only sound to break the silence until the bellicose beat of Yolanda's approaching footsteps.

I spent my first day of work obediently filling in the planner until December 31, as per Honey's directions. According to the daily planner, it was my birthday. I was twenty-eight years old. A little panic fluttered like a trapped bird in my chest when I thought about the passing time. Every day I was gone I receded a little further into oblivion. Each day that passed my scent grew colder, the memory of me fainter, and the idea that I would never return grew stronger. I was certain, on this first birthday of my disappearance, my mother had baked the chocolate marshmallow cookies that she made every year for my birthday, mailing them to me halfway around the world if she had to, and Mindy had selected another sumptuous journal as a gift, just as she had done every year since we had decided that I was going to be a writer. But what about next year, and the year after that? How long until they lost all hope that I was alive and consigned me to the ash heap of history? How long until they stopped baking me cookies and buying me journals?

As I was getting ready for the scheduled dinner with Honey that evening, Yolanda appeared in my room and thrust a green leather box at me. Inside, wrapped around a tiny velvet cushion, was a delicate gold Rolex, the hours marked by diamonds. "She remembered," I remarked to myself in surprise, snapping the slinky mesh strap closed on my wrist.

"Remembered what?" Yolanda asked, gazing with green envy at the watch.

"My birthday," I said, putting my sparkling watch next to her dull, diamond-less one.

Wrapping her hand protectively over her wrist, a gesture that told me that her watch had also been a gift from Madam, she sneered, "I doubt it. She didn't say anything to me about it. She just got you the watch because you've been bitching about not being able to tell what time it is."

Later, over a dinner of pan-fried trout with lemon and capers, I thanked her.

"Every businesswoman needs a watch!" she exclaimed brightly.

But no champagne toast, no cake for dessert, not even a candle in the crème caramel. By the time dinner was over, I knew for certain that Honey had forgotten about my birthday. I tried to revel in the sick irony of it all, that my crazy birth mother didn't even remember the anniversary of the momentous event that had led to this crazy situation she had orchestrated, but I only felt hurt. The watch was pretty and extravagant, but it didn't mean anything, and I would have gladly swapped it for one of Mindy's journals.

To celebrate my twenty-fifth birthday, Mindy and I met for dinner at an Italian place in the Village, the halfway point between our neighborhoods of the Upper East Side and Flatbush. The restaurant was deserted—not a good sign—and the place had the generic whiff of a tourist trap. After we ordered, Mindy gave me my birthday present, the same present she gave every year, a journal, this one bound in full-grain green leather, the pages edged with gilt.

Plopping the journal into my bag without a word of thanks, I whined, "The only thing I want for my birthday is for you to tell me that you loved the first chapter of my novel."

I could see from the apologetic puckering of her brow that she was going to be critical. She toyed with her knife. "It's just that it doesn't feel authentic. It doesn't sound like your voice."

My tongue swelled in anger and embarrassment against my teeth. When the waiter came, I grabbed my drink and swished it around in my mouth, the strong taste of gin replacing the bitter bile of her words. She looked at me pleadingly, and I saw the inky stains under her eyes, her wan complexion, posture uncharacteristically droopy, hair overdue for a trim; medical school had drained all the youth and exuberance from her.

"I mean, why make the protagonist a white guy? You're not white. You're a beautiful young Asian American woman—you need to write about beautiful young Asian American women. What do you know about white men?"

"That's all I know about is white men, Mindy! From Dante to Dickens to goddamn Don DeLillo, white men have dominated my life. Trust me, I know more about white men than I do about beautiful young Asian women."

She exhaled impatiently. "Mmkay. Look, I'm not saying that you write something similar to this, but at the hospital gift shop they are selling a novel by Nicole Richie, about the adopted daughter of a fabulously wealthy Hollywood family who struggles through adolescence and early adulthood, and just as she is about to get her life on track, her birth father comes on the scene to throw her life back into turmoil. It's the write-what-you-know thing. She's using the compelling circumstances of her own life to write a novel. You could do that, but in a literary way. Instead of writing about some pale Victorian poet, you should be writing the Great Adoption Novel, where you unveil universal truths and shit by exploring the adoption story."

Voice high with resentment, I demanded, "How do you know my manuscript won't do all those things, unveil universal truths and shit? All you've done is read the first chapter. There are four hundred more pages to go. You haven't even gotten to the part where you find out he's an orphan yet."

"An orphan?!" she echoed, openmouthed with incredulity. "Seriously?"

She didn't have to tell me why that got her agitated. Orphans were not adoptees like us. Orphans had parents who died, not parents who had abandoned them, shunting them off to be raised by strangers. Orphans were Disney and Hallmark, orphans were a half-hearted gesture, orphans were less than full disclosure.

"I just think..." she blurted out, and then paused as the waiter brought our appetizers. "I just think you need to write about yourself."

"I do write about myself! All the time! In my journals."

"Then why don't you use that to write a novel?" she asked, as if it were as simple as all that.

I clicked my tongue impatiently. "What the fuck do you know about novels anyway? When was the last time you read one?"

"God, Lisa, I'm just trying to help you." She angrily patted at her mouth with her napkin.

"Well, it doesn't matter anyway," I said, the words slipping from my lips with venomous glee, happy to change the subject and avoid having to consider whether Mindy was right about my wasting two years of my life writing about the wrong thing. "Because I'm going to Japan."

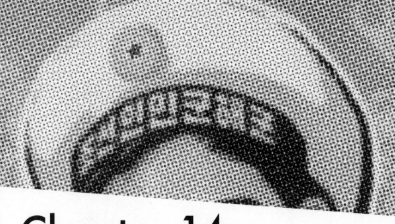

Chapter 14

"I would lose the family I have now
if people found out [about him]."

–Anonymous birth mother of Toby Dawson

Pondering how to use Jonny's glamorous wife on our website, I asked Honey to show me a photo of her. Sally, as Honey called her, was a famous singer who encompassed the Korean ideal of beauty: plump face, half-moon eyes, enameled complexion, delicately molded mouth, and a demure, supportive manner. Honey explained, "She comes from a good family and is already well known throughout the land."

Fingers vibrating like a struck tuning fork from the bluies— which were definitely not the vitamins Jonny claimed they were, but more reminiscent of the amphetamines I sometimes popped in high school—she had to try several times before she typed the right thing into the search engine, retrieving a badly pixelated video of a young woman in a gaudy *hanbok* singing in front of a full orchestra, mouth set in a permanent smile that showed off her fine white teeth whose only flaw was a small gap between a central incisor and a canine, her hair auburn, the color mine used to be.

"See how poised she is, how her face is so charmingly blank, every expression finely modulated to please and not offend? She's the perfect political wife, flawlessly inscrutable. I helped Jonny pick her out. We, of course, had a trusted doctor check for an intact hymen. And she was kind enough to submit a photo of herself in a bathing suit. Actually, Jonny has known her for some years—social circles in Pyongyang are fairly small, after all. Most important, we made a strategic alliance with her father, who is a marshal in the KPA."

Honey searched for the bathing suit photo, awkwardly manipulating the touchpad, refusing my offer to help, the synthetic cocoon of chemical camaraderie only taking us so far.

"Ah, here it is!" Honey announced after a very circuitous route through her hard drive. A photo filled the screen of Sally in a modestly cut one-piece, skin opalescent, legs slightly knock-kneed, plump arms crossed modestly over her stomach, elbows notched with dimples. "Keep in mind that the Koreans like a little meat on their women. It's a sign of prosperity."

"Well, she does have a nice hourglass figure," I said. "But that pale skin! She looks like a piece of whale blubber."

"Oh, you!" Honey scrunched up her face in feigned shock, knocking me hard in the side with an elbow but relishing my criticism.

"Does she have any idea who you are?" I asked, lips sticking to my teeth. The bluies gave me awful cottonmouth.

"No! And she never will, for it would be much too dangerous. Her family has too many connections."

"What if," I asked, rubbing my hands against my thighs, "they have a baby..."

"Oh, they will have a baby. That's the whole point of her," Honey murmured.

"...and he comes out looking Caucasian? You know, with brown hair or blue eyes or something. Then surely she'd guess."

"Why would he have blue eyes?" Honey scoffed. "Jonny doesn't."

"Blue eyes are a recessive gene, which means they can skip a generation."

"What?" Her baby voice deepened. "Where'd you hear that?"

"Adoptees tend to be interested in genetics," I explained. "We like to look for clues that might help us solve the mystery of where, or I should say who, we came from."

"Oh." She rolled her eyes.

"Well, let's look it up," I suggested brightly, always happy to wander the internet, even if it was over her shoulder.

Obediently, she brought up the search page and slowly pecked out "blue eyes recessive gene."

Suddenly, with no warning, there was Jonny sprawled sideways on the couch, leaving just a sliver of space for Honey, who had folded herself up with origami precision to take up as little room as possible as she chatted with a third person slouched into a club chair.

"Ji Hoon!" I exclaimed, blinking from the shock, paralyzed as a fulminating mushroom cloud of nostalgia, shame, helplessness, and anger rose in a column through my body, expanding, spreading, fallout raining everywhere. I saw the sharp interest in Jonny's gaze, the amused expectation in Honey's, and endeavored to mold my expression into sweet complacency, bending my neck as Sally had done in the bathing suit photo to look at them from uptilted eyes, curving my lips into a Mona Lisa smile, masking the murderous rage that scalded me from within.

Scrambling up from the chair, Ji Hoon swept into a chivalrous bow. "Lisa! I hardly recognize you. You look... awesome!"

Without getting up, Jonny held out a hand to me, crushing mine with a painful squeeze. "Love the hair!" he purred. "And what else is new about you?" He tapped the side of his cheek contemplatively as he inspected my nose.

My four-inch heels wobbled underneath me as I quavered out a thank you. I wondered if he had seen the video of my defilement. Had Ji Hoon seen it as well? I gave him a sideways glance, but he was looking at Honey, who was beckoning Yolanda, who was pouring golden champagne into coupe glasses. After we saluted the new guest with a welcome home toast, Honey pouted. "What's this name Lisa keeps calling you?"

His luscious lips quivered into an embarrassed smile. "Ji Hoon. It was the first name that came to my mind when Lisa asked me what my real name was."

Honey turned to me and announced airily, "But, Lisa, Harrison is his real name."

I nodded, forming my mouth into a parabola of sweetness. "You've had a haircut too."

He passed a hand over the tight cap of a crew cut. "Feels better this way."

"Very handsome," I murmured, though it wasn't flattering in the least. Or maybe it was just that I hated the sight of him, this twisted

Adonis who did the bidding of his perverted overlords for the privilege of a Rolex and an Audi.

Yolanda flitted up with a tray loaded with hors d'oeuvres, which Honey waved toward Jonny. "Darling, please eat. You are looking worryingly thin."

He placed a chubby hand on his belly, the soft curve of which pressed up against the thick polyester mesh of a LeBron James Miami Heat jersey. In truth, he appeared to be more bloated and corpulent than when I last saw him just a few months ago, while Honey was the one who looked like she needed the snacks, cheeks hollowed into dramatic canyons, hips sharp under the stretch jersey of her little black dress. "I've been with Father these past few days. His appetite is not strong. I didn't want to gorge myself while he picked away at his food." He stuffed a puff pastry piled high with black caviar into his mouth.

"Oh!" Honey put a humming hand up to her mouth. "But my spies tell me he is looking well. They say he is on the road to recovery."

"How many times do I have to tell you not to trust what those people say? They're just telling you what you want to hear, Moms. The truth is I don't think he has much more time," Jonny observed gravely, fingers fluttering over the platter as he searched for his next morsel.

Pinching her eyes shut, Honey clapped her hands over her ears, teeth raking the lipstick glaze off her lower lip as she whipped her head back and forth. Jonny rolled his eyes, delivered an entire deviled egg into his waiting maw. "So, *Ji Hoon*, how does it feel to be home?" he asked, mashed egg yolk squelching between his teeth.

"Stop!" Honey gurgled.

"Really good!" Ji Hoon boomed, licking caviar bubbles from his fingertips. "I was so terribly homesick every minute of those seven years. I only wish that I did not have to leave in such dishonor." He hung his head, the heroic angle of his jawline trembling.

"There, there, Harrison, you did your best," Honey cooed. "We will always remember your loyalty. And ultimately, your mission was successful, even if it did get a little messy there at the end."

"If only I had taken away her cell phone at the beginning," he moaned.

"Are you talking about me?" I asked.

Honey shook an admonishing finger at me. "That last phone call you made from the airport? It pointed authorities to Jeju-do and the hotel where you were last seen. Harrison had to make a hasty and unplanned departure. One of our best undercover agents out of commission."

This news caused my heart to beat so hard my teeth chattered, a happy rush of blood surging through my veins. Authorities were looking for me! My disappearance was being investigated! I quickly brought my glass to my lips to hide the excited tremor that disarranged my careful mask, hardening it back into place before tilting my head with birdlike coquettishness to inquire sweetly of Ji Hoon, "What about your girlfriend? Did she have to come back too?"

"Girlfriend?" Jonny leered. "Who's that?"

"She means Mi Yung." He sighed, flicking a restless thumb against the cleft of his chin.

Jonny snorted. "She's not his girlfriend, she's his fiancée!"

The three of them laughed as if at a particularly hilarious joke, while I escalated my smile to show some teeth in respectful appreciation of their badinage. "How is Mi Yung?"

"Last time I saw her," Ji Hoon admitted grimly, "she was screaming at me, then she kicked me in the crotch when I tried to kiss her good-bye. She couldn't believe I had been so stupid as to let Lisa hold on to her cell phone."

"She was piiiiissed off," Jonny said with satisfaction. "I could have had you executed, you know."

Eyes squinted tightly closed, Ji Hoon clasped his hands above his head as he bowed low to Jonny.

"Translating for the KCNA is just about a fate worse than death," Jonny teased with a laugh. "No wonder Mi Yung was angry with you. Now she has to come back to marry you."

We had finished the champagne, and Yolanda placed a bottle of Johnnie Walker Gold Label, a bucket of ice, and crystal tumblers onto the elephant-tusk coffee table.

"Ah!" Jonny motioned for her to pour him a glass, scratching at his belly with satisfaction. "It's nice to be out of those damn monkey suits! The high collars really chafe at the neck." He slapped at his, the flesh quaking with the impact. "Dear Leader has been rocking a new cut, though, have you seen it?"

"Not the lapels?" Honey murmured reverently.

"Yeah, the lapels!" Jonny howled, pointing at his mother. "How'd you know? Were you behind that? I should've known."

"Ohhh!" She patted herself on the chest with tiny, rapid flutters. "He wore it! I wasn't sure if he would. Was there a photo taken? Can you send it to me?"

They both looked expectantly at Ji Hoon, who had been gazing with unfocused eyes at a spot in between Jonny and Honey. Becoming aware that they expected something of him, he perked up. "What? A photo of the Dear Leader? Where were you?"

"Mokran," Jonny replied out of the side of his mouth as he wrestled a fat shrimp off a skewer with his teeth.

"Your father is a master of the power of the image," Honey twittered away. "By transitioning from the dour, laughable commie suit toward something more businesslike, he's preparing the people for controlled private enterprise, sending a message that they must stop sponging off the state and get their lazy butts in gear to start making money!"

"Yeah, Ma, whatever," Jonny said, leaning over for another canapé.

Miura-san, attired in a full chef's uniform replete with a double-breasted jacket with COOKIE embroidered over the breast pocket and an absurdly high toque, slipped into the room to announce sonorously, "Ladies and gentlemen, dinner is served," before retreating backward with slow, measured steps.

Stuffing a caviar puff into his mouth and taking another for the road, Jonny lumbered from the room, Honey and Yolanda trailing him, leaving Ji Hoon and me alone. He gently touched my arm. "I just want to say I'm sorry for tricking you, Lisa. I... It's just... I did it because..." His lips worked to get the right words out, but it seemed they couldn't be found.

Now that it was just he and I, I dropped the mask, allowing my features to curdle into a sneer. "You did it because you're a fucking coward, and a tool, and a heartless minion."

"You don't understand," he muttered, petting nervously at the unruly circumflex of an eyebrow.

"You could have defected instead of doing what you did."

"If I'd done that, my whole family would have been executed. And they would have hunted me down. I'd have to live the rest of my life in hiding."

"Better me than you, is that it?"

"Come on, Lisa," he pleaded. "It's not a bad life."

He gestured at the mounted heads staring sadly down at us, the animal pelts padding our feet, the picked-over platter of fancy nibbles.

"That kick that your girlfriend gave you? Did it feel anything like this?" And I drove the pointed toe of my red satin pump as hard as I could between his legs. He dropped to his knees to hold communion with the tiger, two pairs of glassy eyes staring back at each other. "You see what they did to my nose? If I ever get the chance I'm going to do the same thing to your dick, Ji Hoon."

And I swaggered forth toward the dining room with a hip-swinging victory strut, mouth cracked into a most un-Sally-like grin. Face crimson, Ji Hoon waddled in about five minutes later, lowering himself delicately into a chair.

The dinner started with snails poached in garlic butter, and Cookie kept the courses coming, each one paired with a different wine, so by the time we arrived at the venison steak, we were all sozzled. "I shot this motherfucker myself!" Jonny boasted as he sawed into dense, oozing flesh.

"Oh? Are there many wild animals in these parts?" I asked, savoring the duskiness of the meat, which Miura-san had prepared au poivre.

Food reeled about in the little porthole of his mouth like laundry in a dryer. "Did you know that Korea has one of the best game parks in the world? I call it Dead Man's Zoo, DMZ for short." He adopted the dramatic tones of a North Korean newscaster, his voice dropping to a deep bass, trembling with passionate conviction: "Over one thousand square kilometers of undisturbed wilderness with the greatest biodiversity in all of Asia, home to 5,097 species of plants and animals, including many endangered species like the Siberian tiger, the black bear, and the red-crowned crane."

"The DMZ?" I frowned. "But surely you can't hunt there. Isn't it heavily mined?"

"He sends in a platoon to capture the animals," Honey announced with great pride, as if he had done something extraordinarily brilliant, like cured cancer or mapped the human genome.

"No, they're not from the army," Jonny snapped at her, spearing another chunk of meat. "I wouldn't waste our soldiers that way. These are common criminals who are given the choice of either standing trial for their crimes or going on a mission to the Dead Man's Zoo. Funny thing, not one of them has ever chosen to stand trial."

"Funny thing," Ji Hoon echoed in an amazed I-never-thought-about-that tone, and we all laughed.

"They are told that if they survive the mission, they can go home. A lot of them make it home alive. They really do!" His cheeks were swollen with meat, a little trickle of juice leaking out the corner of his mouth.

"But the animals never do!" I joined in the half-wit banter, smiling woodenly, turning my head this way and that like Sally did when there was a break in the song.

"I like to hunt on horseback, with a pistol," he said, nodding with great satisfaction.

"Like a cowboy," his mother crowed, and he seemed pretty pleased with that comparison, pointing a forefinger at her and pretending to shoot repeatedly with his thumb.

As we were being served chocolate ganache cake, the icing so glossy I could see my reflection in it, Jonny hefted his snifter of brandy and bellowed, "Here's to my baby daughter!"

We all thrust our glasses in the air and then let them waver there uncertainly, Ji Hoon, Yolanda, and me waiting for Honey to be the first one to react.

"Is Sally pregnant?" Honey shrieked. "Oh, Jonny." A long, sibilant sigh of relief leaked slowly from her parted lips.

"No, it's not the singer," he said with a teasing smile.

Honey leaned back as if slapped. "What? Whose is it?"

His eyes thinned into new moon crescents as a lecherous grin took over his face, evoking a dimple just like Mindy's that pocked his cheek under his right eye. "Remember that Joy Brigade candidate you didn't like because of her bad teeth and the mole above her lip? Used to be a gymnast but now's a dancer? She's still pretty limber, let me tell you."

"Poor Sally, I can only imagine how she must feel. Married so recently," Honey hissed, pushing her cake away untouched. "Oh, the dirty little slut. I knew she was no good! She had the look of a real backstabber, like she'd do anything for success."

I was surprised at her vehement dislike of the mistress. After all, she was a mistress herself.

"When's this baby due?" Honey fretted.

"Three months," Jonny said, his voice thick with icing.

"And a girl you say?"

He nodded, running his tongue like a windshield wiper over his chocolate-smeared teeth.

"Well, at least there's that. Sally better hurry up and give you a son." Honey nodded seriously at the importance of her pronouncement. She seemed to be studying his face carefully—perhaps worrying about that recessive gene.

"Her name's Sol Ju, not Sally," Jonny growled irritably. "Stop calling her that!"

"Why, Jonny," she gasped, hand a shapely and lacquer-taloned shield over her heart.

"And why can't you be happy that I'm having a daughter? It's your first grandchild, after all! Unless this one"—he jerked his head in my direction—"had a bastard baby she had to give up for adoption too."

Honey cried, "Jonny! How can you be so cruel?" Not that she was standing up for me; she was merely embarrassed that he was bringing up her shameful past. "Of course I'm pleased for you. Only, don't you think you should be paying more attention to your wife? We need that baby boy!"

"Oh, don't worry, Moms. We'll get there. Take a chill pill."

Later that evening, after we had retired to the Versailles room for karaoke, while Honey and Ji Hoon were singing "Reunited," I whispered to Jonny, "I'm not sure if you remember, but you promised to send a computer programmer to help me with that website she wants me to build."

"Of course I remembered," Jonny declared, lips flecked with soggy bits of tobacco from the gargantuan cigar he was sucking on. "I have just the right guy picked out for you."

"Thank you very much." I kowtowed toward him from my seat, my forehead touching my knees. "I'm honored that you remembered. I know you have much more important things to do."

"Not really," he said. "Just waiting now for the old man to kick it. Then the fireworks really begin." He grinned around the soggy butt of the cigar. "And hey, great job with Moms. She used to call me five, six times a day, boo-hoo-hooing about how bored she was and how this wasn't the life she had imagined for herself. These last few months, I've hardly heard from her at all." He clenched his pudgy hand into a fist and gave me a thumbs-up.

"Glad to be of service," I said, folding at the waist once again. "She and I have a lot of fun together. It's been easy."

Life in Japan was easy. Everyone was polite and helpful, the streets were clean, the trains on time, the bars always open. My job was easy too, and the students in my elite Fukuoka high school adored me. I was a celebrity with a coterie of admirers, including a first-year student by the name of Kenji, who even joined the English Club, though he was largely absent because of baseball practice, which was a good thing because his presence ruined the vibe, the rather nerdy girls who made up the rest of the club embarrassed to the point of muteness whenever he showed up, so that it was just Kenji and me talking to each other as they giggled into their hands or hid behind their hair.

The majority of my colleagues in the Japan Exchange and Teaching Programme were fresh out of university, and this was their first real job. But to call it a real job was a bit of a stretch. We were props who were given busywork or no work at all, spending the majority of the day in the staff room rather than the classroom. More care was spent arranging a Friday night out than on lesson plans, and because my apartment was a short taxi ride from one of the entertainment centers of Fukuoka, on weekend mornings all eight tatami mats of my tiny apartment were strewn with inert bodies.

Filling the empty hours of the workday was sometimes a challenge, so I started to bring my journal to school, writing in it until my hand ached, the side bruised with ink. When I finished relating the details of my day, I'd compose sketches of the other teachers, dissect strange Japanese rituals, muse about the dynamics of the student body, ponder the bizarrities of Japanese TV, challenging myself to organize my thoughts into a coherent analysis of any given subject. The Japanese teachers admired me for my diligence and work ethic. They didn't care what I was working on, just that I looked like I was working hard.

During my second year, Kenji asked me to tutor him once a week during lunch. It was not unusual for students to request extra-curricular assistance, but mostly it was a one-time thing: help with an essay, a speech for a competition, or an application that had to be completed in English. Sometimes his friends would crowd against the window of the classroom and make comments that I could not understand, though the laughter that followed needed no translation. Once in a while, one of them would make kissy noises, and Kenji would spring up and chase them away. Even the teachers knew what he was doing, as my supervisor had smiled knowingly when I asked for permission to use the classroom and commented, "That Kenji is a bold one, isn't he?" No one, including myself, thought there was any harm in it.

One cold February day, we had brought photos of our families to show each other while reviewing the passive and active verb forms. His photo showed a jocularly smiling father, as if one moment of family coziness could make up for the late nights he was obliged to spend at the office; a mother with her face obscured under a bucket hat; a chunky older sister in her school sports uniform, glaring aggressively at the camera; and adorable little Kenji, one eye squinted against the sun, the other holding up a Pokémon figure. He carefully studied my photo as I pointed out my mother and Scott, explaining that my parents were divorced. He was disappointed that I had not brought a photo of my father and asked, "Isn't he Japanese?"

"Who? My father?" Shivering in the unheated classroom, I rubbed my hands between my thighs for warmth. "No. He's white. I was adopted from Korea."

"What is adopted?" he asked, reaching for his dictionary.

I spelled it out for him.

"Adopt, adopt, adopt," he muttered, flicking through the tissue-thin pages. "*Yosh!* Adopt!" He read the definition and then gazed at me with such tender pity that I looked away from him with a little laugh. "I didn't know," he whispered reverently. "Just like Toby-san."

I was irritated by his reaction and ready to get back to the warmth of the kerosene-heated staff room. "Who's Toby-san?" I asked curtly.

"He is a famous ski... ski... player? How do you say?" He mimed a slalom with his shoulders, making the noise skis might make over slushy snow.

"Skier?"

"Skier. He won in Torino Olympics." Leaning toward me, he was excited, forgetting to be flirtatious and cute. "Like you, he was Korean baby. He adopted with American family..."

"Ah!" I clapped my hands, glad to get back to grammar. "This is a perfect example of the use of the passive verb form. Toby-san *was adopted* by his parents. His parents *adopted* Toby-san. Do you see? Toby-san had no choice, he was just a baby—"

"He was three years old," Kenji interrupted me eagerly. "He... *nan darou?*" Kenji struggled to come up with the words, fingers plucking at the awkward bristle of his adolescent facial hair. "He was at the shop... and cannot see his mother, cannot meet her again."

"He got lost?" I had become fairly adept at translating high school English.

"*Sou, sou,*" Kenji agreed. "A family from America was adopted him..."

"No, no," I protested. "The family is active. They are the one who take the action. The family *adopted* Toby-san." I hugged myself to convey the adopting as active.

"Toby-san won *buronzu* in Olympics. Because he is like this"—
Kenji pulled the corners of his eyes taut—"he is very famous in Japan
and Korea. Quickly, many mothers and fathers in Korea say, 'Maybe
Toby-san is my child.' Everyone wants to be mother and father of Toby-san."

"Really? He has people clamoring to be his parents?" Talk about
a famous adopted person. This guy was living the adoptee fantasy!
"Did he find his parents?"

"Yes! His father and his brother. They are looking the same, all of
them! Same hair, same earring. It is so surprise."

I couldn't wait to get to the computer to search for the story and
then send it to Mindy, who was planning to register with a group
called MotherFinders to search for her birth mother. "What about Toby-san's mother?"

"It is so sad," Kenji said mournfully. "Toby-san does not meet her.
The mother and father divorce, same as your mother and father. She
does not want to see Toby-san never again."

"Oh." Probably better not to tell Mindy about Toby Dawson after
all.

Six days after Jonny's visit, I entered my office to find a stranger sitting at my desk, a laptop computer propped open in front of him. He
sprang up, pecking at the air with a flurry of bows. "Hello, miss. My
name is Gun Ho. I am here to help you with your website."

"Pleased to meet you, Gun Ho. You can call me Lisa." I stuck out
my hand, and he stared at it for a moment before fluttering into another series of bows. His skin was ghostly white, as if the only light he
ever saw came from the glow of a computer screen. His head was too
large for his body, his face too large for his features, which were oddly
clustered in the center, so he seemed all forehead, cheeks, and chin.

We sat side by side, and though I would turn my head toward
him as we conversed, he never looked at me, addressing the computer
instead. "Please describe what kind of website you would like."

"Well, first and foremost, its purpose is to entertain, but it is also
meant to advise, uplift, promote patriotism, and, of course, praise the

Dear Leader." I gestured at the pin he wore over the left breast pocket of his drab olive jacket. "We want something eye-catching, with bold graphics, lots of photos, fun fonts. A home page that features the buzziest stories, and then different tabs you can click on, one for sports, another for fashion, another for household tips, that sort of thing. Um, can I show some examples of websites whose design we might want to model ours after?"

He bowed toward the computer, which I took as a yes. Fingers trembling with anticipation, I touched the keyboard, the plastic so smooth and inviting, so familiar. As I typed into the browser, he intoned, "Please be aware that it is forbidden to go to social media and news sites. Every stroke you make on the keyboard is being recorded and may be reviewed in order to verify that you are not trying to communicate with anyone. If that happens, the consequences will be very severe, for both you and me."

"Oh, yes, sure." I gulped.

After I showed him the desirable features of several different websites, Gun Ho nodded, his neck a thin stalk to his dandelion head. "I understand, miss. May I ask who will be using this website?"

"The people."

"Which people?"

"The North Korean people."

He blinked rapidly, his eyes squinching into small wrinkles. "Which North Korean people?"

"All of them!" I was beginning to get irritated with him. Perhaps he wasn't too bright. No doubt he was the lowest of the low, the office runt dispatched to help me while his colleagues sweated away at the real work of programming viruses and breaching highly secure networks.

His eyes strobed shut several times before he said, "OK."

"There's one other website I want to show you, but I can't remember its title," I said, speaking softly so that he wouldn't hear the nervous tremor in my voice. My fingers hovered over the keyboard as I racked my brain. I couldn't enter names into the search engine, as that would be an immediate red flag, and even if Gun Ho wasn't bright enough to catch what I was doing, somebody else was sure to be. What phrase might I use that could lead me to what I was looking for, namely that people were looking for me? The only thing I could think of was "famous adopted people." Up came the list, all the usual links to listicles of adopted celebrities. But there on the bottom of the page was a website that was actually called famousadoptedpeople. com. That was new. I clicked on it, summoning a blog, the title a theater marquee at the top of the page, a rotating gallery of images beneath it—a yin-yang symbol, the American and South Korean flags, a mother cradling her baby, a joint, a diary, a typewriter, an American passport—and then, beneath that, text. The latest entry, dated from a few days ago, was titled "Toby Dawson." As I quickly scanned what was written there, I wondered if I were hallucinating. Those were my words, an excerpt from my journal.

> After the Toby Dawson incident, the Korean government began to do a lot of Seoul searching on the issue of exporting their babies to affluent white countries instead of taking care of them themselves. Toby's story is problematic in so many ways. Instead of searching for his parents, the authorities quickly introduced him into the adoption pipeline and shipped him off to the US. But I also suspect that the family purposely wanted to lose him, since apparently no one ever went searching for him. The South Koreans want to get rid of their babies; the Americans want to take them. I think about my own mother, giving up her half-breed baby. Was she coerced by the government? She was definitely coerced by society, because in Korea it is deeply shameful for an unwed mother to bear a child, especially one of impure blood...

"Very nice," Gun Ho said, nodding slowly. "I like the carousel of images at the top. Very eye-catching."

"Yeah, isn't it cool?" I managed to gurgle. "Can I just...?" I clicked on the "About" tab. There was a photo of a woman in silhouette, her face so deep in shadow that none of her features could be discerned.

Hello, adopted people and those who love them! I am a transracial Korean-born adoptee and these are random excerpts from my journals, written over the span of my lifetime, and from the overwhelming response I've had so far, I see that I am not the only conflicted, angry, and maladjusted adoptee out there! I've chosen to remain anonymous for a variety of reasons, but like every adoptee, I'm searching for myself, so if you know anything about my real identity, I'd love to hear from you via the comments page...

"Kenji came through for me," I whispered in awe. From the name of the website and the prominence of yin-yang images, I knew that Mindy had come through for me too. My throat tightened as I wondered if I would ever get to prove myself worthy of her love.

"Excuse me?"

"Just reading out loud," I said, clearing my throat.

"This page is not that interesting," Gun Ho noted. "But I suppose that is typical for an 'About' page. They are not why people go to a website."

"Uh, yeah," I said, reluctantly clicking on the last tab. "Let's just take a peek at the comments section to see how they have organized it."

Expecting to find a sparsely populated page of a few desultory comments, I was amazed to see comments that dated from that very day, a new one even popping up as I scrolled down to view the immensity of the responses. "So great to finally find an adoption blog written by an actual adoptee and not the adoptive parents!" "THANK YOU!" "The entry on how your overdose permanently changed your relationship with your parents just broke my heart." "Shame on you! I hope your adoptive mother doesn't read this. What ingratitude!!!" "Please contact me if you are looking for an agent. This has all the elements for a great memoir." "Methinks thou doth protest too much about not wanting to find your birth mother."

Gun Ho rustled nervously as I lingered there, eyes racing to read as much as I could. "I do not think the comments page is important," he announced, hand inching toward the keyboard.

"But we're going to want a comments page on our website," I protested, itching to type that I was here! in North Korea! and to please send Bill Clinton, or at least Jimmy Carter, to rescue me!!

"It seems unlikely your website will have a comments page," Gun Ho said, and he exited out of the website.

I stared blankly at the screen, nodding as Gun Ho told me what I needed to do for him next, his droning voice lost in the sudden oceanic roar that filled my ears. Mindy was on the case, and she was bringing with her Margaret's Pentagon contacts and Trip's high-powered law firm. They were looking for me and wanted to bring me home. They were signaling to me that if I did my part and found a way to contact them, they would do theirs and rescue me.

Honey instructed me to move my Saturday session with Miura-san to the next day in my daily planner and write in "Fun with the Gang." Sickened at the thought of having to be all chummy with them after they had been such willing participants in my humiliation, I pleaded with her, "Why do they have to come? Aren't I enough company for you?"

"Are you jealous?" She seemed quite pleased with the thought.

"I don't want to share you." I thrust my lower lip out, an unhappy baby.

"That's so sweet. But poor dears, their lives are so dull in Pyong-yang. Besides, I want to show off the new you. I've been putting them off, waiting for the bruises around your eyes to fade away. After all the trouble we went through, it's a shame to just keep you to myself."

Which was just what I dreaded, having to accept their compliments as if they delighted me. Having to see the glee and the pity in their eyes at my comeuppance, me the cautionary tale that kept them all in line. Having to make small talk with the man who had broken my nose with his fist and then ruined it with his scalpel. "Can I have a bluie to help me get through the evening, please? Just to get me over my resentment at not having you all to myself."

Since we were both in the throes of peak bluie at the time, Honey agreed, wrapping a pill in a silk handkerchief for me to take back to my room.

Bluie-blasted when I entered the Versailles room to greet the Gang, the urge to forgive burned ardently in my breast. As expected, they all oohed and aahed at the new me, the women marveling over my nose, the men making stupid cracks about how blondes have more fun, Dr. Panzov assuring me that he knew from a lifetime of experience. Honey stood by my side, petting compulsively at my arm, and I knew that she too had taken a bluie. She was wearing a navy gown with a deep V-neck, her collarbone taut against her skin, chest rippled with breastbone and ribs, and I thought that she better be careful with the liposuction or she would soon have all her insides sucked out of her.

Even the bluie could not make me amenable to Harvey's or Wendell's company, so I chatted with Patience and Lahela, or rather with Patience as Lahela nodded along, smiling when we smiled, laughing when we laughed. Before long, Wendell came to join us, standing just behind Patience and Lahela, head jerking to the side to signify that he wanted to have a word, before wandering away again. When dinner was announced, he and I lingered behind. Hooding over me like a cobra about to strike, he hissed, "Have you thought about my proposal?"

"Forget your stupid plan, Wendell. I have a plan, a real plan, and all I need is five minutes on the internet. Can you arrange that?"

He hesitated, eyes ticking back and forth as he calculated. "Yesss," he considered tentatively. "But it'll cost you a lot more money. Because you still have to get to Pyongyang. And then you'd have to pay a small fortune for my friend to take the risk of allowing you online access, because if he's caught, he'll be executed on the spot."

"How much money?"

"That pretty watch might be enough." He cuffed my wrist, twisting it this way and that to make the diamonds sparkle before I could wrest my arm away. "Big-ticket items, like the gold-plated lighters that are stashed in every room for when Jonny comes for a visit, or the silver salt and pepper shakers, are the fastest way to get your money. Don't forget you also have to pay off Cookie. I've already discussed this with him, he'll explain what you have to do." He finished talking in a rush because we had arrived at the dining room, Yolanda waiting for us at the door, her suspicious gaze traveling from me to Wendell and back again.

When I returned to my room, still jazzed on the bluie, I perused my armoire for items to smuggle to Cookie, deciding I'd start small with a pair of cable-knit tights, which were much too warm to wear in the eternally mild climes of the compound.

Chapter 15

"Every adopted person has to deal with the fact of abandonment, and what that has done to them... I based so much of my being on whatever that was, and the anger that I held to my birth mother, that I needed her to stay in that villain place."

–Frances McDormand

The bluie kept my mind spinning all night, constructing the perfect narrative of escape. I had thrown out the internet to Wendell more to shut him up than anything, but when he said he actually could get me access, my souped-up neurons seized upon that one detail, the gritty heart around which I spun a nacreous shell to form a flawless, shining scenario that seemed not only eminently logical but even inevitable: Wendell's "friend" would smuggle me to Pyongyang, where I'd contact the Famous Adopted People website, returning to the compound the same night to wait for my rescue. Once the news of my captivity in North Korea became public, Jonny would be unable to kill me without triggering an international incident. Meanwhile, Jonny's father would discover that Jonny had kidnapped me without his permission, thereby scuttling Jonny's succession, so I would not only save myself but very possibly the entire planet as well. The ensuing power struggle would trigger the collapse of the whole regime and North Korea would be liberated, all thanks to me.

But in the gunmetal light of the approaching dawn, when the world had lost its bluie iridescence and my body ached for sleep but my heart could not be quieted, my eyelids spring-loaded to snap open every time I tried to close them, a sour taste secreting from my salivary glands and my jaw muscles twitching uncontrollably, I knew it was all delusion. The story was cracked from the beginning. Wendell himself hadn't seen the internet in years, so why should I think he could get me access to it? More likely, Wendell was stringing me along, encouraging me to think there was a higher purpose for my petty thievery than turning a quick buck.

As I watched the first golden rays of sunlight appear across the ceiling, my stomach queasy but my brain finally quieting, I decided on two things: to take the tights to Cookie anyway and to never take a bluie again if I could help it. If, as I suspected, Wendell's scheme was just a way for him to earn some extra cash, then maybe the money I made could come in handy at a later date for some reason as yet unknown to me. It was only prudent to keep all of my options open. As for the bluies, I could see the way that, in just a matter of months, they were erasing Honey, the once brilliant shine of her eyes now a scratched blurriness, her skin papery, pleating loosely across the backs of her hands, arms scored with the red tracks left by her scratching nails, limbs like rope knotted at the joints. I practiced cupping an imaginary bluie in my hand, where it would stay as I pretended to toss it in my mouth before transferring it to a pocket.

That afternoon, Miura-san looked as tired as I felt. "I am happy when guests leave," he said with uncharacteristic vehemence. "It is too much work to feed everyone."

"Do you ever get a day off?" I asked as he sifted a bag of flour onto the counter of the butcher-block island. We were going to attempt to make our own pasta today.

"Only one time a week on Tuesday," he said mournfully, forming the flour into a mound, white particles floating spectrally in the air around him. "But I must make the foods for Tuesday on Monday. It is too much work, Lisa-san. I am old and very tired." And he looked it, lower lids drooping to reveal the bloodshot whites of his eyes, puffy flesh pouched underneath, jowls hanging heavily as if too exhausted to stay on his face. "I miss my home. I am tired of living underground."

"Where do you sleep?" I inquired. "Here in the compound?"

"We have servants' quarters." He pointed at the floor. "Down below."

"Who lives there? Ting and that other woman?"

"Ting, Mei-ling, and others."

"The guards? Is that where they watch the surveillance screens?"

"*Sou, sou.* And others."

"What others?"

"You think only three or four people can run all this? We are many people here."

"Where are they?"

"Where you are not." He snickered, waving his fingers in the air, sending the flour motes swirling in random directions.

"Do you all live together?"

"Yes. We have our own rooms, and a room for playing, and a dining room, and, of course, a kitchen. We have our own chef!"

It was dizzying to think about—a whole community lurking below this one, the shadow world of a shadow world with invisible servants, hidden chambers, secret transactions, the chef with a chef. Remembering my own secret transaction, I offhandedly remarked, "So, um, I didn't know you and Wendell were such good friends."

He paused to wipe his forehead with a sleeve. "He is very friendly, like many Americans. Like you."

I frowned—the comparison wasn't flattering. "He said I should bring you things..." I let my words hang in the air with the flour dust.

He looked at me mournfully, fine white particles scurfing his stubbled cheek. "Yes."

"I have something." My hand patted at my waist.

"Sure, Lisa-san?" His eyes, normally hidden under half-mast lids, probed questioningly. "Maybe more safe not to."

I replied emphatically, "I'm sure, Miura-san."

He nodded slowly, slapping the clinging flour from his hands. "Let me show you where is the garbage." He handed me the empty bag of flour and led me into the greenhouse, saying, "You know already we put foodstuffs there," and pointing to the compost bin. "Here"—he opened the door of a small plastic shed—"we are putting glasses, metals, papers. Just like Japan, no?" A small, sad smile. "This"—he pointed at a large wooden box with a hinged lid—"is for every other garbage, for example, plastic, rubber, garbage from bathroom." He entered the shed, which was too small to hold the two of us, and, dropping down into a squat, tugged at the bottom of the crate, which pulled out like a drawer. He didn't say anything, only pulled it in and out twice, then stood up with a popping of his knees and exited the shed.

The drawer was not as easy to open as Miura-san had made it seem, requiring a good yanking. The tights left a damp patch of sweat where they had been tucked into my waistband. I hesitated, wondering if it was worth the risk, before sliding the drawer firmly back in place. Back in the kitchen, Miura-san was cracking eggs into a crater that he had scooped from the mound of flour. "How will I get the money, Miura-san?"

"Wendell-san give you next time he comes."

"Can I trust him?" I fretted. "How will I know he's giving me everything I'm owed?"

"Oh, Wendell-san is honest man," Miura-san assured me, his cheeks shaking as he strained to work the eggs into the flour with a fork. "He always gives me my money."

"I was surprised that you wanted some money from me as well, Miura-san," I mentioned casually, shoring up the flour that trickled away from his fork. "I thought we were friends."

He shaped the paste into a gooey ball, pressing down on it with the heels of his hands. "Before, I get salary in real money, sometimes yen, sometimes yuan. But now they only give won. I need money for going home. I want to open sushi-ya."

"Can you really go home?" I pressed. "Won't you miss your... young friends?"

His fists pounded at the dough. "Yes," he said, and then again, "Yes."

Heeding the advice of Kang Chol-Hwan, I kept busy, arriving at my "office" on time whether Gun Ho was to be there or not, diligently writing up article ideas like "A Day in the Life of a Salesgirl at the Paradise" or "How to Cook a Kaeson Hamburger in Your Own Home," working the prescribed office hours to the minute. Honey's schedule left me with very little free time, for which I was grateful, and the evenings that I didn't spend with her, I read whichever book she had chosen for me, *King Lear* followed by *The Man in the High Castle*, *Alice's Adventures in Wonderland*, and *Uncle Tom's Cabin*.

Through it all was Honey. We were a dynamic mother-and -daughter business duo, though our business was watching humorous video clips, browsing gossip sites, keeping up with the fashion blogs, poring over catalogs and haute couture websites, reveling in frivolity. The less uplifting it was, the more we worshipped it. If it was self-indulgent, unnecessary, a waste of precious resources, or absolutely useless, we studied it, debated it, endlessly dissected it. Occasionally, I updated her on the progress of the website, showing her a few beta pages that Gun Ho had produced, the text in Korean so I couldn't read a word of it. But it looked good, with neon fonts that seemed to jump from the screen, a carousel of scrolling images, a scattering of animated GIFs.

One morning my knock at the door of Honey's inner sanctum went unanswered. I waited some minutes to let Yolanda finish blow-drying Honey's hair or buffing her fingernails or giving her a foot massage, or whatever it was that the two of them did together behind closed doors, before knocking again. Another long pause, so I bashed hard against the steel, the increased volume disproportionate to the pain that cracked through my knuckles. Putting an ear up to the door, I could hear nothing but the sound of my own breath drawing into and out of my lungs. Yolanda was never behind on the schedule, and I had an intuition—maybe mother-daughter, maybe a more prosaic awareness of Honey's deteriorating state—that something was going on with Honey. I was just about to take off a spectator pump to bang on the door with the heel when it whipped open and Yolanda frantically waved me in. I could hear Honey yelling in the background and then a crash of something splintering into a thousand pieces.

"You must help me with Madam," Yolanda panted, French twist unraveling down her neck, a popped-out button trailing from her jacket by a thread as we rushed together into the one room of Honey's inner sanctum that I had not yet penetrated: her bedroom.

There, standing on an enormous bed that shimmered with crimson satin sheets and coverlet, a deranged Honey, hair in a ratty halo around her grinning skull face, screamed, "How can he blame me? It's not my fault! I tried to warn him!"

One of the many mirrors decorating her walls had been shattered, jagged shards of glass clinging to the elegant gold chinoiserie frame, fragments tessellating the floor, catching the sun that poured in from the picture window in crazy flashes. Glass crunching under our shoes, Yolanda and I flanked Honey. Locking our arms around her, we managed to topple her onto her bed, where she flopped beneath us, slippery as a fish.

"Madam, I have your bluies all ready for you, all you need to do is take them."

"Shut up, Yoyo!" Honey screamed, eyes squeezed shut, mouth an open wound that could not be stanched. "You're not the one who just got called unspeakable names by her own son because his mistress gave birth to a baby daughter with blue eyes! You should have heard the horrible things he said to me! After all I've sacrificed for him!"

Wriggling out from underneath Honey's prone body, Yolanda panted, "Don't let go of her. I'll be right back."

"Have your bluie, Honey," I advised, my voice coming out in jolts as I rode her bucking body like a broncobuster. "That will make you feel better."

"I've sacrificed everything for that boy!" Her voice shattered and came back together again in a tortured howl.

"You're a good mother. Everybody knows that," I assured her in ragged gasps.

Yolanda returned, a plastic box tucked under her elbow. "Madam, Madam," she crooned soothingly. "You must stop! You're getting yourself much too excited."

"Does he want me to pluck my own eyes out? Is that what he wants? Bring me something to do it with and I will!" She dry sobbed, chest heaving, legs flailing like two autonomous life-forms with wills of their own.

"Grab her other arm and lie sideways over her," Yolanda hissed as she struggled to hold on to Honey's arm.

I inched my body sideways to lay my stomach over her hips, pinning her upper body with mine while her legs kicked the air. I put a restraining hand over her womb, touching for the first time that place from which I had sprung. It was a hollow bowl between the twin blades of her hip bones, my palm sinking until it seemed to reach the knobs of her spine. "There, there, Mom. It's OK. Everything's going to be all right. Just relax and let Yoyo help you."

"Try and keep still, Madam," Yolanda grimaced, attempting to line up a syringe with the swollen blue vein that snaked down the inside of her arm.

"I can't keep her down much longer," I grunted, feeling her body, a cyclone of clammy flesh, move and twist beneath mine.

A moment later, Yolanda sank the needle into Honey's arm and depressed the plunger. She stared up at us, hazy and unfocused, her hair a crackling frizz around the washed-out, weary teardrop of her face. I had never seen her without makeup on before and was surprised to see faint freckles, not too dissimilar from my own, spattered across her cheeks and nose. Tiny wrinkles frilled the edges of her mouth; dark circles rimmed the hollows under her eyes. Her lids, bruised with blue, dropped down like a curtain, and when she raised them again, she seemed present in her body once more, as if suddenly waking from a fainting spell or a hypnotic interlude.

"Lisa?" she murmured.

"Honey," I replied, stroking a cheek, the skin gelid to the touch. "You gave Yoyo and me a scare."

"Lisa," she repeated, staring up at my face as I overhung her like a doting lover. "You called me 'Mom' just now."

Had I? I looked questioningly at Yolanda, who nodded that I had. Tugging at the hem of her silk-and-lace nightgown, which had ridden up to bare the desiccated stalks of her thighs, I murmured, "I guess I did."

"Will you say it again?" She gazed up at me, eyes limpid as a mountain stream.

"All right," I said, my breath still coming in ragged gasps from wrestling with her. "Mom." And as I said it, I meant it. For as I gazed down at her, I saw me in her, or her in me, nose or no nose. She was the abyss that I had long tried to fill with pills, drown with alcohol, and paper over with good times. Here, finally, was the link between us that I had been searching for all this time.

"Say you love me, baby," she whispered, the cold radiating from her body cooling the sweat from mine. "Tell your mama you love her."

I didn't love her, but I recognized her, as familiar to me as my own self. She was not a monster, not entirely; she was a human being, with flaws that were all too intimate. By saying it, I was telling myself as well: "I love you."

"Just remember, I love you," my father said, hugging me close as I buried my face into the crook of his neck and took in the familiar scent of Nivea shaving cream, my cheek against his weathered skin.

He was on his way home from a business trip in Indonesia, and we met in Osaka. Now that I was older, the biannual reunions of my childhood and adolescence had slackened, and we hadn't seen each other in more than a year. Since the overdose, something had changed in our relationship; he was more tentative toward me, as if I were something worrisome and fragile, something to feel guilty about. Dedicated to bettering the far-flung lives of those less fortunate than he was, I suspected that he felt guilty for failing to help his own damaged daughter. In turn, I tried too hard to show him how "normal" I was, and both of us knew that we were hiding a part of ourselves from the other in order not to strain our relationship further.

In Osaka, we stayed at a capsule hotel, toured the sights, visited some *onsen*, and ate in cramped, proletarian restaurants under train tracks. He liked to do as the natives did when he traveled, so for his last night, I took him to a dingy *izakaya* that seemed to cater mostly to university students, where we both drank too much, which was par for the course for me but unusual for my father. As I refilled his sake cup, dribbling a path between his cup and mine, I said, "I've re-upped for a third year in the JET Programme, but I already regret it. My life is pretty good here, but the job is a joke."

"Life's too short for regrets," he asserted, a smile wobbling on his lips. "Regrets are for losers."

"I guess I'm a bit of a loser then, because I have quite a few regrets," I bantered back.

But he took it the wrong way. Slapping a hand to his forehead, he groaned, "Oh god, Lisa, I'm sorry. What a stupid thing for me to say. Of course, we all have regrets. We wouldn't be human if we didn't."

There was a reply ready on my lips, but I hesitated, second-guessing myself, wondering if he would see it as a rebuke or a cry for help.

In the meantime, he started to speak slowly, staring into the bottom of his sake cup.

"For instance, my biggest regret is never talking to you about the divorce. I often go back to that abrupt announcement we made just before dumping you off at Korean Kamp and wonder if things would have turned out differently if we hadn't handled it so badly."

I shifted uncomfortably on my haunches. Was he actually agreeing that I was a loser? All of a sudden I didn't want to go down this conversational path that I had started us on, but he had already set off, and there was no turning him back.

"Your mom and I thought it was the best way to tell you, at the time. I always meant to discuss it with you later, but time passed, things kept getting in the way, and then it seemed too late. I didn't want to dwell in the past with you, especially since we get so little time together."

"It's OK, Dad," I said jocularly. "It wasn't the divorce that messed me up; it's just the way I'm wired."

He grimaced, tugging at his ear as he struggled to articulate his thoughts. "I know some kids of divorce blame themselves, and I just want you to know that your mother and I did not break up because of you."

"Dad, you really don't have to..." I murmured.

But apparently he did. "It was just, over time, our goals changed. She wanted to build the catering business at home, and I wanted, no *needed*, to get out and work abroad."

He leaned heavily against the wall, unfolding his crossed legs to stick them straight out under the table, polishing off his cup of sake in one gulp, as if it were rotgut instead of the most expensive drink on the menu. I scooched back against the wall too so that he wouldn't be talking to my back, which he didn't notice he was doing because he was gazing down soddenly toward his own navel.

"It was almost like a drug, and I got *hooked* on this idea that I was spreading enlightenment and prosperity to the underprivileged peoples of the world. I pictured you running barefoot and scabby kneed, chasing crickets and making mud pies with your local friends in some untouched paradise." With a shaky sigh, he brought the sake cup up to his mouth, only to find it was empty. I signaled at the waitress for another. "It was not a dream that your mother shared. She envisioned a childhood of ballet and riding lessons, trips to the mall for back-to-school clothes, cones at Baskin-Robbins, sleepaway camps. Of course, I didn't want to leave you behind, but it was only natural that you live with your mother. Only later did I realize that you might have considered that I had abandoned you, especially after I married Esther and settled in Gaborone for good..."

The waitress excused herself with a "*Shitsurei shimasu*" as she slid a full flask of sake onto our table, thankfully interrupting my father from his exasperating prattle.

"More sake." He chuckled. "Oh, Lisa, I don't know if I should."

"Come on, Dad," I cajoled, lifting a cup in salute to him and feeling a perverse pleasure watching him gulp his cup dry. "You're living like a local."

I waved my hand at a neighboring table—where a young man slumped facedown, drool puddled under his open mouth, while the party raged on around him—and tried to change the subject by explaining the intricacies and different stages of the Japanese *enkai*, or drinking party.

"A change from Indonesia, I can tell you that!" Dad said, and laughed. Then, to my dismay, he returned to his soliloquy, not quite slurring his words but sloshing them together. "Of course, the irony of it all is that the light that I thought I had brought to the darker corners of the world just sputtered out. Pssh!" He pinched the air as if he were snuffing out a candle. "Here we are, a quarter of a century later, and I'm still going to the same countries with the same projects, and some people are benefiting from it, but it isn't the downtrodden."

The drink had relaxed his neck muscles, and his head lolled forward, and I noticed that his widow's peak had now eroded into a monk's tonsure. His head continued to nod forward, and my first thought was he had fallen asleep, and I felt embarrassed for him and somewhat ashamed of myself for urging the sake on him only because I wanted to drink more, but then I was horrified to realize that he was crying, a thin stream of tears rolling down the eroded gullies of his cheeks to drip off the flaccid flesh of his jawline. Was he crying for me, or the fact that the benighted peoples of the world were not getting the help they needed? Was it all one confused jumble in his mind, me and the benighted peoples and his inability to help any of us? Whatever the answer, he had succeeded in communicating one thing quite clearly: my father had regrets, and I was one of them.

At the Kansai Airport the next day, he suggested we should make a date to meet every year to explore an unknown city together, given all the fun we had had in Osaka. This seemed to me like something that old friends or clandestine lovers would do, not a normal father-daughter interaction. I muttered weakly that it was a brilliant plan, painfully aware I had done that—I had made our relationship strained and false—him so unsure of how to relate to me that he drank himself stupid because that was really the only connection that I offered him. It made me sad, and as he was hypersensitive to my moods, that made him sad, so we said good-bye with sadness, not at our parting, but at the tentative nature of our relationship.

"I love you too," I whispered into his neck. Looking back on it, if those were the last words I ever said to him, that was at least one thing in my life that I would not regret.

From the windows of Honey's inner sanctum, I had watched the autumn come and go, the foliage kindling into sparks of color before bursting into a fiery conflagration, spangling the air as the leaves drifted down to festoon the rock garden, curling and desiccating and eventually blowing away, but since the indoor temperature never strayed from that of a soft spring day, it was easy to regard the change of the seasons as something fake, like Muzak playing in the background or a Yule log on TV, and I was shocked when Honey started to discuss Thanksgiving plans. While the thought of Thanksgiving invigorated Honey, who bounced back like a rubber ball from the strange episode in her bedroom, it depressed me, as I thought about home: my mother's moist chestnut stuffing and green bean casserole crackling with fried onions, the table crowded with out-of-town relatives and guests who were far away from their own families, the traditional after-dinner walk along the Little Falls Park trail before returning home for mulled wine and pumpkin whoopie pie.

The Gang arrived in high spirits, filling up the empty space of the cavernous rooms with noise, laughter, and commotion. Resplendent in a bead-encrusted, long-sleeved, floor-length gown that hid her gaunt frame, Honey looked like her old self. Dr. Panzov had arrived early to inject her lips with filler, and maybe he pumped something into her face as well, for it looked firmer, juicier, lambent. And she was up to her old wicked ways, announcing a game of strip Scrabble after our sumptuous turkey dinner. From the start, it was clear that the point of the game was for Lahela, the only non-native English speaker among us, to get naked. It was, for no apparent reason, her turn to be humiliated. Once the game was over, Lahela was not allowed to put her clothes back on, huddling in on herself with arms crossed in an X to shield as much of her nudity as possible.

"Oh, Lahela, now I'm going to have to get rid of that chair you're sitting on!" Honey complained, and I felt ashamed for her, for the broken person that was my mother.

"What if she gets up and moves?" Patience grumbled. "I do not want to accidentally sit on her pussy sweat." The others hooted with laughter, though I did not, surprised and disheartened at Patience's treachery toward Lahela before understanding it was a ploy to get Lahela back in her clothes when she added, "Better let her put her knickers back on. You don't know what diseases we could catch."

"Hey!" Wendell interjected, a look of slow comprehension dawning across his stupefied features. "Thass my wife you're talkin' about! She has no diseases."

Irritated, I studied him. Wendell had not gone through his usual eye-rolling, head-jerking routine to indicate that he wanted a private chat, and now he was getting too drunk to be coherent. If I too had been drinking, I wouldn't have minded so much, but tonight my instinct told me to stay sober. That my instinct would tell me to stay sober was in itself unprecedented, but what was even more remarkable was that I heeded it.

"You know, you're right, Patience," Honey marveled, tipping her lipstick-smudged wineglass in Patience's direction. "It's really not often that you have a thought that is worth listening to, but you've brought up a good point here. Give Lahela back her panties, Yolanda."

Yolanda held them up, old-lady nylon underpants with little worms of elastic wriggling from the waistband, the seat saggy and worn to transparency. "Really, Lahela, did you rob these off your grandmother? Surely Wendell gives you enough pocket money to let you buy decent underwear at the Paradise." She made a great show of turning the underwear inside out, luffing it around like it was a sail. "Eww, Lahela, the crotch looks like a mattress in a brothel in Hillbrow, man. So dirty!" She showed us the faint ghosts of menstruations past that stained the crotch before tossing the underwear. It parachuted through the air like a giant spore, landing about five feet away from where Lahela was huddled.

Hoping to distract the onlookers, especially the leering Dr. Panzov, who followed Lahela's every move as she scrambled back into her underpants, I suggested, "Karaoke?" The more noise, the easier it would be for me to exchange a few private words with Wendell.

"Oh," Honey groaned, "I'm so bored of karaoke!"

Oh god, I thought, *please don't let her choose charades.*

Probably all of us were thinking the same thing, Harvey going on the offense by braying, "I tell you what I used to enjoy on a Saturday night as a young buck in Norfolk: dancing."

"Dancing!" Honey cooed breathlessly in her baby-doll voice, a sure sign that she was captivated by the idea. "What do you think of that, Lilo?"

"I think it's just what we need to shake off the tryptophans," I exclaimed.

Everyone was ordered to clear the floor of furniture except for Wendell, who was dispatched to fetch the CD player and CDs, with me quickly offering to assist him. His absurdly long legs carried him in a spidery scurry down the corridor, forcing me into a trot to keep up.

"Where's my money, Wendell?" I asked as soon as we were out of earshot.

He didn't answer, striding ever faster, his gangling body striking a praying mantis–like shadow up the dimly lit walls.

"Come on, Wendell, how much have I earned so far?" I persisted, breaking into a gallop to catch up with him, pressing a hand against the stitch that had developed in my food-swollen side.

"You're not passing along anything of value, Lisa," Wendell said. "You've only earned about thirteen dollars."

"Thirteen dollars?!" I spat. "That mascara was Chanel, which retails for, like, thirty dollars, and those tights were Wolford, which sell for fifty dollars online!"

"This isn't online," he said. "This is North Korea. And no one here gives a shit about Wolford, or mascara, or silk scarves, or designer perfume, or any of that other shit you've been sending me. They care about sparkly things, shiny things, things that they can see cost a lot of money. Like your watch."

"You really want my watch, don't you?" I laughed bitterly as we came to a stop in front of a door.

"I don't want it. It's what *they* want. I can't force them to buy things they don't want."

The door released after Wendell punched a code into the keypad, revealing a room crammed with all manner of electronics: big-screen TVs, video game consoles, microphones, a portable karaoke machine, a treadmill, a rowing machine, a keyboard piano.

"God, this compound is a never-ending rabbit hole of stuff!" I marveled.

"Exactly," he exclaimed, rapping his knuckles on an unopened Xbox 360. "There's stuff all around here, tons and tons of stuff that never gets used and no one will ever miss. Have Cookie show you the storage room full of china and silverware sometime. She's got settings there that she's never even taken out of their packaging. Oh, and try and get into the linen closet. Towels are in high demand in Pyongyang, the thicker the better. Also there's a rumor that she has a medical supply closet chock-full of drugs. You should check that out. Of course, the best thing would be for you to get access privileges to more rooms. You should really do your best to make that happen."

"So basically you want me to do your stealing for you. Coward," I sneered.

Pulling at his tie—the same black knit tie he always wore, the weave stretched and saggy at the knot—he remonstrated, "Maybe you haven't heard, but we're transitioning to a market economy. I'm merely fulfilling the time-honored role of middleman. Think of me as an offshore account, cleaning up the money and giving it back to you. Oh, and by the way, my friend is asking for fifteen thousand dollars for access to the internet."

"Fifteen thousand dollars?! Are you fucking nuts?"

"Lisa!" His moist lips twitched with the gravity of what he was telling me. "This man is putting his very life on the line for you. If he's caught, instant death is the best he could hope for. Life is cheap in Asia but not that cheap."

"You know what I think, Wendell?" I snarled, poking an angry finger at his pigeon-breasted chest. "I think you see me as your golden goose, and you never want me to leave. If I go, who will do your stealing for you?"

Pointing at the boxes of CDs, he scoffed, "That's ridiculous. We better hurry up. They're waiting for us. We don't want to rouse suspicion."

"Where is my money?" I held my hand out, impertinently waving it under his nose.

Rubber-banding his arms around a CD player and two chunky speakers, he said, "The money is already with my friend. It seemed ridiculous to bring it here and then just take it right back to Pyongyang to give to him. Can we go, please?"

Moving out of his way, I picked up the boxes of CDs and followed him out the door. "I don't trust you. I want the money now."

Stopping in his tracks, he stooped his pale face close to mine, eyeballs gleaming like oysters in their shells, spit-glossed lips shining and smooth. "In this business you're only as good as your reputation, and my reputation is solid. Ask Cookie. Ask Harvey. Fuck, even ask Vladimir. I take my cut, but not a cent more. This is my living, and if I were not a man of my word, I would have been chucked in the gulag long ago." He straightened his back, smiling in a way he probably thought ingratiating. "But I understand, you demand a better accounting. I'll bring it when I come at Christmas."

"I don't want the accounting, Wendell, I want the money. In dollars. Or else I'm not passing anything else on to you." I pushed past him, the CDs already heavy in my arms.

. Now it was him chasing me. "OK, OK, Lisa. Cash it is. And I'll leave the money you've already earned in the drawer, but it'll have to be in won because I cannot get dollars while I'm here. Will that satisfy you?"

It was just as I suspected. He needed me more than I needed him. "All right, but I expect dollars from now on."

"If you want dollars, you have to bring me something the North Koreans want. Not that designer crap. They know a rip-off when they see one."

"What about the bluies?"

"Yeah," he agreed, slackening the pace to say his piece before we arrived back at the Versailles room, whose lights we could see spilling into the crepuscular shadow of the corridor. "That's where most of your thirteen dollars comes from. If you could get more of those, you might start making something."

A slight dusting of snow powdered the world outside of Honey's window the day after the Gang left for Pyongyang. Honey's cheeks were wet, and I thought it was due to the melancholy that settled over both of us when they left, an implacable, gnawing feeling of loneliness and abandonment, of life passing us by while the Gang returned to their busy lives in the big city.

But that wasn't why Honey was crying. She showed me the screen of her laptop, which displayed an article with the headline "LeBaron Donates $50 Million to Yale."

"That's my money he's giving away," she wailed. "My inheritance!"

Yolanda slipped into the room with a glass of juice and the enamel pillbox, placing it discreetly on the edge of Honey's desk.

Leaning over to read the article, I noted, "It says here that your brother, Eric, grew the family fortune from quote 'a modest few hundred million into a ten-billion-dollar multicorporate empire.'"

"Money breeds money like rabbits," Honey scoffed. "If it weren't for the family money, he'd never have gotten anywhere."

She swiveled the laptop away from me while I was still reading the article. I hated when she did that, which was all the time. I showily tapped a pill into my palm and pretended to swallow it down before sliding my hand into the pocket of my Burberry satin-lapelled tuxedo jacket and releasing the capsule. Honey paid no heed to my theatrics as she droned on about her brother.

"He was always the dumb one of the family. He almost didn't get into St. Paul's, if you can imagine that, the first LeBaron in generations. Daddy had to build a whole new performing arts center before they'd agree to take him. And just look at the beast that he married..." She started to poke at the keyboard, typing in a name. "She was my best friend at Choate. At least she pretended to be, but now that I look back on it, I think it must have been a ploy all along to get at my brother. Ha, if only I could tell him now what a miserable slut she was! Ah, here she is!"

She showed me a society page photo of a moderately well-preserved woman with shellacked tresses piled atop her head, a diamond-and-emerald necklace worth the GDP of a small island nation twinkling against time-stippled skin, her aggressively toned body swathed in a gorgeous off-the-shoulder silk confection.

"Look at the work she's had," Honey hooted, "and still she looks like a mummified corpse."

"What work is that?" I squinted at the screen.

"Well, jowls most definitely. Eyes too. And neck. No way that's her original neck." She clutched at the smooth column of her own throat.

"Is that your brother she's standing next to?"

"Yeah, that's Eric. The dirty thief!" She stuck her tongue out at the assured-looking man with a bronze glaze of hair, small smoky-blue eyes buried deep into pink folds of skin. Peering closely at the screen, she muttered, "My god, has he had work done too? He has, the vain pig!"

"Should we look for more stories about him?" I proposed cheerfully. "That might be fun."

"No, this is boring," Honey declared, pushing the laptop away. "We need to discuss Christmas. Jonny has promised to come this year, so we'll have a real family celebration! We'll watch *It's a Wonderful Life* on Christmas Eve, followed by Christmas karaoke. And maybe we'll get a visit from Santa! Ugh, I can't stand looking at that photo anymore!"

As she reached across the desk to fold the laptop shut on her brother and his wife, the ridiculously flared bell sleeve of her dress toppled my glass of juice. She screamed as the juice splattered her dress, and she and Yolanda rushed into her bedroom to do triage.

To keep it safe from the spreading liquid, I snatched up the laptop, clutching the humming, warm machine in my hands. I had only a split second to decide. Putting the laptop safely out of reach of the pale pool of pomelo juice, I seized the enamel box of pills and crammed a fistful of them into my pocket. Not a moment too soon, for Yolanda came hustling out from the bedroom, seizing the laptop with an accusatory glare, me putting my hands in the air to show that I was totally innocent.

The next day during kitchen duty, I dumped six bluies bundled in a scrap of plastic wrap into the false-bottomed drawer, imagining the dollar bills crinkling between my fingers as I stashed them under my mattress with the tattered and stained won that Wendell had left me.

Miura-san was on edge, not paying attention to my instructions, and when he burned the gingerbread we were baking in order to surprise Honey with a gingerbread house for her holiday sideboard, I asked him what the matter was. Tugging hard at his ponytail, he said, "Koreans in servants' quarters are very nervous. They all try to get permission to go away from here."

"Why?" I asked, scraping burned dough from the cookie sheet.

"They are like animals who know big earthquake comes and behave strange. I want to go home before earthquake comes."

I brought up the subject to Honey at dinner the next evening as delicately as I knew how. "Any news on Jon's health?"

Rearranging the food on her plate, which was her way of eating dinner these days, she said, "Some people say he's better. Others say he's worse. All of my attempts to communicate directly with him are being thwarted. Even Vladimir, who usually has good intelligence, says he cannot get a straight answer from anybody."

"You will miss him when he's gone," I said, cocking my head sympathetically.

Her cheeks lifted her swollen lips into a melancholy smile. "Yes, I will miss Jon, but sometimes a woman only comes into her own when she becomes a widow. It wasn't as if I spent much time with Jon anyway. His country always came first. He thought a woman didn't know anything about politics and would rarely heed my advice. It will be different with my son. He listens to me."

"You could go home to America a hero," I suggested helpfully, as if recommending a spa treatment or luxury cruise as a cure for her grief. "You could do all the TV shows, write a book, do a TED Talk, tour the country. America would go crazy for you."

This was a scenario that I imagined for myself, but I generously offered it to her. If she could be persuaded to return home, all my troubles would be over.

But she rejected the idea, as I knew she would. "Don't be absurd, Lisa. Everything I worked so hard for is finally about to happen. Jonny and I know what we're doing. We are now within a few years of becoming the world's tenth nuclear power, which will not only bring us worldwide respect, but also make our nation more prosperous as we sell our nuclear secrets to other countries. As our rightful place in the international order is acknowledged, restrictions will loosen and North Koreans will be exposed to the real world, acquiring the same tastes as everyone else, wearing the same clothes, eating the same food, watching the same films, craving the same brands. One day in the not too distant future, it may be possible that you and I can live like regular citizens in Pyongyang."

It was a measure of my own sick complacency that I actually felt my heart quicken at the thought of moving to Pyongyang sometime in the hazy future of Jonny's golden reign.

Chapter 16

"In some strange way I think [adoption has] given me an open door to be the person I wanna be."

-Debbie Harry

Ahead of me, an unknown figure scurried along the corridor wall like a rat in a subway tunnel. I called out, and the person scampered off into the darkness, footfalls fading into the distance. Possibly a hallucination conjured by the gloomy monotony of the claustrophobic tunnel, like the eerie sound of human voices that the wind that sometimes swept through seemed to carry—but other strange things had been happening lately. A few nights ago, the temperature plummeted, and I woke up shivering under my thin bedspread, forced to ransack the armoire for clothes to layer on. By the next morning, I was suffocating under the mountain of apparel, the temperature suddenly back to normal. A day later, a door had been left open to reveal a room columned with department store catalogs from Saks, Neiman Marcus, and Nordstrom in piles higher than my head. Half the room was empty, delicate skeins of dust skirling against the walls, as if someone were in the process of clearing it out. And just yesterday, I was spooked to find a dead mouse in my otherwise sterile office, little paws curled up close to its pink snout.

These preoccupations were quickly squelched when Yolanda, who was waiting for me at the entrance to Honey's inner sanctum, grabbed me roughly by the arm and frog-marched me to Honey waiting at her desk, hands cupped in front of her as if she held the dark secret of the universe in them. She lifted them up to reveal six bluies wrapped in plastic, plus three loose ones that I had added to the false drawer in subsequent days. My knees turned to water, and it was only because Yolanda had such a firm grip on my arm that I did not collapse onto the floor.

"Honey, Mother, I can explain..." I warbled, leaning with my hands on her desk to keep myself upright.

"Yes, I'd be most interested in hearing your explanation," she said, her eyes the palest blue of the outer edge of a winter morning.

Wondering how much she knew, how much Cookie had told her, I stammered, "I was hoping to exchange those pills for some notebooks. I told you that I've always kept a journal and—"

"You are lying," she solemnly enunciated, carefully bending her fattened lips around each cruel syllable. "After all I've done for you, and this is how you repay me. Dr. Panzov is on his way. I've told him to be ready."

"I th-th-thought he wasn't coming back until Christmas," I stuttered, my teeth knocking sharply against each other.

"On Jonny's order, the Gang is coming to the compound to wait out the mourning period."

"He's dead then?" I gulped.

"Not yet, but soon. Can't you practically feel it in the air?" A shiver ran through her, twitching under her skin like something alive. "The people will be driven mad by their grief, so it's not safe for the Gang to stay in Pyongyang."

She fixed me with her gaze, eyes blazing with the intensity of lightning, and there was no love there, only a fury that pinkened her cheeks and dewed her complexion, restoring the radiance that had faded so quickly with the bluies so that she was once again, like a phoenix rising from the ashes, the flawless goddess who had first received me upon my arrival to Villa Umma.

"This is the very moment for which I brought you here and you have ruined it for me." Her face sagged for an instant, and I glimpsed the human Honey, the woman who craved love, who had only wanted a daughter with whom she could share both the burden and the reward of her good fortune.

Hoping to appeal to that umbilical bond, I collapsed to my knees and clasped my hands in supplication, imploring, "Mother, please. It's me, your very own Lilo. You know how hard I've been working for you. I've been so happy here with you. We've had so much fun together!" And I reached out to wrap my arms around her legs, but she quickly rolled her chair away from me with a kick of her Stuart Weitzman alligator pumps.

"You didn't listen to me when I warned you that Cookie was a pervert and not to be trusted. He's been trying to sell you out for weeks in order to get permission to flee. I told him if he could deliver proof of your treachery, I would let him go. But when he finally turned you in, it was too late, because now no one is allowed to leave the compound."

A sob bubbled from my trembling lips.

She sighed impatiently, pinched the knotted bridge of her nose. "I'm much too busy to deal with you at the moment, Lisa. A great man is dying, and all you're worried about is your own skin." Beckoning Yolanda over with an impatient gesture, she proclaimed, "This has all been a terrible mistake. I disown you as my daughter."

"Mother," I protested, crumpling back upon my heels, as something dark rose from my depths, welling to the surface, roiling through my veins. Anger and resentment and some kind of a release, a snapping of a tether. "You made me in your image, Honey! Just think about that! If I'm a mistake, so are you!"

"Shut up!" she snarled, slamming the desk with her knotted fist. She seemed to glow brighter and brighter before my eyes, puffing up like a piece of paper just before it catches into flame, and when she spoke, her voice hissed with the urgent ferocity of a butane torch, scorching a trail from my head to my heart. "You are not my child anymore and I am not your mother, for a mother cannot hate her child the way I hate you. The very sight of you sickens me. Go to your room and wait for Dr. Panzov."

Yolanda scuffled me out the door as I shouted, "You can't hide from your mistakes!"

Just as we arrived at my door, the walkie-talkie clipped to Yolanda's waist crackled to life. "Yoyo, come back right away! Jonny's on the satellite phone and I need you to take notes."

Shoving me into my room, Yolanda gave a nudge to the door before sprinting off down the hall. Before the door swung shut, I stuck my foot out, then waited until the clatter of Yolanda's running feet died out. As I drifted down the hallway, a fetid rush of air like the foul exhalations of a beast panting in its lair pushed me toward the kitchen, where I banged on the door, expecting a guard to come to drag me screaming and kicking to my room. Instead, the door simply opened, and I stalked into the kitchen to find Miura-san, a large cleaver gleaming in his hand.

"Ah, Lisa-san, I am waiting for you," he said, lips trembling amid the heavy corrugations of his face. "You can kill me."

He extended the cleaver, handle first, to me. My fingers grasped the smooth, stout handle of the knife. He let go, and the full weight of it dragged my arm down.

"I want you to do," he said, nodding seriously. "I should not live. I am a very bad man."

One part of me could easily imagine the blade hacking into his body, the *chung* of it as it buried into the dense mass of his shoulder muscles, the satisfying rip of sharp steel through flesh, the shock of the blade against hard bone, the spurt of blood as it baptized me in a hot vermilion arc. The other part saw his familiar, comfortable features wrinkled into a mask of anguish—the hooded, intelligent eyes; the sensitive mouth a fallen scythe of shame and grief—and quivered with sympathy. He could have played me like just another pawn in the game, as the rest of them did, but instead he tried to warn me, even against himself. But then he looked up at me, a scrim of red curved along the bottom of each eye like another eyelid, and I saw Dr. Panzov sinking his scalpel into my nostrils, peeling back the skin, wrenching the nasal bone from my skull. I imagined him doing the same thing to my eyes, my breasts, my cheekbones, my jaw, until I was a monster like Yolanda, disfigured both outside and in, just another ghoul skirmishing for crumbs and favors, ratting out the others in order to live another day. Miura-san was, perhaps, the worst of them all, the only one who was free to leave but didn't. I ran an experimental finger against the honed edge of the knife. It was sharp, drawing a thin line of blood across the fleshy pad of skin. I thought of my parents, my real mother and father, sick with worry; of missing Mindy's wedding; of the months that had been stolen from my life; and I felt shame for my acquiescence, as I all but offered up my wrists for Honey's handcuffs. It was time to quit being the victim, to let someone else be the victim, to victimize. Opening my mouth for the scream that was already pushing its way out—molten lava erupting forth, blotting out every thought and memory from my mind, transforming my solid flesh to red-hot sludge—I raised the cleaver and, with a tennis-player-like grunt, brought it hurtling down onto Miura-san's bent neck with all of my might. For one brief moment, I saw the blood ooze up, dark and tarry, before I was knocked to the ground, the knife spinning across the black and white tiles of the floor. Something landed on me, holding me down. Raven hair brushed my forehead, and I was staring up at Ting, her face twisted with rage, the zipper of her scar across the bridge of her nose livid against her bone-white skin.

"Fool," she barked, "you must not kill him."

"Why not?!" I screamed in English, recalling the satisfying feel of the cleaver landing on Miura-san's neck. My body shivered to complete its task. I tried to toss Ting off, but she clung to me as if her limbs were suctioned to mine. "He wants it. He wants me to kill him!"

"If you kill him, the Madam and Young Master will own your soul. You will never be rid of them." Her eyes were sharp-tipped daggers, and her sweat dripped down on me like pearl raindrops.

"Ting," I heard Miura-san say, though I could not turn my head to look at him because she had my head pinioned. "Let her go. Let her finish the job!" he screamed in Japanese.

She ignored him, leaning her full-moon face down until our foreheads and noses were touching, her scar against the ghost of my knob. "If you kill him, you will become one of them."

I could feel her heart beating against mine in arrhythmic bangs. Her ribs seemed so delicate, like the hollow bones of a bird, and yet I could not move an inch. Something was leaching from her into me. Slowly, my heart stilled; slowly, her heart did as well, until our hearts were beating in the same, measured beat. She whispered, "The end is near. Just wait for me."

Then she rolled off me and scrambled over to Miura-san.

He wailed, "Ting! Why did you do that? Why did you save me? I am unworthy of you. I am the most useless and unworthy husband in the world."

"H-h-husband?" I echoed, as I crawled toward them on all fours.

"Yes." Miura-san flashed me an anguished look as Ting stanched the bubbling spring of his wound with a dishcloth. "We are husband

and wife. Young Master give me her when I come here, when she was eight years old only. She save me!" His baggy eyes began to fill with tears that slid sideways down his face. "All the terrible things I do to her, but she save me." He began to sob uncontrollably, his head bobbing in her lap.

The door slammed open and in charged two burly men, one wielding a baton that was shooting blue sparks. Miura-san began to shriek at them in Korean, spreading his arms to shield Ting. With a clop of high-heeled shoes, Yolanda galloped in, clutching a walkie-talkie. "What the fuck's going on here?" she shouted.

Miura-san and I began babbling at once. "Shut up!" Yolanda shrieked. The two goons hovered threateningly over Miura-san and Ting, blocking my view of them. I heard a staticky zap, like the noise made when an insect flies into an electric bug killer, and then a high-pitched scream.

"Make them stop, Yolanda!" My scream too was high-pitched. "You don't even know what happened."

"Well, then," she said coolly, though her chest was heaving underneath her smartly tailored jacket, "tell me."

"I ask Lisa to kill me," Miura-san screeched. "She didn't want, but she hit me with knife, and then Ting save my life! After everything I do to her, Ting save my life." He collapsed into anguished bawling, his turtlish mouth yawping, snot slicking his cheeks.

"Cookie, I'll give you something to cry about if you don't fucking shut up," Yolanda snarled.

But he couldn't stop. With both arms wrapped tightly around Ting, he sobbed and sobbed. Yolanda gave a curt nod to the man with the baton. *Bzzzz, bzzz, bzzz!* Entwined together like young lovers, Miura-san and Ting screamed, and the smell of burned flesh wafted through the air. *Bzzzz!*

Leaving school on a steamy Friday, I heard the first cicada of the season, buzzing like an alarm clock. My last summer vacation in Japan was almost here, and I had made no plans, just letting the time drift by, and now it was too late to get a cheap flight anywhere. As I stepped out the gate, I heard someone calling my name. I turned to see Kenji running after me. "Miss Lisa! Do you go to catch a bus? I go to catch a bus too. Let's catch a bus together."

"Kenji! I hardly see you at all these days. How is it to be a *sannensei*?" Unbidden, my heart began to flitter about like a bird.

"I am very tired all the time," he said, though he didn't look tired now; he looked very awake and very attentive.

As we walked down the street, occasionally our arms would brush, and I knew he was doing it on purpose.

"I see you got a buzz cut." I passed my hand quickly over my own hair to show him what I meant.

"Yes," he said proudly. "For baseball team. This year, I am captain."

"Congratulations!" We were approaching the bus stop. "Well, bye, Kenji. Have a good weekend."

He looked at me in astonishment. "You do not catch a bus?"

I laughed. "I prefer to walk today. Soon it will be much too hot, so I'll walk while I can."

He threw his chest out. "I am walking too! I like to walk. I like to walk with Miss Lisa."

We continued past the bus stop, crowded with students in their summer uniforms. Like sunflowers following the trajectory of the sun, they all turned and watched our progress. A few called out my name, a few called out his. I waved, and then so did he. He yelled something in Japanese to one of his friends. Everyone erupted into laughter. After we had left them behind, I asked, "How do you know that we are walking in the same direction?"

"Eh?" he asked, leaning solicitously toward me. A drop of sweat glistened in the soft bristles of his hair.

"How do you know that where I am going is the same as where you are going?"

"Oh! Ah! Ah! Oh!" He nodded vigorously to show he understood me. "I know! I know where you are living."

"You know where I live?"

"*Hai!*" He looked quite pleased with himself. Then, realizing that perhaps he had crossed a boundary, he hastened to add, "Everybody knows. All the students."

With an astonished cough, I yelped, "Do you spy on me?"

"Spy?" His broad forehead wrinkled in puzzlement.

"Spy. Watch me in secret, without my knowing." I pretended to be peering around a corner and then ducking back.

"Oh! Ah! Ah, no. Not 'spy' on you," he assured me earnestly. "But students always see you wherever you go. You are famous."

"Like Toby Dawson," I joked. He didn't laugh, but he looked at me with a smile so confident it was disarming.

We turned a corner and then another corner. We came to a small park. I paused in the shade of a tree. He stopped with me. "OK?" he asked with gentlemanly concern.

"I just want to..." My hand drifted up. "Your hair," I explained sheepishly, as my hand landed on his head. I felt the heat emanating from it. My fingers began to caress the fuzzy nap. "It's so soft. Like a plush stuffed animal."

His whole face steepened into crimson, and I felt I had made a mistake. I pulled away abruptly. A trickle of sweat slid down past his ear and trembled at the sharp angle of his jaw. "Miss Lisa." His voice was strangled, as if he were suffocating.

"Are you all right, Kenji?" I asked as he gasped for breath. "Do you have asthma?" *Oh god, trust me to kill my favorite student with a minor flirtation.*

For some reason, my hand returned to his face, to catch a drop of sweat sliding slowly down his hairline. He grabbed my hand and brought it up to his mouth, pressing his lips against it.

"Miss Lisa," he murmured.

"Oh god, Kenji, I don't know," I stammered.

His lips sent electric shocks pulsing down the length of my arm, tickling through my chest, and crackling lightning forks to my pelvic region. The heat that was radiating from him seemed to shimmer in the air, melding with the sonic reverberations of the cicada's first cries. The noise pushed me against him, his hard chest, his lank limbs, and then our lips met and melted together. My tongue flicked into his mouth. It tasted sweet and warm, like pie fresh out of the oven. It was wrong. I knew it was wrong. But right then, at that moment, and all the other intimate moments that followed over the next ten months, it felt like a triumph, like I was somehow putting something over on the rest of the world, like I was invincible and could get away with anything.

I could feel the whole compound on the move, disturbed currents of air roiling the labyrinthine tunnels, distant hurried footsteps pocking the silence. I thought I heard Harvey's honking voice like the faraway boom of a cannon, more sensation than noise. Non-Ting was at the door to my room, waiting for us with an enormous cart.

"What's going to happen to Ting?" I asked Yolanda as we filed inside.

"That's not your business," Yolanda snarled.

"Ting was only trying to save me from making an awful mistake," I pleaded, watching as non-Ting wheeled the cart to the armoire.

"Bring it up with Madam," Yolanda sneered with a scornful thrust of her chin. "Oh, that's right. You're in deep shit with her. Again. So deep I don't see how you can possibly get your way out of it this time."

Non-Ting began to scoop clothes from the armoire, flinging them into the cart.

Affecting nonchalance, I sat on my bed and picked up *Moby-Dick*, leafing through it to find my place. Yolanda snatched the book from my hands, hugging it to her chest as she chided, "It's a pity you didn't kill Cookie, you know, because you would have taken care of the problem for Madam, and she might have let you off a little easier."

"What do you mean, 'taken care of the problem'?"

"Just what I said, *domkop*. He can't just go home to open up his stupid sushi restaurant knowing everything that he knows, now can he?"

Everything was shifting. Things that I thought I had sharply in focus were becoming blurry, while what was once blurry was now coming sharply into focus. Honey wanted Cookie dead? But I didn't want Yolanda to see my confusion because confusion made me vulnerable, so I pretended indifference, trying to stare her down, but it's impossible to win a staring contest when the other person never blinks.

Once non-Ting had emptied my armoire, she began to method-ically sweep through the rest of the suite, quickly rooting out the small wad of won that I had tucked into the elastic seam of the fitted sheet on my bed. Clicking her tongue against the roof of her mouth, Yolanda deftly unbuttoned her shirt to tuck the money into her bra. "I never would have believed you'd be so stupid. You're just lucky that there is so much going on, or Madam would be dealing much more harshly with you. But don't worry, your long, dark journey is just beginning."

Non-Ting emerged from the bathroom to give Yolanda a nod be-fore wheeling the cart out the door.

"One last thing," Yolanda purred, grabbing my arm to pick open the catch of the strap of my watch. "Madam says this is mine now." Slipping it onto her own wrist, she thrust it under my nose for me to admire, angling it so that the light winked off the diamond chips.

"You wear it like a natural," I noted, feeling strangely relieved to be liberated from Honey's golden handcuff. "It should have been yours all along, Yolanda."

She reached a hand toward my head and, scared that she was go-ing to yank my hair or rake her nails down my cheek, I tried to duck, but I was too slow, because her fingers were gripping the back of my skull, pulling me in close to plant a hard, hungry kiss on my lips, her other hand thrusting something into my pocket. After she let me go, I reeled back while she ran her tongue all around the rigid rictus of her overinflated lips. "We're both sloppy seconds, Lisa. It's a pity that we have to be enemies, but Madam wouldn't have it any other way. You know, I've got a heart too..."

With a final, tender wink, she took a backward step out the door, running right into a man with a squashed, lumpy head and a wide, wolfish smile. Because he was dressed in black, all I could really see of him was his disembodied face, which floated silvery white above Yolanda's, and the black-gloved hand that landed on her shoulder with a *thud*. He said something to her in Korean and she turned sharp-ly to look at him. Since her face was a horror mask anyway, it was the sudden panicked paralysis of her body that told me she was scared.

"Yolanda?" I squeaked. "What's going on?"

He spoke again, his voice not so cheerful this time, like a father giving one last warning to his wayward child before the belt came off.

"Yolanda?"

"Madam needs me," she whispered, stepping out the doorway to give me a glimpse of the man. Wearing a turtleneck and close-fitting pants, he was well fed, chesty like a Spanish fighting bull, with a narrow waist wrapped tightly in a wide belt, from which hung a holstered pistol, the glossy black grip pressing into his side. As the door swung shut, he gave me a genial nod, as if to say that we would meet again, and soon.

With trembling fingers, I pulled out the object that Yolanda had slipped into my pocket. It was my silver necklace with the yin-yang pendant.

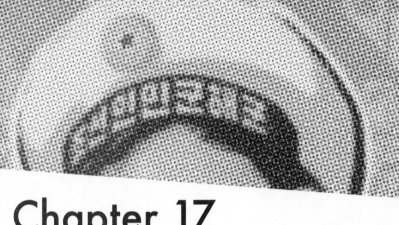

Chapter 17

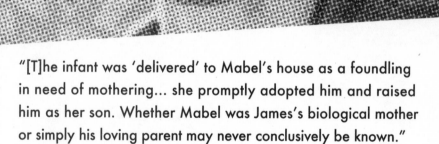

"[T]he infant was 'delivered' to Mabel's house as a foundling in need of mothering... she promptly adopted him and raised him as her son. Whether Mabel was James's biological mother or simply his loving parent may never conclusively be known."

—Stephen J. May, Michener biographer

"Lisa!"

My eyes fluttered open. All night I had been hearing phantom noises of someone coming into my room, creeping toward me with black-gloved hands extended. Had I just startled myself awake from another dark dream? The room was cloaked in thick, velvety darkness, and I could sense rather than see a head bobbing over me like a perfectly round balloon.

"Ting?"

"Lisa." She was shaking me. "It is time. Get up."

Time for what? I asked groggily in English.

"Quickly," she urged me. "Put these on! Hurry!" Folded items of clothing bounced off my arms and chest, falling into my lap.

"Why? What's happening?" My voice flared in the dark room. "Is that man going to come back for me?"

"Quiet!" she whispered sharply. "Comrade Kim is dead."

"Dead?" I echoed.

"Hurry. It may already be too late." She was flinging more clothes at me. "Make sure to put the long underwear on first. It's very cold out there."

"How is Honey taking the news?" I groped at the clothes, trying to make sense of them and of Ting and of what was happening.

"Forget Honey. She soon will be dead. And you will be too if you don't hurry up."

"What?" I pulled the covers closer. "Why will she be dead?"

"The Young Master will kill her."

She said it with such certainty that I knew it was true. "Shouldn't we warn her?" I asked.

"No." So cold, callous, and certain, when we were talking about someone's life here. Someone who happened to be my birth mother, so maybe I owed her at least this one thing.

"We should warn her." I pushed her aside to get out of bed.

She slapped me hard with an open-palmed blow to my cheek, returning on the backswing to strike the other cheek with the back of her hand. "You cannot save her." Then I felt her cool cheek against my hot one as she leaned close to explain to me in a calm, measured voice, "The journey we must make will be very difficult and dangerous. Maybe it will end in death. But if you stay here, your fate is certain. The Young Master brought the Gang here so everyone could be in one place when his men come for the slaughter. You can either come with me or you can stay here. It's your decision, but you must make it now."

Even as I thought about my filial duty to Honey, my body was making its own choice, shedding the pajamas and pulling on the long underwear. Ting exhaled. "Good girl." She knelt to shimmy socks onto my feet. The darkness was just beginning to be erased around the edges, and I could now discern her round head, the outline of her thin shoulders.

"But why, Ting? Why do you take me with you? I have never done a kind thing to you," I wondered as I struggled into a pair of stiff workman's pants.

Her fingers picked the laces loose on a pair of black jackboots like the guards wore. "Because two are stronger than one. And you didn't deserve what they did to you."

"What do you think will happen to Miura-san?" I asked, jamming my foot into a boot sleeve.

"They will kill him with the others," she replied with quiet satisfaction, tugging the leather snug about my calves as she tied the laces in sailor's knots. "Let's go!"

The hall was completely black, the glowing mushroom lights extinguished, air thick and stagnant without a hint of the earlier turbulence, silent as a tomb. I held on to her shoulders as she led me into the obscurity.

"Quiet!" she chided me. "Lift your feet up instead of dragging them."

But my feet were clumsy in their cocoon of socks and the rigid encasement of the new leather, inflexible as steel, and several times the soles squealed against the tiles. At the kitchen door, Ting leaned in for the retinal scan and then pecked the code into the keypad, the beeps piercing the hush, followed by a long, flatlining error tone. Cursing under her breath, she tried again, taking it more slowly this time. The door gasped open. Pausing to grab two knapsacks that were hidden behind sacks of flour and rice, she led me into the greenhouse. At the far corner, near the twisted, ropy skeletons of tomato vines—black veins against the smoky-gray skin of the fading night—Ting dropped to her hands and knees and popped out a bottom pane of glass. She wriggled through effortlessly, and I did as she did, flopping onto my stomach and shimmying forward until my shoulders lodged firmly in the frame and I could go neither forward nor backward. Fluttering her hand, she advised me to corkscrew my way through. Panic rising, I folded myself as small as I could go and tried to ram my way out, my shoulders catching painfully against the steel casement until my feet, scrabbling against the ground, propelled me through with a rip of my new cotton-padded canvas jacket. Expertly, she tapped the pane back into position. Humping a pack onto her back, she handed me the other one. "Keep low," she instructed, before scuttling forward in a crouch as I followed, our breath leaving silvery contrails behind us.

Once we entered the bamboo grove, I turned back for a last glance at the compound, but in the graphite gloom of the predawn light, there was nothing there to see.

The first few miles were exhilarating. The dark was losing its quotidian battle with the light, slowly receding until the last few shadowy holdouts lurked in tree branches, behind boulders, in thickets and hollows. When the dawn finally broke, it was as if it broke in my very heart, as though the very universe was conspiring to bring me into the light after months of confinement.

It was cold, and as day took firm hold of the earth, the sky whitened with a pearly sheen. Ting observed glumly, "It will snow soon. Then we will leave tracks."

Long after the point where I had left exhaustion and entered catatonia, when every step was an existential conundrum as my raw and bloody heels rubbed against the exact same unyielding joints of my boots, I stumbled and landed sharply on a rock with my knee. I lay where I collapsed. "I can't go on," I panted.

Ting squatted beside me. "OK, let's rest," she said grudgingly. "There's food in your backpack. Eat sparingly."

Wiping my mouth after chugging water from a canteen I found in the backpack, I asked foolishly, hopefully, "How much farther?"

She lifted a lip and took a delicate sip from her canteen. "We have only just started."

I wanted to ask more questions but became distracted by a carrot, which I gnawed at with rabbity ferocity. Still chewing, I reached in and pulled out a sandwich wrapped in wax paper. "Oh man, Cookie's roast beef," I said, drooling.

Ting was systematically demolishing an apple. She warned, "Don't forget the carrot top. It's all fuel for the body. You'll need it."

"Mmm," I said, my mouth stuffed with the tastiest morsel of bread and meat that I had ever eaten. Washing it down with another great gulp of water, I caught Ting's eye.

She frowned and shook her head. "Slow down!"

One more furtive gulp before I lowered the canteen. "Where are we going, Ting?"

She pointed away from the sun. "China."

"China," I echoed in wonder, crunching on the woody substance of the carrot's stem. "How far is it?"

She gave me a wary look. "Far." She pulled her black woolen cap more snugly over her ears, eyes disappearing into the shadow of the brim. It was getting cold just sitting there. "We should go. Are you ready?"

Reluctantly, I carefully folded the rest of my sandwich up in the wax paper and got to my feet. "Uh," I groaned, "that hurts. I don't think I have toes anymore, just blisters."

Ting nodded. "I was able to break mine in, but we couldn't risk it for you."

I looked down at her boots, which indeed appeared comfortably creased, already balding in a crescent along the toecap, the soles gently eroded at the back heel. "How long did you think about escape?"

Trudging forward, Ting replied, "Since I came."

"You were a child bride?"

Ting snorted. "I was kidnapped. Snatched in broad daylight from my own village. It's common where I come from. The parents have no money to search for their children, who are taken far away to the mines, or to the brick factories, or to the brothels, which is where I went. I was twelve, but due to the poor diet in my village, I had not yet developed breasts, grown hair, or begun to menstruate. They told me someone special was coming to get me and that I should tell him I was eight. It was Miura-san."

I opened my mouth to ask her another question, but she shook her head. "That's enough talking. We must save our strength."

We marched on, scrambling over boulders and up steep inclines, ascending to an altitude too high for trees or meadows, where it was just rocks and patches of low scrub that we crashed through, our boots breaking the brittle twigs to release an herbal odor that powdered the insides of our noses.

Snowflakes began to flutter down like tiny wisps of the thick, cotton-batting clouds that veiled the late-afternoon sun. "The snow has come for good," Ting observed softly.

Involuntarily, I shivered, even though I was sweating from the upward climb. "Where will we sleep tonight? How will we stay warm?"

She stopped walking and faced me. I knew that it must be serious for her to stay our advance, even if only for a few seconds. "Soon we will search for a place to lie down."

"Where?" I asked, my voice rough with panic. "There's nowhere. All day long, we haven't seen anywhere to sleep."

Gesturing up to the scree-strewn horizon that never seemed to get any closer, Ting said, "We need to get over this peak. On the other side we can find a tree, or the lee of a boulder."

We trudged on. The snow, at first so fine that it was barely perceptible, began to fatten and proliferate. The mountain never seemed to end, the peak hanging tantalizingly above us.

"*Shit,*" I wailed, collapsing to my knees. "*We're going to die, aren't we?*" I started to cry. "We're going to die!" I repeated in Chinese.

She nudged at me hard with a boot. "If we sit down and cry, yes, we will die. If we give up, we will die. But if we keep going, we can live."

The cold air burned my lungs. I screamed at her, *"I don't want to die!"*

"Do you want me to leave you here?" she asked in a clinical voice. As if she really meant she could abandon me.

"Yes!" I ducked my forehead onto my folded arms, tears of anger and frustration dripping from my eye sockets. "I'm going back. I never should have come with you in the first place."

"I'm walking away."

I heard her footsteps puncturing the thin crust of snow, and then a long period of silence but for the steady soughing of the wind in my ears. The cold settled in, covering me like a blanket. Finally, I lifted my head and Ting was nowhere to be seen. For one moment I continued to sit there, watching the snow descend in helix patterns, then I leapt up and started back down the mountain. But very quickly, I realized that the odds were infinitesimal that I'd find my way back. I was but one speck on the flank of a massive mountain, with other massive mountains echoing on all sides of me into infinity. A hot flush of shame brought some warmth to my wind-chapped cheeks as I realized that I had fallen back into my old habit of running away instead of facing up to the consequences of my actions. I whirled back to face the mountain and set off at a gallop, screaming, *"Tiiiiing! Tiiiiiing!"* Up the slope I scrambled, eyes straining to penetrate the scrim of snow. Just as I thought that I had lost her, I saw a black dot way up the rock face of the peak. Squinting to make sure it wasn't an illusion of the falling snow, I screamed her name, and the dot pulsed with movement. She was waving.

We spent that night at the base of a scrubby, long-armed pine tree, curled up into each other, wrapped in gold-foil emergency blankets, the snow pinging off the crinkly material with a sound like breaking glass. Despite my bone-deep exhaustion, I was unable to sleep. The tree's roots dug into my side, I was terrified that I was going to freeze to death, and I yearned for my little dots of pure light. "Ting, I wish I had my pills," I sobbed.

She locked her arms around me, spoke softly into my ear. "I never forgot home. Every single day of every single year, I planned for my escape. When you came, I knew I would take you with me. I pictured the two of us, lying together just like this, keeping each other warm, keeping each other alive. But we cannot stay alive if we do not get some sleep. So please, close your eyes, because tomorrow will be even more difficult than today."

"But they say you shouldn't sleep in the cold, because you may never wake up," I whimpered, my teeth chattering.

"We'll wake up," she said, hugging me closer. "I promise."

Soon, her breath was stroking my cheek in slow intervals and I wanted to shake her awake; I didn't want to be left all alone on this windswept mountain, the snow sifting down to bury us beneath its awful beauty. But I must have eventually fallen asleep, for Ting was patting me on the cheek, telling me it was time to wake up. I burrowed deeper into her chest. "I need more sleep. Just give me a few more minutes."

She pushed me away from her. "No. The snow is deep and will slow us down." Sitting up, she rummaged in her backpack and then held out a hard-boiled egg. "Breakfast. Egg, just like your usual breakfast. It will taste so good."

"I can't feel my toes," I groaned, still curled up on my side. "My bones ache!"

She tossed the egg at me, and it landed with a soft thud in front of my nose. "Your complaining is tiresome, Lisa. I understand that you have never had anything bad happen to you before. But this is it. This is the bad thing that you must overcome. If you don't, you will die, and maybe take me with you."

I scrambled to my feet, wadding the reflective blanket in my fists. *"I was kidnapped too!"* I screamed at her. *"My body was violated, my nose taken away from me. By my own mother."* Bent double, I screamed at Ting as she munched on her egg. *"How can I ever be normal again?"*

"Good," she said, brushing eggshells from her lap. "Keep that anger. It will give you fuel for the next mountain, and the next. The Korean people have a great thirst for revenge. It is the Korean in you that will carry you back to your home."

"Let's go then," I seethed, grabbing up the egg and marching forward. Soon, though, I became aware of the pain in my feet, the weariness in my muscles, the dryness of my mouth. Every fiber of my being was consumed by pain. We were going uphill again and then scrambling down. Over and over, up and down, my muscles trembling with the effort, the sweat popping out on my forehead despite the cold that made my bones feel as brittle as ice. When I was about to collapse, I thought of Honey and, as Ting had said, my anger pushed me onward. If I could survive the abyss that was my own mother, I could surely survive this.

When the dark came, we made our bed in the lee of a jumble of boulders that somewhat sheltered us from the snow and wind. In the morning, I begged Ting to let us stay there one more day. She refused. "We don't have enough food and we must take advantage of the announcement of Comrade Kim's death. Grieving and uncertain about the future, the border guards will be more pliable."

"What if we get there too late?"

"It may be."

"Won't they have the border guards on alert, looking for us? Jonny will do everything he can to have me caught."

"It may be."

"So really, your plan is full of holes?" I accused her angrily.

"Nothing is for certain, but this is the best and only chance that we have. Even if we get caught, we can try to bribe our way across. It is the usual way, and I have things that the guards will want."

Taking off a mitten, I reached into my pants pocket and pulled out the broken necklace and the yin-yang pendant. "Maybe they will want this too."

Ting lightly pushed my hand away. "Keep it."

"No," I insisted. "It is made of gold and silver. The guards will like it."

"All right, but you keep it. You can give it to me if we need it."

"Please, Ting." I stopped walking. "I want you to have it. If we don't have to give it to the guards, then keep it. As a symbol of our friendship. Please."

She must have sensed my determination, for she took off her mitten and let me place the necklace in her hand. "Thank you, friend," she whispered, briefly holding it against her cheek before slipping it into her backpack.

We trudged onward. It was the beginning of another brutal ascent up a snow-swept peak.

"This one is the tallest. After this one, though, there is only one more before we get to the border."

The snow was deep now, and each step was a struggle. "Two more mountains?" I panted. "I don't think I can make it."

"How many times will you say that?" she wondered to the sky. At least it was blue, and the sun was out. "Don't slow down. We must make it to the lower elevations by nightfall or else we will die in the cold."

"How many times will you say that?" I mimicked her. I think we both would have laughed if we had the energy.

When we crested the mountain, the view was hypnotic, like an optical illusion. We were on top of the world, dazzling, cloud-tufted peaks rolling away from us in ever-diminishing crenellations until they disappeared in a lavender haze on the horizon. "How will we know when we get to China?" I asked as I turned in a slow circle to peer into the kaleidoscopic distance.

"There is a river," Ting said, her words curling from her mouth in a vaporous cloud.

"How will we cross the river?"

"With a lot of luck."

Two more days of careful descent—toes crushed against boot leather, knees screaming hinges, thighs quivering like aspic—followed by hard scrabbling up steep slopes—hamstrings burning fiery trails of pain, from aching buttocks down to macerated heels. Two nights of clinging to each other under shiny golden Mylar blankets that made me feel like Tutankhamun in a space-age casket. Our backpacks sagged limply from our backs; we were down to our last rations, a few rubbery dried apricots and a small handful of crumbled crackers. My mind was blank, numb, glazed over, attached to reality by a tenuously thin string. Our water was gone and we nibbled at the snow, but it freezer-burned our digestive tracts, chilling us from the inside out. As night began to fall again, I suddenly realized that my death no longer scared me. It would bring an end to my misery and make my growing anxiety about what would happen once we reached our destination moot. The unknown at the end of our journey terrified me more than the plodding certainty of our arduous march. I could never return to the person I was, but I wasn't sure who I would turn out to be. Would I have the strength and the will to put in the hard work that I knew awaited me? Would things be different with me this time? Better to stay forever in this painful limbo, with my trusty guide. Here it was simple: put one foot in front of another, up the mountain, down the mountain. Be careful not to step in a hidden hole or trip over a hummock. Rest when Ting tells me to rest, get up when she tells me to get up. Follow her, follow her, follow her. Tiny little Ting was my leader, to be wordlessly obeyed, with the reward of a nighttime embrace. Life was simple. No ambition, no regrets, no failures. No drugs, no sex, no rock and roll.

A gray fog was stealing over the mountain, coiling thickly over the rocks, settling heavily into crevices and shallows. I stumbled again and again, the bloody mush of my toes unable to balance my tottering body. Passing my hand in front of my face, I realized it wasn't fog; it was my vision clouding. Reality was a flossy tissue, easily torn. The thin string that connected my head to my body snapped, and I floated overhead, looking down upon two figures floundering in the snow. One of them fell and clutched her ankle as if it hurt her. It did hurt her. I knew that because it hurt me, the pain retethering my consciousness to my body, so that I became aware of the rock, hard and frozen, under my thighs, the wind whining in my ears, the cold a dull and constant ache. Ting extended a mittened hand; I took it. Her grip was iron strong, pulling me onto my feet. For a moment, I leaned against her, testing my tender ankle, before falling in step behind her.

"Mindy," I think I said, "did I ever tell you about James Michener?"

"My name is Ting," I think she replied. "Call me that."

"James Michener's mother told him he was adopted to hide the fact that she had given birth to him outside of wedlock. She denied being his real mother, even though she was." I felt giggles escaping from me in frozen bubbles of air. "It doesn't get more fucked up than that. Mothers! I tell you. What about your mother, Ting?"

"She was disappointed that I wasn't a boy. She would have killed me right after I was born, but my father said no. She never let me forget that I was taking someone else's life, someone who deserved it more. But I don't blame her. If I had been a boy I would not have been kidnapped to be Miura-san's wife. Now I'm going home to help her and my father on their farm, to show her that even though I am a girl, I can work hard, I can look after them."

"They are lucky, your parents," I said. I stumbled and almost splatted down into the snow but caught myself. "If I fall again, I want you to leave me here. You have a chance to make it. Go on without me."

I didn't want to die, but being smothered by a gray fog was an easy way to go. Much better than being slaughtered in five-hundred-thread-count satin-finish sheets, a gold Rolex glittering on my wrist.

"Careful. Let's go slowly," Ting advised as the downward slope sharpened dramatically. "Follow in my footsteps."

The snow swallowed her boots as she crushed through blanketed humps of undergrowth and dodged the fallen boughs of the proliferating pine trees that became taller as we descended. I looked down at the dark smudge of my boots sinking and rising against the sparkling snow, my legs moving even while my mind blotted in and out of consciousness. Thoughts came in on distant radio waves, more static than intelligible phrases. I talked to keep my mind from slipping out of my body, my voice droning and small in the immense clarity of the crystal air. "I've still got things to do, Ting, so I don't want to die. I mean, I've just figured out how to live. I bet you figured it out early, but I was a little slow. A late bloomer, let's say. Recently, I've started writing a book in my head. I have the first few chapters finished already."

Ting plodded ahead, giving no response. I wasn't sure if I was talking in English or Chinese, but I kept going, my words stumbling after her.

"It's kind of a memoir. It starts in Seoul, as I argue with my friend Mindy. But before I sit down to write that book, I have to..." The fog began to roll in again, and I had trouble seeing my feet, so far below. "I have to... put... one... foot... in front... of... the other." I missed Ting's footprint, my exhausted leg twitching my step a little short. Too late, I saw the sunken spot that was disguised by the depthless white of the fresh snow, and I went pinwheeling down the slope, slamming to a stop against a tree trunk. The snow felt good on my bare cheek.

"You go ahead," I murmured, turning to snuggle into the soft bed of snow. I heard her footsteps crunch away and closed my eyes, wrapping myself in the whirling darkness.

But a moment later, something roused me from the soft sucking oblivion. It was Ting batting lightly at my cheeks. "Get up, Lisa. We made it! I can see the river from here. All we have to do is cross it."

She offered me her hand. I took it. One foot in front of another. All I had to do was cross the river.

Epilogue

"You know, if anybody wants me to say it, in one sentence, what my plays are about: They're about the nature of identity... Who we are, how we permit ourselves to be viewed, how we permit ourselves to view ourselves, how we practice identity or lack of identity."

–Edward Albee

First of all, I want to assure everyone that I am OK, and thank you to all who have expressed concern about me over these last few weeks of silence. Some of you have suggested that I've been ill, which is true. Some of you have speculated that there's been a death in the family, which is also true. Some of you thought I went on a trip, and I did. Some of you feared that I have come to harm, either through my own hand or through the agency of others, or that I had gone back to my pill-popping ways. It's all true.

But as adoptees, we know that truth is a squishy thing. Stories are told, myths created, and through constant repetition we come to accept them as real. When we were children, our parents offered us an explanation about how we came into the family, a charming origin story freighted with fate, destiny, and other hazy cosmic forces that purported to join these particular parents with that particular child as if they truly belonged to each other all along. From an early age, we are used to looking upon ourselves as a character in a story, but not the most important one. In the dominant narrative of adoption, the protagonists are the adoptive parents, and the adoptees are the catalyst for the plot, which revolves around the Herculean labors the parent-heroes must perform in order to obtain the object of their desire. Those stories end with a happily ever after at exactly the point that our stories begin, with the baby being brought home.

We all know there is no happily ever after. As children of chance, we understand it's not a kumbaya world out there and that not everything happens for the best. There's a lot of loose talk about fate in adoption circles—we were fated to be adopted by the perfect loving couple, or fated to be reunited with our heartsick birth mother. But sometimes the loving couple gets divorced, or the birth mother's heart is too sick to give us the love that we crave. Fate isn't real; it's a literary device, a retroactive designation: you can't be fated to be something until you have actually become it. Fate is what you make of your own life, and it's hard, dirty work. Every day is another slog up a snow-swept mountain, every day you have to prove yourself to yourself all over again.

From the noxious stereotypes that are still being perpetuated about adoption, it is clear that our side of the story is not being told. In popular culture, either we are a punch line to a joke, a cautionary tale, or a pitiful castaway in need of rescue. In novels, we are a societal anomaly that roils a close-knit community, the vehicle for sappy stories of the power of maternal love, or spunky Victorian foundlings. In movies, we're the neglected but talented child from an abusive family, an adorable alien from outer space, or the bad seed come to wreck your happy home. Everyone, it seems, is telling our story but us.

That needs to change.

Because when we feel like we're not being heard, we get angry. From reading through your comments and letters, I can say with certainty that we're an angry bunch. Anger is a healthy emotion, but it is not an identity. In my recent misadventures, I saw how easy it was to turn people who should have been allies against one another, so that instead of helping one another to escape the bizarre situation we had found ourselves in, we fought and skirmished among ourselves, tightening our own chains with each betrayal. We adoptees are a global community with conflicting opinions that reflect the immense variety of our individual experiences. My story does not negate your story; my journey is no more or less legitimate than yours.

Some of you have demanded to know why I think I'm talking for the whole adoptee community. I don't. I speak for myself. Though we all share some of the same plot points—the death of or abandonment (coerced or not) by our birth parents, the nagging feeling of being an outsider in our own families, the inevitable crisis of identity—each adoption story is unique. The time has come for us to start getting those stories out there. Though statistics vary, there are approximately five million American adoptees, and each one of us has our own tale to tell.

I'm told Famous Adopted People gets enough page views to monetize, and plans are in the works for a bigger, better website, which I envision as a forum and a virtual community center for adoptees. There's still a lot to figure out, but in the meantime, I'm starting a guest blog, which will feature your stories. I want your version of the truth, pustules and running sores and all. I want the raw story: the agony and the ecstasy; the good, the bad, and the ugly. I want to hear you, pushing back against the stereotypes and misinformation.

I'm still writing too, and I know that sometimes the hardest part of writing is where to start telling a story that has no beginning, middle, or end. My advice is to go with the moment in your life when everything changed, whether it has something to do with being adopted or not (if you really think about it, though, I'm sure you can find some connection from that moment to your adoption). My story starts with an argument with my best friend at a Dunkin' Donuts in Seoul the day she was to meet her birth mother, an argument I provoked. Why did I provoke that argument? These are the uncomfortable things I have to face as I write my story.

People have commented that it is hypocritical of me to talk about erasing stigmas while remaining anonymous, as if I'm ashamed that I'm adopted. When I was young, my best friend—she of the Dunkin' Donuts, the shadow behind the shadow of this website and the first major investor—and I started to keep a list of famous adopted people, which grew to an eclectic assortment of individuals: lots of athletes and entertainers, a few businesspeople, some who were famous because of their parents, several writers, a hate crime victim who inspired a civil rights movement... They were living, visible examples of people like us, people who had grown up and, in many cases, achieved extraordinary things. I vowed to become a famous writer, thinking the admiration, love, and respect of people I didn't know and would never meet would make up for me not admiring, loving, and respecting myself. But now that I have a chance for the spotlight, I realize it would be premature to reveal my true identity when my true identity is still a work in progress. There are a few other projects I need to work on first, including this website.

So let's be quiet no more.

Acknowledgments

As an adoptee, I appreciate the roles that chance and luck have played in my life, and it was chance and luck that brought my manuscript to its true and proper home at Unnamed Press. Many thanks and deepest gratitude to Chris Heiser for his insight, wisdom, guidance, and patience during the intense editorial process and for always demanding more than I thought I could give; Olivia Taylor Smith for her support and advice; and Jaya Nicely for a gorgeous book both inside and out. Special thanks to superb copy editor Nancy Tan for cleaning up my manuscript and making it pretty.

Thanks to the first readers whose support and encouragement sustained me through the years: Betsy Stephens, Polly Stephens, Michael Fatsi, Betsy Goldstein, Mercedes Bryant, Ananya Bhattacharyya, and, most especially, James Prochnik, who urged me to bring my manuscript out of retirement after I'd given up on it, took my stunning author photo, and designed my author web page.

Thanks to Geri Thoma for taking me on as a client so many years ago and giving me the confidence to keep at it.

Warm thanks to my writing guru and mentor, Caroline Bock.

Thank you to my parents, Betsy and Ralph Stephens, for their unwavering support and for instilling in me a love of reading and literature.

Thanks to all the adoptees out there who are raising their voices and making themselves heard.

Thanks to Quinn and Auster for the love, laughter, and life lessons.

Love and gratitude to William Pittman for being my rock, my inspiration, my career counselor, my traveling companion, and my life partner.

Sources of Chapter Epigraphs

1. Moses: Exodus 2, *The New Oxford Annotated Bible*

2. Gerald Ford: *Time and Chance: Gerald Ford's Appointment with History* by James Cannon, The University of Michigan Press, 1998

3. Dave Thomas: "Dave Thomas" by Marilyn Achiron, *People*, August 2, 1993 (https://people.com/archive/dave-thomas-vol-40-no-5/)

4. Michael Reagan: *Twice Adopted* by Michael Reagan with Jim Denney, Broadman and Holman Publishers, 2004

5. Faith Hill: "How Faith Hill Found Happiness" by Leah Ginsberg, *Good Housekeeping*, April 2004 (https://www.goodhousekeeping.com/life/inspirational-stories/interviews/a15246/faith-hill-renewed-apr04/)

6. Vincent Chin: "The Ordeal of Lily Chin" by Colin Covert, *Detroit Free Press*, July 7, 1983

7. Liz Phair: "A Conversation with Singer Liz Phair" by Rachel Resnick, *Women's Health*, May 11, 2006 (https://www.womenshealthmag.com/life/a19932276/liz-phair-interview/; http://writersonfire.com/media-press/a-conversation-with-singer-liz-phair/)

8. Steve Jobs: *Steve Jobs* by Walter Isaacson, Simon & Schuster, 2011

9. Soon-Yi Previn: "Soon-Yi: Woody Was Not My Father" by Walter Isaacson and Soon-Yi Farrow Previn, *Time*, August 31, 1992

10. Melissa Gilbert: *Prairie Tale: A Memoir* by Melissa Gilbert, Simon Spotlight Entertainment, 2009

11. Christina Crawford: "Christina Crawford Describes Her Famous, Abusive Mother" CNN Larry King Live, August 10, 2001 (http://transcripts.cnn.com/TRANSCRIPTS/0108/10/lkl.00.html)

12. Greg Louganis: "'The Truth Shall Set You Free'" by Michael Quintanilla, the *Los Angeles Times*, February 28, 1995. (http://articles.latimes.com/1995-02-28/news/ls-37032_1_greg-louganis/2)

13. Nicole Richie: "Nicole Weighs In," by Leslie Bennetts, *Vaity Fair*, June 2006. (https://www.vanityfair.com/news/2006/06/richie200606)

14. Toby Dawson: "Olympian's Avalanche of 'Families'" by Barbara Demick, the *Los Angeles Times*, April 14, 2006 (http://articles.latimes.com/2006/apr/14/world/fg-dawson14)

15. Frances McDormand: "Frances McDormand on 'Olive Kitteridge,' Dropping LSD, and Her Beef with FX's 'Fargo'" by Marlow Stern, *Daily Beast*, September 3, 2014 (https://www.thedailybeast.com/frances-mcdormand-on-olive-kitteridge-dropping-lsd-and-her-beef-with-fxs-fargo)

16. Debbie Harry: "Blondie Bombshell: Debbie Harry Interview" by Nina Myskow, *Saga Magazine*, May 2014 (https://www.saga.co.uk/magazine/entertainment/celebrities/debbie-harry)

17. James Michener: *Michener: A Writer's Journey* by Stephen J. May, University of Oklahoma Press, 2005

Epilogue—Edward Albee: "Playwright Edward Albee, Who Changed and Challenged Audiences, Dies at 88" by Jeff Lunden, NPR Weekend Edition Saturday, September 16, 2016 (https://www.npr.org/sections/thetwo-way/2016/09/16/462191417/playwright-edward-albee-who-changed-and-challenged-audiences-dies-at-88)

About the Author

Born in Korea, Alice Stephens was one of the first generation of transnational, interracial adoptees. Her work has appeared in *Urban Mozaik, Flung, Banana Writers,* the *Los Angeles Review of Books,* and the *Washington Independent Review of Books,* which publishes her column, Alice in Wordland. She lives with her family and dog in the Washington, DC area. *Famous Adopted People* is her debut novel.